Nov. 2010

Regards
A. D. Norvay

WALDENSONG SATURNALIA

A Novel by A.D. Morvaye

Published by

Prince Chameleon Press
www.princechameleon.com

Invisible Cities Network
www.InvisibleCitiesNetwork.org

Published by Prince Chameleon Press

Photo and Cover Design, Manolex Editorial & Design

Legal Deposit, 2009, Bibliothèque Nationale du Québec
National Library of Canada

Printed on recycled paper and bound in Canada

Library and Archives Canada Cataloguing in Publication

Morvaye, A. D.
      Waldensong saturnalia / A.D. Morvaye.

Includes text in German and French.
ISBN 978-1-894967-33-4

      I. Title.

PR6113.O78W35 2009   823'.92   C2007-901452-6

An excerpt from Waldensong Saturnalia was short-listed for the Eastside Stories Competition, London, U.K., 1995.

Copies of this book may be obtained through:
Prince Chameleon Press: http://www.princechameleon.com
Invisible Cities Network: http://www.InvisibleCitiesNetwork.org

To the mythic years

Waldensong
Saturnalia

A novel
by A.D. Morvaye

Part One
Prelude
Chapter 1   Magnificat
Chapter 2   Madonna
Chapter 3   Nightmare in Triptych
Chapter 4   Goddess of the Harvest
Chapter 5   Monday Morning
Chapter 6   No Art is Possible without a Dance with Death, *Céline*
Chapter 7   Stain
Chapter 8   The Merman's Spawn
Chapter 9   Physician, heal thyself
Chapter 10   Last Supper

Part Two
Chapter 11   Litany of Loss
Chapter 12   Die Kamera trügt nicht
Chapter 13   Jewboy
Chapter 14   Deus Invictus
Chapter 15   Artisan
Chapter 16   Star
Chapter 17   Stardust
Chapter 18   The Inhabitants of Walden
Chapter 19   Our Father in Heaven
Chapter 20   Birth Day
Chapter 21   At the Gates
Chapter 22   Cyclops
Chapter 23   Die verlassene Heimat
Chapter 24   Traveling Soldier
Chapter 25   On Lethe's Bank
Chapter 26   Sea Change
Chapter 27   Witness
Chapter 28   Apocalypse-in-Waiting
Chapter 29   Your Boy has Spoken
Chapter 30   Paradise-in-Waiting
Chapter 31   The Lord Giveth

Part Three
Chapter 32   Brave New World
Chapter 33   House of Shade
Chapter 34   Flesh and Blood
Chapter 35   House of Prophecy
Chapter 36   Magus
Chapter 37   Nativity Play
Chapter 38   La Revanche du Berceau
Chapter 39   Belladonna
Chapter 40   Liberation Theology
Chapter 41   Want
Chapter 42   The Hidden Years
Chapter 43   Wilderness Prophet
Chapter 44   Book of Revelation
Chapter 45   Vieille Souche
Chapter 46   Goddess Ceres
Chapter 47   Ignorance
Chapter 48   Fairy Tale
Chapter 49   Second Coming
Chapter 50   The Haunting
Chapter 51   Consider the Lilies
Chapter 52   Chiaroscuro
Epilogue   Prison Ship

Thus, each of us makes,
individually, a personal
illusion of the world,
Guy de Maupassant

The woods around Mile End were once walden and
Walden all woods; and waldensong the delirious
murmur of wood pigeons guarding the gravestones,
the mediaeval black trunks of elms, St. Dunstan's
square tower glazed onto the sky.

I was weaned too soon, I suppose, so I need to travel back now and then to my birth city to feast on its remains. When my soul shrivels dry and threatens to expire in this saturnine land of my adoption, I come tramping back around London's East End, soaking in the sooty streets and hop-reeking pubs, the soft buttery dog droppings plastered over the pavement and the damp, open greens—*O Mum*—the day you tumbled into bed with a 'bloody foreigner,' you condemned me to be an exile in my own land. Thank you, thank you for this double-edged gift—but where will I lay my neurotic bones to rest while I'm still alive? Where is my country?

Drifting through these streets that loop and cross and threadneedle into one another, I eavesdrop on tweed-capped pensioners, pulled strongly along on dog leashes, rumbling out their gentle coughs at every lamppost. I admire the wind-polished faces of the schoolboys as they wade through market trash along Whitechapel. It's where the glassy red phone-boxes, reeking of musk and dog piss, are vandalized by the local Hun.

My salmon-river journey tugs me past centuries' old terrace-houses. Blindfolded. Gagged in plywood. Awaiting their death-row demolition. Pounding the pavement like an accidented soul, I'm newly dead—yet still haunting the track-path of my sudden annihilation. Wedged into this purgatory between worlds, I am a displaced sinner, forever atoning for the loss of the motherland.

Along Walden, most doors and windows are boarded up or cemented shut. Our number is still visible though, painted white on faded blue under an arch of bricks crowning the door and fitted together like dragon's teeth. Our doorstep, the one Aunt Flo faithfully 'redded' in wax, is faintly red still as though stained forever and ever in holly-berries or ox blood. The rib-iron grate guards her disused coal cellar, smeared in cobwebs, now an underground shrine.

A sharp draught pierces my eyes as I peep through the letterbox. The passage, arched at the far end and buried in workmen's ladders, is awash in Walden's mellow streetlight that filters in through wedges of dark glass, still intact, in their half-moon frames above the door. Guarding its aura of privacy, the sitting-room door to my right is wedged shut as though Uncle Albert still lived here. And a few steps further down into the gloom is the ramshackle latched door through which Aunt Flo's black poodle escaped daily into our coffin-like yard.

Standing where I am, on this raised red step, with my 'voyeur' eyes framed by the narrow letterbox, I can see no further than the twisting juncture of the first and second landing where Aunt Flo and Greta, my sister, faced each other eyeball to eyeball, aeons ago, in a blood-curdling duel of screams and punches. I remember, too, the shadowy stairs around the unseen corner that led up to the lodger's bed-sit. And climbing further still, as far as Lily's—my mother's—attic kitchen, the blackened gas stove (if it's still there) must be on the topmost landing. This is where she stood years ago, leaning dreamily on one thin hip, frying steak and chips for Greta's dinner.

"What's the matter, Angie?" she'd say, a shade reproachful when she saw my face, nose wrinkling, seduced by the perfume, the translucent pearl of chopped onion. "Didn't you get nothin' to eat at school?"

My gaze travels upward to what used to be Lily's bedroom window; it's surrounded by a baroque pastiche of sooty mauve slate tiles. Each corrugated segment of roof is partitioned from the next by a slope-descending row of bricks. A drainpipe plumbs straight downward from the eaves, incongruously elegant, while, splashing up the brick façade, is a flat gleaming cataract of moss; an exotic weed, rooted reckless between the cracks, offers up its marguerite blossom to the world.

PART ONE

CHAPTER 1
November 1955

Magnificat

"Get off that wall," screamed Lily. Her voice, shrill and plaintive, more like the neighing of a horse than a human sound, issued from a doorway along Walden.

Directly facing this row of Victorian terrace-houses was a narrow brick wall. Beyond the wall, a steep descent. Here were feathery hillocks green with cabbage grass, bomb-fragments and rust-bitten tins. Glass splinters twinkled amidst the prehistoric fern; they flashed like new-struck florins coining blasphemies at the sun as it sank, staining the length of Walden in a pale gold wash. It gleamed over the roof of the Royal London at Whitechapel, snaked away into the gutter-drains of Bow.

Lily, meanwhile, watched Angie treading that precarious brick ledge. Then she saw her daughter fall, falling ever so slowly as in a dream, floating out of sight. Lily's pitiless imagination was her own torture chamber. Blood surged to her head; her heart pounded. The burning intensity of her angst seemed contagious. Transmitted itself. Even the solid brick, fashioned from rose madder like the kiln-baked soil of Mars, began to shift. Began to tremble and slide—*God, O God!*—Angie swayed, lost her step, almost, yet still daring the devil, tempting the gods. Her skirt fluttered. The stiff November wind braised her skin like a furnace blast, galloped past her like a stallion. Her thin long bones felt like those of a stallion racing into the wind. She failed to witness Lily's pallor flushing to a terrifying purple, hysteria spike. But then again came that 'voice,' a shriek of pure anguish like nothing else on earth.

"Get *DOWN*, Angie! You know you're going to fall, that stinking dump is full of germs!"

Here on this twilight wasteland, this bomb-site 'débris' that Lily stared at so apprehensively, was the spider-ridden ghost of luminous stone and mortar, stamped upon her retina to tremble there forever. Porous as a giant mouldy cheese. Stone-blind. Stone-blasted into catalepsy—that ill-fated terrace-house, dissolved one night during the Blitz into a rubble of brick, wood-shards, snaking wire and charred wall plaster. For years after (in the mind's eye) its phantom-scaffold remained. Yet Time had tamped itself solid since then. Reaped itself fallow. Derelict and unconsecrated, this tiny abandoned hump of land seemed to be gasping for the Flood.

On Lily's side of the street, the *safe* side, Walden's row of terrace-houses appeared to blur, waver, then re-settle gradually into ships of brick moored in a misty street harbour. A single porthole shimmered out of the ochre-brick hull of the corner house; it resembled the eye of God gazing darkly onto the street. The light faded; even the stiff buffeting wind sighed, subsided, relented momentarily. And then a November mist-chill rose like a tide of white fungus from deep beneath the pavement flags, like a writhing sea of unquiet souls, rather, for this entire square lot, this Sheol, was once a *jüdische* burial ground. Clattering past the Christian Mission gate, at Walden's eastern end, a couple of figurines materialized as though out of the grave. Fantastic stragglers, perhaps, from some bygone Mystery Play. Leather-strapped and blinkered, Solly's old mare was dragging a barrow-stall back from market. She seemed wired to invisible strings beneath the gas lit pavement.

"Whoah, whoah there, stop—!" There was a slow crunching of wheel against curb and paving stone as the market barrow ground to a halt. Flourishing the reins with the ghost of old-world gallantry, Solly reached up, compulsive, twirling his Napoleonic forelock, smoothing the last threads of hair still plastered to his head. As he grinned—or grimaced rather—deep ripples traversed his forehead like the wavelets of a fleshy pool. "D'you know what I'm going to do with this old bag of bones, Lil?" he said.

Lily couldn't stop staring at the moths, almost as big as birds, dancing around the fuzz of the gas lamps. A sliver of light locked onto her glasses and flashed them into thick silver coins. Dark-haired, olive-skinned, bone-delicate and trusting, she shuddered like a dormant volcano of quivering wounds.

"Time to pack the ol' girl off to the knacker's yard!" said Solly. Awaft in the fragrance of leather and old tar, he grinned darkly down at Lily.

"Oh, no, don't, she's a lovely 'orse, ain't she, Angie?"

Lovely? Nine-year-old Angie stood shoulder to shoulder beside her mother, Lily, mirror-image darkling to pale, though the lamp-glare made spectres of them all. Her illumined fingers brushed the horse's bulging flank; it glowed darkly, reeking of sweat, mildew and damp. For no apparent reason, the thing reared upward in a sudden clatter of chains and shoddy wood. Head rocking wildly. Hoof-iron singing on stone.

"*Whoaah*, what's a'matter, you silly old nag—!" Solly made an impromptu grab for the reins.

"She don't 'alf smell bad, don't you never give her a bath?" said Angie, already retreating into the shadow; Lily's vague and tentative presence offered scant protection, if any at all.

Taken off guard, Solly launched into a rollicking rumbling spasm of asthmatic laughter, almost painful to witness. "What, you're bleedin' joking, ain't ya?" he said, needled as always by a twinge of distaste for Lily's skinny flax-haired kid. There's definitely something leechy about her, he thought, something artful; as for the elder one, Greta—*Godstruth,* that hellion was sure to come to a bad end.

"Angie, that was rude, come inside now, it's late," said Lily mildly, absent-mindedly. Stooped and shivering, already she was receding, sucked backward like a water lily stem into the twilit passageway. A wan smile—*G'night Solly*—then her seemingly disembodied hand, timid and self-effacing, pushed shut the front door.

The ground-floor strip of hall was narrow, rickety and dim, creaked like a precarious gangway. Was there life breathing in this house? To her right, only the muted murmur of '*Gunsmoke*' could be heard; the invisible telly screen flickered silvery around the woodframe of Albert's closed door. Her sister must be off somewhere, gallivanting again; the steps leading down to Flo's subterranean kitchen were as dark as the grave. Lily halted, gazed martyr-like up the glimmering staircase, embarked on her slow creaking ascent.

Inside the double parlour on the second landing, all the lights were off too. Mr. O'Faolain, their septuagenarian lodger, must be out at the pub, or else stone-drunk in his bed, or perhaps just slumbering in the emerald dream valleys of his long-lost motherland. A gentle soul he was, a melancholy drifter, God love him, no trouble at all. He lived like an anchorite in his cell, co-existing peaceably with a lifetime's worth of memories, breathing silent life into the corners of his sparse cocoon-like headquarters. Of course, thought Lily, at once both envious and pitying, *he being a man*, he isn't flesh-bonded to the earth by a string of famished children—children who race into adolescence, unearthing their own dangerous liberty and power to rebel.

One last creaking turn around the stairwell led up into Lily's attic kitchen. A solitary bulb glared through its sculpted mold of milky glass; unsung graveyard for flies. Lily dropped into her chair, moaned, humped forward. She pulled off her glasses, peered at them intently with an air of bewonderment, as though bewitched by the bottle thickness of the lens. Her spectral gaze, reminiscent of glimmering quicksilver bogs—yet at the same time remote, tragical and queen-like—fixed itself upon the steam-clouds belching energetically from the tea-kettle.

"Angie? *Angie?*" It was a thin rising shriek that no one heard. "Where've you gone to now?"

No answer. The compartments of the house stood like disused catacombs. Lily contemplated the walls, cupboards and antique stove with the air of a saint being flayed into martyrdom, with the faded gaze of a holy picture tumbling from a dusty missal. Just look at the spreading rash of tea stains on her frock, her tense woolly aura of a cardigan, tortured into shape around coat-hanger shoulders—God help her, she'd have to haul herself off this chair now to respond to the hysterical tea-kettle, the incensed fairy-ring of gas jets that hissed, crackled and flared.

Lily curled her fingers around the gas tap and twisted it full circle, aligning it exactly with the other three. There, that was off now, wasn't it? Or should she double check? Twist it back one more time to its full ferocious blast, then dial it slowly closed. There, all safe! No deadly fumes seeping into their lungs to carry them off in innocent sleep. Lily pressed her fingers down again, bruising them against the taps. Good, all done, now to make the tea!

Inside the cupboard, jars and boxes must be shifted with patient, meticulous fingers. There was the Sifto salt—set it back down where it was, perfectly straight, perfectly neat. The open packet of tea biscuits, half-empty and spilling crumbs from its pierced cellophane wrapper—pick that up too, straighten the biscuits. Stack them domino style. Now, put them down again; no, that's not quite right, try again. It must be *perfectly* aligned with the box of salt.

The sugar cubes were already crunching and rumbling against one another like an incipient avalanche in their box. Lily's fingers trembled, hovered like moths—place the sugar box *exactly* adjacent to the tea biscuits. How about shifting it a tiny fraction to the right? Would that be better? Would it, would it? No, never mind, leave it just the way it was. The tea-strainer, of course, must be sodden with old tea-leaves, trapped under a mound of greasy cups and saucers piled as high as the cold water tap. All right then, lift out the unwashed crockery, ever so carefully, plate by plate, cup by trembling cup. Empty the tea-strainer into the dustbin. *Oh, God no,* don't touch that lid—too grimy—just dump the whole lot down the sink instead.

Don't do that, Lil, those tea-leaves'll stop up the plumbing!

There it was again, that familiar outraged ghost-echo of her sister, Flo, who might be scarcely more than a few miles away, probably at the Mare Street Bingo Hall. Never mind, thought Lily—that stubborn rebellious vestige of Lily—just dump the bleedin' tea-leaves, a plague of floating locusts, over the drain and swish them down the antique pipes. Now rinse the strainer under the tap, twisting watery braids through its inverted wire dome. Measure two spoonfuls of fresh tea-leaves—*careful, don't spill any over the sides.* Pick up the kettle. No, that's not right, put it down for a minute. Pick it up again, more carefully this time; then pour the boiling water through the strainer into the cup. Watch the tea-leaves bubble and stir like a foamy pond, then wait for the witchy potion to steep.

For no particular reason, the jade greenish stain around the sink, like a font in an ancient churchyard, the lethargic trickle of the water, the way Lily stood there, wrapped in indecision, brought with it a sudden flash-image of Taddeusz, then he was gone, like the warp and weft of a dream. His smile was the last to fade, as though it were charged with a luminescent energy all its own. Taddeusz—the Unholy Ghost who'd given her all these babies, Greta, Larissa, Angie, Peter, then disappeared into the aether. Taddeusz, her one-and-only love, God damn him. Such distances he had traveled just to come to her. To her. Of all the innocents sleep-walking the back alleys of this fair city, she had been chosen. God, the Devil—perhaps some malignant pact between them—had strewn him across her path.

Taddeusz hailed from the '*Schwarzwald*' mingling into Transylvania. It was a dynamic, if not a happy union—the narrowing fire-yellow eyes, the fleshy nose and womanlips. If he wasn't already underground he must still be in flight, Lord knows where, disturbing nests, scattering seed wherever it fell. They had met at a dance during that bleak Saturnalian winter of '39. Lily danced well, had a natural sense of rhythm, but in this draughty hall of merry-making strangers she was ill at ease, painfully shy. Taddeusz, on the other hand, couldn't have cared less about the dance, the nocturnal fest raging in the blacked-out dance halls and pubs. Even as a young man he was mildly corpulent, luxuriantly rolled into his own flesh and streaming an aura of gold sparkling sensuality. He eyed the women as they entered, whether whores or maidens, as though he expected them to drop like flowers at his feet. But only Lily blossomed for him, offered herself freely on his altar. And how it galled him, a dispossessed émigré, a false aristocrat or an aristocrat falsely disguised, rather, in rags. Didn't anyone recognize his intrinsic worth, his standing? How was it possible to confound him—Taddeusz—with these raw East Londoners, born and bred in damp terrace-houses, to whom a feast was burnt toast with pork drippings, sizzling over a candle flame!

His innocent little Lily was once so funny, so witty, but how was Taddeusz—a foreigner—supposed to have been able to distinguish her broad Cockney lilt from the Queen's English? When did he first suspect that he'd unintentionally fallen into the dregs? True, the eastern wing of the city was cut off like some poor relation from most official maps, which acknowledged London's sprawling growth only up to, and including the mighty Tower. For centuries now, the East End beyond was a place to which the poor, the invisible gravitated. But this was wartime, hearth and homeland up in flames, and Taddeusz just another destitute inmate of the Limehouse seaman's refuge, an ornate stone battleship of a building near the West India Dock Road. Slave and Obermeister, it mattered not; this *accident de guère* had tossed them close together onto a level turf. Lily was a blasted kitchen maid at Lyons Tea Shop, so what was he doing dancing with her, for God's sake? What was he doing sleeping with her?

So be it; they were all in flight, ephemeral.

From his 'beloved' German motherland, the deutsche Luftwaffe was launching raids on English Channel ports. Soon, a pitched battle for the skies would seal their fate—invasion, then Nazi occupation. No wonder the present instant contained its own terrifying liberation. This was no time for scruples, nor self-reproach. An alliance, a dalliance with a kitchen maid! So what? Taddeusz had always enjoyed the company of domestics; in his father's home in Timişoara he'd practically been raised by them. He felt at home.

And Lily? To her, Taddeusz was a divine happening, a mystic icon, shipwrecked and driven to shore. She was intrigued by his exotic attempts at mastering her language, his deep rumbling European tongue doing battle with the words. Even so, he uttered his mangled phrases with flair, with a stern glance of hauteur (Lily managed to stifle her laughter, but used to mimic him out of earshot). Soon he began correcting her, losing his temper when she disgraced the noble English tongue with her *'ain'ts'* and *''ers'* and *''ims.'*

"Blimey, Lil, what you 'anging around with 'im for?" said her brother, Georgie. "A bloody foreigner, and 'e don't 'alf fink 'e's grand!"

She noticed Taddeusz suspiciously scanning her face. She knew she was almost too dark to be a true Briton. Her coal-black hair—too fine, too wispy—coiled into high rolls, her Asiatic cheekbones with their faintly Geisha air, her olive skin paling for lack of sun, her upslanting eyelids veiling eyes that often grew large and murky with fear. Just a harsh word from him, and those eyelids began battering fiercely as though she'd been struck by a shaft from which she instantly recoiled, vainly disguising, hastily pulling down the veil. Her fragility did not make Taddeusz feel tenderer, nor even repentant. It only made him want to strike out, again and again, till she grew so calloused that it mattered no more.

On her mother Renie's side, there was no danger of Jewry. Renie was a hefty matriarch, whose roots sprang from the bottomless Irish bogs, more Catholic than the Pope himself. But then there was Lily's father, Karl, whom Taddeusz had never met. Penned up in a 'Rest Home,' maybe the old man was the wild card they were all concealing, not only mad, but perhaps a mad Jew into the bargain! And her sister, Flo, the eldest—a Jewess for certain, he'd wager his last shilling. That baroque-shaped nose of hers with its wide-fashioned bridge, her gloomy features of wine-coloured stone. She was arrogant too; scarcely a shade above illiterate, surely, yet she strode around this eastern ghetto like some high-born tribal priestess in her own '*Chosen Land.*'

Flo matched Taddeusz in arrogance, intimidated even him by the way she stood guard over her sister, Lily. They all did, the entire freakish tribe, ten or eleven of them, watching over and protecting their own weaklings, moving nowhere but in herds. Should anything happen to Lily, Taddeusz knew they'd all be down on him like a starved pack of wolves. And so he tried to curb his temper, or at least camouflage it, when Lily did something stupid or said something stupid. She was forever in danger of angering him, and sometimes he just couldn't restrain his rage, such as the time she dropped her handbag into the communal dung-trough during an air-raid, and he had to fish it out for her, or worse, the time she went hunting through his papers and discovered a numbered Swiss bankbook, with a scrawled signature at the front.

"Teddy, is that your name? That sounds Jewish, don't it?"

"What did you say?"

"I just asked, don't get upset, there's nothing wrong with being Jewish."

"Shut up, I said I'm not Jewish!" Taddeusz gave Lily a shove, strong enough to send her flying against the wall. She bumped her thin hip against a bureau, almost lost her balance. Her dark eyes opened wide, frightened, pained.

He thought of just dropping her. He knew he should. In his lucid moments he rehearsed the farewell speech he was always on the verge of making. He'd make sure it stung hard—"Look, woman, you're ignorant. So what if you read *Charles bloody Dickens*—(Taddeusz was secretly mortified to acknowledge that even he had trouble hacking through the literary Master's turgid prose, genius though Dickens undoubtedly was)—so what if you're the only one in your family who can read anything longer than a shopping list! You're still dismally stupid!"

True, weak-minded Lily surprised him sometimes with her modest literary flights. She was a passionate reader, although she read little other than schoolroom Classics and quaint Period romances; her passion was reading stories, telling stories, mimicking them into life. Her unschooled speech was inlaid now and then with elegant expressions, plundered from musty volumes on public library shelves. Perhaps she was bright enough, but just needed to be rescued from this swamp of rotting terrace-houses whose insides were clammy with fog and damp and the stench of centuries. But Taddeusz didn't relish the notion of being Lily's Saviour. It was not his calling, not his destiny. He finally did test his farewell speech on her, then watched her disintegrate like a dying flower. She didn't put up a fight, or argue or scream. She didn't batter him with her tongue or her fists. She knew, of course, that she was unworthy. All along she had been awaiting it, fatalistically expecting to be driven out of the Temple, defrocked for uttering heresy, for uttering Cockney.

Her original sin was her genesis, her arisal like a primeval water lily out of the brackish swampland of London's East End.

But then, Taddeusz came back. He was getting inexplicably attached to her, and it worried him. She was too good, too guileless, too easily led, scorned, trampled upon. He knew she couldn't care less whether or not he had a penny to bless himself. Poverty was, in any case, her birthright. She accepted it without question, without reproach. She herself had never owned much more than the sad little rags on her back. She didn't seem to want anything, nor miss anything. In her ignorant, unscheming way, Lily seemed pure of heart. She took him back that first time, then so many more times after that. A faithful hound that caters to its master's whims, that knows it deserves to be beaten, that unconditionally loves. As time passed, for Taddeusz it became a sort of game, a sport, a bloodsport. If he battered her around long enough, he'd eventually break her. Wouldn't he? And that would be better, surely, than dragging out her interminable lament for

14

him. He wished he knew what it was that kept driving him back to those rank, fire-smoky, sunken brick rowhouses on Walden. It was here that Lily's tribe bred and festered together like an open sore, glued to one another, standing up for one another, propping each other up. Taddeusz knew that he was dallying mindlessly, allowing himself to be ensnared on alien ground. He felt stained, dishonoured, grubby, and all for a scrap of comfort, of human warmth marbled with brutish passion. He definitely had to leave her; the next time would be final. Perhaps he might eventually have done so.

One day Lily told him she was pregnant.

Was it a trap? Lily's transparency, her guilelessness came under intense scrutiny again. It was hard to believe such innocence could exist. Taddeusz had never known it before. Certainly not in his own complex world in which multi-layers of deceit were simply an attribute of its sophistication. He himself had never questioned that lying was something you did to get yourself out of a scrape, to evade the nefarious powers of authority, to better your situation or to transform it altogether. Taddeusz had emerged from his chrysalis (circa '33, in an elegant Prussian-style ghetto bounded by east Dortmund's *Kronprinzenstraße*) into that sophisticated political '*ambiance*' in which telling the truth could easily get you killed. The practice of deceit was part of one's armour then, without which one might perish; it was the necessary knee-jerk response of a survival-bent species: it's either him or me. And Taddeusz went one further—lying was a skill to be practised until it was flawless; you had to squash that traitor truth lurking in your eyes, to mask it, obscure it, for in the end that was what gave you away. Truth, in any case, was base metal, needing always to be processed and rendered palatable for the consumption of others; it was neither the birthright nor the privilege of strangers, or even loved ones. Like the wisdom of a Holy Book, its mosaic of baffling contradictions had to be interpreted for those of feebler understanding. Taddeusz had learned to keep his own truth under lock and key, for his own sake—but also for the sake of the world.

When Lily found out she was pregnant, she didn't know what to do. She agonized, she delayed, she was terrified—of Taddeusz, of course, but perhaps even more so of her father. Old man Karl would have to be kept in the dark; although now chemically sedated, he was a volatile, still unknown property to be approached with caution. Urban legend, perhaps, but it was said that as a young man, in a fit of rage during a meal, Karl had stabbed his pregnant wife, Renie, with a dinner fork. Her wound healed, but infant Lily came into the world—by mysterious transference—with four delicate prongmarks in the exact same spot on her neck, a faint perforation, like the foreshadowing of a regal execution.

Lily expected Taddeusz to become hysterical at the news of her approaching motherhood, which he did. He thrashed around, kicked the furniture, beat the walls with his bare fists. He threatened to leave her, demanded blood tests, irrefutable proof of his paternity. Lily gazed at him broken-hearted. Looked away. Wiped her eyes.

"Maybe I can go away and have it somewhere. Maybe Flo can help me—"

"You don't understand," shouted Taddeusz, "if you're carrying my baby around, you're damned well not going to just go away and have it somewhere—*if*—it's mine."

For the first time Lily showed a mild ripple of something that actually looked like anger. It was so uncharacteristic, so rare, that Taddeusz was taken aback. He almost felt like patting her on the back and whispering, "Bravo, girl, that's the spirit—" had it not been diluted at once by the perennial flow of tears.

"Who else's baby do you suppose it is then?" wept Lily. "Who else's damned baby can it be?"

Lily's wedding day. After all these years, it remained a still-life animation flickering steadfastly in the darkroom of her soul. There was the perverse recollection of the graveyard directly opposite where some unknown Victorian damsel, *Clarissa Barnett,* slumbered beneath a large monument of pale stone. In her mind, Lily registered the carved inscription of the girl's epitaph as she herself, weak-legged and light-headed, seemed to float barely an inch from the pavement, past the spiked black railings guarding the burial ground. She knew she was lurching—or being lurched—toward her own destiny; there it crouched in wait for her, in the guise of some malevolent jewel-eyed gargoyle, visible only to her, beshrouding the otherwise non-descript drab portals of the Limehouse Town Hall.

Her younger sister, Ruth, (in those bygone days, still slim, alert and watchful) had already arrived and was standing on the steps beside Laszlo—poor Laszlo, if only they'd known then how close it was to the end. Lily never understood why Taddeusz insisted on a double wedding, how he'd browbeaten his sea-farer comrade, Laszlo, into proposing to Ruth, or even more inexplicable, how he managed to persuade stubborn Ruth into accepting. Practical as always, Taddeusz had secured special nuptial licenses for them both, on sale at two shillings and seven pence each. He wasted no time.

To Lily, however, it made no sense. Here she was, shaky on her feet, hollow-eyed and jaundiced-looking after weeks of relentless nausea. She felt ugly and uncomfortable, masquerading in her mothball-smelling white jacket, her tailored hat with its feather trim and lacy eye-veil, its sprinkling of fake pearls. Secretly, she cursed her aborted attempt at elegance. Taddeusz stood beside her, meanwhile, exuding a palpable martyr-like gloom. His solemn vows seemed to be wrenched from him like extracted teeth. As he put the ring on Lily's finger, his own hands were shaking, his fingernails clumsily grazed her skin. In contrast, tall gentle Laszlo, his dark-haired Doppelgänger, was smiling and oozing pure joy to

17

the world. Later, as they floated outward through the portals, his consort, Ruth, appeared star-struck, even dazed at the suddenness of her nuptials. She stretched out her fingers, stared at her wedding ring, then at her brand-new bridegroom. Joyful. Apprehensive. Certain, well almost certain that she truly was in love.

The tap was still drip drip dripping in its malodorous enamel grotto, dripping over the stains, over the grease. How long had Lily been standing here? Who knows? Who cares? She no longer believed in the tyranny of clocks and watches. What difference could it possibly make in a lifetime of empty teacups and mystical constellations of sodden tea-leaves whether or not she knew how late it was? Half her life had already slipped away. An unintelligible blur, the view from a train speeding through a twilit tunnel. Time might be rushing on still, for some, but Lily no longer clocked its meaningless flight. Her soul had twisted ever so slowly inside out and become imprinted on her flesh. Her pace had slowed to a crawl, her footsteps followed an endless loop through a mental maze. A dragonfly trapped in amber, a horse ploughing through sand. Each day the mist—and the mystery—deepened.

Why go on? Where to? What for?

Lily put forth her thin hand, screwed the tap closed. Screwed it closed again. There, or was it still dripping? She twisted it one more time; then her fingers trembled over a full bottle of milk, submerged, baptized in its cold water pan. *God, this was dangerous*—what if it slipped from her spastic fingers, exploded like shrapnel in her face! She wrapped the milk bottle into a dishrag, as she would a ritual offering, peeled off the glinting silver seal and raised it under the light. Were there any cracks around the edge? Any loose chunks, treacherous as icebergs, any splinters clinging to the rim that might fall unseen into her cup? You couldn't be too careful, the way that sod of a milkman dropped his cartload onto the pavement every morning, rattling his milk bottles murderously against one another in their crates. But could she be certain there were no cracks in this one? Angie would have told her. Angie examined the bottles for her every morning before running off to school, but then where had that kid disappeared to now? Lily twisted the bottle around, full circle, for the twentieth time. Then she removed the tea-strainer and ever so, ever so carefully poured a drop of milk into the cup. There! She'd done it, made the tea at last. Who said she couldn't even make herself a bleedin' cup of tea? The first sip spread like a tide over her parched tongue.

Stone-cold.

CHAPTER 2

MADONNA

"Hello, Lady Macbeth," said Greta, at the open doorway. Her tone was nasal, oily, inlaid in a bedrock of mockery. "Still washing away the evidence, are you?"

Lily's bony hands were smeared in suds of creamy soap. She twisted her sunken head to look at her daughter. Her own voice was high, very light and fragile, trailing away to shreds. "Oh, hello, Greta, where've you been, then?" she said.

"Out."

"Out where, Greta?"

Greta flung her denim jacket over a chair. It slithered unnoticed to the floor. "Wouldn't you like to know?" she said. She loved to tease her mother, Lily, provoke her the way you torture a caged animal with sharpened sticks.

"Are you warm enough in that jacket, darling?"

"No, I'm bloody freezing. Move over, will you!"

"Eh?"

"I said move over."

"Careful, you can do me an injury like that," cried Lily, as Greta shoved her out of the way.

Steadying herself, slowly, elaborately, with just a hint of melodrama, she stared at her daughter. Her weakly glimmering gaze was full of resentment, thin and tepid resentment. Is this why you give them life? she wondered. So that they can turn around and deliberately spurn you, innocently destroy you? Whatever is it that happens in that mysterious eyeblink, that mistily remembered collage of Time which stretches backward

21

like a visionary 'near-death' experience, seeming either so brief or so interminably long, those ten, twelve or fifteen years that elapse from the moment they open their blind, wavering kitten eyes and take in, devour the world?

That's when they begin to feast on you, like maggots swarming over putrefying meat. You become their birthright, their domain, their breeding ground to trample on. They grow and grow into an unimagined rearrangement of muscle and bone, newly formed entities forging their own invincible construct of flesh and soul, agonizingly slowly at first, and then with the disproportionate speed of a balloon swelling suddenly from its slim rubber neck.

Darkly beautiful she was now at fifteen, although with her somber skin, her strong boniness, Greta definitely resembled her grandmother's tribe, Aunt Ruth in particular. From Taddeusz she had inherited nothing obvious, except for a faint gleam of arrogance, a narrowness of the eyes that lent her an eastern look of gypsyish exotica, a touch of Romany. Greta squinted into the mirror that was propped up on the mantelpiece. She pursed up her wide mouth.

"How long've you been washing them hands, then?" she said, peering beyond her own to Lily's quicksilver image, suspended in the rust-pocked rectangle of looking glass.

"Eh?"

"I said how long've you been washing them bloody creepy hands of yours?"

Lily rubbed her soapy palms together, interlocking her bony joints in a slow-motion, oft-repeated ritual. She seemed to be held together as lightly as a bundle of feathers, or rags. "I touched the dustbin," she said.

"What?"

"I said I accidentally touched the dustbin."

"You touched the dustbin? You're joking, ain't you?"

22

"When I wanted to throw away them tea-leaves just now."

"Don't tell me you actually made yourself a bleedin' cup of tea. Well, that's a miracle," said Greta, as she bent her head back to the mirror and began to attack her overgrown eyebrows with a pair of metal tweezers.

"Oh, Greta, be careful, you can poke your eyes out with those, you can. I knew a woman once who lost her right eye."

"And you found it for her, didn't you, Lily?" Greta bared her perfect square white teeth and howled to herself like a moonstruck she-wolf.

"Don't joke, Greta. I'm serious. Her hand slipped just as she was tweezing her eyebrows, just because she was so vain. She wanted two thin lines for eyebrows. She weren't happy with the eyebrows God gave her."

"So God punished her, right?"

"You're beautiful, Greta. You're lovely just as you are. Put away them tweezers, darling."

"Make me." Greta swung around, and poked her face closer to Lily's. Contentious. Victoriously mocking. "Go on then, make me!" she challenged. Then she laughed.

"Oh, Greta, I can't stand looking at you when you put that sharp point up near your eyes—!" all pronounced with an agonizing tremor, exactly what Greta was waiting for; she jabbed the metal spike, abruptly, toward her own eye.

Lily screamed. "Don't *do* that, you fool!"

"Well, just stop staring at me; I'm going out now anyhow."

"What, on Sunday night?"

"Yeah!"

"But you've got school tomorrow, ain't you?"

"No, I ain't."

"How come?"

"I'm on holiday."

"What holiday?"

"I'm taking a bloody long holiday and that means I ain't never going back to them nuns no more."

"What did you say?"

"You heard."

"You ain't going back to school?"

"That's right, I ain't, and it's your fault. I told you I didn't want to go to that school in the first place. I hate it there. And that stupid uniform I've got to wear—that bowler hat with the hat band and the school crest—I don't 'alf look like some mug coming back down the East End wearing that. And if some snotty mole of a prefect catches you not wearing it on the bus, you get hours of detention—it's the fucking Gestapo, Lily. You should've heard the fuss they made about my stockings. I can't have no black lines down the back 'cos I look like some trollop, they said!"

"Who said that then, who dared say that?"

"And then this Monseigneur, or this red-assed Cardinal came to the Prize-giving and we had to kiss his ring. I'm telling you, I wanted to bite off his thumb instead!"

A convent! A convent, my God! The mere fact that Lily had managed to get her daughter into the convent at all was, in itself, a miracle. Greta had wanted to go to Raines Comprehensive mixed, but Lily put her foot down, perhaps for the first and only time in her life. They stayed up, literally the whole night, battling it out. Hour after hour of hollering and arguing—amazing to witness how weak-minded, frail little Lily turned stubborn, remained adamant, actually refused to give her consent.

Was it not bad enough that Taddeusz had refused her a church wedding, cried Lily. Was it not bad enough that, as a civilly married and divorced woman, her religious status was beyond the pale? Her daughter, at least, was not going to be sent to a

Godless school. Although the last time she had even set foot inside a Catholic church was at Peter's baptism, Lily believed her duty was to get Greta initiated, instructed by the experts in the tenets of her own religion.

She finally got the little pagan enrolled in a Roman Catholic convent in neighbouring Hackney where Greta was immediately segregated from her fellow pupils and subjected to intense spiritual coaching in preparation for the Sacraments, of which she had received only one. Instead of being allowed to escape to the leaf-enshrouded schoolyard after the dinner hour, she was force fed the concepts of Original sin, plenary indulgences, Penance, the varying states of grace, the Holy Trinity, cupidity and mea culpa, abstract coinage of a complex and bureaucratic dogma, altogether foreign to Greta, besides being, in her view, a morbid reliquary of pious twaddle.

But this 19th-century convent was an unexpected jewel, hermetically sealed behind a curving maroon-brick wall, a forest of overhanging willows and an elegant forged-iron gate. Its oval lawn of sensually lush grass was purely ornamental and off limits to human feet. Around the lawn ran a mud gravel footpath where the Sisters staged elaborate devotional processions to the Madonna in the month of May. The building itself had a romantic profusion of castle-like turrets, waxy oak doors, and a spacious central hall housing the double-winged main staircase that looped upward from storey to storey. The rafter beams were pierced with a neat row of skylights through which the collective prayers and hymns of the feminine Assembly floated heavenward each morning to reach the ears of God.

"You stuck me in that holy prison for two years and I ain't never going to forgive you for that," said Greta. "I cleared out my desk on Friday and I ain't going back!"

"You're going to have that truant officer coming down here again looking for you," said Lily.

"So what?"

"What am I going to tell her, then?"

"Tell her what you like. Tell her some sheik came and took me away on his magic carpet. Tell her I'm dead, Lily! Tell her you smothered me in my sleep."

"And what if she wants to put you in a reform school?"

"Just let her bloody well try."

"Greta, darling, you're such a clever girl; all them good marks you got and all, just look at that painting you done—" She pointed to Raphael's framed *Madonna of the Meadows,* enlarged and copied slavishly from a gloss-art postcard. A dedicated and skillful likeness, true, by someone so young; to Lily, no less than pure genius.

"Don't try to butter me up, it won't work," said Greta, brushing rapidly through her coarse-gleaming hair and eyeing her mother with malicious glee.

"Greta, darling, listen to me—"

"D'you know what day it is tomorrow?"

"Well, it's Monday ain't it?"

"It's my birthday. What's the matter, are you still trying to forget that horrible day?"

"Of course I didn't forget your birthday, how could I forget that?"

"I don't know, didn't you tell us a hundred times what them nurses up the 'ospital did to you?" Greta pressed her nose close to the glass and reddened her lips with a worn-down stub of greasepaint. Her twisting features leered back at her, delighted her, all tarnished with spots of rust. "All that torture, Lily, I bet it weren't worth it, just to give birth to a bloody ugly monster like me."

"I never forgot your birthday, I was going to send Aunt Flo out for a card in the morning—honest."

"Well, don't bother, Lily, 'cos I won't be here. Don't bother with the cake and candles neither."

26

"Where are you going?"

"Out."

"Out where, Greta?"

"Out, I said."

"Just tell me where you're going."

"Well, I might be going out with Georgie—"

"Who?"

"Georgie—Georgie—ain't you never heard of Georgie?"

"Georgie who?"

"Or else I might be going out with Kenny."

"Kenny? Is he that Teddy-Boy who came around here yesterday on his motorbike?"

"Yeah."

What a dreadful name, thought Lily. Kenny! What a cheap trashy corruption. She couldn't imagine anyone calling that boy Kenneth. Those hulking great shoulders of his, garbed in black leather under a fine film of road dust. The dark-blond sideburns, almost as long as wings, flapping in the wind. She had watched yesterday from her attic window as Kenny roared away from the curb on his motorcycle, clutched onto by Greta, the freshly driven wind blasting up her narrow skirt, through her hair, roughening, obliterating its gleam and tangling it into a nest of dark straw. Where they were going Lily feared to know. She would have preferred to preserve her own self-deceptive image of a chaste kiss exchanged between them on the dark green, the dark common, where the November mists lie low, congealed to the ground, too raw, too chilly to offer itself as a bed for lovers. Lily wished she could somehow evade bearing witness to the obvious danger, the one that years ago had plunged her headlong into her present misery. She could hardly bear watching her own child, her foul-mouthed rebel, her first-born blithely treading that same precarious ledge.

"Greta, I've got to ask you something."

"What?"

"D'you love him?"

"Love him? What the fuck is love?"

"Now, listen here, I'm still your mother."

Greta twisted around, bending to straighten the bold black line down her stockings. "Mother? Did I hear you say Mother? You're joking, ain't you? I ain't never had no real mother in my whole fucking life."

"Greta, darling, don't swear. It's so common."

"But I learned it off of you, Lady Macbeth."

"You learned it off of me?"

"Rinse them bloody creepy hands of yours, will you, for Christ's sake. Ain't you the one that taught me to say bastard?"

"Oh, my God, Greta, don't—"

"I ain't talking about God, I'm talking about Taddeusz, that bastard child-deserter you picked for a husband."

"She won't stop, will she!" cried Lily, rhetorically addressing the walls.

"That *verdammte* no-good son of a German bitch."

"I'll get Aunt Flo in here, I swear I will!"

"You ain't surprised 'e ran away from you, are you, Lily? No wonder. When are you ever going to do the washing up? And what about this filthy floor? The place ain't fit for a bleedin' dog to live in!"

To Greta, living with Lily was like being forced to wander around, straitjacketed inside someone else's madness. The air seemed to grow thicker, clammier, congealed with inertia as soon as you approached within shouting distance of Lily. She drifted endlessly around this grimy kitchen, the collapsing boundaries of her universe, mentally sloshing through something transparent, gummy and swamp-like. The effluvium of a stagnant pool in which her mind kept getting lost, snared, entangled.

Yet Greta could still remember the *Age of Taddeusz*. A page of ancient history. That bygone golden age of Taddeusz, whose favourite she once was. Now her escapist Sire traveled freely through his brave new world, somewhere half-way across the world, moving mountains or else transforming them altogether by the sheer force of his will. Greta, meanwhile, had been left behind to stagnate on Walden, deserted, lumped together with Lily, who was steadily deteriorating. Greta felt no pity for her. She wanted to thrash her mother, martyr that she was—martyr that she chose to be.

"Just pull yourself out of your stinking pool of tears!" screamed Greta. "Stop feeling so bleedin' sorry for yourself all the time. It ain't no one's fault but your own, anyway, and no one can do anything about it. Stop whining about the past and the war and your dead baby!" She seized Lily from behind, gripped her bony shoulders and shook them. "D'you hear me? I can't stand living with you no more, Lily, *I fuckin' hate it!*"

Lily looked around the kitchen, desperate, as though in search of escape. Her lips trembled. Her soapy fingers trembled. Her small head hung limply like a frowsy greying albatross.

"Oh, God, God, how did I get Satan for a daughter—?"

"Just rinse them bleedin' hands of yours," said Greta, grinning, suddenly changing moods and switching into a lower gear. She seemed almost pleased with the reaction she'd managed to provoke in Lily, as though this was some sign of life, however feeble, a benchmark of progress. Snatching up her flimsy denim jacket from the floor, a moment later she was gone.

The timbers of the old house groaned like masts in dry dock as she descended. Down one short flight thumped Greta, then around the second landing. The light-bulb in the passage had blown out, so the last flight of stairs was almost as black as caulking pitch. She made her way past the ground floor sitting-room, yanked open, then slammed the front door behind her, oblivious to the sudden smash of glass on wood that echoed her departure. Uncle Albert's felt-soled slippers pattered over the parquet. His shiny bald head appeared, as the door gaped open with a deep indignant creak. Meanwhile, at the top of the winding staircase in Lily's attic kitchen, Greta's framed *Madonna of the Meadows* rocked on its hook. Warily, Lily eyed its slow glassy shudder, from side to side to side. What if somehow, what if this instant—it crashed to the ground, aiming its deadly splinters through her heart!

CHAPTER 3

NIGHTMARE IN TRIPTYCH

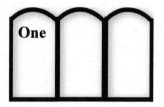

One

Lily was drifting in reverse again. She steadied herself, gripping the iron rail of her hospital cot. Its pallet mattress was as narrow and hard as a cross. Beyond her knees, sheeted in white linen, beyond her outstretched feet, imprisoned in shining metal stirrups, stooped Sister, dour-faced, businesslike, intent yet detached, as though this was not Lily's flesh and bone that she touched with her deftly straining fingers, but a corpse from which a small breathing bundle of life must now be wrenched.

"The gas, Sister," said Lily, "give me the gas."

A humming sound burst over the darkened Thames. The unseen terror rushed down, threatening to rip Lily open at the seams. "Please, the gas…"

"It's for the wounded," barked Sister.

"The mask, please."

Sister clamped her grey lips savagely together, ignoring the rattling windows, the forceps trembling on their stand.

"I don't want it, Sister, I don't—"

"Just be brave, now," said Sister, with a grimly pitying smile. "Just try to be brave."

"I'm going to die," sobbed Lily and, in sympathy, the entire building shuddered. A fountain of glass burst through the air from the upper floors, drowning her screams in brilliant terror. Flaming serpents slithered down the east wall, trailing columns of smoke.

"Be brave, Mother," said Sister, herself all twitching and trembling—eyes, lips, hands.

"O God, O my God—"

"Be brave," shouted Sister, grimacing. Her starched smock was smeared a bright butcher red. In her sterile hands she cradled Greta's frothy matted skull; roughly, clumsily, the wet rubbery little body was plunged into the antiseptic light of a November dawn.

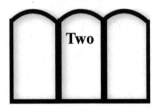

Two

It seemed scarcely a few moments later, yet already the tall windows were filling up with dusk. Propped up on pillows, tough as sandbags, Lily laid the newborn on her white-shrouded knees.

"It bites me, Sister, I can't—I can't feed it."

Sister was gaunt and grey, and as pitiless as a besieged General. She lifted up the baby and, again, nestled its mouth close to Lily's breast; a thin trickle of nipple blood had stained its lips a marbled milky pink.

"Persevere, Mother," said Sister.

"We've got severe fire damage to the east wing and surrounding tenements, about two dozen casualties so far," said the resident surgeon. He paused to glance at Lily, and at the infant malingering at her breast. "Is this the patient who refused to be evacuated? And now she won't feed her baby?"

"Yes, doctor."

"Then smother it."

"Smother—?"

"Yes, that's what I said. Smother it. Then send the wretched creature home."

"But—"

"We need the beds, Sister." He blew past them, hurrying toward some greater peril, swearing and trembling, an angel of mercy with sooty wings.

"But, Doctor—"

"Just smother it, I said."

Three

Strapped to her sickbed, Lily trundled the tunnel length of Walden Street. Propped against her hospital pillow, she was sucked through a spinning kaleidoscope of fire and blood—the intermangled images of hell. Sirens were screaming, driving everyone out of their houses. Women were pushing past her, cradling their babies. A bomb sank through a roof; the ground heaved. Foaming starlight, smoke and flame were whipped into a doomsday glare.

Ever so slowly Lily's sickbed creaked through a drift of smoke, over the shattered pavement, past the Christian Mission gate, beneath the beetling shadow of the hospital, desolate and echoing like a hollow sorrowful womb. Then, all at once, the street filled up again with people and she was swept along in the frantic human stream, crashing toward the bomb shelter. Past her flashed corridors pasted—*V for victory; United we shall win.* Gripping the rails of her cot, Lily rattled headlong down the spiraling steps, then rolled along the station platform. No one paid the least attention to her, inert on her hospital bed. As though it had a will of its own, her rolling cot mowed its way through the crowd and halted at the very end of the platform. Lily stared down the fearful black crescent maw of the train tunnel, then, with a mild shiver of surprise, she felt the weight of a sleeping infant, her first-born, propped against her knees.

It is warm and surprisingly heavy, restless, too. Although its eyes were closed, its body stiffened. Tiny arms thrashed around inside the blanket, as it whimpered, twitched and sighed. Surely it must be hungry, but no, *God, no*, she couldn't feed it; not again, not the breast. The infant's fontanel pulsated steadily under her thumb as—carefully, fastidiously—she rubbed a layer of milk-crust from its fiery mottled scalp.

Then Lily screeched like a startled mare.

Horror rippled through her body. She pushed the thing away, wanted to hurl it onto the tracks. Beneath the tips of her fingers, unmistakably, a pair of tiny lumps, like birds' eggs or horns, were burgeoning from the back of its black hairy skull. Thank God, so far, no one had noticed. People were serenely unconcerned with her; they were chattering, yawning, unfolding blankets and kicking off their shoes in anticipation of this long, infernal night. Not one of them would even glance her way, should she wrap the blanket around the infant's nose and mouth. And nonchalantly smile and smile. Madonna-like—

And quietly smother it.

Not a soul would condemn her, she felt sure; although, when next she looked, they'd all vanished in a blinding swatch of hospital white.

CHAPTER 4

Goddess of the Harvest

"Lily! Lily?" Her sister, Flo, bent her face, purplish as grapes, over hers. "How come it always reeks of gas in here? Don't you never open them windows?"

Lily bolted awake in her chair. "Gas, what gas? Who left them gas taps on, then?"

"And what are you burning all this electric for? Albert'll do his nut."

"Did I fall asleep with the lights on? What time is it, then?"

"Half past twelve."

"Oh, my God—"

"What's the matter?"

"Nothing, I just had this horrible dream."

"Get to bed, for God's sake."

"Didn't Greta come home yet?"

"No, but Albert heard her go out, and he's raging mad!"

"Why, what happened?"

"He said she slammed that front door so bloody hard, his mum's photograph—you know the one he just had framed in silver—fell down off the wall and smashed all over the new parquet. I'm warning you, Lily, if she don't stop her bloody fits she ain't staying here much longer. Now stop that crying, I can't help it."

Flo's own brush with maternity, and much later—her brush with death—had both been freak happenings. She had seen neither of them coming until they were upon her. And she had resisted them both, warded them off; they were not of her choosing, none of her doing, she rejected them.

Hers was a sort of darkly immaculate conception, of carnal knowledge unsanctified by consent. Exactly how it happened was, by now, lost in a faraway blur of African drumbeats, heat, sweat, laughter, shouts, an underground celebration going on down at the end of Walden. One of the revelers, a dark-eyed dark-skinned Bacchus offered Flo a foaming, aromatic drink. That was the last she remembered. She awoke several hours later, lying in the dark on a strange mattress, in a strange bedroom, the tender space between her temples pounding, her stomach churning and, though she didn't know it at the time, with child.

Flo refused at first to believe it. Later on, when her body began to transform itself, swelling in its own accidental maternity, she deliberately refused to connect with it. Albert, to whom she was vaguely engaged, still wanted to marry her. They both agreed that the baby she was carrying belonged to neither of them. The papers were signed; it was consigned to an orphanage as soon as it was born. Bad enough it had chosen her as unwilling host, forced her to bring it forth in pain. Flo refused to see it, to hold it, to bond with it.

"You'd better put Greta away, Lil," said Flo, "before she does you in."

"What?"

"Phone up that social worker, the one who was here this summer talking to her."

"What, that horrible stuck-up bitch?"

"If you don't do it, Albert's going to."

"Oh, no, he's not."

"What can I do? This is Albert's house—he's raging down there, he is."

"He ain't calling no social worker in here."

"Well, you can tell him that yourself tomorrow, 'cos I don't want to have no more arguments with him—*over her.*"

But, in fact, Flo and Albert had hardly had a real argument in close to twenty years. They were like a couple of fixed stars, reciprocal, predictable in their orbit. Albert was tight with his money; Flo spent too much and was a relentless gambler. But, as she said, it was her own pocket money; she earned it labouring in the basement kitchen of the hospital, preparing feasts to feed the pale mouths, the fading bodies that drifted through the wards, breathing in the rarefied stratosphere of antiseptic and aether, wrapped in a pallid aura of dandelion wool, as though rehearsing for their future rôle as angels or ghosts.

Usually by mid-week, Flo's wages had vanished in a toss and a flourish. She kept nothing, not even the child she'd been given, some malevolent tongues whispered behind her back. A sort of blissful carelessness seemed to envelop her. She accumulated nothing in the midst of overflowing abundance. What was the point of it? She was only passing through. She knew that. No, life itself was only trickling through her, but briefly, quickening her with its flourishing munificence. Flo's black cloth purse, too, was always crammed with guineas and shillings—a fluid goldstream that ended in a dribble, then a rush, then a torrent once again. Let it go, she'd say to Albert, frankly contemptuous of his compulsive hoarding, it'll flow back to you, a hundredfold. In the same spirit, she blithely squandered her own non-renewable lifestream for no return, just for the journey, the unfolding, the blossoming, the surprise.

Her husband Albert's grumbling was a deep rippling undertone, sliding in and around the conversation, filling the vacant spaces, like the fussy bric-a-brac of a sitting-room. His grumbling was a pastime, a routine, like a daily walk. He grumbled not because he was morose or angry; for he was neither. Besides, he never imagined that anything he said could influence Flo, for good or for ill. Over the decades, an unspoken pact had forged itself between them. Each ruled over their respective domains, neither impinged upon the other; they complemented each other like death and fertility, like prosperity and want.

Flo now glanced across at her sister. "By the way, Lil, what time have we got to be up the 'ospital in the morning?" she said.

"Er—"

"Don't tell me you forgot Peter's coming out tomorrow."

"Of course I didn't forget."

"Well?"

"Nine o'clock, the letter said nine o'clock Monday morning."

"Right, Lily, and are you getting up early then, or will I have to drag you out by the hair?"

Flo got up, breathing heavily, dragging the huge soft mound of her body. Her voluminous dark woollen skirt, with its fine dusting of lint, concealed the deformity high up on her left thigh, a mass of purplish scarflesh, round and hard as a ball, a remnant, a perpetual reminder of the accident. The accident on the hop fields. In August. She had fallen asleep, in the middle of the field, in the waving shadow of the lush green harvest. A delivery truck circled, then unexpectedly swung across the partly harvested field. Flo awoke in that split second, that indescribable impact when its iron wheels rumbled over her legs, over her chest. For a moment she lay on the hop fields, her eyes glazed like a sacrificial goddess of the harvest, then she was gone, floating across the universe, hovering in the twilit space twixt life and death.

But now here was Flo, despite all the surgeons' predictions, miraculously resurrected in the flesh and fiercely gripping on to life. Lily stared at her sister, bustling around the kitchen, as though she were a heroine of the silver screen. The furious torrent from the cold water tap, the gas flame flicked on, the teacups rattling as though by magic across the table.

"Oh, Flo, how can you make the tea so quick?" she said, in genuine wonder.

"I make it, Lil, *I just make it,*" said Flo. She sounded irritated. "And another thing, from now on you've got to get Peter off to school in the morning or he's never going to learn to read and write."

"He's tired in the morning, Flo, he don't want to get up."

Flo scowled, her voice vaulted to a screech. "Put him to bed early then!"

Lily appeared not to hear. It was always best to ignore Flo's anger, never real anger, not against her anyway, her blood-sister, Lily, whom she fed and harboured and protected.

"All right, sit down and have your tea, love," said Lily, openly in retreat now. Her cringing smile was tinged in guilt, in shades of Uriah Heep. It had the desired effect. Flo's frown relaxed; she relented.

"D'you know I lost ten quid at the Bingo tonight, Lil. If Albert finds out he'll have a stroke."

"What's the old miser hoarding it up for anyway?"

"Who knows, he won't even tell me how much he's got." Flo gave a noisy, anguished yawn. "Now I'm warning you, Lil, I'm coming up here at seven tomorrow morning to yank you out of bed."

Silence.

Flo stared. Darkly. Shook her head in disapproval. Sensed the tacit resentment, the mulish resentment of Lily. O Lily, the eternal child, raising her own children, two, three, even four of them. Here was blind warped Nature again, flowing through tunnels of holy ignorance, curse-blessing the unfit with multitudes of their own kind. Lily had borne Taddeusz four children. Frail though she was, she had nevertheless brought them forth one after the other into the world, her third daughter, Angie, having slipped from her almost painlessly. When Taddeusz could not be found, it was kind old Mrs. Dykes from the next door flat in Bayswater who took charge and prevented Angie from being born in the bathtub, for that's what Lily insisted upon, she must be immaculately clean before being hustled into her clothes and rushed by taxi to the hospital. No time for the ablutions, nor the surgical shave. Lily was whisked directly along the sloping ramp into the birth chamber, where the resident doctor, bemused and curse-whispering, pulled on his transparent gloves to preside over a birth that might just as easily have happened in Lily's bed. But now, at thirty-five, Lily was often seized with needling stabs in the womb. She harboured them like some Divine Right of Queens, complaining incessantly, yet ready to die and sink to heaven before she suffered a surgeon to separate her from her pain.

And Flo, too, was adept at pain. The birthpain of one who had put out spores in dark forbidden places. That one-and-only, meant to be hers, yet not hers, never ever hers. That unnamed unclaimed boychild, whom she'd steadfastly refused to handle. Its fleetingly glimpsed face of crumpled tissue; blood-stained, skin-stained, tear-stained. Features alien, squalid and mottled. Eyelids deep-sealed, stretched upward like tiny bowstrings, eyelashes encrusted with flakes of pearl. True, its imperious nose was undeniably hers. So, too, perhaps were its smooth lips, glistening with spume, its miniature fists with their coin-sized palms clenching and unclenching, agitated, primed to do battle. Perhaps already sensing the need to forestall, to deny the inevitable—her ultimate denial.

Jesusboy, *Jezz,* they called it, the anonymous, uniformed, almost uniform collection of ministrants at the Orphanage. Such a rickety dwelling it was too, with its shanty-like aspect of impermanence, billowing in white muslin, echoing in white halls, reeking of sea salt and kelp.

Back, back to the Sea from which it came, the baby that had no name.

And then came the outstretched hand of the eldest guardian. She had the air of a marooned sojourner from some equatorial isle. Her tough brown hand was scrupulously clean and dry, its palmflesh incised with dark lines of destiny. Between she and Flo, a couple of pound notes offered and taken, a shared whisper:

Take good care of it for me, please.

I will—

I promise I'll come back as soon as I can.

"Now who's that banging on the door down there?" said Flo suddenly, her gaze hardening into the present moment, her expression an enigma, living fossil of imprinted pain or else the permafrost of outrage.

"Oh, Flo, it must be Greta."

"The little tart!"

"Go and let her in, will you?"

"What, after what she's done tonight?"

"But, Flo, it's freezing out there, and she ain't dressed properly."

"Why ain't she got her key?"

"I don't know."

"Let her sleep out there on the doorstep."

"Oh, please, Flo, go down and let her in."

"You'd better tell her what Albert said, you'd better warn her, or else I will."

Lily's timid pleading gaze was suddenly sentimental and full of alarm. "All right, all right, but it's her birthday tomorrow, so just promise me you won't say nothin' about it tonight."

CHAPTER 5

MONDAY MORNING

Flo screamed once from downstairs. Then came the tramp of her footsteps as she mounted painfully upstairs. She paused on the landing, listening for signs of life.

"Lily!" she shrieked again.

But Lily did not move. She lay in yesterday's tatty frock and wrinkled cardigan, wrapped in profoundly tortured sleep beneath the bedclothes. Greta raised her body on one elbow and leaned across the mattress.

"Wake up, Mother," she said, poking Lily viciously in the ribs. "Don't you hear Flo calling you down there?"

Lily groaned feebly and stirred, flicking her dry tongue over her chapped lips. "What, Greta? What d'you say?"

"I said get up. Flo's screaming her bloody head off down there."

Lily's features were sculpted in agony. "All right, I'm getting up now, O God!"

Greta heaved herself off the mattress and headed for the kitchen. She filled the tea-kettle with tap water and put it on to boil. Then she pushed aside the unwashed dishes and ran cold water over her hands.

"Greta!"

"What?" said Greta, dabbing her toothbrush into the small round tin of Eucalyptus powder.

"Make me a cup of tea, darling, I just can't move."

Greta fished for the dissolving wafer of Imperial Leather soap. Carefully she washed her face and neck, then ran back into the bedroom with a towel around her neck. "Are these clothes clean, Lily?"

"Yes, darling."

Greta grabbed a rumpled flannel blouse from the linen mountain next to Lily's bed; it was the colour of frail eggshell spattered in chickenshit. "So what are they doing on the bloody floor, then?" she said.

Lily groaned and rolled toward the wall, shielding her eyes from the agonizing light pouring through the windowpane.

"I said what's this chest of drawers here for? A decoration?"

"I was going to put them clothes away yesterday, I was, honest."

"They've been on this floor since last year, and you know it."

"Put that woolly cardigan on. Auntie Beattie sent it over for you. That'll fit you, that will."

"I don't want nothing from no one, specially that bitch!"

"You'll freeze if you go out like that!"

"So what!"

"Where you going, then?"

"Mind your own business," said Greta. The tea she had made was too hot. It scalded her throat. She brushed her hair violently into place.

"Greta?"

"What?" Greta pulled on her nylons a little too roughly. Her toenail pierced a hole at the toe, which slowly snaked itself into a narrow ladder all the way to her knee. Greta noticed it a moment later, and swore. She clipped the top of her stockings onto her garter belt.

"Is my tea ready yet, darling?"

"It's on the bloody table, come and get it," shouted Greta, from halfway down the staircase; then she was gone, slamming the front door behind her.

The Social Security Office was just around the corner on Settles Street. That's it, thought Greta, gazing, with a stab of apprehension, at the scratched gilt lettering above the door lintel. The reception desk on the second floor was presided over by a lady whose dull gingery hair was laced, at the temples, with masses of kinky silver.

"Is this where I'm supposed to apply for a job?" said Greta.

"Your name, please," replied the lady, with a magisterial air. She poised the nib of her fountain pen over a pad of yellow forms.

"Greta Morvaye."

"Date of birth?"

"The fourteenth of November, 1940; that's today."

Greta grinned foolishly as though she expected the pallid lady to smile and break into song.

"Previous experience?" said the lady.

"I ain't never, er, none."

"I see; well, would you please fill in your address in block letters?" said the lady, handing her the yellow form. Languidly she waved in the direction of the waiting room, a dilapidated space lit by three dome-shaped windows. Its pock-marked raw brick walls were clad in off-white institutional paint and graced, here and there, by a handful of antediluvian posters. Governmental edicts. Cautionary notices. Fissured bilious-looking charts of house Rules & Regulations: *Kindly take a seat until you are called; Strictly no alcohol to be consumed or brought onto the premises.*

"'Ow long we gonna have to wait?" whispered someone. "They don't never answer the telephone, neither, what do they care, they'd let you rot—wicked, i'nit?"

A fleshly apparition, reeking of booze, lurched aimlessly alongside a bank of glassed-in cages. It was here that the long-suffering officials on day duty sat safely enshrined away from the rambunctious multitudes. A second grey-bearded inebriate, a blaspheming prophet in a trench coat, stood up abruptly and stumbled toward the exit portal; a pool of thermos tea or piddle shone quietly beneath his seat. On his way out, he crossed a wild-haired female of uncertain age, a ragged earthling carrying her assorted grave goods, a damp sleeping-bag rolled up with cord, a bag of woollens, fruit, biscuits, a tin bowl. Bumping into Greta, she bathed her briefly in a miasma of raw onion and stale tobacco; a feathery black runt, her familiar, came scratch-tapping across the floorboards after her, settling onto her spilled-open carpetbag.

I ain't waitin' in this piss-hole, thought Greta, eyeing the plaster-pale teenaged Madonna seated directly opposite her, who shivered steadily, clutching onto her comatose infant as though in a vain effort to keep warm. But already Greta was absorbing the dusty living scent of the place, the broken-spirited humming and sighing, the grotesque consensus of desperation exuding its own peculiar currents of lit darknesses. Her thought-fingers trembled, twitched in artisanal empathy. This scene with its living, traveling scents and sounds glowed white-hot in her mind and fused itself into the eternal.

"What can you do, Miss Morvaye? Have you any skills?" said Mr. Norton, upon ushering her, more than an hour later, into his stuffy, slightly mangy looking office, which was half buried in stacks of antiquated letter trays, overflowing cardboard boxes, mildewed folders and files. Highly doubtful, he might have been thinking—(given his penetrating gaze, rendered awesome by magnifying lenses, his unfathomable leer)—aside from dragging her saucy little ass down Cable Street.

"Well, I—"

Mr. Norton took the rumpled yellow form from her hand, and perused it rapidly. "You see, it's not very easy to find a place for you if you have no skills. What was your last school year completed, Greta?"

"Third form at St. Victoire's Covent Grammar School."

Mr. Norton looked startled. "I see, and you're—?"

"Fifteen."

"Fifteen? I see, well, Greta, do you have any special talents? For example, do you—"

"Painting, I can paint. I paint in oils."

"Oh, you're an artist?" Mr. Norton was really surprised now. He pushed back his chair, adjusted his spectacles to take a second look. Pretty. Very pretty, he thought. And a saucy little tart she looks, too. Contentious dark eyes under low straight brows. Deep spots of blood speckling the cheekbones. A squarish, sensuous tip to her nose, and a resentful slant to her sullen mouth. "All right, Greta, here are a couple of places you might try. There's a factory on Fenchurch Street where they're looking for someone who can hand-decorate pottery."

"Well—"

"Or here's another one. Perkins' Laundry on Philpot Street. That's in your district, isn't it? They need a counter girl immediately."

"So should I—?"

"Apart from those two, Greta, I don't have anything else at the moment. Just take these addresses and tell them Mr. Norton from the Employment Office sent you."

"Thanks ever so much, Sir," said Greta, in her high-pitched, nasal, deliberately genteel Cockney voice. All that polishing they'd rubbed into her at the private boarding school in France;

she'd surprise the old bastard with a bit of breeding. She folded the note-paper and stuffed it into her breast pocket.

"Oh, and Greta, if you don't get the job, come back and see me, won't you?"

"Yes, thank you, I will," said Greta, loitering at the door. The shaggy haired receptionist, distracted momentarily from her correspondence, fixed her gaze upon Greta's scuffed heel, the traveling obscenity of her laddered stocking.

"That's right," leered Mr. Norton, scribbling into Greta's newly opened file. Sunlight laced the autumnal tweed of his jacket, creating around him a sort of haloesque canvas-glow. "You just come back, dear, and see me—*any time*."

CHAPTER 6

NO ART IS POSSIBLE WITHOUT A DANCE WITH DEATH, CÉLINE

Angie, pale as the morning, was running toward the tinkle of the school bell. Her windblown hair was as fine as flax; her lank, bony body, more spirit than flesh. It seemed to be a body moving steadily onward, wrapped in its own envelope of mist—miraculously blinded, miraculously shielded from the precipice ahead. Blunt knifestrokes hacked through her lungs as she ran, a seemingly endless underwater ballet. Surely, if she ran fast enough, Time itself would graciously stand still—for her alone—so that she wouldn't be late, she daren't be late. The universe whirled, curdled and spun around her; she was no longer running now, but floating, floating around the corner of Walden. Past the iron-spiked cellar grates of Turner Street. Into Ashfield.

Rutland School was a three-storeyed monument resembling a Victorian Dosshouse. Red-brick walls. Cement-tipped posts set at intervals along a gigantic wire fence enclosing the games court. What windows there were, ever melancholy with dust, remained mostly closed except in summer, when a hooked wooden pole was sent the rounds of the classrooms to push out the topmost transom panes for an invigorating breath of East London air. A street-tough assortment of urchins came straggling, singly or in clutches, through the arched school gate, then across the forecourt, which was paved with uneven swells and hollows, like a silted-up valley of ashen cement.

At the piercing shrill of the drill whistle in they filed, an agitated squirming sea serpent being sucked into an underwater cave. A twilit space. Tranquil and safe, with its distinctive reek of school benches, musty vellum, chalkdust and lead. Past the ancient lukewarm radiators, enshrined beneath the windows on each landing, poured these ragged panting little bodies, each with its particular scent blending into the common medley, swelling the low-ceilinged passages of dim antique white, clamouring, whispering, pushing, tugging, flooding the main hall in a vast square rocking sea.

Of silence—a lull, a tempest becalmed. Headmistress, Mrs. Myles, glided to her throne on the raised dais. Soberly elegant, immaculately perfumed and powdered, her graceful little coils of auburn hair were permaset into a burnished crown; her eyes, lips, her entire being blazed with the conviction of royalty to rabble. She eyed the mute, assembled staff and their rag-tag charges with authoritarian severity, gloomy disdain, the iron curtain of intimidation. It worked wonders—above all, never to smile, lest it be construed as leniency or weakness. As was the custom, with her solid oak ruler tucked between the pages of the Old Testament, Mrs. Myles addressed the morning assembly:

The Lord is my shepherd. I shall not want. He maketh me to lie down in green pastures. He leadeth me beside the still waters. Yeah, though I walk through the Valley of the Shadow...

It was this image that always blew a grim draught across Angie's baby soul. Where was it, the valley of the shadow of death? Perhaps the gloom-corridor between Walden and the sprawling London Hospital, inhabited—surely—by one-eyed trolls and cloven-footed devils, wandering ghosts of slain harlots, their throats hacked open by the Ripper's knife. Perhaps even the sable shadow of the phantom Aunt Flo swore she'd seen stooping across her bed on certain nights.

Thou preparest a table before me in the presence of mine enemies...

Enemies, indeed—there was hateful Jennifer Markham with her flaming orange pigsknot, massive bully body and viper's tongue. One day vengeance would be hers. Next time Jennifer bounced up to collect first prize for the egg-and-spoon race, Angie'd stretch her plimsoll just far enough across the aisle—

Thou anointest my head with oil...

Angie hadn't bathed, nor washed her hair last night, of course. There was time only to splash a little cold water over her face this Monday morning, tug at her ankle-socks and lace up her grungy plimsolls. Now, shrinking like some miniature Alice among the mushrooms, she swallowed the acrid after-taste of tea on her tongue, and prayed that the sphinx-like gaze of the headmistress should not fall upon her anointed head.

And I will dwell in the house of the Lord forever...

Within the solid mass of steaming bodies, Angie sensed an uneasy rustle, a collective tremor as Mrs. Myles stepped down from the platform. She moved forward; her oak ruler swung downward with a *thwack*, stinging the grimy knucklebones of two unfortunates near the end of the front row. Simon Geldblum was seen blowing hard on his fingers; his ears were brick red above the tide-line of yesterday's grime.

"We have repeated continually that there is *no* excuse for any pupil to come to school unwashed," declared Mrs. Myles, transfixing the entire assembly with her steady, green-glittering gaze. "Always remember, children, cleanliness is next to godliness," she said.

At the head of Angie's class stood Mr. Levy, his desert-olive skin taut and shining around his smooth hooked nose. Tiny tucklets rigged the corners of his eyes to his balding temples and his lips into a beatific smile. Mornings, he struck the pose of a martial hero, dry as a sunbaked fig, still humming the canticle of Moses in a timeless desert war. Given a romantic black patch strapped over one eye, he might have passed for a weather-beaten old Mt. Sinai general presiding over guns and tanks and suicide commandos, or else a diminutive rod-bearing Moses leading the Children of Israel into the Promised Land. But his borrowed troops were just a column of East End ragamuffins who tumbled up the footworn staircase into the classroom after him, and who sprang to attention only at the flesh-raising squeak of his chalk on the blackboard, or the occasional swish of his wooden cane.

The pupils now settled down at their desks, yawning and scratching their heads with alarming vigour. They thumped down their battered copybooks, then sidled into a queue to begin grinding and regrinding their tiny pencils at the sharpener, once in a while staring at Mr. Levy with the collective hostility of thirty pair of Monday-morning eyes. It was time now for Angie's weekly martyrdom, the collecting of the dinner money. Ringing coppers, shillings and ha'pennies delivered up, one by one, from grubby fists to be locked into Mr. Levy's desk drawer.

"Lionel Anthony, Joey Bernstein, Rosanna Barnett, Simon Geldblum," sang out Mr. Levy. His melodious voice flowed from lips as colourless as sand. "Benjamin Isaacson, Margaret Kirk, Jennifer Markham..."

Sensing that familiar firebrand on each cheek, Angie mentally trudged up Calvary behind him, waiting for that pregnant pause which encircled her name, saw him glance up tactfully to check the presence of the non-paying 'welfare' kid, flush-faced and nailed to her wooden seat.

"Shirley Nollings, Mary Peate, Eleanor Schiller, Barry Segal, Janet Wylie," chanted Mr. Levy, rolling calmly downhill.

Mr. Levy now flicked open the pages of the Old Testament and launched into the story about the Red Sea. In they all tumbled after him: first, Jennifer Markham, brashly wide-eyed, twitching her phosphorescent orange pigtails as she went. Behind Jennifer came Eleanor Schiller, raven-haired, with droopy eyes aglaze in her wan sleepy face. And further back, entrenched as in a dugout, Simon Geldblum, having recovered his composure, even his bravado, flexed his rubber-and-twig contraption, targeting Angie's left temple. She, oblivious to danger, wandered trustingly on the virtual coat-tails of the schoolmaster into the foaming surf. Her mind, responsive and malleable, like putty or primeval mud, soaked in the Biblical spoken Word, obediently absorbed the ordained image; already a rolling crescented salt green spray seemed to be thundering, dangerously, above her head.

But the children of Israel walked upon dry land in the midst of the sea, and the waters were a wall unto them to their left and to their right...

Mr. Levy paused and glanced up. Someone stifled a giggle, although a universal grin had stretched itself across the room as though yanked by a common thread. The schoolmaster's shrewd yellow-speckled eyes, like those of a sun-wary lizard perched on a crag, glinted solemnly at the would-be offender.

"Master Geldblum!"

"Yes, Sir?"

"Sling-shots may well have had their uses in the days of Goliath, but you are aware, are you not, that in my classroom they are strictly forbidden!" A benign potentate, satisfied for the moment, Mr. Levy returned his attention to the Holy Book.

And I will sing unto the Lord for he hath triumphed gloriously. The horse and its rider He hath thrown into the sea.

It was this verse that reminded Angie of Solly, their next-door neighbour. Draped in robe and desert sandals, he'd be cursing and pulling his scruffy nag between the trembling walls of water. She imagined the beast's hysterical whinny, its refusal to take another step.

The depths have covered them. They sank to the bottom like a...

"*Mr. Levy!*" It was Miss Thayne's voice, a piercing stage-whisper that sizzled above their heads from the half-open classroom door. "D'you think it would be possible to send your pupils to the gymnasium a little early this morning?"

"*...like a stone,*" intoned Mr. Levy, frowning darkly. He thumped his Bible shut. "Early, Miss Thayne?" he echoed, openly contentious, challenging, displeased.

"Yes, a little early, if you please, as Monday's the *only* day I can have the hall free for a full hour—what with the easels moving in and out, and the recorders, and choir practice and the workmen painting down there, and the assemblies!"

Miss Thayne, fretfully pale, tightened her lips and glared, not an auspicious omen. In a heartbeat she grasped control of the class, appearing as triumphant as Caesar at the gateway to Rome. Coiled like a wire spring, her slightest whisper electrified the ranks with its breathy timbre. Her dun-coloured feathery eyebrows shot skyward, her eyes glittered urgently, consuming the wayward souls of her pupils into rapt attention.

"Listen, children, do you realize that we have scarcely four weeks left to practice? Now, I'm sorry, but if you cannot perform your Xmas dance properly this morning, I shall just have to strike this class off the program."

Fifteen minutes later in the ground-floor assembly hall, the music ceased, abrupt as death. Miss Thayne's fingers trembled as she swung back the needle-arm of the gramophone; perhaps, on days such as these, the awesome power she wielded over the life and death of the dance overwhelmed her, too.

"No, no, no!" Her voice resounded, mist-hollowy, striking the walls, which reverberated with outrage. "I said, no, that was wrong *again!"*

The whirling dancers froze in mid-step, confused, fidgeting and groaning with irritation. Angie trembled all over, her wan overstretched calf muscles, her ribs smouldering around lungs ripe for bursting, her swift-hammering heart that seemed to be squeezed inside a nutcracker. *It was no use.* No matter how hard she tried, she could not master the temporal, spatial and aerial complexities of Miss Thayne's dance drills. Angie was neither quick-thinking nor physically adroit enough to execute those graceful little twirls, leaps and skips; neither could she get herself positioned precisely where she was supposed to be, whenever the violent hammerstrokes exploding out of the old school piano signaled the merciful end, or beginning of each round. Miss Thayne didn't appear to understand this ingrained flaw in Angie's nature; at any rate, she sincerely believed it was nothing more than laziness, stubbornness, inattention, something that could and *must* be corrected.

"I said no, Angie, no, no, no!" Miss Thayne seized Angie by the arm, her blood pressure rising, her crusty-dough complexion flushing like a dull grape. Side by side they stood, palms clasped, an unwieldy cross-hatched pair, fearsome giant linked to recalcitrant flax-headed elf, chins high, backs straight, knees raised, right foot pointed outward. "All right, we'll practise this again together," declared Miss Thayne, "but this time watch me carefully, *and follow!*"

O blessed moment. The time had came when it was all over. Well, for another week, at least. Angie's heart was beating so violently on her way back upstairs that she had to pause for a moment on the second landing to catch her breath. Through the tall windowpane, darkened by its perpetual mist layer of soot and dust, she caught a glimpse of her mother, Lily, arm in arm with Aunt Flo, crawling along the shadow-strip of Ashfield toward the hospital.

Bird-breasted Aunt Flo, jacketed in black Persian lamb, was strutting painfully forward on injured legs. Hump-shouldered Lily, a surrealistic figure from a Dalian landscape, was shrouded in an old cloth coat of musty olive, like unsloughed skin. Together, they vanished beneath the glassed-in walkway of Edith Cavell Pavilion, past the outpatient clinic, around the windy corner of Whitechapel Road, and up the wide stone steps of the hospital. The marble-black façade of the portico was framed by squat sandstone pillars. A clock hung inside the pediment. As they paused inside the double front doors, Lily felt weak. She leaned on Flo's arm.

"Which way's the children's ward, Flo?"

"Down this way, don't you never remember?"

As always, whenever she entered this hateful place, this place of Judgement, she was assailed by the nauseating reek of antiseptic, the smell of sickness, the pervasive perfume of death. Labyrinthine corridors forever aswarm with cripples, cancers, consumptives hawking, coughing, streaming their way through Surgery. Meanwhile that privileged breed or caste, almost another species, glowing with health, were the snowy-capped uniformed nurses floating all around them; on their white wedged soles they moved through the wards like silent eddies, dispensing opiates, disinfecting wounds, spoon-feeding cripples, collecting befouled bedpans and dressings for the sluices, flicking down thermometers, cranking up mattresses, whipping shut bed-curtains or turning death-sheets.

"Oh, I hate this place, Flo, you don't know how I hate it."

"Now, pull yourself together, will you?"

Coming towards them, an angelic white-robe was trundling an unwieldy trolley full of fresh linen. Lily faltered, shrank backward, froze momentarily in her tracks, as though confronting the gun turret of a Panzer tank.

"Flo, why was that nurse looking at me just now?"

"No one's looking at you."

"Oh, yes, she was, Flo, I ain't blind."

"Now stop that, Lily."

"D'you think my coat's too shabby?"

"There ain't nothing wrong with your coat."

"All I've got is this old rag to wear."

Flo's tone rose a pitch. "Well, why d'you sleep in it, then?"

"I've got to, it's bloody freezing upstairs. The roof's leaking again. You've got to tell Albert before it bloody—"

"Lily!"

"—before it snows on our bloody heads."

"All right, I'll ask Albert to find out if he can get that roof fixed, and then he's going to ask me when's the last time you paid your rent."

"Effing tightfist!"

"Albert ain't putting no more money on the house, Lily. We got another letter from the London Hospital last month. They said they're going to start tearing all the houses down by next spring."

"Tearing them down? Don't you believe it; them houses ain't never going to be torn down. Besides, where do they think we're all going to live, then?"

They lease them out to us like damp leaking coffins, thought Lily, cramped oblong boxes—with their walled-in yards and outdoor 'privies'—to be reclaimed at will. Almost since the war's end, Walden's dank, unsanitary terrace-houses had been marked for demolition, then granted an interminable stay of execution. It was now just a question of time, the existential masonry of Time. The hospital would expand its domain; some day it might well overflow its banks, submerging them all in its antiseptic well, sucking to the bottom the frail multitudes, those too weak to flee, to keep pace with the rest of mankind.

"Lily, what are you standing there for?" Flo's voice rose again. In barely suppressed fury, she bit her top lip which was elaborately rounded out with lipstick. Her cheeks, like harsh-veined marble, flushed dangerously. "Peter's been waiting for hours already, come on, for God's sake."

Lily stood her ground, muttering. "Bloody death landlords, they ain't gonna pull no houses down, they'll bury us all underneath first."

When they finally reached the children's ward, Peter was marooned beside his packed suitcase, looking like a sulking cherub on the hospital bed. His spiked chestnut hair, mother-of-pearl smile, and 'drop-dead-gorgeous' eyes were tragically mismatched to a stunted, dwarfish body—heir, as he was, to that randomly scarred gene, wreaking its careless, its cosmic effect on his body.

"How long've you been waiting here all dressed up?" said Flo. She stooped, like some clumsy bird, to swallow him up in her woolly black embrace.

57

"Two hours."

"Oh, my poor darling!"

"I thought no one was coming to get me."

"Of course I was coming to get you, you know that, I just couldn't get your mother out of bed."

"Ain't she come, then?"

"She's outside, signing some papers for the doctor."

"Two hours I've been waiting for you—"

"I'm sorry, love, how're you feeling?"

"I ain't never coming back here no more, I hate it."

"Godstruth, you ain't half pale, what've they been doing to you?"

"Taking tests, Auntie, tests for my blood, tests for my heart, tests for my stomach, tests for my lungs, collecting whole bottles of piss from me every hour—"

"Never mind that now."

"—and making me drink this yellow medicine that tastes like piss too."

"All right, you're coming home now, and guess what I bought you for Xmas!"

"What?"

"A brand new watch. Seventeen jewels. Cost me five quid down Hessel Street, but don't you go telling Uncle Albert, will you?"

Peter's misshapen fingers clawed at Flo's knobbly black coat sleeve. "Can't I have it now, Auntie? Let me have it—please."

"Oh, no, I can't do that, love, not before Xmas. Here's your mum coming. Ready, Lily?"

Lily trembled. She trembled with the effort it had cost her to sign that intimidating form, that cryptic maze of black and white, that *Open Sesame* magically releasing her son from the *Gates of Hell* to her. Carefully she formed the letters of her name, licking her ash-dry lips, deliberately scoring over her pen-strokes as though engraving eternal letters on her tombstone. Then she gazed on Peter, almost afraid to look, yet clinging to the lines and shadows of his face. His huge deep-set brown eyes, his chopped dark hair, his skin, water white, transparent over temple veins of sluggish blue.

"All right, darling, I'll carry your suitcase. Don't make him walk too fast, Flo."

"Can I have my new watch today—please, Auntie, please?"

"He's going to be all right, ain't he, Flo?"

Lily shuffled her thin haunches over the scrubbed hospital tiles. Flo didn't answer. She gripped Peter's hand and steered him through a maze of dreary corridors, down two service elevators, up a rubber ramp, then out through one of the innumerable back passages connecting to Walden.

CHAPTER 7

Stain

"Angie, get your nose out of that book and get your lazy arse up off that chair," said Greta. As she came rattling in, reeking of wind and damp, she dumped a small cardboard box on the kitchen table. Inside was a baby tortoise, thunderstuck, traumatized, laid in a bed of lettuce leaves and grass. Its exquisitely formed shell was inlaid with striated sections of polished jade. A wave of reptilian terror arose from inside the box.

"Where d'you get that from?"

"Down the market. Someone wanted to get rid of it, so I took it."

"Oh."

"Didn't you hear me, I said get up off that chair!"

"Don't start on me, Greta, or I'm going down to Gran's."

"Oh, no you're not. You're making me a cup of tea first. Ain't there nothing to eat in this place?"

"I don't know."

"You don't know nothing, do you? Not even what day it is. What's the date today, eh? Tell me that, you prawn."

"It's Monday, ain't it?"

"No, it's Monday, the fourteenth of November, 1955."

"So what?"

"So nothing, you bitch. Where d'you get them apples from?"

"From down the market."

"What with?" said Greta. She rummaged through the cupboards, and knocked down a couple of boxes. "How d'you pay for 'em—with buttons?"

"With the money from Saidye's washing."

Greta smashed the cupboard doors shut again. "That's it, from now on Lily's going to cook me a bloody steak every day," she said. "I got this job at Perkins' Laundry. Two pound ten a week."

"A job? What, a real job? Ain't you going back to school, then?"

"No, I ain't, hurry up with that tea, will you. I'm fifteen, right? So, it's legal. They can't do a bleedin' thing about it."

"Perkins' Laundry?"

"Yeah, any objections?"

"Ain't there nothing else?"

"Yeah, there's painting a bunch of clay pots down on Fenchurch Street."

"But don't you like that, aren't you good at painting?"

"Yeah, I'm good at painting. But when I decide I want to paint something, like your ugly mug, I'll paint it. And not when some fat arse-hole of a boss tells me to."

"Oh, I don't know, Greta, I wish I could paint like you."

"I wish you could make a cup of tea too; what's this piss?" Greta poked into the teapot with her spoon. As the tortoise began creeping around in its brave new world, she stared into the box and grinned. "Here, look, it moves faster than Lily, don't it? Where's she gone to, anyway?"

"She just went round to Gran's."

"Didn't she get her Assistance Money today?"

"I don't know."

"Well, ain't she gone shopping yet?"

"No."

"Bitch!"

"What did I do?" whined Angie.

"Not you, *her.* Is there any biscuits left?"

"No."

"Can you smell that? Flo's cooking a fucking feast downstairs. Peter always gets fed, but there's never anything left for us. What's that you're doing?"

"Homework."

"What's all that shit you're reading? Don't you know the whole Bible's a pack of lies?"

"What d'you mean?"

"That fairy tale in there about the Virgin Mary, for instance, what they don't tell you is she got knocked up by a traveling soldier."

"Knocked up?"

"Yeah, it's written in the Jewish Bible. Don't tell me you didn't know that, Christ!"

"But, Greta—"

"What?"

"What does knocked up mean?"

"Oh, you stupid—!"

"Well, tell me."

"It means she got pregnant—see—by a traveling soldier. That's what it means."

"Oh."

"What're you staring at me for?"

"Nothing."

"Well, then open your eyes, for Christ's sake, just look at this shit-hole you're living in, just look at it!" Greta barged into the bedroom and came back with an armful of laundry. Ragged knickers, blouses, brassieres smashed against the wall. A sock landed in Angie's tea. Greta buried her fingers in her sister's hair as though it were a harvest of unripe wheat, and yanked viciously.

"Ow, that hurt, y'know—"

"Now just stop reading your comics and your bleedin' Bibles, and start cleaning up this shit-hole instead."

"You leave me alone, or I'm going round to Gran's."

"Stop that sniveling."

"I hate you."

"Me too, 'oy, where d'you think you're going? Come back here, you prawn, I just remembered something. Didn't I never tell you about that mad lodger who used to live up here with his wife before you was even born. Didn't no one ever tell you what happened?"

"No."

"Well, this creepy lodger, he murdered his wife right near that chair where you was sitting—don't get scared, silly, they never found her body, poor cow, just this bloody ugly bloodstain on the floor right where your foot is now."

Angie jerked her foot away. She blanched a shade more ashen than usual.

"They think he must have bricked her up behind the wall, that one over there. I saw her ghost once, sliding through—*it was horrible*—her eyes were wide and staring, and her blood was pouring all the way down the walls!"

The fat clock on the mantelpiece had long ago been struck dumb. It was lodged for Eternity at 17 minutes to seven. Greta pulled down the sleeves of her denim jacket. There was a roar outside; Kenny was revving up the motorcycle engine, loudly agitating at the curb.

"Watch out for that bloodstain," said Greta, peering slyly at the clock. "It comes back every year on the fourteenth of November, that's the night she was murdered, at exactly a quarter to seven—"

"Don't go, Greta, *wait for me!*"

"Oh, dear, now is that Kenny down there waiting for me?" said Greta, picking up her handbag. She grabbed the tortoise in its box. "Think I'd better put it downstairs in the shed, it might catch something nasty up here, eh?" she said, followed by that dangerous laugh of hers.

"Greta, wait, wait for me—!" Angie's fingers fumbled spastically with the grimy laces of her plimsolls. Her chintzy frock flew behind her like a balloon. She descended the twisting inkwell of a staircase like a firefighter at his pole; touched down at every second or third step, like a rampant heart murmur. Her ankle folded neatly under her at the very bottom, knees scraping against the gritty rug. Stumbling through her sister's vanished shadow, she smashed her way almost bodily through the front door.

CHAPTER 8

THE MERMAN'S SPAWN

Lily's father, Karl, was a Teuton from Heligoland, a blond emaciated seaman who jumped his fishing trawler at the London docks and bedded down at the first derelict hotel that opened its seedy arms to lost souls and ancient Mariners. One day in 1918, he tumbled down the suspended causeway, reeking of cod and pitch, testing his sea legs for the first time on firm land after weeks of rolling at the spumy edge of the earth. He now couched down with the bedbugs, prior tenants to his mildewed berth. They tickled lovingly over his shankbones, tapped deep his warm thighs and buttocks, and left blood splotches of themselves each time he twisted inside the nightmare strips of sacking that served as sheets.

But grandfather, Karl was not, at least not yet. He was, in 1918, a thin-chiseled youth with a wild netted look about him. Like a merman with a borrowed soul, he floundered up and down London's east dockside, never seeming to trust the solidity of the pavement beneath his feet; drifting through the obscurity of the fog, whilst ravenously sniffing out work—potato boy for a while in a fish shop at Limehouse, coated in grease drippings and loath to loose his Danish tongue for fear of being mistaken for a bloody German. The 'Great War' was smouldering to a close, but London was still an outraged city.

Karl rubbed in his home-made pomade—a smearing of cold chip grease and potato water, deliberately dulling the beacon glow of his platinum temples. He examined his skinny jaw, pocked with adolescent pimples, reflected inside the fragment of a mirror he'd retrieved from a bomb-site on Salmon Lane. His flaxen hair he ruled flat from his temples; his blanched lips were barely distinguishable, lost in wisps of blond swansdown. Pale narrow teeth, an inordinate number of them crowded neat and close into his jaw. There was no fixed colour to his eyes, they blended grey or else spume green into the atmosphere.

Girdled in a fishstained apron, his hips thin as an unformed girl's, Karl plunged his blond hairy hand into the batter, reeking of cod as usual, watched by Renie who was leaning up against the shop counter waiting for her newspaperful of fried fillet and chips, sensing the tremulous quiver of fish-tail deep in her own gut. She gazed up and down Karl's narrow flanks, shrouded in fish-linen, and fantasized upon his Nordic alabaster limbs bestriding virgin floes and Jungfrau peaks. Deep in December she made him her lover, soon to be teeming with eleven, twelve, or was it thirteen little fishlings? Flo, Lily, Ruth, Raymond, Tweetie, Georgie—four decades later, Renie could scarcely remember all their names.

Renie and Karl were married beneath the white turrets and spires of All Saints' Church, a sweeping flat-roofed barge, a holy stone white ark moored alongside East India Dock Road. It was a Catholic mass, Renie sentimentally attached to her Irish blood-roots and Karl scarcely comprehending his vows and barely acknowledging the very Catholic God that joined him—a lapsed Lutheran—into sacred Matrimony with this passionate Mädchen from Water Close. He guessed she must be older than him by perhaps four or five years. Renie was, in fact, twenty-three and enveloped already in a bountiful and fresh Pre-Raphaelite plumpness; still, he could not have imagined her as she was now at the age of sixty, ensconced between bed and table, her snuff-stained fingers straining to extract the insides of a fowl for dinner, slicing cucumbers into a glass bowl full of vinegar, her head trembling noiselessly on its flaccid ringed neck, a bloated old Titan in perpetual motion.

A massive Victorian bedframe of scarred reddish wood seemed to hold up the wall. It was beating heart and soul of the room. Easy chair, confessional, sofa and crib. To its crumb-gritty blankets gravitated dozens of grandbabies; the mere touch of its snuff-fragrant pillow and deep rotting mattress floated them instantly away. It was steamy hot heaven itself to close one's baby eyes, propped between the sustaining wall on one side, on the other, the shadowy hulk of a tender giant.

Renie was presiding over the square wooden table, laid with a shiny white chequered oilcloth and drawn up close beside her bed. Everything was executed in this spot, runner beans clipped, chickens disemboweled and their stillborn egg yolks collected in dishes, potatoes soaked, peeled and sliced into chips. Her bed-sitting-room was large; it had a fireplace, and its tall wood-framed window opened midway along Walden. The antique beige-flowered wallpaper was stained with greasy palm smudges as high up as the children's hands could reach. It was a comfortable shabby old cave, smelling of snuff and coal and chicken broth, a tribal field-camp through which the scattered remnants of Renie's offspring tramped in and out. True, the Herman tribe had diminished in number. Quite a few had migrated to serener, greener pockets of the city. Those left behind were the ones who couldn't or didn't want to go, or the ones like Lily who had once been uprooted and torn away, only to be sucked back in.

Renie's sister Georgina, aged sixty-eight, sat perched beside her on the bed, dark and frail and melting away like a translucent cake of soap. Strips of thinly rationed hair, coal-dusty in colour, were soberly arranged around her skull. She held her head expectantly high, listing a little to one side and trying to fix her flickering gaze on whoever was speaking. Georgina was blind. Eternal cataracts poured over her eyes, filmy white streams that plunged her into a world of whiteness, shrouding everything behind a permanently milky veil. But Georgina could still hear the lyrical babble of the grandchildren; despite the familial diaspora, quite a few of Renie's adult children had never truly left home.

This, as everyone knew, was because Renie was an eternal font of tenderness. An infant, no matter whose, was almost always being 'minded' nearby, oblivious to the clatter, safely anchored behind Renie on her voluminous day-bed. Young Peter, just this morning discharged from hospital, had sunk into a restless sleep beneath her comfort blanket. Then Angie had come tearing upstairs and was soon wrapped in a foetal coil around her brother's body. The kid was too scared to go back alone to an empty house; however Lily, who was warming her thin behind in front of the fireplace, showed no sign of wanting to go home.

"Here's your tea, love, be careful," said Renie. Her own head shook back and forth incessantly, rhythmically; her benevolent half-smile was placid, compassionate. Georgina's fingers groped for the handle; with a trembling great effort, she navigated the enamel rim to her lips.

Their brother, Henry, was there too, sitting close to the fireplace. Usually he was verbose and cheerful, but tonight he seemed low, dejected, sitting with crumpled shoulders, head bent, gripping a bottle of Guinness between his knees, paying attention to no one, just grumbling softly to himself. A fine-looking man he once was, if one recalled the old photos of Henry in his smart army gear, although he was never the same after the first 'Great War,' *began wandering around in his mind,* as they say. Now he was an unquiet presence, full of soaring imaginings, obsessed with the latest possible sightings of flying saucers, legendary spaceships headed for the remotest wrinkles of the universe, where sickness and even death had been conquered. A Super-tribe of Aliens scarcely distinguishable from earthlings were walking the earth this very moment, believed Henry, kept eternally alive by a top-secret blend of chemicals, a sort of space-age elixir granted to mankind, at last, after so many centuries of searching for the Philosopher's Stone.

Tonight Henry was silently sunk into his cups, and Renie was reminiscing through one of her favourite ancestral tales, the one that sent ice thrills down Angie's back whenever she heard it. One gruesome night, years ago, Renie's own mother, Clara, had made her way on foot to the hospital, carrying a baby in her arms. The infant had been taken ill with the croup and was coughing itself breathless.

"Which one of us was it?" said Renie to her sister. "I can never remember if it was you or Vicky or Henry; in any case, just before mum turned the corner, she was stopped by a stranger, a man. She said she'd never seen anyone like him before. He didn't look like he came from the East End, he was too well dressed for that. He was wearing some sort of black cloak and cape, although it was the middle of summer, and tall leather boots—you know the kind with them fancy brass buckles—anyway, with that cape of his, mum couldn't see his face until he was right in front of her. He asked where she was going in a soft gentle sort of way. His voice was very low, and that eerie glittering look in his eyes gave her such a scare, to her dying day just the memory of it would cause a rash of goose pimples all the way up her arms.

"Anyway mum said that she was taking her baby to the hospital because it was sick, and the stranger looked at the baby, pulled the blanket away from its face as though he didn't believe her, as though he wanted to make sure. He was wearing dark kid gloves so she couldn't see his hands, but they looked as though they must be long and bony, like his face, and all of a sudden he reached inside his cloak, perhaps into a secret pocket or something, then he smiled, shook her hand like a real gentleman and pressed a shiny gold sovereign into it—*I swear, honest to God, this is what mum told us*—she didn't know what to say, she didn't even know if she should take it, but before she could thank him he was gone, disappeared around some corner. It wasn't till next day that she heard some other poor girl's body had been found not far from the hospital, with her throat slashed to bits by the Ripper's knife."

Georgina, too, remembered that story. She had heard it countless times and was nowhere near as fond of it as Renie was. Being old and blind, she was doubly vulnerable and at the perpetual mercy of the world's mercy. To preserve a peaceful state of mind, she preferred to populate the irrevocable mists that enveloped her with saner, more comforting thoughts, sounds and smells. Renie's fragrant chicken broth, for instance,

71

mingled with the damp hairy *'pong'* of Prince, the Alsatian, who was almost lame and on the verge of being put to sleep. Prince bumped against her legs, he slipped and his claws scratched the floor as he laboured to get up. Although he tried, he didn't always make it to the yard in time; tonight Prince had dropped an unsavoury mess downstairs on the corridor rug.

"Godstruth, Mum, I almost slipped on a pile of dogshit," cried Flo as she came upstairs. Tower-dark and imposing, she was standing at the door in her posh Astrakhan jacket, wrathfully examining the sole of her new shoe, looking as though she regretted her impulse to drop in on Renie, on route to the Bingo Hall.

"Didn't you clean it up, Lily?" Renie's head trembled steadily; her mildly ironic smile seemed to say, *I should have known.* "What was you doing downstairs all that time?"

"And what's this?" cried Flo, furious and recoiling from the stench of feces, smeared over her hand and wrist. "What's this white stuff—it looks like flour—bloody'ell, she didn't clean it, Mum, she just dumped a whole packet of flour over it—*LILY!*"

"I was going to clean it up in a minute!" said Lily. "Flour absorbs the smell; I read it in a book, it makes it easier to shovel up."

"Shut up, Lily, bollocks!" said Flo, turning around to Renie. "Mum, she's just pretending to be stone mad so we'll never ask her to do anything, but she's cleverer than any of us. Just look at her, warming up her arse and talking about books, while I almost killed myself coming up them stairs."

The powerful timbre of Flo's voice pierced Angie's slumber. She opened her eyes, yawned, crawled off the bed and went to sit in Prince's hairy armchair. Her mother, Lily, was still perched close to the fireplace, skirt hoisted slightly above her knees, trying to soak up the warmth. The look she gave Flo was filled with venom, insofar as Lily was capable of venom. Her eyes watered, steaming up her lenses.

"I was going to clean it up, Flo, but you don't understand, I was going to do it me'own way."

"Angie, you shouldn't sit so close to the telly," broke in her Aunt Beattie and, as usual, at the sound of her voice the general chatter subsided almost to silence. A taut, mildly hostile silence.

Beattie's leonine mane was what struck you at first glance; although fuzzily unraveling like raw wool, it was still somehow majestic, a sort of tribal headdress. Her serene, wide-apart eyes were the colour of amberdrops set within jaundiced circles and shaded by wispy-thin, magisterial eyebrows. Low, authoritative, grumbly, her voice seemed to scrape its way through rocks. Beattie wasn't from the East End. She came from somewhere up around Birmingham and was an alien of sorts. Perhaps she mildly despised her husband Georgie's family, being—as she was—a prisoner of circumstance, entrenched here in the East End against her will.

"That child's going to ruin her eyes," continued Beattie, glancing mournfully around the room. "Lil, you ought to get her vision checked up at the eye clinic."

"It's no use, you know you can't tell Lily nothing," said Flo, flushing rosy-purple, her face hardening with rage. The maddening reek of dogshit enveloped her, making her want to throttle her sister, or else butter a handful of the stuff down her skirt. "She don't listen to no one. She's got to do things *her* way, and her way means—*fuckall*—who gets Peter to school in the morning? Who gives him his dinner? Not Lily! I'm the one with the injured leg, but she's the one who sits in state and sends me out for the shopping. She's bleedin' lazy, Mum, just look at her, and now she's crying. Crocodile's tears! I'm going to murder her!"

Beattie sighed and went on scribbling her crossword puzzle. Soft-hearted Henry reached over to grasp Lily's hand in sympathy. In his dilapidated jacket, trousers, and limp buttonless shirt, he reeked of tobacco smoke, fermented hops and irreparable bodily decay. He didn't blame her, he declared, in his deep roiling bronchial croak; after all, who likes to shovel up dogshit? When was someone going to finally take that old wreck, Prince, and have him put to sleep?

"D'you know, Lily, one day during the Great War—" Henry's bottle of Guinness slipped between his knees, and hit the hearth.

"Don't drink out of that bottle, Uncle, you'll get a mouthful of splinters!" said Lily, her eyes still glittering with tears.

"Ah, Lil, give over, I said once during the war—"

"Listen, when you came upstairs tonight, Uncle, were you careful not to catch your eye on the nail?"

"Eh?"

"On the first landing, just over on the right side, before the stairs, there's a nail sticking out about an inch. It's bloody dangerous, someone ought to hammer that nail in before it takes someone's eye out!"

Henry's voice rose a full threatening octave; he plunged in again.

"One night, while the last few blokes from our regiment were stuck in those filthy French trenches near the enemy lines, I could hear the bastard Germans patrolling just a few yards away; they couldn't see exactly where we were, but I knew the swines were laying land mines ready to blow us all to Kingdom Come."

"Just a minute, Uncle, when you came upstairs, did you remember to switch on the light?"

"Yes, Lil, I did—"

"And did you walk up on the left side or the right?"

"I don't know, Lil, will you just shut up, I'm telling you something important."

"But this is important too, before you keep on with your story, will you just tell me whether you walked upstairs on the left side or the right?"

"Now, how d'you expect me to remember that, for God's sake?"

"Because if you walk upstairs on the right side, Uncle, there's a killer nail in the wall, waiting to take your eye out!"

There was a splutter, a choking sound from Henry. "She's stone mad," he shouted across the room to Beattie, "she's raving, how can anyone talk to her?"

"But I was only worried about your—" There was an abrupt crash, like a bomb exploding, as Henry picked up his beer bottle and smashed it on the hearth. Deliberately. Lily screamed; she backed out of the way. "You bastard, Uncle, you did that on purpose! You tried to injure me, just because I didn't want you to lose an eye."

But Henry was already gone. They heard him curse as he ploughed through dogshit. The front door smashed shut behind him. Beattie surveyed the remaining débris—a shallow puddle of brown glass shards—with a jaundiced eye.

"I hope no one expects me to clean that up," she said. "Angie, go fetch the dustpan, will you? The one under the stairs."

"Be careful, don't touch that glass, Angie, you'll cut yourself to bits."

"No, she won't, Lil. Go on, Angie, that's a good girl, sweep it up."

"No one has any compassion for me," said Lily. The mere sight of Angie bent over the broken glass evoked a furtive glance of horror; she forced herself to look away. "No one understands the terrible life I've had, what with the husband I had—"

"*That* was your own fault," remarked Beattie grimly, "why didn't you pick one of your own, instead of that foreign bastard?"

75

"All right, never mind, stop crying now, Lil," said Renie, with an ironic glance that seemed to say: *Leave off, there's nothing to be done, she's the way she is.*

From Beattie's throat escaped a low growl, a murmur of disgust. She had scant patience with her sister-in-law, Lily, a fretful child clinging on to Renie well into her thirties. As soon as Lily's babies were out of nappies they were expected to raise themselves and look after their mother as well. In Beattie's view, Renie was far too indulgent with her grown-up daughter, pampered her beyond all common sense. It was sickening. Besides, Beattie was thinking, although she daren't say it, Renie herself had married a foreigner, a bloody German, no less, although he called himself Danish, from Heligoland, not even a Catholic, and just look what had happened to her. It was said that even their parish priest had come close to refusing to unite them. It was bad blood, he'd declared; he had seen it too often before. No good could come from welcoming heretics into the ranks, diluting the Catholicity of his own Church. Whenever he presided over one of these cross-hatched nuptials, his conscience smote him; he repented his rôle as unwilling conspirator to certain tragedy.

Consider the fate of Lily's sister, Ruth, whose name was rarely mentioned these days, and certainly not in front of the grandchildren. *Auntie Ruth wasn't feeling well, so she's gone away for a long rest,* the grandchildren were told whenever they pestered anyone with questions. Lily turned away, too, hid her flushed face, her tears. But Beattie, grounded as she was in the bedrock of prosaic sanity, observed all this from the discomfort of her shabby armchair. Her expression harboured a glint of self-righteousness. Perhaps she disapproved of Ruth's spurious frailty, an indulgence she certainly couldn't permit herself, given her three small boys, born scarcely eighteen months apart, to look after and a virtually absentee husband who materialized only to wolf down the desiccated dinners she kept warm in the oven for him, or else to toss his work overalls on that familiar trail along the passage floor.

Georgie tended the pigeon shed. This was his passion and premier duty, training his homing pigeons to shoot up to Scotland and back in record time. There was also his passion for fishing, which took him away every weekend. Beattie was just biding her time until things got better. He was a good enough husband, within the realm of his limitations. He provided—minimally, shabbily—but he provided nonetheless. They ate proletarian fare, but they did not go hungry. Although the house reeked of decay, it was a shelter. Beattie soon understood that there was no sense trying to disinfect the smell out of the wood, out of the walls—the smell was *inside* the wood, inside the walls. Like a water-damaged book irredeemably warped and speckled with mould, their terrace-house on Walden would go on basking in the damp rot of centuries, for at least another century, unless put to the torch.

But then, the Devil you know! Beattie, at least, had the sense to pick one of her own. Perched securely in her niche like one of Georgie's homing pigeons, marked with an ankle-bracelet, Beattie was programmed for brief domestic flights, hopping steadfastly from target to target before winging her way home. She was not unhappy. She was not even lonely. Hers was a community of strong women and weak women, withdrawn, impassive, deranged women. Women without men.

Beattie noticed that Lily was picking at her food again. On a plate in front of her was a small piece of haddock, a handful of chips.

"What's the matter, Lily?" said Beattie, although she already knew.

"I'm checking for bones."

"There's no bones in there," said Renie.

"It's the tiny ones you've got to look out for. They're like little needles. Treacherous. I got one stuck in my throat once, years ago; I almost died!"

Stealthily, Lily pushed the plate away untouched. With a large handkerchief she began wiping her glasses, reverently gripping the stem as though it were her greatest treasure. But her hands shook; she dropped them—*O horror*—onto the floor. The brittle frame cracked. One lens fell out. Lily went hysterical.

"All right, Lil, calm down," said Beattie heavily.

"Calm down? I can't see anything without them, don't you understand? Where's that lens? *Oh, my God,* where is it—don't move Angie, you might step on it!" Lily bent down, groping on her hands and knees, methodically searching, caressing the pock-marked linoleum with the tips of her outstretched fingers. Up she gazed, her weak eyes glittering with malevolence. "What a curse, *what a bleedin' curse it is to be almost blind!"*

Blind Georgina stirred on her perch, releasing an intake of breath, like a sigh. Renie reached out to touch her sister's hand; with her head shaking gently, rhythmically, she glanced down at Lily in affronted silence.

"I see it, it's right over there next to the armchair," said Beattie, who was blessed with hawkish vision. "Angie, look, can you get that lens for your mum?"

The lens was then glued back into the broken frame with some of Georgie's industrial glue. Beattie's patience was at an end. She looked as though she wanted to push Lily bodily out the door.

"I'm tired, I want to go home," whined Angie. It was a good thing she'd slept through Renie's revival of *'Jack the Ripper.'* Already her heart was skipping, fluttering, remembering the phantom pool of blood, the female corpse bricked up, lurking in wait for them behind their kitchen wall.

"Don't wake Peter up now," whispered Renie, yawning and rolling the blanket over the boy's shoulders. "Leave him be, let him sleep, poor little sod."

Meanwhile, mother and daughter stepped reluctantly into the nightstreet; the cold gripped them, sliced into them like knives.

Thank goodness, just three doors along and they were already home. As they crept along the passageway and up the tottering staircase, the spindle-like rungs of the stairwell breathed damply at them like live things, like the slow-decaying timber shard of coffins. Approaching the bewitching hour it was, and a couple of fat-bodied mice, guilty revelers, bolted across the floor as Lily switched on the attic light. Instantly it blew out again, gave up the ghost in a sudden, hallucinatory flash. It was then that Lily screamed, lunged backward without warning, almost crushing Angie against the wall.

There was a face. A grinning, disembodied face. The ghastly flash of narrow eyes—like Taddeusz's eyes—lit by a candle-flame. Crouched cross-legged atop the corner alcove cupboard, like a floating visitation, like a malevolent Buddha lying in wait for them—was Greta. Only her face glowed; her predatory teeth flashed in pitch darkness. In the hollow pit of her lap nestled the remains of a skullbone from the bomb-site. Its eyesockets were steeped in darkness, its dusky row of ivory still intact. Greta raised it like a torch or a grim trophy in the palm of her hand. Then she laughed, that thin maniacal laugh which was uniquely hers. The candle-smoke flickered upward, souring, blackening the air.

"Bitch!" screamed Lily. "What d'you think you're doing? You almost scared us to death!"

But Greta, wedged precariously above the cupboard, was now howling with laughter. One hand clutched her flat growling stomach; the other gripped the flickering candle. The skullbone dropped, rolled drunkenly between her knees; her bony shoulders shook. Convulsively. Hysterical tears glittered at the corners of her eyes and down her cheeks.

"You horror!" screamed Lily, brandishing her thin arms, thrashing them like impotent weapons through the air. "You're the Devil incarnate, O Jesus, *Jesus,* how ever did I give birth to a horror like you!"

CHAPTER 9

PHYSICIAN, HEAL THYSELF

Angie came home from school a few days later to find her mother weeping in the kitchen; her face was grey with shock. Flo was pressing ice-cold flannels against the back of Lily's skull. She looked furious, driven almost out of her wits.

"Let the doctor look at it, Lily," said Flo. "You've got a swelling the size of an egg and it's still bleeding. I'll take you down to 'Emergency' right now."

"NO!" Pure terror shone out of Lily's eyes at the mention of the word doctor. "She did it on purpose, Flo, she tried to kill me!"

"Oh, Lil, for God's sake, will you stop that!"

"What happened?" said Angie.

"Your mum was in the yard, supposed to be hanging out the washing, but you know how long that takes her."

"That had nothing to do with it, Flo," interrupted Lily, "I was standing in my own yard, minding my own business, not doing no harm to no one and suddenly—"

"You must have been daydreaming, you know the way you stand still for hours at a time, like a bloody statue, like a pillar of salt."

"She knew exactly where I was standing. She was watching me all the time from that creepy porthole window of hers, and then she came downstairs with that bone—"

"Now look, Lil, she don't keep mutton bones up on the landing. Stop imagining things."

"Well, how else could she strike me right here, smack on the back of my head?"

"It was an accident, Lil, she tried to explain, she didn't know anyone was standing there, she just tossed the bone over the wall for the dog—"

"Who throws mutton bones that size over the wall? She could have killed the dog, and all. When that thing struck my head, I heard a crunching sound—*Oh, my God, the pain, the PAIN*—I thought I was going to die. Everything went black, then I saw these shiny lights dancing in front of my eyes."

"Who, Mum, who threw the bone over the wall?"

"Saidye," said Lily, her voice breaking, "that horrible jealous cow, all because she don't like Solly talking to me."

"Poor Saidye came over to apologize, but your mum wouldn't let her in."

"Stop defending her, Flo! Why doesn't anyone ever believe me? Of course I wouldn't let her in the house, not after she tried to murder me! She's my sworn enemy, Angie, you're not doing her washing down at the launderette any more, and no more switching on her lights on Friday night, neither. Let her rot in the dark from now on."

Whatever it was that Lily said to the itinerant nurse, summoned to the house by Flo, must have thoroughly baffled and alarmed her. In a postscript to her official report, Nurse Chiswick recommended that Lily's case be followed up by the Psychiatry Department at the hospital. She suspected a full-blown case of clinical paranoia, although not wishing to pronounce on matters outside her jurisdiction, she referred Lily's medical file to the appropriate authority. A few weeks later, one of the resident psychiatrists, well versed in psychological-trauma symptoms, dropped by to offer his help. Of course, Lily had to be lured downstairs; her panic-driven eyes were those of a feral creature cornered in its den.

"God forbid that he should set foot in that filthy cave of yours upstairs," hissed Flo, tugging Lily forcibly by the arm. "There's someone from the hospital come to have a few words with you."

"From the hospital?" Lily's voice was trembly, indignant, breathless. "What for? What did he come here for? Who told him to come?"

"I don't know, Lil, it must have been that nurse who came over to look at your head."

"Oh, that bitch— "

"*Shush,* keep your voice down; d'you want him to hear you?"

Lily was ushered into Flo's neat sitting-room, an alien unfamiliar place with its paneled mahogany side bar, upholstered chairs, lacquered Japanese prints and gilded China porcelain on the antique television cabinet. It had a ceremonial air, lace-curtained, dimly lit and faintly smelling of wax like an unused altar; this was Albert's private sanctuary from which a riff-raff stream of visitors was consistently barred.

"Don't go, Flo!" said Lily. The panic was rising up in her chest again. "I want you to stay here with me."

"Lil, you and the doctor can have a few words in private," said Flo. "I'll just be downstairs in the kitchen if ever you need me."

Sitting on Flo's sofa, his long arm flung casually over the backrest, was Dr. Radzinsky. The bottle-thickness of his spectacles, eloquent witness to decades spent poring over textbooks, actually rivaled Lily's. His black hair, his beard, despite his relative youth, was already whitening, a cluster of unpruned tendrils curling over his collar. He looked as though he had sprung into the world fully formed, had forever and always been garbed in that thin tailored vest, shiny with age, whose buttons split and dropped to the ground like seeds, under a wrinkled jacket of faded black. As soon as Flo disappeared, the doctor stood up and shook Lily's moist hand.

83

"Hello, Mrs. Morvaye, I'm Dr. Radzinsky. I hope you're feeling better now. That was quite a nasty accident you had!"

"Accident! That was no accident, Doctor, that was deliberate; she tried to murder me."

The doctor sat down again on Flo's sofa. He gazed blankly at Lily like a spectator in the front row, waiting for the performance to begin. "Well, perhaps you'd like to tell me exactly what happened?" he said.

Lily's thinning black hair was snowy with dandruff. Her paling skin glistened with oil and sweat. She looked as though she hadn't washed in days, perhaps weeks. Crouching in Albert's ornate armchair, she seemed embalmed in a film of hopelessness, her head sinking on her meager bosom, her thin shoulder bones collapsing, folding inward like butterfly wings—as though she had long ago relinquished the will to live. It seemed that, lingering on the force of its own inertia, only her ruined body refused to die.

"As if I haven't had enough suffering all these years," said Lily, "and now that jealous bitch is trying to murder me in my own back yard."

"But why would she—?"

"First it was the bombs, Doctor, the sirens going off in the middle of the night, and me having to run to the shelter with one baby on each arm—no time to stop for milk or blankets or medicine. I was always running, running, the babies screaming, their heads flopping and bouncing backward over my arm. How many times did I trip into some bloody great bomb crater in the pavement and almost drop them! And my husband? Where was he? When he wasn't locked up with the other aliens on the Isle of Man, he was running around with actresses and whores. Some people think I'm mad, Doctor, but that's because they don't understand; not one of them has been through what I have."

Dr. Radzinsky said nothing. He looked at Lily and pinched his lips together in a sort of helpless aborted smile. His smile seemed to irk Lily; it kindled in her a flash of hostility, a spark of life.

"Well, don't you think I've got a *right* to go stark raving mad? How many children have you put on this earth, Doctor?" Lily's lips quivered, her skin flushed rose-grey; under her thick lenses her eyes suddenly glittered with tears. "How many—have you laid underground?"

It took him aback. A retort sprang to his lips, but he checked himself in time. He wanted to say, "But, my dear Mrs. Morvaye, you are not alone. All of us, sooner or later, have to face up to tragedy. Most of us, in time, manage to overcome—" But, no, these were false and pernicious platitudes. One man's sorrow can never alleviate another's, as well he knew. Besides, Lily was simply not 'most of us'— Lily was Lily, unique.

Not long before his flight from the Medical Faculty of the underground University in Warsaw, Radzinsky's own parents had been rounded up and annihilated in the gas chambers of Treblinka. Since then, he'd had his own terrors to face and beat down, and the effort made him weary. Like Lily, he, too, waged his own daily war against the seductive desire simply to lie down and die. Why should either of them struggle on?

Where to? What for?

Behind him yawned the cave of history, stretching back and back to the days of Abraham. His gaze reflected the instinctive empathy of a persecuted race. But he doubted there was anything he could do for this woman. Like him, she was prematurely aged. Her spirit was broken. Her fears had fossilized inside her bones, her condition irreversible. He knew that for Lily—perhaps also for himself—there was no hope.

Barely ten days later, wearing her brand new National Health wire-framed spectacles that pinched behind the ears, Angie stepped out of the second-floor Eye Clinic in Vallance Road. Its shadowy ravine of a staircase gave a kaleidoscopic shudder. Angie gripped the handrail to steady herself before going down.

"They look really nice on you, Angie," said Lily, when they got downstairs. She had the grinching smile of an unwilling liar; her own suddenly misty eyes said, *God help you, Angie, you've inherited the curse.*

They hurried past the hospital. Lily's terrors multiplied. She thought of Dr. Radzinksy and his legion of white coats lurking behind closed doors. Lily could not stop poring through her memory, through the patchy remnants of their defunct conversation. What sort of carelessness might have incriminated her? She hadn't admitted with her own lips that she was mad, had she? When she lost her temper with Dr. Radzinsky, *bloody hell*—she couldn't remember exactly what she'd said.

No matter what happened, though, they would not get her to take pills. She would refuse them, hide them under her tongue, spit them out. Compressed poisons they were, tiny land mines waiting to blast open her brain or soak it in chemically induced forgetfulness, obliterating patches of it at random, distorting her perceptions, freeze-drying her feelings, impairing her alertness, her radar-sensitive instinct for survival—after all, *the Devil you know*—Lily couldn't articulate her mistrust of the all-powerful healing hierarchy, yet she knew she preferred to go on living in uneasy alliance with her angst, rather than trade it in for something worse.

"Is it possible, Mrs. Morvaye, that you might have misjudged Saidye's intentions. Could it indeed have been an accident, as she says?" Lily's voice descended an octave, mimicking, reviving the spectre of Dr. Radzinsky, with impotent venom. Somehow she managed to capture the timbre of the doctor's voice, his trademark tic, the delicate clearing of the throat, the rhythmical forward thrusting of the chin, like an erudite pigeon.

"No, doctor," I says, "that was no accident. That murderous bone-hurling bitch is afraid I'm going to run off with her husband, Solly, (although, between you and me, doctor, I wouldn't have him, baked). I've noticed her evil eye at the porthole window of an evening, whenever Solly stops by to chat, poor sod, he just enjoys a bit of gossip, a bit of company, but she—*I call her the Eye-of-Death*—she can't stand it, doctor, she's deathly jealous. That mutton bone was just a warning! When is anyone finally going to believe me, when my corpse is laid out on the mortuary slab? The next time that bitch tries to kill me, doctor, she ain't going to miss!"

Dr. Radzinsky hadn't believed her, of course. Lily knew that. To think that her fate, and the fate of so many other innocents, was in the hands of this man, whose eyes had gone hard and beady-looking from too much studying, who believed himself infallible, who secretly scoffed at her distress even as she tried to explain the danger, implore his help. Over Lily he wielded the power of liberty, life, perhaps even death, this learnèd simpleton who spoke with a silver-forked tongue of false comfort, although he clearly believed that she was mad. And what frightened Lily most, this was exactly how it had started with her sister, Ruth. First it was the interviews with one doctor, and then another. Later, it was the questionnaires, the examinations and consultations, the electric shocks, the succession of tablets—red ones, striped ones, capsules looking like tiny time bombs that made her not better, but worse, much worse. When they finally came to take Ruth away, Lily was crying. Tears leaked from the corners of her eyes and she dabbed at them with a large paper towel. Gone was Ruth's ethereal beauty, the soulful eyes, the lavish dark hair curled high into a bun and studded with glittering pins. Flanked by her white-garbed custodians, Ruth moved slowly, lethargically, her cheeks unnaturally bloated, her eyes swollen and masked like a lake in winter. She drifted. She drifted away from them, unaware of their tenderly plucking at her arms, which were as limp as stone-weights, a bevy of tugboats straining to bring their half-sunken wreck to shore.

In another page of ancient history, secret history, Ruth had been Taddeusz's first love. Then, and even now, Lily was eaten alive by jealousy, a profound living wound that would not heal. How had Ruth so casually managed to push him away? After all, Taddeusz was a virtual stranger to rejection. He was born and bred in the primeval cult of maternal adoration; it fired his indestructible energy, his intelligence, the turbulent waves of sensuality that streamed from his body and irradiated Lily's like the halo-aura of a Saint. But somehow, early on, Ruth had mistrusted Taddeusz. She turned cold, stubborn. Some equally powerful force of soul made her drive this foreign menace, this seductive stranger, off her life's path. Did she know? Could she divine the fate she was escaping by her refusal?

When Ruth rejected Taddeusz, he settled on Lily; soon afterward—who knows why—he cajoled Ruth into accepting his sailor comrade, Laszlo, in a double wedding. And it was from this tragi-comedy of errors that all their fates were sealed; the names and shadowy faces of the next generation, their forked and fledgling destinies were determined, *by default,* in that resounding 'no' from Ruth's lips. For the following winter, the men's merchant ship went down in the North Atlantic. In the resulting chaos, Taddeusz, it was said, was forced to abandon his comrade kinsman, Laszlo, fast asleep, perhaps, or else punch drunk in the hold; his prematurely snow-white hair, according to legend, harked back to those infernal hours spent, frozen to the soul, clinging to a heaving lifeboat before being rescued by the same British convoy that had mistakenly caused their sinking. The SS Kronenberg a Norwegian merchant vessel, on route from Reykjavik to Kirkwall, was reported lost. Eight months after the sisters' twin wedding, Lily was already mother to her first-born; Ruth was a 19-year-old widow.

After Laszlo's body floated to the sea bottom, Ruth was tormented for months with identical recurring dreams. He wasn't really dead. She knew because he kept coming back, penetrating her dark hours with corporeal visions of overwhelming force. *'I'm not dead, my beloved, see!'* he whispered, brushing back his long wet hair, plucking strands of seaweed off his arm, and floating into bed beside her, stroking her body with fingers that were at times, icy cold, at times, searing hot.

For months, even years, Ruth couldn't bring herself to look at another man. Was she a faithless whore? Laszlo was constantly tracking her. She sensed his penetrating presence in the most banal of places, peering over her shoulder as she fried herself a rasher of bacon and cherry tomatoes, gazing at her as she took her sponge bath, even trailing her to the draughty outhouse, as though to partake vicariously of her life. So often without warning, whilst sitting beside Renie's baking fireplace, Ruth's fingers, arms, her entire body abruptly shuddered and frosted over, signaling Laszlo's presence, his comforting and *oh, so familiar* attempt to pre-empt her own pulsating bloodstream in place of that which he'd lost. It was only after six years of such tenacious haunting that Ruth finally accepted Stanley, her sterling-silver lover who worshipped her with an almost preternatural intensity.

"I'm never having any children," she thought, the day they buried baby Larissa in Kensal Green Cemetery.

Ruth had lived through Lily's perpetual state of confinement, shackled as she was by a succession of sick babies; she watched her sister losing ground with each birth, submerged in a debilitating maternity that saw no end. *Enough, enough!* Her own body, which needed to stay intact and undefiled, was also under assault. A large pulpy mass had been growing inside her for weeks, perhaps months, before she realized what it was. And as the body turned traitor and sickened, even her face seemed no longer her own. Every feature seemed harsher than usual, separate, prominent—not a harmonious landscape, but one of discord. The forehead too high, too broad, marked by its long wrinkle between the eyes, the paling sunken cheeks, the nose, usually so regal but now, like Gogol's, standing absurdly alone. There was no glow to her face, save for a filigree of thread-like veins, burst in a moment of ancient fury, to lace her white cheeks. Raw. Strained. Devoid of artifice. Not a touch of rouge relieved the skull-like craterland. Even her soul-dark eyes seemed to be bleached of their intense colour. Within weeks, a medical verdict was called, and her womb sentenced to be sliced away, along with all its suspect nodes, tubes, growths and mushrooming polyps, sealing off the entrance to the tomb.

Ruth's detached irony during this ordeal was something foreign, even intimidating to Lily; the disconcerting habit she had acquired of withdrawing her own soul from its fleshly sepulchre, while she watched, from afar, with a deep impassive smile. Was it a matter of indifference to her whether she returned to inhabit her body, or whether that fragile thread would stretch and snap, releasing her to the darkness of the larger universe? When she finally awoke, the peril was over. Her fate was sealed; she seemed content to drift away from them all on her sickbed of resignation. Only Stanley remained by her side, night after night, raging and mourning like a dumb creature, snared within a trap.

Lily's agonizing week wound down to a close. Then another week passed with no disquieting messages from the hospital. Dr. Radzinsky's spectre failed to rematerialize, so perhaps he thought Lily wasn't worth the trouble of snaring. When time came for the Sunday night cleansing ritual, she began to breathe easier; she was almost jubilant.

The drained metal bathtub, caked in soap scum, was carted upstairs by the handles. It contained Angie's sopping wet school blouse, which—*with all this terrible upset*—Lily had abandoned outside. For days, the blouse had been rusting beneath layers of melting snow. Oh, well, never mind! Time to start boiling water for the bath, a mammoth task that would go on for hours. Firing up the water kettle, a brilliant blue wreath of flame roared from the gas jets, one shilling's worth at a time, gradually creeping lower and lower, then dribbling forth in gasps until it was little more than the ghost of a fairy-ring, valiantly flickering to death in the midst of the dim grey landing.

"Oh, no, not enough hot water, and that was my last shilling—"

"Fuckin' hell," said Greta, "not again!"

She hoisted the broom out from behind the gas stove, and a single red flea leapt, knee high, from the dust. Rarely, if ever, had she tolerated the indignity of Lily's Sunday night ablutions. Instead, she barricaded the kitchen door with a couple of chairs while she took her sponge bath in private. But Angie and Peter still had to undergo the torture ritual. One after the other they were dunked into the metal tub, where they sat cramped and shivering, knees cradled to their chests, one wary eye on the door. As usual, Peter was crying. Lily was frothsoaping and fretting—"*one, two, three, four,* now watch me while I do this, four times on each side, *one, two*—" As always, her mind, her fingers drifted into a slow-motion dream.

"Oh, Mother, hurry up, will you?" said Greta.

Lily began soaping Peter's skin at the collarbone—"*One, two, three*—" meanwhile, his body had already taken on the patina of blue-veined marble; his cherub features were distorted with rage.

"Let me finish washing him," said Angie.

"I'm telling you, he's going to freeze to death," said Greta.

"Now wait a minute!" Lily was swishing soapsuds up and down Peter's back. "*One, two, three*—"

"Hurry up, I said I'm cold." Peter gripped the metal handles; he raised his thin haunches, intent on escape.

"No—*not yet!*"

"I can't stand this no more, it's the same thing every poxy Sunday night!" screamed Greta, flinging down the broom.

"Listen, you're going to the doctor's tomorrow, will you just sit still and let me wash you properly!"

"Give me that!" Peter grasped at the towel on the chairback just beyond his reach. He stood up, shuddering, dripping bathwater, hunching his shoulders together, veiling his cold-shriveled little penis from view.

"It's no use, I'm going mad," whimpered Lily, her face pinkish-grey and shiny with sweat, her bottle thick eyeglasses steaming from her exertion. "Just finish him up, I'll give you a shilling tomorrow, Angie, promise, as soon as I get my Assistance Money."

"No, I don't want no shilling—" Again, Angie couldn't bear the sight of Lily begging; it flooded her with something indescribable, something toxic that scoured her insides like famine. "All right, he's ready," she said, sloshing a saucepanful of tepid rinse water over her brother's head and shoulders, a sort of clumsy baptism for a dying child. "Give me that towel, quick now—he's finished, he's finished, he's finished!"

CHAPTER 10

LAST SUPPER

Beside Mrs. Myles's shadowy dungeon-cell of an office, to the right of the ground floor stairwell, hundreds of schoolchildren tiptoed cautiously past on their ascent to the upper floors. Angie, along with a ragtag band of fellow crusaders, was gathering coppers for Dr. Barnardos' orphans; true to a hallowed Xmas tradition, they stood a-caroling off key outside Mrs. Myles's beetle-browed cave.

> *Star of wonder, star of night*
> *Star of royal beauty bright,*
> *Westward leading, still proceeding.*
> *Guide us to thy perfect light...*

There followed a moment of collective apprehension; someone stifled a giggle before the grim Lioness herself opened the arched wooden door, a shiny half-crown pinched between her polished nails, which she dropped with a leer of contempt into Angie's sweaty palm. Miss Thayne, meanwhile, goose-stepped past them clutching her lists, hauling the dancers from their classrooms for one last briefing in the gymnasium before the Xmas concert.

"What is that stain on your blouse?" she said, hoisting Angie out from amongst the furtive carollers. She examined the pale brownish streak on her collar before twirling her around by the shoulders, like a marionette. "Why, it's rust! You'll have to run home at once and change that blouse; you can't come to the concert like that!"

"I don't—" said Angie; her voice got trapped at the bottom of her throat.

"What? Speak up, we haven't much time!"

93

"I don't have—nothin' else, Miss."

"Jesus, Mary and Joseph! What do you mean you don't have *anything* else?"

Flushing, Angie stared down at her plimsolls; her voice had completely disappeared.

"All right, children, this is not funny!" exclaimed Miss Thayne, whirling around, almost blowing them all away in a blast of dragonfire.

That afternoon a specially chartered school bus deposited the juvenile dance troupe on the pavement of the Embankment. From there, they were frogmarched across the Hungerford Bridge footpath to the Royal Festival Hall, a post-war extravaganza of rising cement and glass. Wracked by tension and secret misgivings mingled with pride, Miss Thayne braced herself for the challenge ahead. "*Shush*, I said *SHUSH!* Now you must remain in your ranks at all times, and keep perfect silence when we enter the building. It is an exceedingly great honour to perform at the *ROYAL* Festival Hall. I expect you *ALL* to be a credit to your school!"

In their plush offstage trenches, lightly veiled by velvet hangings, the dancers cowered together, hypnotized by the radiance of the empty boards. Thunder-struck, they registered the trilling oceanic murmurings of the audience which couldn't possibly—but sounded just like thousands spiraling up the tiered staircases. All around was the discordant hum of the unseen violinists. The thunder, clash and keening of kettledrums, cymbals and oboes. The silent cellos laid like sepulchres upon their sloping sides. Then a burst of applause, all shrieks and whistles, as the musicians took their seats behind each lectern, and the silver-flash of camera bulbs traveled, from here to nowhere, like sparks from a fairy wand. Hollow and alive, the hall glowed and breathed like the belly of a Leviathan. Celestial organ pipes, massed behind the stage. Starlit circles, countersunk into the ceiling. Rows of balconies and loges that seemed to be trussed, high up, across a darkened sky.

Angie gazed at the wooden stairway jutting upward from their side of the stage, which itself was layered, tier upon tier—*Oh, all the more to stumble on.* Miss Thayne then gripped her by the shoulders and pushed her toward the back. "We can't have you up at the front with that awful stain, Angie," she whispered, "and for heaven's sake, make sure you remember to exit *on the left.*"

The pupils were marshaled to attention; they waited for their *Führerin* to lower her baton. They knew their cue. As soon as the music began, the instant the dance mistress's eyes flashed triumphantly, her muscular arm sliced a command through the air, they began shuffling forward as though to a battlefield, like the collective might of a nation defending its freedom. Marching forward en masse, shuffling, squeaking, clip-clopping over the boards, trussed in their fresh white blouses, navy trousers, regulation skirts with cross-bands and white socks.

"Fine, so far so good," hissed Miss Thayne under her breath. She surveyed Angie's group from behind the velvet curtain. Her insides convulsed in an agonizing knot. Sweat cascaded down her back. Her left eyelid twitched with emotion. "*Jesus, Mary and Joseph,* that little twerp, where's she going now?" She made frantic signs—"*Back, back*"—but it was too late; there was Angie, exiting solo across the lonely stage, pirouetting toward the wrong side of the wings.

Like the last soul on earth, she tottered under the brilliant stage lights. The universe darkened; the world came to an end. Overwhelmed by the shame and humiliation of the moment, she was swallowed, whole and alive, down a deep black hole.

As Angie pushed open the front door later that afternoon, the sudden draught started Peter wheezing again. A shallow pond of phlegm seemed to float at the bottom of his lungs. He coughed and coughed, then wiped his palm down the front of his shirt. Sitting at the bottom of the staircase, he was tinkering with the Xmas gift that he'd managed to wheedle out of Flo and had already taken apart. With his thick malformed fingers, somehow he was miraculously reassembling the tiny screws, the wafer thin gold-plate, the bulbous glass frame. Obsessed by the exactitude, the inexorable ticking of watches, Peter had taught himself to tell the time, although he could barely read. Chronically sick, and the baby of the family, he was Flo's undisputed darling. An unspoken law—only he was allowed into the inner sanctum of Albert's sitting-room. Meanwhile, Angie, still looking downcast and teary-eyed since the morning, trudged up the stairs to Lily's attic domain just as Flo's shadow appeared on the stair.

"Auntie, can't I watch telly now?" whined Peter.

"Yes, darling, but shut the door behind you, will you?"

Housed in solemn state, inside a dark-wood Victoriana cabinet, was the black and white television set. Peter sat hunched on the cloth-covered settee, drummed almost into catalepsy by the monotonal B.B.C. testing signal while he waited for the on-screen arrival of *Andy Pandy, Whirligig,* and *Bill 'n Ben,* followed by the craven, bespectacled *Billy Bunter,* waddling back to Greyfriars School, his pockets bulging with booty from the Tuck Shop. Flo then summoned Peter downstairs into her kitchen, trying to tempt him with delicacies from her bountiful shopping bag, tender fat-free baby veal slices, a strip of smoked salmon. *"No Rye bread for you, darling, here's your special gluten-free buns"*—(as insubstantial as holy church wafers)—a pared tangerine, a couple of dates followed by three heaping tablespoons of choke-powder, processed from hog's glands, as well as Tetramycin at bedtime for his delicate chest.

"Look how thin he's getting," said Lily, basking uneasily with her cup of strong tea. "How come he's losing so much weight?"

At around half past six, they heard the front door slam as Greta come in from work. Yesterday was payday, sweetened with a small Xmas bonus. Already she had splurged, recklessly spent the whole lot, and was wearing a smart new red dress and pale grey jacket, gypsy gold-bangle earrings, and a whiff of 'Evening in Paris' perfume.

"Bloody hell," she said, when she reached the top of the staircase, "Flo's cooking up a feast downstairs. What's there to eat up here?"

She rummaged around in the kitchen cupboards. The fried eggs and tinned tomatoes she dished out resembled jaundiced eyeballs swimming in blood. Angie couldn't touch hers, although she was starving. Her hunger was a nauseous knot coiled in the pit of her stomach, spreading outward and scouring her away from the inside. It was always there, that lingering sickly sweet ache in the gut. She crawled onto the mattress and dozed off for a while, then dreamt she was feasting on Christ's carcass, His own precious 'Flesh and Blood' stretched out before her on a slab, a morbidly literal Last Supper. When she awoke the hunger was still there, gnawing at her, flooding her with an intensely thrilling wave, the onset perhaps of a mystic trance.

Lily then came upstairs into the kitchen, looking depressed. Steeped in guilt, she was brooding on the image of Prince, the Alsatian, faint from hunger, almost lame, staggering up the steps to the gas chamber. "That poor Prince, I went out to get him a treat, his last supper, but when I got back it was too late. Your Aunt Beattie, the Death-Eater, had already taken him to be put to sleep."

"Yeah, and what about our dinner, Lily?"

"I didn't have nothing left over, Greta, you know I'm short this week."

"You're short? What about the extra pound I gave you yesterday? D'you mean to say you spent my money on a treat for the dog, and you was too lazy to even give it to him, and now the shops are all shut and there's nothing to eat in this bleedin' house again, and it's almost Xmas—!"

"You don't understand, just listen to me."

"Just because you don't eat nothing, Lily, don't mean we have to go starving too."

"It ain't my fault, you know I've got this—thing at the back of my throat."

"Yeah, yeah, yeah, so you're wasting away on soup and tea. Just look at you, you're a bleedin' skeleton, skin and bone! *Oh, Christ, I hate you, Lily*—!"

Angie was sitting on a mattress in the bedroom, absorbed in a comic book, when the screaming began. She jumped to her feet as soon as she heard the dense thump of something hitting the wall. Greta was flinging open the kitchen cupboards, one after the other. The mere sight of those tottering piles of empty dishes seemed to enrage her as she thrashed and lunged like a rabid hound. A crazed tempest of plates, bowls, cups crashed against the walls, imprinting crescent shapes of themselves like multiple rising moons on the creamy stippled wallpaper. Lily stared as glass and porcelain exploded like arsenal all around her.

"Greta, stop it, *stop it*—"

But Greta now had the bread-knife in her hand. Her eyes glittered as she tested its serrated blade against her fingers, lovingly, as though she wished to sacrifice Lily to some wrathful Old Testament God; it was a gruesome ritual, almost biblical. Greta turned on Lily and pushed her toward the bedroom. A moment later, they were both sprawled on top of the mattress. The blade of Greta's bread-knife was pressing against Lily's throat.

"All right, prepare yourself, you're going to die, Lily," said Greta. She pressed the blade even closer.

Angie screamed.

"Are you ready to meet your Maker, Lily?"

"You just stop that, *stop it*—!" Angie tried to wrench her sister away; Greta kicked her repeatedly from behind.

"O God, O Christ!" whimpered Lily, stretched across the bed like a limp bag of feathers. Like a lamb for the slaughter.

"Get your suckers off of me, you little leech!" shouted Greta, prying Angie's fingers off her arm and giving her one last determined shove that sent her slithering across the floor. "All right, Lily," she said, turning back to her mother, "when you meet Saint *fucking* Peter up at the pearly-whirly gates, just tell 'im from me that you got sliced up because you was too lazy to feed your kids—" Greta made a dramatic flourish, wielding the bread-knife as a curved sabre, a pirate-like gesture. "Ready, Lily? Your time's run out!"

Lily gave up a sigh, a long-drawn-out tremulous whimper, a sort of premature death rattle. Her eyeballs seemed to be rolling backward inside their sockets.

"Good-bye, Lily—"

The bread-knife swung up into the air like a guillotine, just as Flo appeared. Breathing hard, she'd heaved herself up to the topmost staircase, gripping the banister for support. Now she stared at the chaos, the ruined walls, the shattered glass and porcelain all over the floor; it resembled the inexplicable wrath of God in his own Temple.

"What's going on up here?" A powerful wave of indignation swelled in Flo's throat, exploded in her voice. *"What's she doing to you, Lily?"*

Lily lay still, inert upon the mattress, like a starry-eyed corpse gazing at its own coffin lid. Greta moved backward. She dropped the bread-knife. With a cold ripple of laughter, she turned around to face Flo.

"You little bitch!" Flo was panting, both with rage and fatigue. "Your mother should have put you away a long time ago. I'd rather have no kids at all than one like you."

"But you had one, didn't you, Aunt Flo? You had one, but you put it away!"

"Shut up, you, or I'll smack your bloody lip."

"You didn't like the colour, did you, Aunt? Just because it was black."

"No, Flo! No! Don't hit her—!" screamed Lily, rousing herself from her torpor.

Kindled emotion had turned Flo hideous—a metamorphosis of damp-glistening forehead, flaring nostrils and harsh wineskin cheeks. In her eyes shone a sudden fire-flicker, raw memory perhaps of a blasted harvest. Empowered by heroic rage, she heaved Greta down the staircase, kicked her sideways until she slipped against the banister. Then lifting her injured thigh, she descended heavily, step by step, and reached Greta just as she pulled herself up, half laughing. half crying; with her mighty shoulder, Flo forced her all the way down the stairwell.

The sitting-room door opened, just a crack. It was Albert, wanting to shield young Peter from all the fright and commotion. Frowning, displeased, with that shiny pink complexion of his, a radiance of health and prosperity, his abrupt appearance beside the door jamb seemed about as incongruous as an apple blossom out of season. "Now, what's going on here again, for Christ's sake?" he growled.

"Stop it, Flo, please—*Oh, God*—stop hitting her!" Lily watched, inert, from the second landing, like a timid grey angel crouching behind a cloud.

But there was no stopping Flo as she smashed into Greta, again and again, with the back of her massive stone fist. Greta's nose was bleeding. On her right cheekbone was a raised welt, the imprint of Flo's ruby ring; she edged backward, twisting and crouching to protect her eyes.

"Now get out of my house, you *bitch!*" screamed Flo. "And don't you ever come back."

100

PART TWO
CHAPTER 11

Litany of loss

In late autumn of '47, Taddeusz's mother Mitzi had arrived in London with nothing but her melancholy dimpled smile, her pure white hair, the pearl drops hanging from her ears, and her fierce cleanliness which she clutched onto in the midst of chaos like a battle flag. In one silken pocket of her handbag, tucked behind her *deutsche Reisepaß* and her small silver and lead crucifix, she kept the listed inventory of her possessions destroyed by Allied bombing raids—*zwei Bettstellen, ein Kleiderschrank, eine Wäschetruhe*—a litany of loss, and her dead husband Yosef's water colour sketch of their beloved '*Heimat*,' their homeland, preserved under glass.

Yosef had died twice; at least, Mitzi had mourned him twice. First when she saw his name printed in the national newspaper's obituary list of officers, fallen in battle in 1917. The shock had made her feel ill, violently ill. Dressed in her peaked white nurse's cap, that flamboyant nun-like wimple, and striving to contain her turbulence of grief and anger, she made her way into the lobby of the military hospital, the Schloss-transformed-into-Lazarett on the outskirts of Vienna.

She remembered on that particular morning, the red-headed boy soldier from Ceglèd had smiled forlornly at her as she entered the ward. It was the eerie, wayward smile of a floating nightmare. He had been carried in, blood-soaked and barely conscious, fated to lose his damaged left eye before departure from the Infirmary. The chief surgeon had trained her, and she'd learned to conceal her initial repugnance at having to massage, with extreme gentleness, the empty shell of healing flesh, former shrine to that visionary organ. The youth, still masked in bandages, tried to clutch her hand, grasp at her halo-aura of starched cotton as she passed his bedside, as if reassuring himself, dolefully, time and again, that her flesh was not surreal, and his own life not merely the substance of a soiled dream to be washed away by sleep.

Nearby was Herr Morvaye, an older officer from the Imperial *Kavallerie-Korps*, who still retained an air of innate authority, despite his bandaged neck and leg wound. Was he a cavalier thrown vengefully, perhaps, by a dying horse? Sooner or later Mitzi was to hear all their stories, their missed or mistaken triumphs, their lapsed destinies within a nation at war. But now her own betrothed, Yosef, had joined the ghost-ranks of the disappeared. It was no surprise, in fact, it was a wonder that he had lasted as long as he did. Yosef, whose Sunday-artist fingers were soiled and toughened by daily contact with a rifle barrel. Yosef, the youngest love child of an indolent and bejewelled *jüdische Mutter*, milk-fed in opulence, basking in ancestral tenderness, stranger to any random or decreed acts of brutality, of course, he would be among the first to fall.

Although Yosef's mother, Frau Stahlman, surely preferred that he should select a Jewish *Mädchen*, her capacity for maternal indulgence was deep enough to have embraced Mitzi, a pure-bred native Teuton with the commonplace white-blond hair, gilded skin and fiery marble-blue eyes of her kind. During the early days of the couple's engagement, she invited young Mitzi into her boudoir, where the bewitching dressing table was overladen with antique heritage *Schmuck*. Ornate chains of old gold. A torque of pearls. Lucent fire opals and tiny blinding flashes of diamond. Mitzi chose a sapphire-studded silver necklace, slightly tarnished from its long residence within Frau Stahlman's jewel casket. Such generosity astounded her. As a young girl growing up in the working class home of a mid-ranking employee of the *Deutsche Reichsbahn,* it was more usual for Mitzi to inherit the damp, grainy boots of brother, Franz, and latterly—the feminine cloth-pile of rejects from her sister, Else.

She wondered, at the time, why they should go to such lengths to welcome her, an impoverished Christian damsel into the fold. She observed that they were hardly of the orthodox brand; their family excursions to the grand domed Synagogue in the heart of Dortmund Stadt were occasional and formal rather than frequent and devout. Besides, the Stahlmans were of a benevolent disposition; they had more than enough wealth to share. Thanks to several generations' worth of toil and prolific investment, they were now estate and property owners, well on their way to founding a Diaspora dynasty. Mitzi traced her strong infatuation with *'Luxus'* and graceful living to those first romantic months at the residence on Friedensstraße, pressed deliciously close, hip to hip, beside Yosef at the dinner table, fingering the family's hallmarked Hanukkah candlesticks, semi-hypnotized by the sheen of the crenellated silver plate.

At this moment, Officer Morvaye was struggling to sit up against his pillow. He demanded to know why Mitzi looked so stricken, particularly why her eyes looked as though they'd been rubbed in salt and why she neglected to remember to bring him yesterday's newspaper as well as a mug of very weak coffee, with dry biscuits, which the doctor had allowed. His near fluent German was laced in Magyar accents, harsh, guttural, the intonation forceful, swift and choppy. His features, although not unattractive, were plain, seemingly bloodless, with the aspect, almost, of a living death mask. Not the sort of face to whom one might confide a personal heartache: the vision of her beloved Yosef, still warm, clutching stupidly to his useless gun and sinking, sinking somewhere beneath the foul rivulets of imperial mud. Mitzi turned away, deliberately, reckoning that this stern looking Hungarian must be an oaf if he couldn't guess her trouble. At any rate, he sank his head back against the ivory-coloured bolster roll of a pillow, disgusted and morose. It was the first flicker of antipathy between them. An undisguised tension-bond of mutually repugnant curiosity—*during the next few weeks, months and years, a rough and blinding patch of time, it metamorphosed, slow-burning into a harshly requited desire.*

Herr Morvaye was Taddeusz's natural father, the stern-looking officer who first seduced Mitzi within the sick-chambers of the Lazarett, then spirited her away with him, pregnant, to Timişoara. This was a provincial town, cosmopolitan and prosperous, situated along the River Timis. Fabled seat of resistance to oppression, notably the peasants' uprising against the Magyar aristocracy of the Middle Ages, Timişoara was now home to a blend of border Hungarians, grafted Jews, transplanted Germans and modern-day Romans.

War being over, this border territory had shifted its allegiance yet again, much like a child's toy being wrenched from hand to hand. Eventually, quite soon in fact, Herr Morvaye might need to transmogrify into Domnul Iliescu or some such distasteful thing. Passport, birth certificate and travel documents would need to be renewed, given the necessity for ethnic versatility and pragmatic circumspection. And there was more; the Jewish banking class, to which the Morvayes belonged, were keenly at risk from nationalist firebrands and misfit anti-Semites said to be leading rogue attacks on isolated villages in the Moldavia and Transylvania regions. Mitzi, however, understood little of this and, besides, why should she care? She was homesick. Even now, she had not managed to settle in comfortably with her in-laws, with whom she found herself sequestered. The family spoke a blend of Yiddish and Hungarian, with just enough utilitarian Romanian to suit the edicts of the times.

But amassing money—blood-out-of-a-stone usury—that's the language, the coinage they understand since birth, these Yiddish bankers, whispered the disfranchised day labourers, disgruntled tradesmen and farmers, native Romanians since birth, they'd like to remind you, who'd struggled to keep their businesses prospering despite one tumultuous invasion after the other, whether it be ancient Roman, Magyar, Avar, Turk or Prussian. This chunk of land they all shared had so often been wagered, held to ransom, then reluctantly handed back and forth between successive military victors and between wars.

Mitzi soon discovered that her new, and newly Romanian kith and kin were struggling, up-and-coming-Jews, still far from that level of opulence already attained by the Stahlmans of Dortmund Stadt. Nevertheless, their family home on Calea Aradului was large enough, almost too large for Mitzi who was expected to help with the household chores, relieving the regular housemaid on Tuesdays, Sundays, and special holy days on the Roman orthodox calendar. It is true that Frau Morvaye attempted to be welcoming, even kind, but winter and summer for several years now she had suffered from *'the saintly vapours'* so common to women in mid-life. She also suffered from depressive black moods, mysterious bodycramps and blinding migraines, as though she had gazed too frequently into her occult crystals and divined the worst.

More honey, lemon in your tea, Mitzi? she asked, her ashen fatigue-ridden gaze reflecting the pool of gravitas in which she was steeped. Her familiar sounding Yiddish tongue might have helped Mitzi to feel at home, except that Frau Morvaye was unusually taciturn for a woman, often given to harsh pronouncements, flashes of sternness; overly sensitive to noise, to clatter and chatter, she rarely showed any pleasure even when handling her infant grandson—*'Oy, dos iz eyn kleyn tayvl, Mitzi mach dokh di tir tsu.'* It was disconcerting, offensive even, but Mitzi learned to remove her cherished little 'devil,' often spied clutching a handful of stolen silverware, from his grand-dame's sight.

I just don't like the way your father looks at me, Edi, I don't like him touching me.

Of course Mitzi couldn't say this, not openly. It seemed that Herr Morvaye Senior considered all females fair game, even the wife of his eldest son: Woman is woman, as the saying goes, and whatever your country of origin, land is land. Disgusting—and it frayed at her nerves, as well, to be abruptly dropped into the uneasy tedium of peacetime Romania, lukewarmly adopted into a household wherein she vied in status with the housemaid, most often with only a tyrannical, hyperactive toddler for company.

Not long ago, she'd been a respected and beloved nursing sister, a specially appointed *Krankenschwester* to the Surgeon at the field hospital, hand-selected, head and shoulders above the rest. Yes, she could disembowel a slaughtered kitchen fowl, but she could also watch unflinchingly as suture lines were stitched together, or anesthetized human limbs were sliced from their damaged parts.

Mitzi missed her family, as well. She wanted to go home, at least for a visit, and it was this first nostalgic return to Dortmund in the summer of 1922 that provoked the ominous start of the domestic schism. The circumstances could hardly have been more bizarre. Thirteen days after she arrived at *Steinstraße 11a* (before even her mother Wilhelmina had ceased marveling at Taddeusz's energy, genius, beauty and determination of character) a special delivery, franked with exotic looking stamps, arrived from Timişoara. Plummeted through the stratosphere onto their worn, ancestral table. Mitzi trembled with shock as she scrutinized the document, addressed to her and composed in German, Romanian and the lingua franca of legally sanctioned intimidation.

Frau Mitzi Morvaye, having unlawfully deserted the conjugal home and taking away her son, Taddeusz Morvaye, aged three and a half years, all without the consent of her lawful husband, Herr Edi Morvaye, Frau Morvaye is herewith served notice that official divorce proceedings have been initiated against her by her husband. Herr Edi Morvaye is empowered by law to retain the legal guardianship of the aforementioned child. However, he agrees that Frau Morvaye should be granted custody of the child for the greater part of the year until he reaches the age of twelve years, at which time he may be summoned back to reside at the family domicile on Calea Aradului, Timişoara. The boy will thereafter reside in Timişoara for the greater part of the year, with regular maternal visits allowed, at least twice yearly, but always at the discretion of the Morvaye family. In the interim period, a reasonable monthly allowance is to be agreed between the two parties for

108

the child's maintenance and upkeep. Once the 'Decree Absolute' has been granted, given the grounds of calculated desertion by the aforementioned spouse, no financial or other kind of support may be sought by Frau Morvaye', nor by her appointed advocates, from her former husband, Edi Morvaye.

Although in later years, Mitzi considered herself to have become almost shock-proof, with the present humiliation came its attendant poverty. What work could she find other than hiring herself out for domestic service? How repugnant! Sometimes she managed to find piecework as a seamstress (at least she was gifted in sewing, fine crochet and lace work) but sometimes, very often in fact, there was nothing to be had at all. Still, Taddeusz lacked neither food, nor love, nor shelter. His maternal grandmother Wilhelmina Hölke seized upon him with a dedicated, almost sensual passion. She welcomed Mitzi and child back into her dim rattling hollow of a nest and it wasn't long before Taddeusz learned to shadow her like a shrewd familiar. He knew Grandmother to be his grand Protectress for even Mitzi herself was reprimanded—fiercely reprimanded—if ever she raised her hand in temper against her own son. But in the years that followed, there was to be nothing but separations, as Taddeusz was shunted back and forth between Vater und Mutter. Accompanied to the station and placed on the train by Mitzi. Bathed, brushed and polished, hanging on to a wicker basket of cold sausage, Apfelstrudel and spiced custard, he was consigned to the temporary guardianship of Rolf, a senior rail employee and trusted colleague of Herr Hölke into whose hand Mitzi slipped a few notes or coins, and into whose ears she whispered, both in humiliation and maternal angst: *Möchten Sie bitte, auf meinen Jungen gut aufpassen, sein Vater, Herr Morvaye, soll ihn in Rumänien direkt vom Bahnhof in Timisoara abholen.*

Taddeusz's fascination with trains flourished especially during those last years Grandfather Hölke worked for the *Deutsche Reichsbahn*. Their first storey apartment on *Steinstraße* was housed in a crumbling, stone-fronted building, the colour of rancid butter, situated halfway up the slope to the railway embankment. This was a grassy mound, resembling a prehistoric dolmen, springy and fragrant, chaotically sown with dandelions and clover. At the summit of this hill, through the chinks of a stalwart steel fence, Taddeusz was allowed to watch the regular parade of steam-driven juggernauts, forged in unforgiving steel and iron, blasting their way toward Timişoara.

Still, he was barely old enough to understand the strange and ominous mood that infected the house one winter evening, the sight of Wilhelmina, crumpled, ash-grey upon her day-bed. Mitzi, heave-sobbing, with her plump back turned toward the kitchen dresser. Then came the urgent flurry of doorbells ringing, the priest offering a token of divine comfort, a bevy of flushed and grave-faced relatives, *Tanten, Onkeln, Kusinen*, plodding or scurrying about carrying ornate cut glass dishes of funeral food, gifts and flowers, the hoarse whispers and suppressed sobs of women, even grown men weeping in the wake of the cortège. A cheap sealed coffin contained (as Taddeusz was later told) Herr Hölke's human remains, both limbs severed five inches above the knee. He'd been discovered along the track and wooden sleepers—a signal failure, perhaps, or was he pushed, did he fall?—on some mist-befouled night, struck head on by the ironblind train-wheels of the *Deutsche Reichsbahn*.

Mitzi met Yosef again while crossing *Marienkirchenhofplatz* on her way to Reuben's Haberdashery. The day was dry and wind-dusty, with scraps of litter buffeting the road cobbles. As they mirrored one another, face to face, Mitzi trembled like on that day in the Lazarett, seven years beforehand, when she'd heard the news of his 'death.' Her skin was suffused with a dangerous flush of blood; she sensed an otherworldly pressure at the crown of her head. His immediate reflection was a look of bafflement, of wariness, of hurt.

"Yosef!"

"They told me you'd married some foreign military, gone away to Poland or Hungary, or something."

He touched her hand. It felt cool, distant and formal. He turned abruptly as though wanting to fade out of her life again.

"And my letter?" It was an afterthought, almost an accusation. "Didn't you get my letter?"

"What letter?"

He sighed, a loud impatient gush of breath, as though exasperated at his own stupidity. All around there remained traces of the universal blood-letting, the broken spires, ruined fields, the desolation of the cities. *Fein deutsche Jugend*, blond-haired comrades of his had fallen on crop-fields and pasture land, now renamed as notorious battlefields, shredded and pierced, to the right and to the left of him, in less than an eyeblink—yet he had expected his letter, with its cream-coloured envelope inscribed with urgent postscripts, crumpled and smeared with palmsweat and spots of grease, his fragile love letter, that artifact of passion and paper, he'd expected it to find its way across blood-drenched potato fields, bomb-sites and battle shelters, had expected it to reach her, reach her safely, and preserve her.

"Then are you here in Dortmund visiting your family—?" It was a questioning look, a polite and guarded query, betrayed by the angst in his glance.

Mitzi noted the intervening lost years that had scored themselves across his forehead like rings of bark. His thick coarse hair, a sort of dry ash mixed with brown, was being blown about by a wind of dust. He looked older certainly, more fragile, pale and grave, and she wondered—anxiously—whether he was thinking the same of her. It made her flush dangerously again. Her eyes glittered, reddened, as she beat back the tears. Inside the smooth scented lining of her jacket she instinctively buried her wedding ring. She shook her head.

"No, I left Romania, I've come back to stay."

Did the light of his eyes flicker? They were still of a translucent light brown, ever fragile and revealing. She noted a swift inclination of the head, a spark of mildly hostile curiosity. He seemed about to speak, then flushed darkly, a purplish corpse-like flush.

"—with my son."

"Oh!"

Silence.

Mitzi wanted to cry out, *Yosef, Yosef, I thought you were dead; I would never have married that man, I could never have loved him.*

Would he dare to kiss her? No, he edged away from her into a safer space.

"Some day we must meet again, you must tell me everything that has happened to you—*aber es tut mir Leid*—I must go now, *entschuldigen Sie bitte, Auf Wiedersehen!*"

CHAPTER 12

DIE KAMERA TRÜGT NICHT

At Reuben's Haberdashery on Ostenhellwegstraße Mitzi's sister, Else, was making lunch in the back room behind the shop. Her son, Karl, was imprisoned in his home-made playpen, fast asleep in a stinking cloth nappy, surrounded by his half-empty milk bottle, an old rubber teething ring and a few pitiful donated toys. Poor little bastard, thought Mitzi, no father to speak of, and a bitch-goddess for a mother. Chestnut-haired Else, second eldest of the Hölke brood, raising hell wherever she went, intimidating her widowed mother, outsmarting her two younger brothers, had been vanquished—finally—by the fertility of her pleasure-seeking body.

But, characteristically, Else had confronted her pregnancy with the duplicity of a spymaster. Who else but she could have persuaded an old school friend, Rolf, a clerk at the *Dortmunder Stadtarchiv*, to embark on a brief union of dual convenience? From his perspective, as a latent homosexual, it was the means of fulfilling society's expectations, whilst furnishing a legal identity for her illegitimate son. At the age of 32, with her first marriage conveniently behind her, Else was a single mother long before it became acceptable, even modish, to be so. Her new lover, Reuben, traded in textiles and household linens at the Ostenhellwegstraße Haberdashery; eventually the couple set up housekeeping together, she working as his general shop-assistant, cook, charwoman and extra-marital partner.

As the *jangling* of the shop-bell announced Mitzi's arrival, Else thrust out her head from the curtained back-room. Motherhood could hardly be said to have softened her. By now Mitzi was accustomed to her sister's offhand manner of welcome, the paradoxical air of resentful contempt that she rarely disguised. It hardly suited the demeanour of a shopkeeper's mistress. *She must drive away all the customers, I wonder why Reuben puts up with her?* she thought.

"Oh, it's you, Mitzi, I'm busy right now, can you—?"

"I've just come to pick up the duvet and the bedspread, the green silk, you know the one I ordered."

"I don't think they've come in yet, I have to check, but did you have to order that expensive top-of-the-line import; what's wrong with those ordinary ones over there? They're good quality, from a local *deutsche Fabrik*, they don't cost a fortune, and they aren't a pain in the arse to get hold of."

"That's nice, does Reuben hear how you talk to his customers?"

"Go to hell, Mitzi," said Else, with a mildly guilty smile. "And stop putting on those wealthy madame airs, you may be wearing your brand new wedding ring but, believe me, I'm not impressed."

This time it was Mitzi's turn to flush. After a painfully renewed courtship with Yosef that had begun tentatively, almost breaking off more than once, then lasting more than a year, it had been agreed that Mitzi's wedding band should not be selected from her mother-in-law's jewel casket. It was to be a unique and irreplaceable bond, personally inscribed: Mitzi and Yosef, 15 November, 1924. But the 18-carat gold ring that Mitzi was wearing had been melted down and recast from the self-same wedding band that Edi Morvaye had placed on her finger almost seven years before. Ironic, really, for hers was, in truth, a destiny recast. Yet why waste perfectly good gold, when it wasn't necessary, thought Mitzi, keeping her own counsel and secreting away the cash that Yosef had given her. Not a soul would ever know this, not even her mother Wilhelmina and certainly not Else, whom she was sure she couldn't trust.

"How are you getting along, do you need anything?" said Mitzi. Else's baby started to grow more restless; they could both hear him whimpering, searching for his mother, shifting around in his playpen amongst a chaotic scattering of toys.

"No, not a thing but I've got to go now, I need to change the kid." Else lowered her voice at the rhythmic clang of the shopbell, and called for Reuben to come out and serve his customer. She withdrew abruptly behind the curtain, taking shelter from the icy flow of wind.

For all of them, it was these weeks, months, years that were to be remembered, later on, as a perilous time of grace. For Mitzi this was an unaccustomed luxury, almost an acquired taste. Life, that is to say her daily life, became predictable, comfortable and secure, even if no more exhilarating than in Romania. Here in Dortmund, at least, she was on safe ground, surrounded by the stolidity, the permanence of its Prussian-style architecture, the familiarity and ease of her own language, her own anarchic tribe of siblings rooted, spreading, flourishing nearby.

Elderly Frau Hölke was still possessive of Taddeusz and would have liked to entice him to spend days on end at his early haunt and shelter, abutted to the fenced-off railway embankment on *Steinstraße*. As the boy grew older, however, the *Eisenbahn* lost much of its thrilling impact in favour of a new symbolic significance—escape. There was nothing particular to escape from, however, unless it were the discipline and tedium of his studies at the *Bismarck-Realgymnasium*. This was a grand, ochre façade of a building on *Münsterstraße*, massively ornate, a well-regarded private academy, dedicated to the training of the élite.

Mitzi had personally cut and sewn his school uniform, his shirts, blazer, trousers, even—despite Taddeusz protesting—his school tie. It was not that Yosef hadn't sufficient means to employ a suitable tailor. On the contrary, he owned several houses on nearby *Leopoldstraße,* which were rented out to locals of the more affluent kind. But although Mitzi enjoyed the occasional extravagance, she detested waste. She'd been through the wars, literally; a fierce dread of poverty was endemic to her, which she would bequeath to posterity through her genes. Never was she likely to forget she was the eldest child of a working man, who had earned his living—and also his death on the *Deutsche Reichsbahn.*

115

However, it must be said that as time passed, a certain degree of luxurious indolence crept into her day-to-day life. To fill the inevitable void, ornament, domestic ornament became an obsession. First and foremost, decorating herself with scarves, silk blouses, autumnal cloche hats, fox-fur mantles lined with thick imprinted silk, essential for the biting winters of northern Germany. Then every corner of their roomy flat became a repository for her handiwork. An explosion of frilly edged bolster cushions materialized on the armchairs and sofas. Reel upon reel of white or beige cotton thread was twisted through Mitzi's restless crochet needle, metamorphosing into tablecloths, dripping with snowy or creamy lace.

Yet it was tiresome the way dustlayers collected over everything, over the furniture, the velour drapes, the alcoves full of books. Mitzi pressed her two nieces into service, luring them with rich cream and custard cakes, sprinkled with brandy or *cerises glacées*. She could afford to be indulgent in this instance. Teenaged Liesl and Lottie were, after all, family and they were grateful enough for her tokens of affection, whether it be a slightly worn blouse, a cast-off silk bodice, a pair of discarded earrings or a jade bangle from her jewel box of ornamental baubles. Mitzi's relative state of plenty had helped her waistline spread to more generous proportions. Sometimes as she regarded herself in the mirror, half criticizing, half admiring, she saw that she was beginning to fatten sleekly like a cream-fed cat.

But here again, as in Romania, came the disquieting signs. The remains of a custard tart thrown against their stone-and-glass fronted real estate firm on *Leopoldstraße,* widely known to be of Jewish provenance. A long splintered crack, disfiguring their shop window, caused by a stone, a brick perhaps? Some hotblood venting an inexplicable aggression on a business establishment, retired for the night. A faint whiff of urine, perhaps the first tentative marking out of territories, the outward push, now notorious, toward a greater *deutscher Lebensraum.*

In time, this was followed by a name-and-shame campaign known as *Rassenschande*: a rash of poster images of degenerate hook-nosed *Juden*, bare buttocks bristling, ravishing pure-bred German girls—no German sluts. Such obscenities, ripped from the nationalist news-sheet *Der Stürmer,* confronted young Taddeusz as he walked along *Münsterstraße* not far from the school gates. They made him redden, furious and fearful, his heartbeat quickening with repressed terror and disgust. For this represented, supposedly, the likes of Mitzi and Yosef. Yosef, who—thank God or the Devil—looked nothing like such stereotypically lampooned Jews. He was even-featured, blandly handsome in a conformist, indistinguishable sort of way, of solid yet slim build, moderate, unremarkable, except perhaps for the subtle pearluxe sheen of his wide trimmed fingernails. Mitzi had never known a man to be so fastidious, and she his eager and willing familiar, kept his shoes polished, his suits laundered and brushed.

Yosef ambled off to the family firm's headquarters, not dreadfully early of a morning. They always took the time to enjoy their first coffee together. Yosef liked the deft way Mitzi sliced the breakfast rolls, heaped them with cream cheese and olives, *Leberwurst* and spiced marinade. They weren't bound by the rituals of kosher, and for this Mitzi was grateful. They agreed on most food at their intimate dining table, agreed on most things, in fact, except on the occasions when Taddeusz burst in on them like a famished wind, gorging himself under the disapproving gaze of Yosef. Of course Mitzi sensed and understood their conflicted body gestures, the mild to vibrant antipathy between the two—no, the three men in her life.

But paternal disciplinarian he was not, and Mitzi wondered sometimes how effective Yosef's presence was in the family firm, supposedly supervising his two veteran agents, Malkie and Heime, as well as Yutta their girl Friday, who tended the office more devotedly than her own poky little flat above stairs. Yosef, when he did appear, was a mild-mannered benevolent figurehead, a patron saint. So it had been since the end of the war when he returned, darker of mood, more melancholy, exhausted and frankly detached from the everyday graft of getting and

117

spending. Perhaps the privilege to which he was born had seeped into his neurons, into his genes, a condition unknown to Mitzi, who felt distrustful of the ease with which they seemed to slide through life in this precarious, this ephemeral time of grace.

For her brother, Franz, a year older than vagabond sister, Else, had begun to don the colours of an *SA mann*. His pale blemished face, dun-stubbled and ill fed, his harsh young eyes glittered with ill- and well-founded resentment toward the undeserving rich. He had fallen in at the tail end of a demobbed military gang, at large, most of them seeking work and finding none, perhaps seeking adventure or a least a cause, trained to hate and to kill and now aimlessly beating their vigilante patrols through the heart of Dortmund Stadt. Franz's small unit of stormtroopers spared Reuben's haberdashery shop on the Ostenhellweg, but only just. In any case, as a small merchant, Reuben had seen better days. His customers, the stalwarts, the old-timers, the faithfuls still came, but the newer ones were a fickle crowd, picking over his narrow selection of tablecloths, bed linen and drapes, slightly hostile and mocking in the face of such odd bedfellows as he and Else, tending their dimly lit, snuff-and-must-smelling little shop.

"Just tell Franz if he shows up at Lottie's Confirmation Feast wearing his fascist gear, I'll throw him out," threatened Else's brother-in-law Hans Witte, father of teenaged Liesl and Lottie. He was a tall, unyielding man, gruff, proud and unrelentingly just, a sort of working man's *éminence grise*.

"Well, don't expect to see me, either," said Else. "I'd rather not run into bloodhound Franz, even if he is my own dear brother, and as for her ladyship, Mitzi, and her retinue of grandees—thanks, but no thanks!"

Yosef was aware of this underground microcosm of inter-tribal warfare. He was too astute not to divine its motives but too languid, too deliberately remote to involve himself in its manifestations, its flashpoints. He had wed Mitzi, not her family, which he regarded as a cross-hatch of indigenous toughness, pride and poverty, profane rebellion laced with banditry. Although Yosef had, with some reluctance, inherited Taddeusz, he rarely felt close to the boy. More and more, he sought a tranquil existence in which he could, without undue strain, superintend his family's commercial interests while still finding time to think, to read, to paint and to sketch. The walls of their home were crammed with his framed landscapes, watercolour field-flowers, *nature morte*. His life—his reclaimed life—waxed and waned in a rarefied atmosphere of privileged 'tristesse,' even as he basked in the security, the luxury of Mitzi's aromatic feast table, her unfailing caresses, effusive and erotic, her strength.

So it was some considerable time before Yosef awoke to the realization that in this slow poisoning post-war environment he was becoming a glass man, on the verge of becoming invisible. He rarely used the local library, usually purchasing books, whether fiction, biography or fine art reproductions whenever he needed or desired them, but now all Jews were being denied this essential civic civility. A senseless and offensive gesture, as was the Nazi-inspired edict barring them from Dortmund's public trams, bathing houses, park benches, cafés and eating houses, theatres and museums. Jews were soon afterward denied driving licenses, jobs within the civil service and even state medical care. From 1933 onward a raft of repressive edicts rained down with increasing malevolence over this once mediaeval bastion of a city. They appeared as typewritten notices nailed, stapled or pasted onto fences, posts, shop windows and public entrances: *Kein Eintritt, für Juden verboten.*

It fell to Mitzi to shield her family from the effervescence of Nazi fervour. She was, after all, undeniably Aryan, although her pure blond hair was beginning to whiten. She was still fit and strong, maturely beautiful and forever vain, primped, perfumed and bedecked in high high fashion—bejewelled fur jacket, cap and muff, brown leather lace-up shoes—her inflamed varicose veins strapped into prescription stockings. No grocer demanded to see her identity card, or refuse to part with his wares, even for hard Jewish coin. It was certain that the SA now patrolled the marketplace, watchful that each fresh edict should be enforced. Almost everything she owned was to disappear during the bombardment of the coming war but for a long time Mitzi treasured a copy of that ill-focused photograph of herself printed in the *Nationalsozialistische* newspaper '*Rote Erde.*' Below her image, the caption: *Nicht bei Juden kaufen—Die Kamera trügt nicht.* She, in her coquettish fox-fur cap, windblown skirt and jacket, her shapely legs swathed in elasticized stockings, clutching onto her 'illegal' parcels and shopping bags as she stepped down onto the wide sweep of pavement outside Reuben's Haberdashery on the Ostenhellweg.

And this, in time, was to be followed by the loss of her brief-lived ancestral seat beside Yosef; as they had expected and feared, his property, land and assets were taken in custody. The couple were moved out of their flat on *Lortzingstraße* and sequestered in a *Judenhaus* on *Kronprinzenstraße*, forced to share with one other mixed-race couple and their child. It was here, ghetto-style, that they harboured reluctant Else and her infant Karl, as well, once Reuben, also a glass man, vanished abruptly, abandoning his long-standing establishment on the Ostenhellwegstraße to be plundered. Although senior members of the SA would have preferred to grant it to some deserving German citizen on the official reward list, they turned a blind eye when '*begeistert*' young enthusiasts tossed a small amount of paraffin through Reuben's broken shop window, followed by a lit match. From then on, Mitzi kept watch over their foundling, their little nephew bereft, when hothead Else slunk away—regularly—to meet the exiled Reuben at a secret tryst, somewhere under cover of the dangerous fragrant woodland along the Belgian border.

"Don't, Mitzi, don't do it," warned Irmgard the 'sensitive,' her visiting friend and neighbour from earlier days. *"Whatever happens, don't let Yosef go into hospital."*

What on earth was she talking about? Her crater-like eyeholes, unhealthily purplish, her glittering eyes and earnest emaciated face frightened Mitzi. Likewise, did the sight of

Yosef. True, he had been ailing for some time now, and with no recourse. Like Napoleon on his island, he continued to languish and sicken in the pernicious atmosphere of their urban prison. Could it be gallstones, bowel disease, stomach ulcers or a damaged liver? Or was it—as was whispered and believed long afterward—caused by a slow, deliberate and self-administered poison?

"Just remember what I say, don't let Yosef set foot in that hospital."

As if one truly needed second sight or precognition to divine his fate, his second death—*Die Schändung, die Schandtat die mein Mann erleiden musste!*—with a frisson of rage and dread, Mitzi wondered, in those final hours once they forced her to leave, had his Aryan physicians—themselves—finished him off?

Yosef was buried one day in October when the earth was wet, the sky morose and tearful. Tiny raindrops blew against Mitzi's face; the wind battered the stone-grey clouds over a tiny woodland, steeped in green gloom. Breathing incense of mould, pitch, ancient growth, anarchic garlands of wild ivy draped themselves around the bones of the trees that were as tall as gallows. A quietness, a sadness lingered over the damp curls of the oakleaf, the beechleaf, decomposing amongst the stones. And then—the final profanity—a handful of armed stormtroopers, ranged like archangels at heaven's gates. With harsh orders, they separated and held back the Aryans from amongst the assembled family of mourners. Only Mitzi was allowed to follow behind Yosef's coffin, between the twin rows of Lombardy poplars, to his grave.

CHAPTER 13

JEWBOY

"Thank God, thank God you're here, Mama," said Taddeusz, embracing her when she arrived in London, one year after the war. It hurt and amazed Mitzi to realize how much her turbulent, headstrong son had aged in just a few years. Having driven himself almost to the breaking point, he was marooned and battling to stay afloat in an alien country, constantly calculating, planning, plotting his next move. Fuelled by virulent coffee, night after night, he crammed a secret double life into his few spare hours, studying newspapers, business journals, textbooks, novels, pacing frantically over the floorboards, smoking, cursing, scribbling God-knows-what until all hours of the night. He seemed to be consumed by a restless hunger to devour the world. Over the years, it had taken its toll.

He was now barely thirty, yet his hair was completely white. The fiery glimmer of his eyes was progressively dimming. He had already crossed the borderline between luxuriant corpulence and mild obesity. Trapped in Lily's unwholesome cave of dank primitive domesticity, he looked humiliated, angry, scared. "You've got to help me," he whispered privately to Mitzi, "since the baby died, Lily's gone completely to pieces."

It wasn't long before Mitzi's silky black umbrella, unfurled, stood guard over little Angie's crib, which was cobbled together from remnants of blue taffeta glued around a robust cardboard box. Of course, there was no extra space for a nursery, so Mitzi stowed her grandchild in a corner of the kitchen. Evenings, she banished everyone from the room. *"Careful, don't—!"* she cried, prying Greta's nimble fingers away from her baby sister's eyelids, before pushing her away. *"Verflucht, noch mal!* That child has a touch of the devil—of Taddeusz—*um Gottes willen,* she mustn't be allowed to run wild!"

Remoulded in Mitzi's image, their cramped little cottage on Headstone Lane was soon reeking of disinfectant, spiced apples, sauerkraut. Home-sewn curtains clothed the naked windows. Crocheted lace doilies appeared on the polished furniture. Bountiful order was restored to the larder, the linen closet, the shed. By the following summer, giant strawberries blossomed under their furry leaves, French runner beans crawled up posts, mounds of radish leaves appeared magically above ground.

"Never mind, Lily, leave that to me, you just sit down," said Mitzi, whenever Lily wandered into her own kitchen to see what was cooking. Mitzi had very quickly mastered the rudiments of the English language, enough anyhow to deal Lily. With Taddeusz she spoke German and, of course, the absorbent minds of her grandchildren intuitively soaked it up. *"In diesem Haus wird Deutsch gesprochen—German in this house,"* she declared, emphatic, impressive, and not to be disobeyed. If Lily resented Mitzi's presence, the authority that she had usurped over the children, she was obliged to do so in secret. Hacked away, displaced from her own roots, she was as good as helpless now. Taddeusz had finally triumphed, wrenched her away from her familiar world of the East End. For her own good he'd raised her out of the squalor, hadn't he? A mark of grace bestowed on the unworthy. And, at the same time, he'd managed to elude the vigilantes amongst the Herman tribe.

Yes, he had transplanted his entire family to this bland north London suburb of tidy gold-lettered little shops, up-market schools and lavish green parks. Still, Taddeusz could barely stifle his rage at Lily and her trundling caravan of babies. No matter where they camped, she would forever hinder his meteoric flight, restrain and cripple him, hold him captive in her narrow world of chamber pots and stinking nappies, sinking sinking sinking into her own maternity, with its mushroom reek of damp, of sweat, of souring milk. This dark humid cult of life, of raw bloody pulsating life, had completely enveloped Lily in a world he raged to escape.

124

For Lily had delivered into the world yet another sick baby, Angie, whose cheeks were still streaked with lingering jaundice. With her tuft of white-blond hair and her father's narrow eyes, she resembled a tiny yellow bird. *"Morgen früh, wenn Gott will, wirst Du wieder geweckt..."* Mitzi sang, rocking back and forth and anxiously scrutinizing the baby's lilac-swollen eyelids, the fleshy twirl of her ears, the familiar wide bridge of her nose. It was an ethereal lullaby, but gruesome, had she ever paused to reflect. When Angie became old enough to grasp the lyrics of Brahm's Lullaby, they never failed to incite a keen malaise: *Morgen früh, wenn Gott will...*

After all, what might happen to her one morning, should 'The Almighty' fail to bid her wake?

Mitzi was not a woman to wallow in painful memories. What good could come from lingering, masochistically, among the bones of history, forever exhuming the dreadful past? When she buried her husband, Yosef, it was with the mournful fatalism of having survived two great wars—great in atrocity—the last, tainted with a macabre touch of lunacy in which whole tribes were torn asunder, brother turned against brother, and distinctions blurred between enemy and friend. Not only had her birthplace Dortmund, beating heart of Germany's coal and steel industry, been flattened to a desolate moonscape; worse, even the notion of a 'Fatherland' in its universal legendary sense was—for Mitzi—no more.

Now, even her anger belonged to the past tense. It died with Yosef in the winter of '42. In a bittersweet way, perhaps, it was a relief to let him go. She couldn't live with his *jüdische Angst* any longer. It reeked around him like a shadow, like the aura of a shroud. She sensed it, late at night, as he double-bolted the front door. She knew what he was thinking: *maybe it'll be tonight, they always come in the dead of night.* So many hundreds, maybe thousands, had already disappeared, interned in the *Steinwache,* the former police headquarters, behind whose barred windows terrifying screams were sometimes heard. It was said that after so many desperate prisoners flung themselves from the highest

125

stairwell, it became necessary to stretch a thick wire netting between the railings, so as to prevent them. Others, still hoping for their release, had been herded onto specially marked trains at the *Südbahnhof,* never to be seen again. *How much longer, God, how much longer before they came for him?*

The lamp glow, which pooled onto Mitzi's open book, inscribed in church-like gothic script, had once seemed to comfort Yosef. Her warm solid body anchored to his, the breath of life stirring beside him, the gentle rustle of a page turning, the illusion that as long as she remained close by him, nothing bad could ever happen: *Brauchst keine Angst zu haben, keine Angst.* His loving warden always, she vigilantly kept the wake. Mitzi sensed the moment Yosef slipped into his first anxious doze. The silky green coverlet slid away. An involuntary tremor shot through his limbs, as though his soul were struggling to leave his body, or else he'd pulled himself up, just in time, from the edge of the nightmare abyss.

Mitzi cursed even louder than she sobbed, the day she had to stitch the yellow cotton star—now a profanity, a sacrilege—to Yosef's jacket.

"Verdammte Scheiße, ich kann es gar nicht glauben, I can't believe it—and this in my own beloved country!" she screamed. Denied the right to work, forced to appear in public with the jaundiced Star of David affixed to his breast, Yosef was counting his last few coins and banknotes.

"Mitzi—(Yosef was turning his wallet inside out)—did you take any money? I'm sure I had more than that yesterday—"

"No, of course, I didn't. You must have spent it. Where did you go yesterday? Try to remember, what did you buy?"

Taddeusz knew that his mother, Mitzi, had stolen the money for cigarettes; he watched her hunt through her husband's pockets every day. Any moment now (just let him dare!) Yosef would probably start accusing him. Tonight Yosef was furious with him, anyway, over an incident a few days ago—a few drinks, a few girls. After supper Taddeusz had been confined to quarters, banished to his room, but he'd climbed out of the window anyway, scrambled over the balcony and crash-landed in the garden. It was risky, true, but he would show his stepfather that he fashioned his own rules, that he would allow himself to be oppressed by no one. He plunged headlong through Dortmund's wild and moonlit night breezes, its familiar darkstreet architecture. Hitler's '*Hakenkreuz*,' his potent swastika, was tattooed all over the gas lit terraces. It dominated the high flying façades of Prussian coat of arms, Pharaonic eagles, Romanesque hammocks pregnant with vine-leaves and flowerets of stone. At the market square, the frail goldleaf arrows of the clock-tower shuddered forward, punctuating Eternity; too late—too late to catch a streetcar, of course.

Especially to Linienstraße.

Its covert rear façade faced onto the blank backsides of shuttered, shamefaced buildings, whose inhabitants were all too aware of the provocative red lanterns, suspended above adjacent front doorsteps. A shrouded passageway to this 'Holy of Holies' was accessible only to the 'Initiated,' for immense flowering trees, growing along the inner courtyards, protected the anonymity of the denizens of this brief sidestreet, seven or eight houses at most, all straight as a plumb line. At the soft-lit windowpanes were the watchful eyes and perfumed lips, the bejeweled fingers and bosoms of those inviting the supreme act, the ineffable ritual of manly self-regeneration.

Linienstraße—it inspired in Taddeusz a quasi-religious awe. And no less so did the 'Initiated,' that single-file of menfolk continually pacing its stark pavement, hanging fire, those who had already breached the forbidden altar, the magic circle—not even a true circle—for it was nothing more than an arrow-straight line of dwellings with steep cement façades, beatified in pastels, romantic rose and lavender. Beyond the porch steps, up the old stairway and creaking banister were the scented side altars, pearlescent candlelights, draped hangings, rugs and couches. The house breathed an atmosphere of perfumed rot, a whiff of decrepit timber, massaged in magnolia. Arabesque lamps hung from chains; a row of tiny footlights guided his footfalls through the warren toward the cell-chamber of a youthful street goddess. As he entered, she was combing her white-blond Aryanesque hair, slightly shadowed along the roots.

She was young, too young, perhaps fifteen, and with the air of a less-than-accomplished acolyte. So then, what might she be doing here? In this place. A veil of awkwardness, of embarrassment dropped between them. Taddeusz lowered his gaze, stepped backward. Doubt, apprehension cascaded over him. What was one supposed to do, faced with the immediacy of the Sacrament? Was it not going to be that easy, after all, this long-desired communion of the body? Some preparation must be needed; something spiritual, perhaps, was supposed to happen? He had certainly dreamed of it, fantasized often enough, yet now he stood, hesitant, in the perfumed dimness of this femininity of a dwelling, face to face with the unknown arch-goddess: she, the nameless virgin, he, the unaccustomed supplicant.

Nevertheless, there was something of the fugitive about the girl. Polish? thought Taddeusz; Hungarian, perhaps? The whole of her meager slim-whittled body was on the defensive. Her skin, despite its subtle lashings of rouge, seemed to be fading out of existence. In the half-light, even her eyes seemed colourless but for their huge pupils which glittered like swift-darting swallows being driven from the nest. Taddeusz hesitated, then peeled off his jacket, his body armour, the *Hitler Jugend* uniform that was salutary to be seen in. In response, the girl flinched visibly as though prepared to defend herself against assault. That gesture unnerved Taddeusz, made him flush, so that he was grateful for the subtle dimness of the room. What was she doing here, damn it, if she wasn't inclined to entertain her customers? Hadn't he paid his money, as required, to the maternally buxom grand-dame of uncertain age who had greeted him at the door? He stepped closer to the young girl, reached out to touch one of her bony wrists, which was parchment white, faintly perfumed, sculpted small, yet strong.

"What's your name, sweetheart?" whispered Taddeusz, aware that all that transpired in this perfumed 'House of Flesh' might well be overheard by a legion of concubines and their clients to the right and to the left of them.

"Alizia," she whispered in return, betraying herself in a word. A Pole, stranded here far from home, perhaps. More of a refugee than a good-time girl. She was about to say something more but he stopped her with an abrupt kiss, he hadn't bargained on sharing a life story. Yet the embrace shocked Taddeusz; it was both thrilling and repulsive. Her sharp hot electric breath, her moist lip set his teeth on edge and he recoiled, as though kissing himself—his own flesh image—young, alien, vulnerable and in danger.

"What are you doing—*here*?" he asked, in a tone both curious and indignant. Their mutual revulsion was unmistakable, yet the girl was a beauty, unformed, but a future beauty, at any rate.

"What can I tell you?" She paused; eyed him with bleak anxiety, spiked with defiance. "At the coal mine they arrested first my brother, then my father, now we have nothing left, nowhere to go."

The coal mine! Taddeusz understood at once. Working class Dortmund, the '*Rote Hochburg*' as it was becoming known, was a festering ground for locals and foreign '*Fremdarbeiter*,' day-labourers transformed into fledgling unionists, demanding more security, better pay. The most vociferous among these were targets of the local SA Corps, as were the city's gypsies, communists, foreign-born slave labourers, splinter religionists and Jews.

As for the girl, she now turned deliberately away from him. He could see that he irritated and disturbed, without overly threatening her. He sighed, refraining from glancing at his wristwatch, although he knew how late it must be. He visualized Mitzi, flushing and pacing the domestic boards, exclaiming rhetorically to Yosef: *Aber wo ist er denn?* He made an abrupt move of irritation, of impatience, and the girl turned around to gaze at him, like some sort of reluctant Queen in her chessboard redoubt. It was a glance of anger, of questioning, of futile despair.

Taddeusz returned home late that night, trying vainly to suppress his trepidation. His breath rasped in his throat; his clattering footsteps slackened, dragging themselves up the broad stairwell, hewn from ancient stone. A reluctant shadow, he flickered past the uniform row of square-cut windows, opaquely shielding the inner gardens, which themselves seemed to be draped in deadly nightshade. Beyond the unseen garden wall of sculpted cement, trailing in ivy, the rising terrace-houses loomed like ghost-mountains. On the second floor landing even their nondescript front door, securely barred and ominous-looking, seemed to be muffled in an almost heart-stopping silence; still, the lights burned steadily in the smoke-filled lounge and, with a lurching heart, Taddeusz realized they were both still awake, probably waiting to haul him over the coals. Mitzi was in his bedroom, actually packing his suitcase.

"What are you doing?" said Taddeusz, with a gloomy guilty look. He hated her snooping through his things. He was angry and alarmed. It was no small thing, granted, to disobey Yosef's orders, but now to be thrown out of the house—what a swine!

"You're going to Timişoara tomorrow," said Mitzi. "There's a train leaving at seven; you need to change at Hannover and Berlin."

"Why?"

Mitzi stared at him, recoiled slightly as though she could breathe the clamorous reek of sex in which he felt steeped.

"And where have you been, crawling the streets at this hour? You know you were forbidden to go out, but you don't listen to anyone, do you?"

"Hell, I just—"

"It doesn't matter now, just listen to me, Yosef has bought your ticket already, it cost a fortune; make sure you remind your father to pay us back. He promised to meet you at the station."

"I said why do I have to go? For how long?"

"I don't know, a few months, maybe longer."

"What's the matter?"

"Did you hear what happened yesterday?"

"Of course, I was right there."

"You were there? *Du verdammter Idiot,* you could have been killed! Did you know two people were shot?"

"I didn't know what was going to happen, did I? Hell, I just saw a crowd gathering so I ran across to see."

"See what?"

"The storm-troopers marching north. They came face to face with the workers, tried to break up their rally."

"And then what?"

"The workers managed to drive them off, *God knows how,* then people started pouring out of the houses. You should have seen them, there must have been hundreds of SA goons armed with clubs. Jesus, I had to run like hell!"

"O, mein Gott!"

"It's all right, Mama, nothing happened to me!"

O God, she felt weary. And this was her child. Her son, Taddeusz, the tearaway. Right now, on the verge of being expelled from the select *Gymnasium* on *Münsterstraße.* In her pocket was a recent letter from his father, Edi.

You've both spoiled him thoroughly, you know; I have no end of trouble whenever he comes here. He needs discipline and clearly he's not getting that from you—or your husband, so-called. Okay, okay, don't tell me he's still jealous, haven't you told him all that was over long ago? Just say what you want this time. Schokolade? Cognac? Leberwurst and cigarettes? All right, I'll be sending you a package, but I'm warning you, I won't pay another penny toward the boy's schooling next term unless he comes to live here. And that's final!

"It's getting too dangerous for you to stay in Dortmund," said Mitzi. "You've got to get out."

"What are you talking about, dangerous?"

"It's dangerous for Yosef," whispered Mitzi, recharged by her anger, by her alarm. "It's dangerous for foreigners, for unionists, it's especially dangerous for Jews."

"I'm not a damned Jew!"

Mitzi stared at him. It was a look of reproach, of fear. "*Shhh,* keep your voice down, *Dummkopf!*" Abruptly she shut the bedroom door.

"I SAID—I'M NOT A JEW!"

Taddeusz was staring at his own reflection, incensed and aroused, in the beveled mirror-pane of the antique wardrobe. His was a face spawned from immaculate conception, surely. Scarcely a trace of Edi's ancestral or patriarchal attributes, just Mitzi's shapely roselips blended with his own fair, glowing, seductively fresh Aryan flesh, the unmistakably Hanseatic mould of nose, chin and cheekbone. Only those live-amber eyes of his which were narrow, shifting, restless and gitanesque, might possibly give him away. Like the archetypal divine Half-Caste, Jesu Xristus—that mysterious earthbound demi-god—few suspected that he was, in fact: Son of Jew, *kategorie Mischlinge ersten Grades*, according to the precise theocracy of Hitler's Third Reich. Yet, despite this blessing of physique, Taddeusz's outrage was spiked with hysteria; he scowled as the shadow of Mitzi's hand crossed his face. "I am not a—"

"Shut up!"

Down came her hand, imprinting rose-dark fingermarks across his cheek. He lunged forward, about to strike her back, thrusting his face close to hers, bellowing, flaming in fury. "I said I'm not—"

"Oh, yes, you are, *mein lieber Sohn*," said Mitzi, "yes, you bloody well are!"

Yosef opened the door a crack, timidly. His face was a pallid shade of grey, he looked sick. "What's happening? What is it, *Liebling*? Taddeusz, what—?"

"Nothing, nothing," growled Taddeusz contemptuously, turning his back on Yosef. He had expected punishment; instead his stepfather's sunken head and shoulders were those of a craven foot soldier in retreat. The door closed again. Mitzi went back to her packing. Taddeusz watched her angrily, nervously. "Let me do that," he said.

Mitzi ignored him. She strode over to his wardrobe and fished out his best jacket, the expensive one that came from Timişoara. Energetically she began to beat a fine layer of dust off the shoulders.

"What's this?" she said, bending down to examine a dense oblong parcel, secured by cords. It resembled some sort of contraband stowed away at the back of the wardrobe.

"Leave that alone," said Taddeusz.

"Well, what is it?"

"Look, Mama, this is my room, can't you leave my things alone?" Mitzi pressed her fingers against the parcel. Abruptly she ripped open one corner of the oilpaper wrapping. "*Scheiße!*" said Taddeusz. "Shit!"

"*Du verdammter Schweinehund!*" said Mitzi.

"Shit shit shit—"

Mitzi was staring at her son. Motherlove marbled with resentment, and fear. Here were at least a thousand printed posters, obscene and secret, in her loved one's possession. What treachery! In her own beloved country, no less, and in her own house. The brooding eyes of the *Führer;* a swastika armband around his outstretched arm—the classic *'Hitlergruß'* of brotherhood'—enclosed within a triple border of black, red and white, the trademark colours of the *Reich.*

"*Du Schweinehund du*—" whispered Mitzi, her icy sky-blue eyes amazed and staring.

But all was lost. She knew only too well that she could no longer fight him. Even as a small child, he had been powerful, as though he knew some invincible force was behind him. Watching him stride around the house, driven by furious energy, Mitzi had sometimes had the uncanny sense, a fleeting conviction rippling coldly through her, that Taddeusz was somehow infused with the spirit of his unborn half-brother, that mangled handful of bleeding flesh that—years ago—Yosef hadn't allowed her to bring, whole and alive, into the world. Behind Taddeusz's eyes, lurked those of a warped, unborn, unholy ghost burning for vengeance, burning for a life.

"*YOU* brought this—*Dreck, this Hitler-Scheiße*, into the house?"

Taddeusz leapt forward, shielding the bundle of posters with his arm. "I had to do it, what do you think?"

"Never mind, leave it now, just make sure Yosef never sees it," said Mitzi, in a voice suddenly crippled and broken. Taddeusz cringed at the sound of her stifled sob. "I'll make sure I get rid of it, as soon as you're on that train."

CHAPTER 14
Summer, 1949

DEUS INVICTUS

"Lily's pregnant again, she's too scared to tell you," said Mitzi.

"Oh, Christ!" said Taddeusz.

Lily was sitting in her chair, facing them both, pressing her palm against her stomach and staring at three-year-old Angie with the usual blend of fear and resignation on her face. The child was lightweight, perennially pale, with bluish hollows around her eyes. She came into the world sick, and it was Lily's own fault. She had tried to snuff her out, drive her out of the womb, and now she was punished. Those searing hot baths, the full glasses of gin she kept sipping until she was fainting, the innocent looking pills the doctor had given her in the vain hope—but no, they had just made her violently sick and still little Angie had clung on for dear life, blossoming inside the impregnable shelter of her mother's terror, forcing her way at last through the portals, damaged but alive. It was Lily's own fault, she had done it, and God had punished her.

"After Larissa died, I didn't want no more," said Lily. "I just couldn't bear it, but then look what happened!"

"Oh, Christ, Christ—" said Taddeusz again. The lines on his forehead disappeared, his eyes narrowed and flashed, the tips of his ears wiggled in a way that might have seemed funny had this familiar metamorphosis not signaled another outbreak of Olympian rage.

"After all the doctor's warnings," said Mitzi, "God, O God!"

That was perhaps the day, the very instant Taddeusz decided to leave Lily. The noose was tightening, he was gradually suffocating. Harpooned flesh-to-flesh with herself and hersickness, he was

135

being dragged to the very bottom. He had no choice now. It was either break away or die.

And Taddeusz refused to die.

This was the day of his 'blessed Resurrection,' as foretold by destiny. Taddeusz allowed himself the luxury of floating, yeasting in a surge of power that instantly energized him. He had just perceived the way out, reclaimed his life. How monumental, yet how simple. The desperation of the moment cleared his mind's eye, revealed at the same time the stark outlines of his bifurcated destiny. Razor-sharp, black on white. He knew now what he had to do. *God, O God, why hadn't he acted sooner*—he gazed around fatalistically at first one, then another of his blossoming progeny—*before all this?*

From this day onward, Taddeusz plotted tirelessly toward his own deliverance. He had to be cunning, needed a good lawyer, had no intention of relinquishing what was his. He laid his plans cautiously while awaiting the birth. But he had to be careful. No one must suspect, not even Mitzi, until it was all arranged, a *fait accompli*. He smiled, felt elated, looked gentler at Lily now, moved toward her, stroked her hand while she, poor bitch, gazed at him gratefully. It was just a matter of biding his time. A matter of patience, of secrecy, of cunning! Had Taddeusz been a religious man, he'd have thrown himself down on his knees to his liberating God, and uttered a prayer of thanks.

Years ago—*he would never forget it*—Taddeusz had spent many bleak months of internment as an Alien citizen on the Isle of Man, where he whiled away the time, trying to absorb and perfect his English. Lily was sometimes allowed to visit him, bringing writing paper, books, dictionaries. Soon he could read well enough, but his pronunciation was, at times, barely comprehensible. Each time Lily came, she related to him in a terrified whisper about the last visit from the Authorities. They had brought a search warrant to ransack their flat on Crellin Street. They had confiscated what remained of Taddeusz's bank documents and identification papers, hacked apart the mattress, ripped up the linoleum, even rifled through a pile of stinking nappies. Voluminous reports were being compiled on him. The two men from National Security wanted to know where Lily had met her husband, what he did, where he got his money, who were his friends, whether he traveled overseas, received messages, letters or telegrams from foreign countries.

"This is wartime, Mrs. Morvaye, and you are married to an ethnic alien. Do you understand what that means? It means that you've knowingly allied yourself with *'the Enemy.'* We have every reason to suspect that your husband may be a secret agent, working for Germany."

But then just as suddenly without warning, the Authorities underwent a change of heart. After having been investigated and interrogated to within an inch of his life, Taddeusz found himself recruited to the British War Office. His assignment was top secret, of course, his position highly sensitive, and he was sworn to secrecy for decades to come. And it was around that time, with the bombs still shuddering through the heart of London, that Taddeusz was gripped by a feverish sense of haste. A torrent of ideas erupted in his brain and spilled out of his gut; he began writing raw poetry, stories, drama in a language that was not his own.

Barely a year after the war was over, he published his first novel, *Permission to Land, Denied,* and a year later his play, *Adieu to the General,* was staged at the Cripplegate Theatre. Although the babies had sometimes gone without milk to subsidize the operetta, it was a splendid flop. It broke his heart; well, wounded his pride, certainly. As for those so-called theatre critics, a pox on all their houses—*morons and cretins all.* He'd even composed the musical score, and had a brief scalding affair with the leading lady before the play-run was canceled; his stack of glossy playbills became useless even as toilet paper, and the histrionic escapade ended for Taddeusz in smarting disappointment, to be acknowledged by scarcely an asterisk in the annals of theatre history.

Nevertheless, he was swimming in another current now; he was author, poet, playwright. Having at last dragged himself out of anonymity, he began to weave his own public mystique. Again, the speed of his metamorphosis, his transfiguration, took even him by surprise. Dazzling contacts lit up for him all over London. Letters of congratulation, queries, offers of contracts, invitations began to pour in. From the lowly untouchable he once seemed, he had climbed into the Brahmin caste. Here were all the earmarks of a potential victor, a brilliant multilingual young émigré smouldering with intelligence, creativity and latent power. And the women—he never lacked for women—models, actresses who secretly or openly coveted the leading rôle in his next dramatic script.

On the stark cold February night when baby Peter came into the world, Taddeusz was lying in bed beside dark-haired Lena, whose exotic stage name matched her ambitious zeal. He heaved his heavy body over hers and gave her a quick kiss, clumsily fondling her small breast in an act of contrition. His wavy forelock flopped over Lena's swan-like neck as he took the phone out of her hand.

"Taddeusz, is that you?" It was Mitzi. She was raging. "*Was machst Du denn mit dieser Hure? Du musst ins Spital!* Lily had the baby two hours ago, it's a boy."

"All right, I'm coming—" The deep wavy lines in his brow disappeared again. The tips of his ears twitched. The receiver shook in his hand. In the quiet of their transient bedchamber, Lena detected the outrage in Mitzi's tone.

"Lily's hysterical. They gave her something to calm her down. The doctors are doing tests on the baby right now—"

"I'm coming, Mama, *I'm coming!*" said Taddeusz. He slammed down the phone.

Lena felt his massive body roll off the bed. Sweat poured from his temples. He began fumbling around in the gloom for his shoes and socks. She switched on the lamp, pulled the bedsheet up over her naked breast, pushed her tangling black hair off her forehead, and stared at Taddeusz provocatively under her arrow-straight, thick brows. Her trained stage voice was penetrating, breathy and metallic; like tolling church bells, or sharpening knives.

"You're going? All right, but remember if you leave now, don't bother ever coming back."

God's wrath continued to storm over Lily. As she opened her eyes next morning, tentatively shifting her body and sensing, once again, that deep chafing soreness between the thighs which signaled her deliverance, the first thing she remembered was Larissa. The vision immobilized her like Christ on the crucifix, like a butterfly on a pin. The indelible image of ginger-haired baby Larissa coughing in her little box crib, the rumbling thunder in her tiny lungs which seemed to be more powerful than she was, forcing her to cough herself to the verge of extinction. Lily had memorized the sheet of notes handed out by the doctor to two Pediatric students, studying her case: *Cystic Fibrosis: A hereditary disease with no known cure. It produces a thick mucus that clogs the airways of the lungs and bronchial tree, causing victims to suffocate. Respiratory therapy and antibiotics to ward off lung infections, and enzyme supplements to aid digestion can slow the effects of the disease. One in twenty people is a carrier. For some unknown reason, males survive longer than females.*

Lily knew what they were doing. They were weighing it, measuring it, beaming tiny floodlights into its eyes and ears, watching for the first signs of respiratory distress, recording the bumpy echoes of its heartbeat, scrutinizing the beads of salt glistening on its forehead. Lily already knew what they were coming to tell her: this baby, too, was destined to die. Peter, the most beautiful of all her babies. The solemn seemingly watchful eyes, almost black, the sward of straight dark hair, the fleshy cherub's mouth. Who did he resemble? Certainly not Taddeusz. Lily had held her breath as the Angel of Death swooped over Angie, then passed her by; now here was its dreadful shade once again, hovering over her last-born.

But when Peter survived three months, stopped losing weight, gradually stabilized, then grew almost plump, Lily herself began to revive. The child definitely has all the tell-tale signs of CF, but they seem to be less severe than before, said the doctors, perhaps with treatment we'll be able to keep him alive a lot longer—well, we can only hope.

Taddeusz rented a hotel room for himself in the West End Princes Square. He was now building the foundations for his career, needed to devote his full attention to his work, to his studies, to the profusion of manuscripts spilling out of his typewriter. Impossible for him to concentrate in that tiny barred playpen of a suburban cottage, piled to the rafters with women and children. He came by occasionally with the household money for Mitzi. From Lily he became openly estranged. As time passed away, and she managed to drag herself out of the Valley of the Shadow of Death, it dawned on her that Taddeusz hadn't so much as kissed her in weeks, perhaps months, that he no longer visited their conjugal bed. During his sporadic duty visits to the house, he had the air of an increasingly remote and impatient stranger, eager to be on his way. It was so gradual, so imperceptible, so treacherous, this leave-taking. It was almost a year before Lily realized she was virtually a widow. It struck her with a harsh pang of clarity that first Xmas Taddeusz no longer celebrated with them. He was going to be away on business, he said, giving them each a cold, almost angry kiss; it was unfortunate, he was sorry, but it couldn't be helped.

'Oh, Tannenbaum' was playing on the radio. Mitzi had trimmed and decorated the pale little fir tree with white scented candles. German biscuits, little crescent-moons powdered with sugar, miniature nut-cakes spiced with saffron and cloves were laid out on the lace-edged tablecloth. Sated by the extraordinary abundance, no one had yet touched the special frothy egg pudding crowned with red currants and sprigs of holly. Greta ransacked her Xmas stocking, then dragged her gifts up to bed. Angie dropped asleep early, and baby Peter was slumbering on Lily's lap in front of the space-heater in their chilly sitting-room.

140

Appearing festive and chic in navy-blue silk, Mitzi primped her creamy white hair, fresh out of metal curling grips; it was swept across her head like a perfect cirro-cumulus in the heavens, marred only by a faint streak of ochre-yellow, mute witness to a lifetime of relentless smoking. Her pale blue eyes were alight with unusual gaiety, her childlike dimpling smile seemed to dispel all trace of the mournful decades she had survived.

After all, she couldn't weep forever, could she?

Life had a way of picking itself up and trudging on amongst the living. Besides it was Xmas-time and she loved to drink an occasional glass of Schnaps and gossip in German with Anton, their Hungarian neighbour, a carpenter, who sometimes came over to unplug the kitchen sink, or else (since Taddeusz was unable even to knock a nail into a piece of wood) attend to repairs around the house. By now Lily could understand a good deal of their conversation; they were talking about the glorious old days, the bygone era of pre-war Europe with its big band concerts, opera houses and balls where Mitzi had waltzed with her first love, Yosef, in the autumn of 1913.

Anton laughed, glancing often at Lily as though in mute expectation. His rough, mountainous voice reminded her ever so slightly of Taddeusz, as did the comforting aroma of stale tobacco, the characteristic scent of maleness. He was probably in his mid-forties, muscular, with ropy tendons along his arms and an abundant growth of black hair that was silvering rapidly. He had been trying for years to bring his wife over from Budapest, but you know how long these things take, this terrible war was, *Gott sei Dank,* over but it was sad, again it was Xmas, and he was still waiting.

"Give me the baby, Lily, I'm going to put him to bed," said Mitzi, when the clock on the mantelpiece struck one.

Anton rose to leave, but Mitzi waved him back to his seat. Lily, who didn't want to be alone, poured him another glass of Schnaps for the road. That made Anton laugh. All he had to do was hop through the front porch and garden gate and he was home. Another glass for good luck then, said Lily. Her eyeglasses became misty; her lip trembled just a little. After all, she had nothing left to lose—or gain—deposed queen that she was, lingering in the darkness and the dubious freedom of the Dead.

"Yes, life is sometimes very sad," sighed Anton. It was Xmas. He was all alone, and she was—well, surrounded by babies and old women. His eyes twinkled quizzically; hers filled with tears. He moved closer and raised his glass. "Merry Xmas, Lily," he said, pressing his hand warmly, comfortingly around hers. "You're a very beautiful woman, did you know that?"

My God, it was all a plot, a conspiracy, thought Lily, barely a few weeks later. They must have hatched this up between them, I'll bet Mitzi deliberately set me up! And then another thought struck her, which hurt almost as much. *My God, what if they actually paid Anton to do it?*

But no, she couldn't believe that, not of Anton. His embarrassment was as great as hers when, eventually, they crossed paths in the courtroom. He flushed in shame—or was it anger—the day he was subpoenaed into testifying and was forced to watch Lily stand trial in the dock.

"The accused, Lily Herman Morvaye, has been charged by her husband, Taddeusz Morvaye, with several counts of fornication, between the dates, December 25, 1950 and March 14, 1951 with corespondent by the name of Anton Romvary. Does the accused plead guilty or not guilty?"

Taddeusz sat in the courtroom, buttressed by his barrister who was decked out in undertaker black, a slightly dishevelled gleam to his curled white wig. 'What an assembly of the venerables' thought Lily. Their reptilian reek of cunning assaulted her from

142

across the courtroom. Taddeusz ignored her, except for that abrupt hostile glance of his as she was called to the witness stand. She managed to catch his eye just once; that look, that fleetingly naked look, revealed what he truly was, her implacable enemy.

Nevertheless, he was agitated. He had the aggrieved dishonoured air of a cuckold and although he may have believed this trial was a necessary evil he, too, raged in the spotlight of public humiliation. Taddeusz hadn't set foot in the house since Xmas. Lily began receiving lawyer's letters in the third week of January. How had he found out, if Mitzi hadn't secretly told him? Of course, he must have plotted this, even welcomed it, it fit in so well with his plans. At last she understood, now that it was too late, she had innocently blundered into his trap.

But then came the shock. He wanted the children, all of them. Their grandmother had declared herself willing to accept the interim responsibility for their welfare, explained his lawyer. Unfortunately, their natural mother, Lily, was incapable of taking proper care of the children, ergo, she was unfit to be awarded custody.

"No!" screamed Lily. "Don't let them take my children away."

The Judge then glanced over in her direction and requested that Lily becalm herself. Since she had no lawyer to represent her, she would certainly be allowed to testify on her own behalf, on the condition that she comported herself with decorum; otherwise, she would be forcibly removed from the courtroom.

With the shock, Lily's thoughts, her instinctual flashes of understanding blitzed across her mind, then were gone. She understood what was at stake and suddenly the intimidating presence of the black-robed, white-wigged High and Mighty Lordships evaporated. She realized, too, that from Taddeusz, perhaps also from Mitzi, she could expect no mercy. She could think of one thing only, and that was her babies. She pulled herself together and seized her last, her only chance.

"Your Honour, please, they're trying to make me out to be a monster, but it's a conspiracy."

"Would you please explain what you mean by conspiracy?"

"They want to take my children away, and get rid of me."

"Do you deny the charges brought against you, Mrs. Morvaye?"

"No, Your Honour, I don't deny them, but that's got nothing to do with it. Infidelity? I could lay my own charges of infidelity against him. I don't have to prove it, because he does it openly. My husband has been unfaithful to me almost since the first day we were married—"

Lily voice rattled a little. She stopped to wipe her eyes. The Judge looked gloomy. Oh, God, he was thinking, these divorce cases are so slippery, you never know what's going to surface, what deadly Machiavellian games are about to be played between once-eternal lovers, torn asunder. Taddeusz muttered something to his lawyer, who was rapidly scribbling notes.

"Objection, your Honour. The purpose of this hearing is not to cast aspersions on Mr. Morvaye's character or reputation. The evidence we are considering today concerns the accused and not the defendant."

"Your Honour, I don't care what he says against me, I know in my heart what I am," said Lily, and then she broke down.

Oh, hell, thought the Judge, how pathetic, and now we're sinking into the dregs of bathos.

"My husband, with his string of mistresses, his whores—"

"Objection, Your Honour!"

"Sustained."

"I've known for years that my husband was unfaithful to me, but what was I supposed to do? Just don't take the baby away, Your Honour, he could die, he needs special treatment, special medicine every day—"

There was a pause. Lily tried to get a grip on herself. She felt the deep need to sob, forcing its way upward. If she let go now, she'd be swept away in a tearstorm, out of control.

"Before we render a judgment, we will require more details on the health of the youngest child," said the Judge. He scribbled a few notes into the dossier, then glanced again at Taddeusz, then Lily. He appeared flushed, even perplexed, although stern. "Mrs. Morvaye, before the Court adjourns today, is there anything further you wish to say?"

But it was all to no avail. Two months later, Lily found herself almost completely alone, a post-nuptial refugee seeking refuge in her sister Flo's basement kitchen.

"I know the Judge would have given me the kids, but then that German bitch testified against me, said I was an unfit mother, said it was my fault Larissa died—" wept Lily. Flo listened to Lily's lament, repeated day after day and consecrated anew in tears, but could find nothing of comfort to say. "He's a murderer, Flo, he wasn't supposed to take the baby away. He knows Peter could die without his proper medicine, but now he's gone off, disappeared. Maybe the baby's dead already and they're afraid to tell me."

"Now, Lil, stop that, you'll drive yourself mad. You know Mitzi wouldn't let anything happen to the children."

But Lily, abandoned, felt as desolate as a child, lost in a crowd of strangers. Day after day, she drifted through an unbearable well of coldness, an aura of darkness, of disconnection. As the months passed with no news of the children, she began to drink.

CHAPTER 15

ARTISAN

Lily's natural gift for mimicry was also a gift for song. Greta still remembered her mother singing a favourite cradlesong, *Woody the Woodpecker,* in bygone days, that is, before Taddeusz left them and Lily still had enough spirit in her to sing. Taddeusz rarely sang, except during that summer when he composed the musical score for his first and only stage operetta. Usually he remained buried behind a great wall of books and newspapers, surrounded by an intimidating veil of cigarette smoke. When in a mellow mood, he sometimes glanced over to see what Greta was doing, studying her child-like scribblings with amusement.

"Look, Lily, your daughter is ten times cleverer than you, she's a little artist."

Greta's gift for mimicry was in the hand. She could sketch her father even from memory, managing to catch the evanescent glint of impatience in his eye with just a stub of charcoal on a sheet of dingy newsprint. The light was not good in his study but that didn't matter, she captured him anyway in all his aspects, mornings, lying indolent in bed, waiting for Mitzi to bring his coffee, half slipping out of his towel as he stepped from the bath, now and then raising his fist in menace, his forehead all of a sudden terrifyingly smooth, his hairline actually shrinking backward, his fire-eyes flashing and blitzing, a kind of stormwind around a weathercock, heralding thunder. No matter! Somehow Greta seemed to apprehend things from the inside. Her fingers gripped around a pencil, instinctively rediscovered the world; as it materialized effortlessly under her hand, she felt she'd always known it to be so. And being strong-willed, she instinctively allied herself with the stronger, with the victor. It infuriated her to see Lily crying, her impotent self-pity, her lamentations. She, too, would have struck out gladly against Lily's martyred gaze.

Sometimes Taddeusz called for Greta, his favourite, the one whose Celtic darkness exuded the aura of gypsy. He sat her on his knee and told her some of the legends of the old country, with its horseshoe ring of mountains and its far eastern border along the shores of the Black Sea.

"Long ago there was a craftsman, a builder named Manole, and one night he had a dream. He dreamt that he had to build a monastery in stone, the most magnificent monastery in the land, but his work would be blessed only if he promised to obey the Master's command: when he awakened from his dream, the very first person Manole saw would have to be buried alive inside the walls..."

"Stop telling her those horrible stories, Teddy, she's going to have nightmares again—"

"Shut up, woman," half-growled, half-grinned Taddeusz, cuddling Greta closer to his great fleshy chest, matted with gingery-white curls.

"...and so Manole promised to obey the Master, and when he opened his eyes next morning and looked out into the distance, he thought he saw his wife coming back from the well, carrying a jar of water on her head. That made him very sorrowful, so he called on the heavens to pour down a torrent of raindrops that would delay her return, but still she came closer. Then he called on the earth to toss boulders onto her path, but still she came closer. And then he implored the mist to envelop her so that she would not find her way home, but still she came closer until he saw clearly that she was indeed his beloved wife. Manole cursed and wept, but he dared not disobey the Master. Deliberately, he closed his ears to his wife's lament as he buried her alive behind the foundation stone of the monastery. But the Master kept his promise; he blessed the building. After more than a thousand years, it is still standing. If you look carefully, even today, you can see a faint trace of bloodstain running down the wall."

Taddeusz had a fondness for the macabre. It haunted his fiction, which some critics sneeringly dismissed as turgid gothic melodrama, teeming, as it was, with poisoned wine chalices, tragic drownings, savage duels, and wretched criminals swinging from the gallows. In his heart, in his gut, although he wasn't yet prepared to admit it even to himself, Taddeusz knew that he would never be another Tolstoy. What mysterious quality, he wondered, what impenetrable magic made it possible to sift through the dross of language, the millions of banal words available to everyman, and forge a masterpiece! It wasn't enough simply for him to lust after it. Like the tantalizing fantasy of a forbidden pleasure, it eluded him. Nothing Taddeusz had written so far rose above the mediocre, and he knew it. He had a rainbow range of extraordinary talents, that he knew, but now he was searching for other stages on which to shine. He had, for some time now, begun to throw his energies into the brave new world of business. His 'Father's Kingdom,' the wealth that he had always taken for granted, was no more. Creating, playing, dabbling self-indulgently in the arts would, at best, bring him nothing but illustrious poverty, not the lost fortune which he craved to restore. Even Lena had grown weary of ploughing through his bulky manuscripts, suggesting changes, correcting his grammatical lapses and striving to tame his fiery emotional style.

"If you think I'd act the part of the Contessa, think again!" she said. "That last scene you showed me stinks."

In the backstage dressing room after Lena's performance, crouching silently over her sketchpad like a guilty stowaway in a ship's hold, Greta stared in fascination as Lena exchanged her sequin-and-lace period costume for a bathrobe, and creamed away the stark greasepaint from her glistening-milk skin. Greta idolized this woman's arrogant swan-like beauty, the very antithesis of Lily. She seemed to be about the only one in the world who wasn't afraid of the great Taddeusz, who dared look him directly in the eyes and speak her mind.

"And I am not taking responsibility for your children, forget that notion."

"All right," growled Taddeusz, "if you don't want my kids, I'll find someone else who does."

Nevertheless, a few weeks later, Greta was standing with her suitcase in the lobby of a Parisian boarding school, located within view of a serpentine bend of the River Seine. The place had the chilling atmosphere of a fortress blending into a prison. Taddeusz must have felt it, too; his face, his whole body was full of agitation and gloom. In his eyes glimmered a blend of guilt, annoyance and relief. He kissed his daughter—it was brusque, even off-hand; he promised to write as soon as he could, then disappeared. Mademoiselle Déry, *'la gouvernante'* then came rattling down the staircase, all in a sweat, her stiff oily grey hair springing loose from its chignon, her enormous breasts bouncing inside her pearly ribbed-silk blouse, her thick downy arms loaded with towels. Greta detested her on first sight.

"Vite, vite, jeune fille, tu dois monter au deuxième étage. Je vais te montrer le dortoir," said Mademoiselle, prodding Greta up the stairs.

"Eh?" said Greta, resisting at every step.

"Ton papa veut que tu apprennes le français—your daddy want that you learn the French—*alors on doit commencer tout de suite! Allez, monte, monte, et dépêche-toi!"*

Soon she would meet fifteen-year-old Luc, the Director's son, a somewhat privileged fellow inmate at the *Pensionnat.* Greta painted a chiaroscuro portrait of him, glowing soft around the edges, in her mind—'The Bathers'—an impressionistic, resurrected Luc, a naked God and destroyer of hearts, surrounded by his comrades in the communal tiled showers, steamy mist floating around rows of diminutive white buttocks, pale limbs slippery with soap, a turgid blending of grime, sweat and lavender. Long, long afterward, she grinned wickedly at the memory of her first day in this rambling institution when she'd mistakenly invaded the bathing chamber of the boys' wing, and the youthful bathers howled with indignation, pelting her with pink slippery cakes of soap, swearing and sprinkling her with watery scum.

Since then she'd waited, apprehensive, yet impatient for Luc to come marching downstairs with the others at exactly half past nine every Tuesday, as she sat at the piano practising the first bars of Beethhoven's *Für Elise* with the music master, Monsieur Laroche. Luc always grinned and winked whenever he saw Greta, recalling perhaps her look of startlement as she'd stepped over the threshold of the forbidden bath chamber. And his seductively cocky grin was, for Greta, his essence; from that vision alone she could conjure him up, whole, warm and alive. It was solely for Luc's sake that she was struggling to penetrate his outlandish language, poring through *La grammaire française*, copying in her minute, deliberate handwriting *Les Fables de la Fontaine*, trying to decipher the first pages of *La Petite Princesse*. She realized, at last, that months had elapsed without contact from either of her parents—except for the delivery of an ornate Indian doll-statue, clutching a miniature dagger in one of its many waving hands; it arrived in a wooden crate one day, accompanied by a terse note from Taddeusz, half-buried beneath the straw.

For already it was Xmas and the school abruptly emptied, except for a handful of boarders whose parents weren't able to fetch them away. All the teachers, the cook and Mademoiselle Déry departed, and Monsieur de Peyrac, the aging scion of the house, was obliged to put up with the remaining stragglers as best he might. He worked, most of the time, in his study with the door shut, preferring not to supervise them too closely, having an entire schoolful to watch over throughout the year, which clearly sufficed. So the Xmas orphans spent these days like unschooled gypsies, all regulations suspended; the freedom that they had always dreamed of and plotted for was now granted nonchalantly by the Director himself.

"*Viens, petite Anglaise,*" said Luc, "I'm going to show you the Master's quarters."

151

Greta followed Luc who was stalking forward on his long legs, his bony shoulder wings jutting energetically from his back as though he were about to take flight. They hurried to the far end of the corridor, up the back staircase which boarders were forbidden to use, along another wider corridor with a row of windows through which Greta could glimpse the family's private indoor courtyard with its conservatory and frozen rose garden. Then they crossed over the lobby into the West wing.

"How old are you, little girl?" said Luc, suddenly glancing around.

"Thirteen," lied Greta. Although she was not tall, she was already metamorphosing, rapidly being remoulded as though on a potter's wheel. Her miniature woman's waist, her green little rosebud breasts, still hard, like twin tumours or unripe fruit, were proof undeniable of her crystallizing womanhood.

"Admit it, little Gretchen, you barged into the boys' bathroom on purpose, didn't you?"

"No, I didn't mean to, but if you don't stop reminding me, I'll do it again, just wait and see."

Luc laughed. He stopped outside an oak door, twisted the door handle and opened it wide. The master bedroom was the kind she'd seen only in films. Here was a secluded world that Greta would never have suspected, a sort of breakaway planet occupying the West wing of the building. A world of opulence, of gilt-framed paintings, mediaeval tapestries, stained glass windows pouring patches of rainbow over the window ledges, elaborately canopied four-poster beds that looked as though they ought to be cordoned off with ropes. Greta knew she shouldn't be here. Along with her mingled fear and exhilaration was an over-riding defiance—what's the worst they could do to her, anyway? She was only following Luc; if need be she would hide behind Luc, who always got his own way, whose presence intimidated the hired staff, even the teachers, who treated him with a strained deference, turning a blind eye to his transgressions. What purpose would it serve to haul Luc into the

Director's study, his father's study? It was an unspoken law that no instructor worth his salt needed to bother the administration with petty conflicts or disciplinary lapses. Either a schoolmaster was capable of extorting obedience from the pupils, or he shouldn't enter the schoolroom at all. Luc was probably thinking the same. Still, he took the precaution of fastening the old-fashioned lock from the inside. Greta watched in mingled excitement and alarm.

There was an aura of haste blowing around them, an insistent breeze flapping at the hem of Greta's skirt, whispering through the strands of Luc's dark hair, a psychic wind of high-voltage excitement, magnetically tugging them closer together. Greta was concentrating on the precise delineation of Luc's lips, his mild, as yet unbearded skin, his squarish chin, the theatrical mole high up on his left cheek, the scented fusion of heat and lavender.

"Ever been kissed before, Gretchen?" said Luc, moving closer, flashing his incandescent grin.

"What *d'you* think?" she replied, immersed suddenly in an invisible glow. She stared Luc directly in the eye, determined to match him, cheek for cheek.

"You know what they call you around here, don't you—*la Duchesse de Glace!*"

"Yes, I know," said Greta, half rueful, half proud. "And all because that fat cow, Mademoiselle Déry, can never make me cry."

Luc began to laugh; he couldn't stop. Greta felt alarmed again. What if his raucous noise attracted the attention of Monsieur de Peyrac? She raised her finger to her lips and hissed at him to be quiet; instead, Luc tossed himself, an ungainly projectile, onto the ornate bed. Strands of his glossy dark hair fell like waving kelp over the aged silken coverlet. Nonchalant, he closed his eyes, then gazed up at the coffered ceiling. Stretching open his arms, he gestured at her audaciously.

"*Toi, que le diable t'emporte!*" said Greta, showing off her newly acquired French. She'd spent considerable time with the *Dictionnaire Larousse,* committing to memory the idiom of insult. It was useful to have a few invectives up one's sleeve, some choice verbal ammunition. It made Luc laugh even more.

Greta stared at him in defiance, her endemic Self. She wasn't sure that the present thrilling situation was altogether comfortable; however, she stood her ground.

"She's a great fat stupid cow and your father goes to bed with her."

Luc froze; his laughter abruptly ceased, his carefree glance infused by a subtle dusk of anger.

"That's not true, now you're telling lies as well."

"It is true!"

"Who says so?"

"Everyone, ask Julia, ask Maria Constanza."

These were two teenaged daughters of a Guatemalan strongman whose government had suffered a coup and he, himself, been driven into exile. Prematurely wise, canny and proud, these natural daughters of intrigue seemed endowed with intuitive perception into the intangible infrastructure of their surroundings. Already Greta was their kindred ally, drawn into the inner sanctum of shared confidences.

"What do they know?" said Luc. "They've only been here a few weeks."

"Well, believe what you choose, see if I care."

Through the leaded glass panes, the midwinter sky was a flush of pink, like watered wine. A saturnalian darkness crept over the walls, the tapestry, the furnishings. In the silence that followed, the romantic excitement of just a few moments ago had been thoroughly poisoned. She felt desolate. Why, why had she done this? Why had she attacked Luc when she'd been

154

yearning for him for weeks, for months? It was too late. He was standing beside her suddenly, grip-locking her wrist. His sublime features were overwritten in ferocious contempt; he whispered something into her ear, and Greta screamed out in pain. A spurt of blood trickled along the side of her neck.

"You insulted my family, *petite sotte*," said Luc. "Now you can tell everyone what I did to you, as a punishment for lying."

CHAPTER 16
Calcutta, 1952

S<small>TAR</small>

Six-year-old Angie was lying under a tree. She herself was made of wood, she could not lift her head. Her shriveling body, consumed in a 'satiesque' funeral pyre, was smoking, floating gently upward through the branches. Higher than the crowns of all the trees, the flat glittering roof of the building. A lone servant boy vanished into the courtyard shade. Bedsheets were sunbleaching outside the laundry room, perfumed spice-clouds escaping from the kitchen. O God, there was baby Peter, screaming, almost drowning, as the pitiless Ayah soaped his skull, re-christening him daily in her open-air tub. Down sank Angie as well. The surface of a black sea—dead calm—closed over her head.

"What do you mean, the Ayah thought the child was sleeping? Didn't she go and see, didn't she check?"

The sound of her father's voice. Enraged, as usual. A coarse sea-sponge hissed against her blistering forehead. Eyes still glued shut; thighs like living logs. No longer floating, she was inside the house now, under the crushed ivory mosquito netting, safely back in her bed. The air, scented with petals of orchid, breezed over her body, making her sleepy again; the black tide rushed over her eyelids, swallowing her up.

"Goddamned bloody idiot, I'll murder her, the kid could have died!" howled Taddeusz, banging his way through the living room, knocking over the bamboo chairs and venting his fury by flinging ashtrays, books and newspapers to the floor. He summoned the Ayah who was supposed to be taking care of his children, so that she might witness a typical outburst of his rage. He threatened to drive her out of the city, beat her to a pulp with his bare fists. She remained unmoved, stared him down unflinchingly, as dark and sinewy as a mangrove tree. Her

responsibility was to feed, bathe and look after the children; she was not a doctor, she said, therefore unaware that the little girl had such a serious fever. It had happened very quickly, in a matter of hours. She regretted the danger, but it was not her fault. If the Sahib was displeased with her work, he could dismiss her—*The arrogance, the astounding arrogance of these people!*—Well, he certainly would dismiss her, once a replacement could be found, but he was oppressed now by a lingering sense of anxiety. What if, despite vaccinations and inoculations, the kids got sick again; how could these paid domestics, these ignoramuses, be trusted to take proper care of them? Something had to done, and urgently.

"LENA DARLING CAN'T LIVE WITHOUT YOU STOP!" For an entire month Lena was inundated with trunk telephone calls, letters, telegrams. *"WIRING YOU A TICKET STOP GET ON THE NEXT PLANE TO CALCUTTA STOP WAITING ANXIOUSLY STOP ALL MY LOVE STOP TADDEUSZ."*

Lena was in the last week of her play-run at the Adelphi Theatre. It had not been a successful season, and she had no idea what she would be doing next. True, she had auditioned for a more important rôle in a new play—an intriguing 20th century minimalist revival of some obscure Greek tragedy. If selected for the part, she would be leaving London for the next ten weeks while the Company went on tour. These dramatic messages from Taddeusz, this flood of bizarre invocations made her frown and then laugh. Reflected in the drizzling milk-glass of an English morning, her pale features churned themselves into a fragile sneer, and then—feeling revolted at herself—she actually wiped away (she couldn't believe it) a tear. All because of a memory, a sudden treacherous image, that of the Great Goddamned Taddeusz, one frigid winter dawn, vainly struggling to fire up the hot-water geyser, the look of bafflement on his face as he tossed a half-dozen charred matches into the sink, the sickening reek of gas leaking through the kitchen until she dragged herself out of bed, at last, to rescue him.

Lena was irritated, disturbed, yet intrigued by this uncharacteristic outpouring of emotion. Nevertheless, his words rang like false coin, *and she should know, shouldn't she?* Looking back now, she repented the time she had spent with this man; her uneasy alliance with him was a trap, fraught with malaise, perhaps even danger. It was his unabashed egotism she detested the most, his boorishness and open contempt for women—*she liked to think of herself as a rare exception*—but then, why had she continuously faced him as though across a battleground, ever prey to his volatile temper, his flights of hysteria more flamboyant than any woman's? How could anyone live with the man! It was absurd, did he take her for some blasted fool?

You'll live the life of a Grand-dame from now on, all you have to do is supervise the servants, amuse yourself, stage your own theatricals for the British ex-pats. Darling, if you wish, you can even have your own theatre! Hitch yourself to my star, Lena, I promise we'll have a glorious life!

"They offered me the part, I lost my chance," Lena said, as she disembarked in the searing, blinding heat at Calcutta's Dum Dum Airport, and almost fell into Taddeusz's arms. Was it better or worse, braving one's unique personal tragedy rather than feigning or representing it? There was no eluding a sense of fatalism; through this premeditated act of free will, she'd precipitated the beginnings of her own destruction. Almost from the very moment she allied herself with this man came the certainty that her life would resemble a miniature 'Court of Intrigue' in which she must always be the cleverer, anticipate the surprise assault from the rear, the innocent looking dish of poison—otherwise she would not survive. Shunted onward by some abstract and powerful force of destiny, she looked on impassively, watched herself do it. But why?

They were formally united in a civil ceremony a few days later. It was very rushed, very cold. Lena barely had time to pick out a suitable wedding dress; Taddeusz seemed so impatient to get it over, like some dreaded ordeal, as though the aura of nuptials was distasteful to him, brought back cursed memories, mocked

159

his lapse in wariness, his better judgment. Among the brief train of hangers-on was their flower girl, Angie, a blondish version of Taddeusz, silent as a shade, who at first glance evoked in Lena little more than lukewarm dislike. Then there was his youngest, Peter, toddling at the feet of the wedding guests, tugging at the stiff white edges of the tablecloths, trailing in his wake the odour of freshly laid feces and bath powder.

The wedding feast, a glorified garden party, was held in their large rented estate, through whose ornately carved and airy corridors a multitude of house-servants wandered in and out. The cook and her two skinny Hindu servant boys, the solemn truculent Ayah, the laundry and domestic staff, the white-garbed bearers who served the platters, a cornucopia of white and jewel-coloured rice, gold lentils, steaming flatbreads, sweets and curries perfumed with fiery spices that burned Lena's mouth and stung her eyes. Taddeusz ushered her over the pinkish-grey flagstones of the bamboo-shaded terrace, introducing her to a stream of acquaintances and colleagues, a surprisingly large crowd, considering that he himself was a virtual newcomer to Calcutta. Lena could see that he was striving to be his most elegant, his most gracious, an uncomfortable rôle for Taddeusz, it warred against his naturally ingrained carelessness, his everyday contempt for the artificial trappings and constraints of social finesse. But for her it was child's play to suddenly glide into stride beside him, to rise to the rôle she'd just been handed. She was bloody magnificent, she thought, (so did they all) as his brand new hostess-bride.

"Christ, I thought they'd never go home, especially that bastard, Ghosh. Why the hell did you spend so much time talking to him, didn't you see me making signs to shut up?" snarled Taddeusz, as Lena lifted aside the mosquito netting and the newlyweds retired to bed. "You've got to be careful what you say in front of that swine, I don't trust him," said Taddeusz, glaring intently at his new bride.

Lena stared back at him. Coldly. So nothing had changed, and why should she have expected it? They had never been true bosom lovers and now, here they were, bound-in-the-flesh adversaries once again.

"Somehow, I can't think why, I'd imagined our wedding night would be a little more romantic, a little tenderer than this."

"Oh, hell, spare me the theatrics, I'm bloody tired!" said Taddeusz, as he rolled to his side of the bed, favouring her with the shadowy view of his bare back and shoulders.

Damn him, he won't make me cry, thought Lena, as she lay awake beside her surly bridegroom for what seemed like hours. I've no one to blame but myself, I know; why the hell did I ever come here? Oh, God, how am I ever going to get out!

As the sky paled, Lena drifted off to sleep; it seemed scarcely a few moments later although, in fact, it was almost ten the next morning when she awoke. Someone's dense body was balanced at the edge of the bed, tightly pulling down the sheets near her bare toes. She heard the murmur of masculine chatter; occasionally someone laughed. Taddeusz was already sitting up in bed like a bare-chested, crossed-legged, chain-smoking Buddha in deep consultation with a couple of his Anglo-Indian office fellows. They held sheaves of documents in their hands. Their open briefcases were propped around the bed. One of them was scribbling notes.

I'm dreaming, thought Lena, this can't be happening.

Her amazement and humiliation rendered her speechless, robbed her of courage, robbed her even of anger. *What am I supposed to do now? I know what I ought to do, but how can I get up, half-naked, and kick these goddamned strangers out of my bedroom! My God, what sort of hell-hole have I come to?* She waited until they'd all gone, managing with a supreme effort to temper her agitation. Above all, she must not lose control, nor succumb to the temptation of matching Taddeusz's own lyrical bouts of hysteria.

"This may well be how you normally conduct business," she said in a distinct and glacial tone, "but if you ever invite

161

a stranger, *I don't care if it's the Maharaja himself,* into our bedroom again, just remember this, it'll be the last you'll ever see of me!"

"What!" cried Taddeusz, genuinely astonished, "what the hell are you talking about? You, who make a living prancing half-naked across the boards, for the benefit of strangers, every night of the week, suddenly you're prudish!"

"There is a vast bloody difference, and you're too damned intelligent not to know it!"

"Well, that's just the way it's done here."

"Not in my house, it's not!"

"Listen, it's thanks to my 'business' that we're able to live like kings here—where are you going?"

"To get dressed, in private, do you mind?"

"Well, in future, you'll just have to bloody well get used to it, or move out of the bedroom, Madame!"

CHAPTER 17

STARDUST

Taddeusz had been hired as consultant to the Maharaja of Ramgarh, landowner and overseer of one of India's most important coal mines. Having impressed the Maharaja with his intellectual prowess, his silver-tongued speeches, his polished-for-the-occasion charisma, he managed in a few months to seize responsibility for the company's regional sales and international exports, as well as for developing long-range plans to modernize its rather antiquated production methods. Obsessive as he was with all undertakings, Taddeusz threw himself into this new challenge with a poet's passion. He devoured the latest trade reports on the mining industry, personally visiting the coal pits, helmeted with a flaring torchlamp—Mephisto-like—his amber eyes glittering, face coated in coal dust as he descended within the rickety cage-lift, boring deep into the bowels of Mother Earth for a glance at her riches. Yet, at the same time, to his surprise and dismay he found himself constrained by the axiom on which this entire sub-continent seemed to repose—*as above, so below*—the shifting locus of human destiny as foreshadowed in the stars, the embedded cult of prophecy.

It amazed and infuriated him that no important business decision could be taken without first seeking the advice of the Maharaja's personal Astrologer. This supremely holy man appeared to have succeeded in detaching himself from all earthly labours, joys and woes. Little more than a modest shelter from murderous sun and monsoon rain, a dhoti and prayer mat, a bowl of fish, fruit and rice sufficed for his existential needs. Taddeusz considered the man as well as the practice itself ludicrous, a tyranny of illogic spawned of superstition. But as he delved deeper, he was troubled by the apparent accuracy of so many of the Astrologer's predictions, the multitude of troubling coincidences—or were they just coincidence?—that occurred. As an experiment, Taddeusz began calculating the celestial charts of his children and noticed with a shock that three of Peter's planets were retrograding at birth, that he had a debilitating planetary conjunction in the Sixth House of Health. Scrutinizing his own chart, he found no less than four planets lodged in the seventh House of Marriage and Partnerships, one of them being Saturn, definitely a bad augury. Whereabouts within this powerful constellation was his own little starlet, Lena?

Months elapsed. Taddeusz became more and more fascinated by astrology's web of complexity, the duplicate jurisdictions of the ruling Houses, the contradictory astral projections which had to be reconciled, the potent side-effects of planetary divinities in their debilitated or exalted states. He found himself psycho-analyzing his colleagues, his loved ones, his friends, on the basis of their Solar, Lunar or Ascendant positions. He tried divining the Stars in the faces of strangers, empirically testing his abstract knowledge in the material world around him. Suddenly, for Taddeusz, all mankind shuffled itself into a dozen distinct planetary tribes, within the seemingly arbitrary construct of the Zodiac.

And, like everything else, star-gazing became an obsession, a means to power. That arse-hole Ghosh, for example, whom Taddeusz had always distrusted, showed up clearly in his own Twelfth House of Exile, Secret Enemies and Self-Undoing. He sensed it distinctly in the man's exaggerated surface politeness toward him, his glittering malaise, his almost palpable aura of mild agitation whenever their paths crossed. Ghosh was short and stout, of unusual girth for the traditional Hindu Warrior Caste. His imposing skull was squarish, ram-like, with a hint of the clipped-back horn. Deep pox scars engraved his cheeks, a fleshly testament to the diabolical endurance of the man; even his hair flourished in an oily swirl of black and silver. Repulsive—and triple-cursed with halitosis, thought Taddeusz, evidently from countless reincarnated lifetimes of ingesting Mother India's mouth-watering vindictive spices. But then, too, his own gut was prone to gaseous bloating and temperamental spasms. Despite, or perhaps because of his voracious appetite, Taddeusz fared poorly under the new gastronomical regime.

It was further aggravated by this newborn malaise, a rare experience for Taddeusz. Intense and unrelenting. He felt sure, *wasn't it also clearly indicated in his chart?* that his colleague Ghosh maligned him in the Maharaja's hearing, complaining, most probably, of his slave-driving zeal, his overbearing manner with the mine foremen, his responsibility for the increasing discontent among the overworked coolies who worked the pits. The man was a puritan, as well, casting a frankly jaundiced eye on Taddeusz's overt flirtations and scarcely concealed amours that blossomed in the never-ending round of garden parties for Calcutta's élite.

"You're sleeping with her, aren't you?" said Lena.

"With who?"

"I don't know her name. I don't need to know her name. You've betrayed me, and the whole of Calcutta knows about it!"

"Rubbish, who have you been talking to?"

"No one."

"I know who it is, my bosom enemy, Ghosh. You two have always been so damned friendly since the first day you arrived. And now you're both concocting a bunch of lies, inventions! Are you sure you're not trying to cover up your own transgressions, your own indiscretions, Madame?"

It is true that Ranjit Ghosh knew, only too well, how unwelcome he would be on the grandiose estate, fringed by shade palms, temporarily granted to Taddeusz by the Maharaja. But, earlier that morning, he had something of profound importance to communicate to Lena for whom, at least, he felt strong anxiety and concern. His unsmiling glance at the Chief Bearer suggested that he wished to speak to the Memsahib in private.

Oh, God, what now? Lena had thought, aware that Taddeusz quizzed the servants regularly on the identity of even casual visitors to their domain.

"My deepest respects, Memsahib," said Ghosh, greeting her with traditional crossed palms, his forehead slightly bowed. Here again was the stiffly controlled elegance of his black and silver mane, the elongated darkfish eyes of those legendary forebears of his (portrayed all around in ceramic and stone), the squat and rotund body, smooth, agile and supremely confident. "Your husband is not at home?"

The extreme heat had already transformed her milk-like pallor to an unwholesome blotchiness, suffusing her cheeks, her throat. Ghosh observed her damp black curls, chaotic, resembling a sprawl of magnetized thread. She appeared dizzy as she sat in the cane chair on the verandah. From somewhere around the house, came the sound of a baby crying.

"I hope you are not feeling unwell," said Ghosh.

"A little, yes, but excuse me, I must speak to the Ayah. She's bathing the children and if I don't watch her, she almost drowns them."

Ghosh looked stern, revealing the benevolent concern of the childless man that he was. He disappeared for a few moments. By the time he returned, Lena felt much worse. She could hardly lift her head.

"I have told the Ayah she must obey you strictly at all times, otherwise she will be replaced," said Ghosh. "We can find you someone much better."

"Oh, thank you, Mr. Ghosh, that's so kind of you."

Why on earth did Taddeusz continue to rant against this man? Wasn't he genuinely kind, obviously seeking to be her ally? Although she was careful not to reveal it, somehow Ghosh already knew that Taddeusz was planning an expedition to certain well-known Lamaseries in Darjeeling, the Sikkim and the Himalayas. It was clear that he did not approve. An occidental, a temporary guest, determined to delve crudely into the transcendent mysteries of their ancient land. And for what? For voyeuristic curiosity, for sensationalism, for some sort of profit or gain? An experience of the sacred to be exchanged, no doubt, into hard coin!—Ironic, thought Lena, having several times traveled through the heart of Calcutta only to be faced with the city's transcendent poverty. She'd dropped a few *'paises'* into the outstretched hand of a teenaged boy, shaded agonizingly by his rag-encrusted mother and surrounded on all sides by the crowding clamour of desperation. It was the boy's duty, his untouchable karma: to extract a handful of greenish, hollow-ringed coins from the pale hand of a foreign Memsahib whose rickshaw was briefly halted at a corner crossing, one of those strange all-white goddesses who were sometimes seen traveling through the tumultuous streets.

But it was later, once Ghosh was gone, having confirmed her suspicions by his polite although humiliating disclosures, that Lena realized she had never felt this scared. Peel off the costumes, all the shining skins, and where was Lena? She couldn't dig into the well and find herself any more. She, who thought she would always be able to put on a good show, put up a good fight, was now on the run. Taddeusz had summoned her here as his handmaid, *in the service of his goddamned Immortality,* yet this man, whom she'd once felt strong enough to be able to salvage, was unable to love.

Of course, it came as no surprise. For months now, she'd been hoarding the few rupees left over from the household expenses. Although beget in relative wealth, Lord Bountiful he was not, and she would not humiliate herself begging for any more. Whatever extra cash she could scrounge she sewed inside the hem of a pillowcase that was tucked at the bottom of her trunk. Saving toward her freedom, the thought comforted her. Maybe one day soon she'd be able to pack her valise, without even a farewell, and vanish. But lately, she felt oppressed by something, by a thought that she wouldn't even put into words for fear of making it real. She always believed, even hoped that she was sterile, deliberately purifying herself after each encounter with stinging vinegar douches, purging herself of the very idea. But for weeks now—perhaps she was only imagining it—there was an unfamiliar feel to her body, as though it was no longer just her own, as though she were secretly sharing it. *Oh, God forbid, no, please, not a baby, not now, not with him!* Lena smashed her head against the pillow, as though it were a rock. The certainty grew as each day elapsed and she felt slightly nauseous upon awakening, a little light-headed, a little weak. Above all, Taddeusz must never find out. Her tiny clutch of savings would have to be used for something else; thank goodness Ghosh had already confided to her the name of a reputable Indian doctor in the city who might be of help.

On the morning of her deliverance, Lena was past caring whether Taddeusz knew or not. She hoped for a sharp influx of courage, once this was all over. Joshi, their chauffeur, had been given his orders; he was up early, prepared to drive her into the centre of Calcutta and wait. Did she appear as agitated as she felt while their shiny black borrowed vehicle, resembling an English taxi, rolled northward beneath the giant palm trees shading Strand Road? With a crushed linen cloth she wiped the sweat from her forehead and upper lip again and again, while young Joshi's gaze, both curious and concerned, fixed upon her intermittently in the rearview mirror. He did not, perhaps dared not speak. His fine black hair and thinly coiled moustache shining with palm oil, his air of serenity and white-laundered freshness were among the last images, subliminal, which impressed themselves upon her lightly, as if on wax, then were gone.

Meanwhile Taddeusz, his eyelids burning with road dust, his body fatigued and his mind disturbed, yet exhilarated, by what he had witnessed at the Lamasery, was at that very moment traveling southward. He arrived in Calcutta three hours later that afternoon. It was the arresting stench, dense and sour, that startled him as he entered her room.

"Lena, what's the matter, are you sick?"

168

She didn't answer. Her eyes were closed, her sweat ice cold. The mattress, the sheets were soaked. Across the flagstones, flowing, sticking to his shoes—a dark pooling stain. He knew at once. He understood. The knowledge surged through his body, thrashed upward like a bird in a grate, knocked inside his throat, stopped his breath. Perhaps liberated now to the stage-darkness of the universe, it was Lena who smiled, fatalistically, while the Great Goddamned Taddeusz sobbed.

CHAPTER 18

THE INHABITANTS OF WALDEN

Angie came home to Walden with her powder-blue sari studded with tinkling bells, her gold snake-banglets that Lily was later to pawn, and a head full of lice. After their ephemeral vision of the Godhead, the Morvaye children were plunged back, once again, into the anarchic darkness of Walden; in his wake, Taddeusz left behind a memory, a mystery, a mythology, a glittering souvenir of Himself to carry back on their return passage to the bleak, mushrooming heart of Whitechapel.

This was an isle within an isle, a dense habitation built on clay and woodland, alongside which the boundaries of world-class London were drawn, perforated and snapped. The forgotten wasteland lay beyond. This was the Eastern land of public baths and free school dinners. Of gas-taps dribbling forth in gasps, a shilling's worth at a time. Of moss-caked turf. Dug-over clods and climbing roses. Brick outhouses and hand-cobbled pigeon sheds. Tenement flats and laundry strung from wall to wall; the land of gaping brickwork, sunken railings, bomb-struck witness to the wars.

Despite or perhaps because of this, life in the East End is a street-philosopher's existential exercise, a day-to-day affair. The milkman comes clattering past the doorstep each morning, dispensing his slender-necked bottles of milk, capped in their silver seals. Fires are already lit from newspapers and clods of coal in the ash-swept open hearths. Women are out and about, selecting this day's dinner from amongst the barrow-stalls, wedged alongside foaming pickle barrels and layered with fresh farm eggs, bread rolls, baked tarts, fish fillets, meat chops, poultry, fruit and greens along the Watney Market lane—it is their diurnal saturnalia of smiles and tears and gossiping.

Mid-winter, and the moon rises by the hour of four. Needle shops closed, the lights of Sabbath-eve glow in scattered rivulets across the 'Mittel East.' Whitechapel's ancestral pubs, *Murphy's, The Blind Beggar, The Grave Maurice* open wide their doors. Lamplight flickers amidst Dickensian darkness and the overpowering perfume of malted hops. Fermented oblivion. Thick-handled glasses of ale froth-dribbling over tile-porcelain counters. The universal communion of talk and laughter sinks and rises; the essence of the moment drifts into the aether—no matter—tomorrow's a yawning chasm from today, and life is but a dream.

A few streets away, in Renie's bed-sitting chamber on Walden, a fierce fire crackled in front of the metal hearth plate. Lily and Flo sat Angie down on a plain wooden chair, wrapped a towel around her shoulders, and attended to her pale thread-like hair with a cake of black soap and a 'nit' comb.

"Have you finished? Hurry up and give me them scissors, Lil."

"I can't believe the state he sent them back home in. Both of them, thin as rakes—and crawling!"

Flo reached across and grasped the scissors from Lily's hand. She began to chop Angie's hair just above the right ear.

"Who do you think's been taking care of them all these months?"

Flo didn't answer. She continued to snip till she reached the top of Angie's other ear; then she swept the wheat-coloured little piles of hair onto a newspaper and tossed them into the fire. Meanwhile Lily continued to gaze at Peter, her youngest, returned to her like a changeling. He no longer recognized his mother. Yelping and screaming, he resisted Aunt Flo's strong fingers, reeking of carbolic. The sight of the crossed blades, the simple act of cutting his hair seemed to terrify him.

"Come, darling, it's all finished now," said Flo, gathering up the shorn head, the writhing bundle of flesh and bone to her

172

opulent breast. She held him awkwardly, as though he were borrowed or stolen. If she was reminded of her own castaway child, Jezz, her expression, always so intense, so overwrought, showed no outward sign. Instead, this déjà vu of the hair-washing flashed onto a memory, deeper still in Time.

"D'you remember that air-raid during the war, Lily? The sirens went off around ten o'clock at night and we all had to run to the shelter."

"What air-raid, which one, what are you talking about?"

"Look, she don't even remember, mum," said Flo, turning to Renie. "And I almost got killed because of her. What do you think she did, the minute she heard the sirens go? She started washing her hair, *washing her bloody hair!*"

Lily glanced around with an air of guilt, as though required to atone for her many failings, even those decades hence; but there was a Puckish resentment in her, as well, as her lips twisted forcibly into a grin. A shade light-hearted for once, she relished the attention of Flo's rekindled outrage. As the years wore away, Lily had become thinner, Flo heftier. Although sisters, born just a few years apart, their only common feature, whether Irish or Iberian, was their straight black hair. Lily kept hers short and plain, with a wayward fringe and elfin wisps silvering above the ear. Flo tinted hers powder black and twisted it into elaborate double rolls above her forehead, making her look taller and even more formidable than she was, au naturel. Lily's waning olive complexion contrasted with Flo's high-blooded duskiness. Her nose was petite and streamlined; Flo's was imposingly Neroesque.

"Did anyone ever tell you that story, Angie? I had to throw a potato sack over your mum's head and drag her outside with me," said Flo. "If I'd gone and left her behind there on her own, my mum would have killed me."

Renie laughed. Steeped in the fragrance of snuff, her imposing head, with its dunnish-white hair rolled into a bun, rocked steadily, peaceably. After all, she was too far gone now to be troubled by memories; more than three-quarters of her lifetime had been spent in this pauper's Eastern demesne. Through the fogged-up windowpanes of her sitting-room cum bedchamber, pitch-black out there under the lamplights, sunk beneath a regenerating anarchy of crabgrass and rubble, was an authentic World War II memorial, the gaping earthwound left by an exploded bomb. After the war, as a governmental gesture, this bomb-site débris had been fenced off from the pavement by a narrow brick wall. To walk the length of this wall was the feat of an acrobat, a coveted rite of passage for the vagabond youth of Walden. Occasionally, a child fell into the dump and had to be hauled out, bruised and dusty, by an elder from the gang. There was also the minor ritual of 'playing two-balls,' against the wall. Pocked rubber-smelling globes springing off the red brick, elastically hurtling back and forth, criss-crossing one another, bouncing smartly, heavily to gripped palm, then back against brick again. More than just an act of skill, it signified acceptance into the herd life of the street. Accidentally losing a rubber ball to the dump meant derision from street clan and anger from parent.

"Stupid bloody butterfingers, Angie!"

"How many times've we told you bleedin' kids not to play near that dump!"

The bomb-site débris was a matter of perception; one could divine whatever one wished in its rank tangle of rust and weed. For the older kids it was a forbidden junkland to navigate and explore. For Beattie it was a potentially dangerous magnet for her growing sons. For Greta, a grim treasure-trove of scattered human remains. For Flo, it was an eyesore; for Lily, a constant re-creation of the receding Apocalypse. For most long-time residents, it was also the permanent reminder of a selective 'miracle.'

The bomb had taken out only two houses, leaving the rest of the street intact, and killed only two, an ancient couple whose legs could not deliver them safely to the shelter; they had

174

probably died instantly and, it was hoped, humanely, transported from earthly sleep to eternal rest. Once the warden arrived, he ordered the whole area sealed off, but Lily slipped back into the house amid a torrent of screams and curses to rescue the cat. A squad of hastily trained 'experts' managed to defuse another object of terror—from its bizarre soft landing—a live, unexploded 500-pound bomb; somehow they dragged away the steel-encased object, resembling a beached baby whale. For Georgie, who had served on a minesweeper in the Atlantic, this was an obsessional tale.

After the war there was a suggestion of erecting a stele, or a small plaque to the memory of the dead couple, but the notion was seen to be impracticable, upon reflection. Thousands of plaques would have been required to commemorate the many dead throughout the city. It was first necessary to rebuild homes, schools and places of worship, whilst housing their living memory, for as long as one could, in the mind.

Lily's mind, for instance, which was an accumulating storehouse of terrors, recrimination and lament. Occasionally, for brief interludes, she shut the door to this storehouse, hoisting herself in front of Renie's fireplace to soak up its transient warmth-energy into her seemingly bloodless body. Her past and future receded and dimmed; the present moment offered its warm cup of tea—made, of course, by someone else's nimbler mind and fingers—and comfort. The love-burden of her several children slid into oblivion, the memory of her brilliant bastard of a former husband vanished without trace. Lily was one of the few inhabitants of Walden who became mildly inebriated on a strong cup of Brooke Bond tea.

Bridgie, who sat facing Lily near the fireplace, found not comfort but bare sustenance in her concoction of a raw beaten egg mixed daily into a pint of ale. Nine years ago, Bridgie had lost the ability to swallow solid food. 'Neuritis Tongue,' a nervous affliction sometimes occasioned by grief, was the medical verdict. Regrettably, there was no treatment and there was no cure. Bridgie's husband and all six of her sons had failed to return from the war. To augment her widow's pension she earned a few bob cleaning other people's houses, and she regularly lent a hand to Renie in exchange for the privilege of first place beside her dependable coal-fire; the alternative was to spend the remainder of her waking hours, brooding alone in her hovel-like quarters above a Jewish clothes factory on New Road. On Bridgie's gryphon-like brow, in her flickering eyes was the essence of sorrow fermented to bitters. Her paste-white face, etched and dripping with wrinkles, both mesmerized and repelled. With her calloused claw she grasped flax-haired Angie by the sleeve, as she muttered into her ear.

"Get out o' here, you nasty little foreigner, who's your father, *eh*, who is he? Go back to where you came from, you treacherous little *Bosch!*"

Lily, wafting in her cups, for once remained oblivious as Angie tore herself abruptly from the old woman's grasp as though shy of a stranger's caress. Oddly enough, as time moved on, Angie might be said to have virtually raised herself. She busied herself with schoolwork, fantasy tales or incomprehensible scribblings. Instinctively a loner, she showed no inclination to run with the herd. When allowed outside, directly in view of Aunt Flo's waxed red doorstep, she soon vanished around the corner of Walden into New Road. Freely roaming the East End from Whitechapel Library to Watney Market to Shadwell Park, she grew accustomed to following the locus of her own internal planets; so much so, that Lily tended to forget her daughter's existence, or so it appeared. In time, she no more concerned herself with Angie's wanderings than she questioned the sun's intention to rise and to set.

Similarly, at home, Angie had the quality of transparence, of sponge-like porousness, moving silently, reflectively around her little world. While the variegated '*Theatre*' of Walden unfolded all around her, she seemed oblivious or unconcerned, neither commenting, disputing or interrupting. The stalwart Aunt Goddesses and their chosen consorts who encircled Renie's familial altar rarely felt the need to lower their voices, to censor their words or their acts in her presence. Angie was rarely ordered to play in their sepulchral backyard or banished to bed. Her earliest recollections were those of the tolerated 'voyeur.' Small wonder that, given the reflective non-expression on her wax-like face, she was ignored or unconsciously cast—by the principals of the drama—as of hardly more consequence than the 'Village Idiot.'

Temporarily backstage, as it were, Aunt Beattie was for the moment confined to her own two-room dwelling, just off the shadowy second landing. She sat in her plump mushroom-coloured armchair, elevated by cushions and protected from draughts by a hairy brown horse blanket. Beside her was a tray of souring milk bottles, biscuit crumbs, half-empty teacups, teaspoons and teething rings. Within the aureole of her mild brown hair was a flurry of silverine threads that crackled, like bonfire sparklers, under her hairbrush, for with each successive confinement, unaccountably, its abundance grew thicker and wilder as if in celebration of her relentless fecundity. Illuminated by the constant glare of the ceiling lamp, her offspring, three pale comatose cherubim, were curled close together in a rag-tangle of couch blankets and pillows. Sated and inert, her newborn lay with its head flopped against her breastguard, a stiff hollow contraption resembling a plaster cast.

"I'm going to need a clean nappy in a minute, Angie," said Beattie, cautiously shifting the infant to her other raised fortress of a breast. "No, not there, go get me a clean one from the cupboard."

As always, the dank cavernous bowels of Beattie's cupboards, the familiar stench of dry rot in the walls of this room engulfed Angie like a depression. By the time she ceased noticing it, she was wrapped up in its lethargy. The unfathomable blue-beige of Beattie's carpet had seen many seasons and many dogs. Above the mantelpiece, the damp-speckled wallpaper was pinned with this year's Xmas cards. A *'trompe-l'œil'* reproduction of *'The Last Supper'* stamped onto a postcard. A ceramic pig with a moronic grin. Some ugly trophies. Large and small clocks, each pointing to a different hour. Cloth roses, curled in sleep, within their grimy cellophane coffins, all basking in the warm stink radiating from the glowing bars of the electric space-heater. Through the murky waters of the fish tank, a solitary giant goldfish stirred and flickered amongst the clammy seaweed, its prehistoric carpet of the deep.

Through the adjoining galley entrance, Beattie's kitchen was laid down in pale marbly-blue tile; its morgue-like walls and cupboards were a blank, eyesore white. Serving out its life sentence, a neurotic canary flapped about in its cage, shooting woodshavings and birdshit over the crockery that was set to dry in the rack directly beneath: a heap of scalloped gilt-edged porcelain, burnt enamel pans, knives, forks and spoons forever tarnished under a film of grease. Every nook and fissure from wainscot to ceiling seemed steeped in the scent of embalming fluid. Whatever battles may have been fought were lost; the permanence of grime occupied Beattie's world like a peevish relation who'd arrived, uninvited, long ago—and lived there still.

CHAPTER 19

OUR FATHER IN HEAVEN

Nearby on Walden lived Flo and Albert, tenant-landlords of the terraced dwelling owned by the London Hospital. In their second-storey bedroom, within a brick tenement of honeycombed catacombs, Albert slept, grunted and sighed in the spirit of glum plenty. Flo, unnaturally charged and wakeful, tossed on her side of the matrimonial bed. Bathed in the night sweats of her menopausal alchemy, her 'change of life' that had descended on her—*some said far too early*—her body seemed be racing out of its transient connection with motherhood to the twilit pastureland beyond. It wasn't her fault, was it, that sixteen-year-old Jezz had run away from the Orphanage? The boy's pocket money that she sent faithfully by postal order each month had been used for a train ticket from the Suffolk coast to the bowels of their eastern necropolis. Jezz managed to wend his way from Liverpool Street to Whitechapel Underground Station, then through the unfamiliar labyrinth of streets to show up, unexpected, uninvited, on her newly waxed doorstep, unrecognized for the moment—*thanks be to God*—by the neighbours. Once her fierce heart ceased its erratic thumping, she sat him down at her shiny white oilcoth-covered table, and fed him like a long-lost stray.

Flo's bountiful hand and heart would not have turned a destitute stranger from her door, much less her natural-born son. Her son, undeniably hers, although she felt no urge to embrace him; on the contrary, she was constrained by a feeling of awkwardness, of strangeness, of instinctual revulsion. It was not her fault that Destiny had caged them together, then wedged them apart. He had her strongly forged profile, pimply as all adolescents manage to be, too sensitive and impressionable by the looks of things, his almondine eyes questing, furtive looking; above all, she noted his strong, brilliantine teeth and tragic smile. Although he'd ceased his childish habit of streaking his cheeks with white finger-paint and shearing away his bush of black hair, no fear that Jezz would trespass unnoticed along Walden. Albert grudgingly allowed him to stay overnight. It was not her fault—*was it, was it?*—that long before the week was up, she had to send him back 'home.'

Beside her, Albert continued to snore, shifting his dense bulk toward the recessed wall. She supposed he was dream-traveling through subterranean banquet halls where the Xmas barrow-stalls of Watney market had been ransacked into a feast for the Gods: cascading purple grapes, blood oranges, downy apricots, and chopped pomegranates dripping nectar into their bitter honeycombs of yellow pulp. It was his recurrent nocturnal visitation—inexplicable, really—a lavish banquet presided over by some gigantic dark-skinned dream deity wielding a ceremonial silver knife, whereas Albert, forever parched and famished, could only gaze and stretch out his hands in vain.

Flo was not the only wakeful one in the house that night. Presiding one storey above them in her attic kitchen, her sister, Lily, was resisting sleep at midnight as determinedly as she resisted waking the next morning. Clutched between her bone-like fingers was a letter from her father, addressed strictly to her, which had arrived recently from the Rest Home for Elders in Kent. Each word, each line had to be read and re-read with infinite slowness. Focusing through her thick, coin-shaped lenses, Lily examined the well-spaced, confident flow of the handwriting, the misspellings, the smudges and blots of ink. *Dear daughter Lily, I was verry pleased to hear from you. As for myself, Im feeling quite well and Im quite alright. The only thing is Ive got a boil on my forehead, a carbolic uncle on the back of my neck, reumatism in my sholder, lumbago right down my leg, and pains in my knees, so you see, Im quite alright, and Flo only comes down to see me every time I have to have an opperation, so I think it's time I had another one, don't you think? The other night I dreamt I was dead and I was frightened to wake up in case it was true. Well, dear, I can't think of any more lies, just now, besides it's getting late. We just had our breakfast, so good night and god bless you all. I hope to see you one day. XXXXX.*

There was little chance of that. Flo, embittered by decades-old grievances, refused to take Lily to visit 'our father in heaven' as she called him, languishing in his chosen soul-rest in the bucolic wilderness of Kent. "I'll visit the day they carry him out in a box; don't ask me to go there, you know I don't want nothing more to do with him," she said. If Lily protested, albeit faint-heartedly, Flo launched off again on the strength of remembered outrage. "You remember, don't you, how he used to drink himself sodden on a Friday night, then roar his way home, vowing to kill mum? She used to call out for me: *'Flo, Flo, I can hear him already at the top of the street—go get the littl'uns and run over to Nan's.'* You know he almost did kill her once, with her favourite aspidistra plant, an'all, he chucked it over the banister of the top storey and almost brained her as she was running away downstairs."

Yes, thought Lily, but it was also true that Karl never laid a violent hand on his children when they were small. He particularly doted on Lily, his avowed favourite. In those early days, fatigued and fresh out of her confinement, Renie often foisted her into her husband's arms—'Here, take her, I can't stand her whining no more.' Of course, Lily had been a fretful infant, from the onset lamenting her unsolicited arrival into this world, a world of perishing cold and perishing hunger. Of sober outrage and Bacchanalian wrath. When sober, proud and scrupulously honest Karl browbeat his children never to accept a penny of other people's charity. Although beget in some quasi-mythic isle of the North Sea, he was destined to be landlocked for most of his long life. He and his germinating family squatted in derelict tenement buildings and, when evicted, transported their jumble of belongings from street to street in a borrowed wheelbarrow. For years he worked as a road-sweeper, trying in vain to earn even a subsistence living for a family of twelve.

181

Lily now scrutinized the recent photograph of her father, enclosed in this missive. It was a crinkly-bordered snapshot taken by one of his carers— *'Smile, Karl, come on, old sport, say cheese'*—the result was a wan, wasted look, a furtive half-smile escaping from the bones of his cheek, with just a hinting glance of his many fish-like teeth, his natural white-blond hair streaming into the photo like a flattened halo, uniform, metallic-looking, like the teeth of a curved wire comb. He looked sad, he looked child-like and abandoned; yet, burdened with remorse, Lily could not summon the strength and resolve to visit her old man if it meant traveling alone beyond the limits of her Eastern demesne. Her sporadic trips to Watney Street market were about as much as she could muster. Food appeared and disappeared, needing to be replenished by the heroic efforts of her threadbare hands and wallet. The supply of eggs, tomatoes, cheese, bread, greens and fruit which she dragged back home on Monday had dwindled by Wednesday, was completely gone by Friday. Sunday was never a day of worship for them; it was a day of famishing. Lily hadn't the strength to drag herself or her children to church either. Whenever she felt the need, she invoked Almighty Jesus, mercifully released into Spirit, to come to her.

Occasional tokens of grace in the form of letters from Taddeusz began to arrive, each containing bank orders for ten pounds sterling towards the upkeep of their children. These were soon halted, however, to be replaced by messages both condescending and bullying. He admonished her not to waste any cash on trifles; he might soon be in severe financial straits. His once-glorious post as advisor to the Maharaja of Ramgarh having been terminated due to recent—tragic—circumstances beyond his control, he was now in-between fortunes and planning his imminent return. Not to the East End, that's for sure, thought Lily, too fatigued even to feel embittered. Where would he alight next? St. Petersburg? San Francisco? Berlin?

I suppose he thinks the kids don't need to eat every day, only when he's flush—which never lasts—it's either feast or famine, God help me, I married a simpleton-genius with an overdose of brain cells and too little heart. As far as she knew, Greta was still being lodged in a boarding school in Paris. At the age of twelve she'd been dumped and virtually forgotten there by Taddeusz. Lily received exactly two letters from her daughter, enclosing a couple of charcoal sketches 'of her honourable jailors' as Greta called them, a grotesquely leering Mademoiselle Déry, *en décolleté,* and a stooping cane-like figure with mauve-sunken eye sockets, Monsieur de Peyrac. '*We drink watery wine at supper time and hot cocoa before we go to bed, but I'm learning nothing at all here, except French and piano,*' wrote Greta; this was followed by a silence of several months.

Of course, Lily knew she ought to reply to her daughter. She desperately wanted to reply, if she could just gather her splintered thoughts, together with the necessary envelopes, paper and pen, she could begin to commence to make a start. Paradoxically, this very thought sufficed to halt her in her tracks. The over-burdened mind, flooded and wreck-sunken, started its slow *slow-motion* drift into reverse. To write a letter to Greta, yes, but how would she go about it? Where was that unused pad of sky-blue airmail paper, where had she last seen it? It would take her at least a day or two to sift through her stash of buried treasures, in order to lay her hand exactly upon it. And a good pen, one that wouldn't leak all over her fingers as soon as she applied it to paper, where would she find that? Of course, she needed to delve deep into her subconscious, to visualize herself going through the motions of searching and finding the paper, the pen, the stamps; of sitting herself deliberately down at the kitchen table to inscribe the lined onion-skin letter paper with her school-girlish handwriting, penning her distinctive signature above a row of x-kisses, carefully copying out the exact address—*God forbid that it should go astray*—licking the Myrrh-like gum of the seal, forging a path to the post office on Philpot Street. All this was a heroic undertaking, the very contemplation of which could gainfully occupy several weeks. She was not lazy, she was not heartless—and this was what most 'normal' people could not understand: the necessary aeons it required for Lily, unique, irreplaceable and timeless Lily, to complete the simplest of tasks.

With the exception of Flo, that is; battle-toughened Flo had long ceased expecting Lily to cope, given the decades of psychic turmoil engraven into the neuro-landscape of her brain. Flo set up a temporary cot in one corner of her own bedroom for Peter to sleep in this winter, since Lily's attic dwelling was derelict and lamentably cold, and the abrupt change in climate brought on the child's endemic cough, his hacking and rasping, as if his fragile chest were filling up with glue. Already Flo had claimed him, had begun to love and possess him, though she knew one day she would pay dearly for this. Thank God, at least, that Peter was still too young to comprehend the original defect of his genes, his own flawed *Book of Genesis* for which no salvation was promised. From across the room, sporadically, came his plaintive child-whimper; his transient cradle creaked as though threatened by a gust of wind. Still caged within his own famished dreams, her husband Albert grunted and heaved beside her. Flo, too, was to find little repose during this, her own dark night of the soul.

What was she going to do about Jezz? His keepers at the Orphanage planned to send him to a Safe House in north London where he could pursue his studies or, it was hoped, take up a trade. That was surely when he would migrate back, instinctively, to the scene of his origins. Then how was she going to be able to explain him away to the extended community of the street? To Saidye and Solly next door. To woe-begone Rachel at the corner of New Road. To Frieda, their less-than-puritan Welsh-born neighbour, renowned for the in-house brothel she kept for servicemen during the war. Now, constrained in a wheelchair by some mysterious degenerative disease, Frieda watched at her open window, exposing her dusky head and still-alluring gaze, her plump, freckled arms resting on the window sill that served as look-out post over the comings and goings of Walden.

Flo knew that little remained secret for long in this porous little street village. Jezz's imminent presence would only confirm what was already rumoured, that her illegitimate past had returned to reclaim its dues. But she rejected this notion as well. Was she just too strong-headed and too cynical to perceive the event as divine retribution or justice-in-waiting? Whatever the injustice, it had been done to her, thanks to the bungling of poxy Fate which had first pushed her into misfortune. So be it, she was weary but, most of all, resentful of all these years of useless fretting—*let them do their worst*—all hurts, all wrongs, whether past or future, should be as impotent as they are irrelevant. She'd be damned if she was willingly going to hump the exponential burden of the past—as Lily did—into her own Sacred Present.

CHAPTER 20

BIRTH DAY

Yet another half-winter spent and Beattie was brought home to convalesce as best she might. Miscarriage—a blessing in disguise, as was said by some—wasn't it enough, four small boys crammed into two tiny rooms; surely the doctors might have intervened, for the greater good, to set a seal on her alarming fertility? Although her once-sturdy body was becoming lightweight, losing girth as well as strength, Beattie herself showed no sign of discontent. Comfortably invalided for a time within her mildewed cave, she resumed her slow imperturbable march, enveloped in the grey-lit grace of resignation and apparent indifference to the timeless similitude of her days that streamed into one another, as over a bedrock of boulders.

Beattie's babes-in-arms appeared in swift succession, uniformly limp, pink-skinned and inert, a mewling litter, useless, helpless, larger than dolls and far more troublesome. Angie's Xmas gift from Aunt Ruth, a tartan-frocked doll with a head of crinkly gloss-curls and glass-button eyes was of scarcely more interest. What could anyone do with a rigid plastic object, vaguely reminiscent of a human child, whose painted mouth could neither taste nor cry, whose arms and legs squeaked as they swung around in their sockets? Instead Angie treasured her over-sized lady's handbag—a throwaway gift from Aunt Beattie—in which she kept her miniature compact case with mirror, scented face powder and 'pretend' lipstick, her library books and comics, her writing tablet, pencils, metallic sharpener, eraser, and an empty package of Woodbine fags stuffed full of crayons. Without remorse, perhaps even with a touch of malice, as soon as Aunt's back was turned, Angie tossed the gift-doll into the dump.

She didn't know, neither would she have cared, that Aunt Ruth's mild and decorous hands had wrapped the uncherished gift and secreted it, with all the others, in a chest of drawers tucked into a shade-recess under the staircase, somewhere in Grandmother Renie's tenement house. Returned home from the asylum—the 'Rest Home' rather, as the children were told—Aunt Ruth herself moved like an over-sized doll, stiffly, without haste, her tone muffled and genteel, her original features recaptured by their former beauty, her placid eyes contemplating, once again, the domesticity of poverty. The arcane blend of chemicals to be self-administered daily, the dreadful yet therapeutic lightning bolts, decreed by the gods of medicine, seemed to have worked their magic to her brain; she was—*almost*—herself again. Once resettled with husband, Stanley, in neighbouring Varden Street, Ruth made her way around the corner each day to serve as willing lady-in-waiting to Renie, whilst vicariously trying to mother the eldest of the brood, hatching from Beattie's nest.

"But I don't understand, why do we get presents for our birthday, Auntie?"

It was a question that truly puzzled Angie. Just because the planets revolved in their solar orbits and the seasons drifted after one other as, each year, the wall calendar revisited one's date of birth, why should anyone deserve the ritual cascade of flowery embossed cards and gifts, the sparkly iced cake and candles, the balloons and coloured serpentines strung from ceiling to wall? Aunt Ruth was swift and emphatic in her reply; it was to celebrate the passing gift of one more year upon this earth, still safe and well, thanks be to God. Peter's birth day, for instance, which fell today, in mid-February, St. Valentine's day.

This was hardly the sentiment of old Bridgie, the fireside gargoyle gazing malevolently at Lily's two foreign kids—one a detested Teuton, the other a dark-haired sickling. Neither should have been born at all, in her view, they had no business being here, she hated the very sight of them. It was necessary to mince her words, though, for Lily herself was sharp of hearing and acutely sensitive. The old woman had witnessed her fly beyond the pale of hysteria whenever she thought that she or any of her benighted offspring were being attacked. As if that weren't enough, Flo had elected to become Peter's second earth mother, a formidable shield of protection. In the absence of her own illegitimate, equally foreign 'darkie' son—which she liked to delude herself no one knew of or even remembered—Flo claimed her sister's child as her own, making it her business to clothe and to feed him with nothing but the very best the market could offer, mind you, the sort of delicacies that Bridgie, with perpetual grief lodged inside her craw, could only gaze upon without tasting. Voluptuously feeding death, lavish waste upon waste, for everyone knew that Lily's youngest was marked for an early grave. Her own brave sons, too, had been consumed but, as some well-meaning imbeciles said when they tried to console her, at least they died fighting for their country. What sick-sentimental nonsense; the truth was that *her* boys had died so that these brash penniless migrants, and their decrepit spawn, could march in here and inherit the earth.

Not that the indigenous inhabitants of Walden were exactly prosperous. It was midwinter and, predictably, Georgie was again laid off by the flooring company despite the fact that Albert, his brother-in-law, was under-manager. Georgie wasn't dismayed, though, to find himself with a little free time on his hands. His backyard shed, crammed full of homing pigeons, occupied many of his daylight hours. The cleaning and feeding, the selecting and training. His prime racers, with tagged ankle-bracelets on their forked crimson feet, could fly to Scotland and back in record time, fast enough to earn him the raucous admiration of his pub-mates and a few quid from their informal 'bookie' who collected the bets.

His eldest, Jamie, toddled around the yard after him, shadowed by Peter, for whom the towering pigeoncote was a cooing fascination of fluff, birdshit and windstruck feathers. Their benevolent keeper dragged open the pale wooden doors to liberate his aery captives and, in an instant, there was organized

189

tumult across the sky. As the children watched, the damp sloping roof became encrusted with pigeons. A windy clamour of beaks and tail feathers, iridescent collars and sharp circled eyes. Then one by one they fluttered downward, as though responding to the will of gravity, beginning to peck around the paving-stones in search of grain or seed. An amorous bird, with puffed-up throat feathers of luminescent vieux-rose and bottle green, pursued his chosen mate across the pebbles and pools of rain. Having renounced their dubious freedom and already resettled on their perch inside the pigeon coop were three plumed dowagers, one, alert and curious, the other dowdy and limp, the third preening her delicate overlay of cape feathers fashioned like rounded shingles on a roof. When examined with the awe-struck attention of small children scrutinizing their world, each feathered inhabitant of this House of Pigeons became a distinct and charismatic personality. This was equally true for Georgie, who acknowledged them by name and lineage, gold-necklaced Cleopatra, for instance, pale Moonfleet and Ben Hur.

"Georgie, I've got to talk to you."

Beattie stood at the half-open back door, tugging at her cardigan, trying vainly to shield herself from the rawness of the draught. Her tumultuous brown hair, flecked with silver, was restrained for once by a sort of ornamental hairnet studded with fake seed-pearls. A discontented baby was perched on one arm, another had latched itself to the hem of her skirt. Georgie could tell from her unnaturally charged state of tension, her somber judgmental look—of a dark, unhealthy rose colour—that trouble loomed. Granted, they were tight, he was out of work and the dole was hardly enough to live on. Why else would he spend so much time tending his racers; just a couple of wins each month was enough to provide the extra they needed. It wasn't often that Beattie shut the door to their antechamber of a dwelling; about the only time they enjoyed such privacy was during their brief sacramental acts of procreation, but this time she dragged him upstairs by the arm, deliberately softened her fierce tone to whisper a long and painful confidence into his ear.

190

It was risky and difficult, but Beattie needed to speak her mind. As for Georgie, he found it exasperating trying to understand women at all. So many of them seemed to be 'touched,' including a number of his own sisters. He'd married twenty-nine-year-old Beattie, formerly a doctor's receptionist-typist, partly because of her emphatic matter-of-factness, her steadfast unflinching sanity, yet even she sometimes revealed incipient traits of 'feminine' hysteria, that unique paranoia which afflicts women during their early child-bearing years. Let them serve on a warship, for God's sake, for a few weeks—even a few days—and guaranteed they would return home, grateful to set foot on terra firma, blown clean of the cobwebs that clung to their brains, capable of judging the distinction between real danger and the fabulous constructs of their imagination.

"What's the matter with you? She's just trying to help."

"I don't trust her around the babies, I'm sorry, Georgie, I can't help it."

"But Ruth would never harm anyone—" *except herself,* an uncomfortable thought that his mind skittered around, without pausing.

"Well, I trust my instincts, you'll have to find a way to tell her, I want you to do something!"

"Godstruth, Beattie, what can I do? She's only just come home from the hospital, d'you want to start a bleedin' war in this house?"

It was Sunday morning and in the adjoining chamber was Renie, apart and untroubled, presiding over the brief unnatural quietness of her familial court. The bare, cobwebby ceiling was ornamented with twisted balloons, rainbows of glued paper chains and feathery glitter-trinkets; on the decorated feast table, drawn up beside her bed-cum-sofa, thanks to Flo's bountiful largesse, was a collection of glass shell and leaf platters filled with deep-fried salmon patties, smoked salmon and cream cheese bagels, crushed sardine-spread and fishpaste on dark rye bread, black olives, sliced pickles and horseradish, mashed egg and ham stuffed into floury rolls, cordial of grenadine, orangeade, lime and barley water, strawberries and Devonshire cream, miniature baked custard tarts, candied almonds, shell walnuts, biscuits, wrapped sweets and, as blazing centrepiece, a frosted coconut cake spiked with three twirly-red wax candles. Raymond, her son, his Portuguese-born wife and their three hefty children were arriving from Kent on a rare, ceremonial visit. This was a twin celebration. For Peter, a significant rite of thanksgiving for his third complete year of life, albeit crossed with sickness; for Ruth, a merciful return to Herself—*please God forever*—and to her familial world.

Just before mid-day, Great Aunt Georgina was delivered from the Blind Home by Josh, a family friend from Nelson Street, and his fourteen-year-old son. She was assisted up the pitched staircase, then along the first landing like a long-lost treasure in crates by her compassionate hauliers, transformed on each side to human crutches—*Careful, son, just watch that corner, don't you worry, love, we'll get you upstairs safe all right*—then propped upright on cushions, beside her sister Renie on her made-up day-bed. Here she hunkered down, as though into some familiar odoriferous nest of snuff, feather and cotton, gripping the enamel handle of a teacup that was placed into her wasted, sinewy hands. She had the air of a rescued blackbird, small-boned and alert, although sightless, with her thin irregular beak of a nose, her glittering off-focus gaze, faint ridges of shade beneath the eyes. The family snapshot taken this day captured her, for all time, as the aged female ancestress of dark-haired Georgie, her favoured nephew and namesake, the one who resembled her the most, frail and spare as he, too, would one day become.

By one o'clock, Raymond and his family drove up in their new car. They dragged in a crate of Guinness, plum brandy and Madeira port, a carrier bag of fresh prosciutto and Hungarian salami, goat's cheese in thin round wooden cases, home-made biscuits, chocolates and twirly-gold wrapped presents. Raymond also brought along an unexpected treasure to show them all. Having recently placed a down-payment on a small cottage on the outskirts of Dover, and also launched a flooring business, which he drove around the clock with the help of his miraculously resourceful wife Esmirelda—obviously he still had money to burn. From inside a gold-foil cardboard case, he pulled out a padded maroon-leather volume. Their family's genealogical tree. Professionally researched and dating back to 1759. Perhaps he had hoped, secretly, to establish a lineage of distinction, perhaps he simply needed to lodge himself and his descendants somewhere along the graph of Time; at any rate, one distant branch of their tribe, apparently marrying 'beneath them,' were shown to have emerged from pastoral Suffolk, whilst others co-mingling into Karl's Teutonic blood-line hailed from London's East End or as far away as Cork in a sort of vanishing mystery play of lace and parasol makers, mat-weavers and bootfinishers, horsekeepers, ostlers, servants, dockworkers and coachmen.

No surprise that it was Lily, sophisticatedly literate and romantically awestruck Lily, who fell upon the leather-bound volume and eyed it, first through her bottle lenses and then a second time, without them, her nose almost grazing the pages of mock parchment, while her eyes and brain committed to memory as many details of her departed ancestors as she could. Was it possible to obtain her own copy of the book? Regretfully, no. Would he give her time to copy out some of the more interesting pages? Raymond smiled, only too aware of his sister's unique gift for procrastination. He promised to try to get the important parts copied at the printer's, just for her, but he would have to take the book back home to Dover today. She must understand that this was a treasured family heirloom, irreplaceable.

Of all Renie's sons, Raymond most embodied the Hanseatic gene-line. His tawny gold hair with its natural wave, his strong fleshy nose, intensely blue eyes and outdoorsy, flesh-padded cheeks, his irrepressible vitality. Lily noticed again how much he reminded her of Taddeusz, perhaps through the synchronicity of chance or simply an accident of shared tribal genes. He was the only one, too, who refrained from condemning Lily's foreign-born 'ex'; if anything, Raymond bestowed on Taddeusz the sort of grudging hero worship that would surely have amused, perhaps even gratified him. "You married a genius, Lil," he said. "All right, I know he was no good to you, but I wouldn't mind having just a quarter of his guts, and his brains."

Today, Lily responded to the contagious spirit of the moment by setting aside her ingrained angst to shine on stage for a moment or two. It was opportune, since Ruth and Stanley were at this moment on their way back from rehearsals at a reconstructed theatre space in Mile End. Opera was Stanley's passion and his pastime; he belonged to a troupe of operatic thespians who staged performances for a handful of spectators every season.

"Listen, listen, this is Stanley!" cried Lily, ducking her small dark head, stretching her bony neck, repeatedly clearing her throat, which was Stanley's gesture of mild stage fright before each show. She stroked her flat Adam's apple, mock-mimicking his characteristic starts and pauses during the interminable practice sessions in the draughty sitting-room on Varden—"Wait, just a minute, that's not right, that bar starts on a lower chord. *Tra la la*—how's my voice, Ruth, is it strong enough, does it ring properly? *O my darling, your tiny hand is frozen...*" Some verses from the classic German operettas Lily could recite, even sing, letter perfect and in perfect tune, thanks to all those years of living under Mitzi's thumb. Before long, her captive audience, the little kids, the uncles and aunts, even Grandmother Renie was giggling shamefacedly, all of which incited Lily's meager body—unbelievably—and the timbre of her frail voice to gather strength; her cheeks became distorted by a skeletal grin, her pallor transformed itself to a lukewarm flush of Puckish malice.

"Go on, Lil, do it again."

"Ain't she a performer, *my life*, bleedin' Sarah Bernhardt, she is, an' all!"

194

"Yeah, and when she don't want to get up in the morning, she makes out like she's ready for the undertaker."

"A right old piss-taker, she is."

"Now she's takin' the piss out of poor old Stan."

"Can't even boil a poxy egg, but she can quote Shakespeare."

"And Charles bleedin' Dickens."

"Ne'mind, Lil, they'z just jealous, cos' you'z cleverer than them; go on, do it again."

"Oy, *psssst,* watch out, is that Stan coming up them stairs?"

But it was Henry who appeared in the open doorway, disheveled as always and somewhat vague, as though he weren't quite sure he'd entered the right front door. Here was a vestige of the Great War, phantom halberd clutched in his fist, the mists of Passchendaele still clinging to his coat tails.

"Hello, Uncle, come inside, have a cup o' tea."

A respectful and compassionate welcome for this solitaire; long ago abandoned by whatever family he may have had, he eked out his present days in a spartanly equipped 'sheltered' room in a group home for the dispossessed on Commercial Road. Nevertheless, with his coming, a mild chill descended over the gathering. Lily ceased her impromptu solo on the pocked linoleum boards. The children stopped playing and stared at Great Uncle Henry. His engraven face and solemn aura had the quality of stillness, the negating chemistry of inertia, until their next-door neighbour, Solly, uncapped a bottle of Guinness and brought it across the room.

"Here, old sod, forget the tea, here's some mother's milk for you."

Henry's grim-flushed, minimalist gesture of a smile was clouded by overtones of disgrace. He had to be careful of drinking too much these days, a problem of mild incontinence, deterioration of the bladder lining, and also the sphincter muscle was weakening for no apparent reason, his doctor said, except for the obvious: it must be Super-Aliens directing laser beams at his kidneys.

"Impossible, they can't beam lasers through a brick wall, Uncle, and not through glass windows neither," said Georgie.

"They can't! Are you sure?"

"Absolutely sure."

"How do you know?"

"I read it in the newspaper just yesterday, it was on the front page."

"*My life,* where is it, can I see it?"

"Yeah, I'll go downstairs and get it for you in a minute; now go on and drink your beer."

Flo bent down and lifted Peter onto her lap; then she began feeding him fragments of mock sponge cake, the one she'd had specially baked without glutenous wheat flour by the Jewish baker on Hessel Street. At least, the kid should be able to taste a piece of his own birthday cake, something that he could just about manage to digest.

"Here, drink your milk, Angie," said Beattie, once she had finished feeding her own brood. "You shouldn't give her any tea, Lil, she's too young."

Renie gazed around her, laughing soundlessly, age-old stoic and ceremonial head of state that she was, perched side-saddle beside her blind sister on the quilted day-bed, a rash of age-spots on her mildly trembling hands, voluminous flesh bound by a bedraggled apron, carpet slippers enshrouding stone-nails, foot-soles propped against an old bolster cushion, head steadily rocking on her plump ringed neck.

> *There was an old woman who lived in a shoe*
> *She had so many children she didn't know what to do—*

Significantly missing from today's gathering was Renie's third eldest, whose baptismal name was hardly remembered, Tweetie, they continued to call her even when she grew older. Why, who could remember? Perhaps because she'd loved birds, and kept caged birds, perhaps because of her bird-like nature. Left behind, after her passing, was her fleshly imprint, her genetic witness, two living daughters, Miriam and Jane, relegated to the care of their widowed father and dollybird of a stepmother—grim lines of a contemporary un-fairy tale; for, two years earlier, riddled by a malicious claw-like growth, Tweetie, aged 31, had died. Nonetheless, on this renaissance of a Birth Day, within the dark-winged recesses of the old house, Renie's bedsitting-room—now with standing room only—dazzled and glowed like a proscenium. Spectator, Angie, having beguiled and vanquished hunger, somehow survived the famishing, perhaps even flourished, imbibing not milk, but Theatre.

CHAPTER 21

AT THE GATES

A bitterdamp night, and a moulting tapestry of snow encrusted the bestilled terraces of Walden. Almost empty was the gas lit street, but for Lily who moved like a revivified corpse, fending off the icy cut and thrust of the wind as she beat her way past the bomb-site towards the draught-corridor of Philpot Street, off the Commercial Road. With her she dragged an empty kerosene can. She resembled Queen Wenceslas trailed by her reluctant Page, for Angie was crying; there were holes in the soles of her shoes.

"Don't cry, darlin', I'm sorry, I forgot to fill it up and tomorrow the house'll be perishing—"

It was of no comfort. Even once their derelict space heater came sputtering back to life, Angie awoke in the dawn-hour dampness, knee to shin spiked with the familiar lingering ache of rheumatism. Fascinating, the way frost burrows a tunnel and sets up camp inside a human leg bone—its winter quarters—resistant to slathering layers of Vicks petroleum jelly. Impossible to reach the invader, to contain it or coax it away. Intriguing too, how Walden's surrounding night-streets dissembled those of the day.

The garment factory-shop at the corner of New Road, for instance, Fair Maiden Fashions, where machinists, messengers, Obermeisters and tradesmen trundled in and out. From cellar to rafters, the entire building vibrated with the harsh arrhythmnic clatter of machinery, the hiss of the steam press, the windy crash-rattle of doors. At the second storey window, a dilapidated mannequin—in the disarming guise of *Venus de Milo*—presided over a giant metal rack stuffed with a chaos of unfinished garments; by nightfall, these windows were shuttered, the front doors barred behind a link-chain portcullis safeguarding its miniature keep.

The church on Ashfield, high Anglican, was a compact mass of rust-coloured brick, rose window and shade cranny. By day, a few lone souls were seen leaving and entering through side doors; by night, its steep-shingled roof wings and stained arches might entice a legion of pitch-forked demons to hide in. Swept clean of all its children, Rutland Infant-Junior School, had the benighted gaze of a Victorian almshouse whose begrimed glass panes entrapped the many hunger-ghosts of centuries past. The Chevrah Shass Synagogue, robbed of its candle-lit mystery, reposed behind the tottering doors of an old carriage house. Nearby was an impoverished Lyons Tea House with drab muslin nets beshrouding a shopfront of timbered glass.

These mazy lanes and lozenges of side streets were transformed, by night, into shade-paths blockaded by cannon-bollards. A meandering street village bordered to the south by Commercial Road, to the north by Whitechapel. At the angle of New Road and Turner Street, Nathan's Sweet & Tobacco shop slumbered in the shade of a padlocked grate. Once the Grave Maurice and Blind Beggar pubs had closed their doors, only the hospital remained lamplit, charged and alive, night after night after night, with the constancy of sickness.

Meanwhile, hundreds of miles away on the tourist sands of Tenerife, Flo and Albert had gone native. A week-long holiday in the Canaria—ancient islands of wild dogs—granted them a fervent glimpse of the sun to strengthen and bless little Peter and help dry up the bubbling mucus in his lungs. Albert managed to secure an occasional parasol, a small beach mat and a couple of deckchairs. After all, the subtropical coastline of Puerta de la Cruz should at least provide the convenience of a Butlin's Holiday Camp and the quintessence of the British strand at Margate, minus its choppy ice-wind and flirtatious sun. All he wanted was to soak up the sun's luxuriant rays, browse through a couple of 'Agatha Christies' and his favourite trade mag on home repair. He also required his regular unadventurous meals, the minimum of enforced excursions to the ancient rock formations and fumeroles, the freedom to drift at will into pockets of sleep. It was Flo, designated tour guide and pack camel, who humped around their sandwiches and crisps, their thermos of tea and bottled drinks, their flannels, tissues, medicines, beach toys, biscuits and sweets.

On cooler days Peter was swaddled in an extra pullover, a wind-jacket and corded brown dungarees. A red plastic scoop and bucket lay part-buried; his dream castle of glistening desert and shellbone was foundering, fish-damp, heavy and burrowed by holes. Lodged in a shallow depression beside his disintegrating masterpiece, cheeks braised and hands parched by salt and sand—hands that had already begun to gnarl, twist and swell like those of an old man—he contemplated Flo and Albert, his Carer Gods who, in his gaze, loomed as large as the earth itself. Albert was a truculent slow-moving planet enmeshed in the gravity of Flo's magnetism—he, inert and silent; she, high-blooded and voluble. By week's end, Albert's complexion had somehow retained a degree of its nordic pallor; Flo's harsh features were wind-whipped and bronzed like a commemorative coin. Peter's twinned idols were reduced either to feet or faces depending whether he trailed along the stony sandpath beside them or was hoisted onto a massive knee or shoulder. From the worm's-eye view, Albert's shoes were neat, round-toed, of sandy pale dot-pierced leather. Flo, of course, was unwisely shod in wedges of raised heel, too narrow, flamboyantly shiny and costly, often an acquisition of impulsive regret.

Speaking of which, she herself hadn't intended to bring her troubles along with her—better they should remain behind where they belonged—but here, shored up by her borrowed family, she stood within a few hundred miles of that enormous dark continent where all her sorrows had begun. On this flourishing volcanic isle, the beaches and towns were bleached white, the people burned black by the sun. The same poxy sun which, at home, flickered and danced, pierced its rays briefly through raindrop, fog and ice cloud, neutral and mild, ensuring that the indigenous Celts, Scots, Angles, Saxons, even the rogue descendants of Normans, Goths and Romano-Brits grew mik-coloured skins and hides, exotic only by virtue of their variant black, ash blond or reddish-gold beards and hair. This geoclimactic fact, in itself, was sufficient to create an outcast, not of her son, but of the unwanted by-product of that accidental bygone coupling. She knew that Jezz had deserted the Safe Home and was now forging his precarious path through the world. It was said that he worked as a dancer or storyteller, at any rate, some sort of entertainer in the cabaret clubs of the West End. Even more curious, he'd adopted the stage name of Candy—or perhaps it was Candide—while embracing the cross-dressing ritual commonplace in the age of Shakespeare.

So what, she thought, pausing to toss sand out of her shoes, would the Immortal Bard himself have made of her twisted, cross-hatched story? Of all their stories? Were there any Negroes in his dramas? Any sick people? Any poor, mad, blameless, helpless, anonymous people? Come to think of it, were there any bastards? As far as she knew, the Bard's hand-written words were a bastard mix of old and contemporary English, contrived to wrack and addle the brains of grammar school pupils. Greta (who thank Providence was, for the moment, walled up safely in some Parisian boarding school) used to fling her school notes over the topmost banister in a raging whirlwind of ink-stained fragments. Flo herself had never read a verse of Shakespeare's, knowingly, that is, although so many of his sayings had apparently wormed their way into the language—pure as the driven snow, for instance, was that his original coinage? If so, then even a Cockney might find himself innocently, ignorantly quoting Shakespeare; yes, indeed, God bless and pity her sister, Lily.

Back home, across the Thames from Greenwich, the sky over East London—a somber whirlpool of iron-blue, pitched high into thunderous cloud—made the contrast between these distinct parts of the world, despite their common time zones, seem like night and day. Twilight swam into the house, flowed into Lily's heart and head, the twilight-deep of desolation through which the hours trod, backwards and forwards, without leaving an impression, and night fell unnoticed in the abnormality of quiet. Of quiet and of absence. The absence of Greta, of Flo, of Peter, an unbearable, expansive hollowness that crushed her from the inside out. Feeble, yet alert, Lily half sat, half crouched at the kitchen table. She felt chilled despite her ratty olive green winter coat—of pre-war vintage—and those fleecy-lined tan suedes that were all she could tolerate on her rawboned feet. Feet that were all but immobile; toes that morphed invisibly into claws, rooting and gnarling into the floor. In sympathy she sensed the mind and body of old O'Faolain, the lodger, on the landing directly below, vegetating the final season of his existence behind closed doors. She, too, was *alone, alone, alone.* Even Angie, the only one she had left, revolved secretly at a vast distance from her like a dark planet.

Lying inert on the common mattress in the next door bedroom, eyes closed, Angie stepped precariously along the 'verboten' brick ledge. A spiraling dreamwind smashed and tore at her flannel nightgown, braised her skin like a furnace blast. As she looked backward, Lily's angst-ridden face appeared at the attic window. A silent scream—then Angie was falling, floating out of sight. Downward past the familiar earth-ridge of crippled undergrowth. Miniature hillocks. Depressions. It resembled the bomb-site débris, yet it wasn't. Her feet skimmed over a bedrock of rust-metal, cracked glass, moulding refuse exhaling the breath of swamp witch. Strewn along the ground were chunks of slate, brick and cement, fragments of bone; beneath the giant feathery umbrella of a weed-bush, Angie's rejected Xmas doll, besmirched with mud and gravelstone, was alive and weeping amongst the rubble.

And it seemed, too, that the whole dump was alive with the spirit of Taddeusz, her progenitor, inhabiting some cave overhung with rotting purple buddleia fuzz and dead needles of gorse. A wizard's cave, potent with good and evil; she was too fearful, too suspicious to enter, despite its lurid invitation, it reeked of mould, of an untouched future, an unlived life. Flying low, without effort, she grazed the uneven surface of the sluggish pit with the ruined soles of her shoes, precipitating a startled flurry of newt and lizard tails under bramble-roots and over fossil sands, sands which smoothed gradually to immaculate ochre yellow—like Ramsgate or Ryde. A colony of live babies, heads bent, bare feet submerged in the foamy transparent tide, were fingering multitudes of sea creatures, gelatinous and squirming in their bed of sand, rainbow-tinted seahorse, glittering starfish and mother-of-pearl—NO, don't, don't touch them, Angie screamed, awakening, startled at the impact of her own voice.

"What's the matter," called Lily, plaintive, from the kitchen next door, "you ain't having them nightmares again?"

Was it merely coincidence or precognition that, a few days later, Grandmother Mitzi arrived, secretly, at the gates of Rutland School? She had the air of a 'bent' prison warden with an iron file in her basket. She was agitated, though, Angie could see that. *'Schnell, mein Liebchen, komm mit mir!'* she said, clutching her by the hand, her cherished one, the one born with the nordic skin, flyaway blond hair and mottled green-blue, slightly iridescent eyes of her own mother, Wilhelmina. They sat together furtively. Angie sensed that these assignations were illicit, and so she yearned for them as she would a lover, the miraculous scent and touch of Mitzi's silk, face-powder and fur materializing at this secluded table in the ABC Coffee Shop at Whitechapel. Mitzi ordered a takeaway bag of cream-filled doughnuts, a couple of Danish-buns and two cups of *café au lait* without sugar. In her handbag was an urgent message, an airmail letter from Taddeusz. He'd sent travel tickets with instructions and cash for Lily to collect Greta from the *Pensionnat* at the end of the winter term.

The provenance of this news, no less than the news itself, sent Lily into turmoil, propelling her around her two-room attic dwelling in a state of exhausted excitement. How despicable of him to send his mother to spy on Angie, to use her as go-between, to bribe and lure her away. She, herself, wouldn't be able to take her kid into the nearest shoe shop and buy her a brand new pair of shoes on the spot, as Mitzi had done. Besides, how was she going to manage to travel to the continent anyway, *the continent,* good God! If she couldn't even make her way into the wilderness of Kent, how on earth was she going to cross water, *to cross water all alone* to collect her eldest child?

Still vibrant and sun-bronzed from her winter spell on Tenerife, Flo stepped into the fray—'*Just ask for directions, for God's sake, hail a taxi at the station, you've got the bleedin' address, ain't you? Stop making out like you've got no poxy brains!*' After much commotion, resistance and unholy blasphemy unleashed from all sides, she frog-marched Lily down to Petticoat Lane and bought her a decent looking navy-blue suit, bargained down off Josh's stall, a pair of almost-new black leather shoes, and a fleecy plaid jacket with buttoned sleeves. Then she made arrangements for the journey, personally escorted Lily to Victoria Station, and steered her aboard the right train.

CHAPTER 22

CYCLOPS

Although the last she saw of her father for many years was in the gloom-lobby of the Paris boarding school, Greta, being the eldest, retained the vividest memory of him. She never forgot Luc either and, as the years elapsed, their images, their potency fused in her mind. She couldn't explain, neither did she really want to know what made them resemble one another.

Clutching a telegram from the elusive Taddeusz, her mother, Lily, appeared at the *Pensionnat* one afternoon. Tuition fees were no longer being paid, so she was obliged to travel to the *City of Light* to collect her daughter. Miraculously—*indeed this odyssey, too, passed into legend*—Lily managed to make her way there alone. They had to rush to catch the returning ferry. No time to say good-bye to Luc, to any of her friends. The breach, the unexpected exchange of worlds, had all the abruptness, the disorientation of a flight in space.

Walden itself, when she returned, seemed dark, uneventful, shrunken. Grim terrace-houses cast their uniformly long shades over the coffin-yards. At the far edge of their narrow plot, on the left hand side, was a draughty spider-infested outhouse. Even the brickwork reeked of decomposition. Someone had planted a lone rose-bush that bore nothing but withering purplish-black blossoms; somehow it managed to co-exist alongside Aunt Flo's adored and pampered child-poodle. Released daily from the cellar kitchen, it went snuffing, squealing, frisking across the shadow of lawn. Greta abhorred—perhaps this is too strong a word—intensely disliked the temperamental creature. She resented the way it lorded over the turd-strewn land. Tore up the grass. Ritualistically buried its treasure-bones under the soil.

Viewed from their attic bedroom, facing south onto a girdling of brick-terraces, housing estates and sluice canals was a townscape that inevitably slipped down to the north bank of the River Thames. Only this shingle-towered space of theirs rose high enough to be irradiated by the flush of sunrise; as it blazed in through the begrimed wrinkled nets, which Lily never noticed the need for washing, it gilded the naked mattress piping. Dropped flatly over a dust-encrusted armoire. Exposed a flurry of limp blouses, frocks, snaked undergarments piled like the tempest-tost remains of a shipwreck in one corner. To Greta, its cheap and cheerful brightness, its glittering swirl of dust-motes, the utter brazenness of the room was an insult, a migraine-inducing eyesore that revolted and depressed her, made here recoil like a tender shade-plant, too easily damaged by excess of sun. Instead she welcomed the shade that was driven and banished to the rear of the house, like natural twilight reclaiming its domain.

Here beside the blackened gas stove on this, the topmost landing, yawned Lily's grey-lit shadowy space. Her attic kitchen housed one spindle-legged table; this was overlaid with a parchment-grainy oilcloth and surrounded by three vintage chrome-backed chairs. One's first impression, coming into this place, was that of the essence of bareness. Of barrenness. Its lack of ornament, even of utility, gave it the air of some disused station-shed, a bestilled and shut-in waiting room whose denizens were only lately arrived, yet on the verge of decamp. Unsurprisingly, little of value was ranged along the narrow mantelpiece, below which traditional coal-fires no longer blazed. There was one diminutive frameless mirror, an erosion of rust and quicksilver, in which tarnished images lost more and more of their substance over time. A defunct and silenced clock. A maudlin cluster of vieux-rose petals, fake-blossoming in their mother-of-pearl vase. A dull, yet delicate piece of Victorian silver plate dredged up from some charity shop. A lone *Get well* card. A couple of flashy postcards (their exuberant overleaf messages a mockery) from Benidorm or Tenerife.

Lily's few treasures were an archival collection of ancient photographs, rustling onionskin letters refolded into their notched-blue aerogramme envelopes, historic telegrams: *ARRIVING AIRPORT DECEMBER NINTH STOP TEN FIFTEEN AM STOP WITH CHILDREN STOP.* Although she appeared not to have lost faith, her papally blessed rosary had yet to work its mysterious blessing. Her curio collection of newsprint cuttings—rendered brittle as old tobacco—was stacked beneath gigantic birthday cards, each embossed with the flowery gold-lettering and identical blown rose. From church and convent came gilt-pinked holy pictures and black-bordered memorial cards to their numerous tribe, deceased. Too unique, too precious to suffer the indignities of kitchen grime and dust, all of these were concealed by Lily in cracked flattened handbags, stuffed into suitcases within the gloom-recesses of wardrobes, undisturbed by layers of Time.

It was here at the kitchen window, recessed and dim, that Greta kept watch over their narrow plot of so-called garden, according to antique city maps, a bygone Necropolis to eternal Judea. From this vertiginous height, its moss-stained soil had an unsettled air, lamenting perhaps the loss of its forest of tombstones. Its starred and gilded icons. Its etched hieroglyphics: *In memory of, never to be forgotten, dear Chaim, Golda, Leah.* This was death, indeed. Contagious, slowly spreading death. And to think it was already two whole years she'd been imprisoned here, two goddamned stinking years. Greta hovered at this watchtower, agitated, restless, vaguely registering from the corner of her eye the resolute progress of a lone ant, scurrying between the cracked, flaking fissures of paint. She was Rapunzel, *la Duchesse de Glace,* absorbing the deathlessness of Death itself.

Consider her mother, Lily, the remnants, the living shade of Lily, Greta's alter ego, perchance—*God, no*—was it possible she, too, might end up like this, a fast-forwarded mirror-image of herself, half-whittled away, bled-white, drained even of soul.

I won't stay here, I'll run away.

Where will you go? mocked the silenced voices from beneath their long-removed gravestones. *Just where will you go?*

The air itself was already dead, a still translucent envelope of grit and grime, lethargically swirling inward upon itself, limp wavelets of an aery pool entrapping the life forms that almost passed for human, along the nearby streets of Ashfield, Turner, Philpot. It congealed itself around them as though they were fruit in aspic or jellied mutton, slowing down, gently crushing out their breath, their heartbeats, their footfalls.

Bloody hell, I won't stay, I won't—! Greta smashed the full weight of her hip against the rickety kitchen table, and it shuddered nervously, groaned like an alarmed patient. Rattling its veined porcelain cups and saucers, its knives and spoons, and leaking, between folds of oilcloth, lone rivulets of rust-coloured tea. Unbearable! For this was permanent house arrest. And Lily herself, pathetic and powerless Lily, was somehow fated to be her deranged Keeper in this mockery of a domestic Gulag.

After all this time, Greta still grieved. She grieved for Paris, the Paris she was forced to leave behind. Citadel of Art and haven for artists. Decorous Moorish domes, sloping roofs encased almost like snakeskin within shingles of slate. Filigree ironwork girding the sheer-façades of buildings; tall narrow windows, withdrawing discreetly behind antique shutters. With its plane trees, scabrous and peeling, guarding the avenues, this was the city of starred intersections, ultra-wide streets connected by zebra crossings, immense stretches of road to traverse; even now, below ground, pushy Parisians were elbowing their way on and off crowded metro cars, hurtling insults right and left—*Pas besoin de pousser, putain!* Their last school outing was to the honeycombed rockface of Montmartre, the forested steepway to the *basilique du Sacré-Cœur*. At its portals, a final glimpse of the brilliantine blue sky, pure elixir of wind, before plunging headfirst into the holy darkness that transformed, gradually, as the eye adjusted, to an immense stone-lantern of a cupola, inset with gothic glass. All around, forests of white tapers flickered and burned in their iron brackets like wayward souls.

But the enduring mystique of memory resided, in fact, within the sandstone walls of *La Salpêtrière*, in the shadow of *Gare d'Austerlitz*. Former military storehouse for the city, now restored to past grandeur, it was reached by a short pathway, shaded by a hospitable avenue of trees. To think that this huge solid dwelling was once crammed with arsenal, reeked to the rafters of soot, iron and saltpetre. Greta recalled the echo of footfalls on the pockmarked flagstones; yet in the half-light it was the extraordinary silence that awed her, the dense, potent silence of the void.

Brass-filigree chandeliers hung on invisible wires from the ceiling vaults; they seemed suspended—miraculously—in pure space. Near the entrance, you could dip your fingers in a granite baptismal font of holy water. The central chapel, a hollowed-out circle of gloom, soared heavenward on blocks of earth-coloured stone. On guard, within their altar niches, were its sculpted wardens, *St-Paul, St-Jacques Mineur, St-Jude, St-André, St-Pierre*—but what about the holy women, where were they? One modest side altar housed a statue of the grieving Virgin, a carnivalesque gilded Mary clutching a plump, lacquered Sacred Heart. And, of course, there was the inevitable crucifix, nailed to its grotesque divinity of plaster flesh, twisted bone and leaking blood. Whose ancient sins and imagined terrors were once whispered here? What counterfeit absolutions granted within its towering confessional of oakwood, perfumed slightly by rot? Courtesy of France's Sun King, *le Roi-Soleil,* this was once Paris's notorious Prison-Palace, a gigantic holding tank for the Impoverished and the Insane. Even today, it felt like a household of unquiet '*Shades*,' condemned perhaps for all time.

Speaking of which, imagine living in that place hundreds of years ago. The smells, the noise, the eerie whispers, howls and blood-curdling mirth of liars, cut-throats, orphans, lunatics and whores. Here ended up all the riff-raff, the human waste routinely banished from Parisian streets. Hundreds, perhaps thousands of lost souls crammed into the building, vainly shielding, defending their own particular vice or virtue. How many rapes, thefts, silent murders were destined to be enacted behind whatever makeshift curtains or rags? This was one great enforced community of the *Living Damned*, yet Greta would rather have existed there, even in captivity. She'd have survived somehow—surely—kept watch with a blade tucked beneath her pillow. Hell, she'd rather be anywhere but where she was now, this open pauper's grave on Walden, the frigid, filthy, leaking dereliction that they called their home.

Inside her sketchbook she pasted a handful of glossy postcard paintings, precious souvenirs from the *Musée du Louvre*. She showed a strong talent for exact imitation, almost slavishly meticulous, and the art tutor praised her highly, even preserved the best of her oil reproductions under glass. But, as the weight of time compressed and matured her style, Greta's freehand sketches became gloomy chiaroscuro, shadowy women with Gorgon heads, thalidomidic hands and dwarfed, sloping shoulders reflected in flawed wavy mirrors, as the light came bombarding, stabbing at their eyes like darts. Headmother Celestine of St-Victoire's Convent thought her drawings unquestionably powerful but, at times, almost demonic. True, hers was a unique, God-given talent; at all costs, she ought to stick to her faithful reproductions of Virgin Mary and the Christ Child.

"Keep the inner eye fixed on the light, Greta, shun the darkness," she said.

But then (as Greta already knew) what is shade but the defining essence of life's chiaroscuro? Its emergence of pattern; its ambiguous, ever-fluid construction and deconstruction. In the absence of shadow how can life, this involuntary exile of planetary existence, enfold either depth or meaning? For two bleak years, since her return from Paris, she had existed here. It felt like two hundred.

And so it was in the evening gloom of December '55, that Greta, barely fifteen, school truant and domestic outcast, found herself trudging along Walden's frigid pavement with no money, no coat, and wearing her tight new shoes with the cardboard-thin soles. Almost Xmas, *and no food in the fucking house again,* high time that someone witnessed a serious outburst of her rage! That terrorist bread knife scraping at her mother's throat, what a bleedin' lark, the memory alone induced a faint, macabre grin. She would never have done it, of course, *or would she?* In any case, that bitch, Aunt Flo, had stormed her way upstairs and beaten her out of the house.

The right side of Greta's face was paining, just beneath the eye where Flo's ruby ring had smashed into her cheek and punctured the skin. There was a throbbing in her jaw; her teeth felt as though they would drop out. She stopped outside Grandmother Renie's. The upstairs light was on, as always. Aunt Beattie must be knitting placidly in her moulting armchair beside the fireplace, with Gran perched on her bed, guarding one of the sickly grandchildren. The telly was on, Xmas carols were playing, or else the inevitable Ebenezer Scrooge, resurrected between cathode and screen, was traveling backward yet again through an endless wreath of so many Xmases Past. It must be warm, the fire blazing, its pure gold heat escaping up the chimney. Greta hesitated, one hand clutching the doorknob—*no, damn it,* she wouldn't give them the satisfaction. She walked on. By the time she reached Kenny's house, her teeth were grinding against one another, her body convulsed with cold. In the lamplight shone the faint spectral mist of her breath, the purplish blue of her lips.

"No, he ain't here, I don't know when he's coming home," said Kenny's mother, a thin, but powerful looking woman towering over the dim passageway. She stared hard at Greta, taking note of the dried streak of blood between nose and lip, the bruised flesh rising to a point over her cheekbone.

"Well, tell him—just tell him Greta was here." *Goddamn, I'd rather die than beg!* she thought, almost tumbling off the step as the front door slammed in her face.

On Commercial Road, she stopped outside St. Mary's and St. Michael's Church and pulled on the door handle. Its twin arched doors, resembling the entrance to a barn, were studded with square-headed nails and bound by crescent iron bands, sweeping from hinge to handle. Greta rocked the doors again; they opened scarcely a crack. She kicked at them viciously, denting the shiny point of her new shoe. "Goddamned Taddeusz—*some fucking father you are*—this is all your fault; why *the fuck* did you give me life? And where *the fuck* are you now?"

Long frail echoes encircled the stone, rebounded from the mute iron bells in the belfry. Down at the corner pub, a couple of Xmas revelers stood for a moment on the threshold, then stumbled into the street. Wading through darkness, they passed the church, trailing behind them the pungence of frosted hops and malt. "What's the matter, love?" called one of the men. His unmistakable leer, his reek of intoxicated maleness disgusted her. "Ar'you all alone tonight then, are you?"

Greta twisted her head, glancing backward over her shoulder. Her dark eye glittered malevolently in its bruised hollow of flesh. "*Fuck off!*" she said.

She kept walking. It was worse when she stood still. Should she go back to Renie's house? No, they could search all over the East End for her and if she died here on the street, let Aunt Flo have it on her conscience for Eternity. Visions of her own funeral blitzed across her mind. The macabre chiaroscuro images pleased her, seemed even to warm her slightly. She could see the brief box notice printed in the *News of the World: Battered woman found dead in abandoned building,* her death notice rolled and limp with oil and steam, wrapped around someone's fish and chips before she herself, her mortal remains were scarcely cold. *No, God damn it,* she wouldn't allow herself to be extinguished that easily, she'd live to see Aunt Flo pay, and pay dearly for this.

Trudging back, she hoped Kenny's motorcycle would be parked outside the door. It wasn't. She drifted aimlessly in the direction of Shadwell.

No one slept that night. Lily stayed awake, paralyzed with angst at the prospect of her first-born, trudging the streets, half-dressed, bleeding, penniless, prey to murderers and mad men. When Kenny came around on his motorcycle searching for Greta, and she couldn't be found either at Gran's nor at her cousin Rosie's, Lily began screaming that someone should call the police. "Don't be ridiculous, Lil," said Flo, angrily smothering her own misgivings, "she'll turn up like the bad penny that she is, when she's good'n hungry enough."

That started Lily crying again, so Kenny said he would drive around the streets for a while and keep looking, although he never knew what sixth sense finally made him drive down in the direction of the docks. The powerful roar of his motorcycle drove a couple of lone wharf rats leaping across the dark road, and suddenly he caught sight of Greta, standing guard like a miserable sentinel in the shadow of a barricaded doorway. If she was glad to see him, to her dying day she would never have said so. She shivered, beat off a patch of mealy dust from the front of her skirt and glared at him, murder in her eyes.

"Where were you when I went round your house tonight, Kenny? Where the *fuck* are you whenever I need you?"

"Shut up and get on the bike, or I'll leave you here with the rats."

Greta disliked Kenny's long sideburns, his limp dark-blond waxy hair, his flaxen pimply skin, his pleading bovine eyes. About the only thing he had to recommend him was that he loved her with an indelible passion. She knew he would have driven around all night in search of her. No matter what he said, no matter how often he lost his temper, he was a gigantic muscle-bound weakling, a soft-headed prawn; it strengthened and comforted her to know that she could wipe the floor with him.

"I ain't staying at your house," she said, as they drove back across Commercial Road. "I hate your rotten bitch of a mother!"

"I know, and she can't stand your'n neither, I'm taking you round to Rosie's for the night."

And so, overnight Lily experienced a change of heart; Kenny could do no wrong. Teddy-Boy though he appeared to be, in his grainy black leather jacket and knuckle-dusters, he was now her heart's darling, Sir Lancelot in disguise, having rescued her errant daughter from the terrors of the night. Greta refused to go back to Walden, so eventually she and Kenny found themselves a cellar flat on Varden Street a few houses away from Aunt Ruth. They scrounged around for some second-hand furniture and moved in together. Granted, the light was hardly ever good enough for painting, but on mornings when the sun beamed in faintly, illuminating the coal-chute grating above their only window, Greta set up her easel and dabbled around in charcoal and oils, using Kenny as her nude study. Mostly, he dozed off while she was painting him; once he awoke, in the deepening chill, to find himself transformed on Greta's canvas to an enraged Cyclops, staggering out of an ancient cave.

"*Godstruth,* don't show that fucking thing to no one, if I didn't know better, I'd say you was loony!" he shouted.

Greta didn't answer. She stared at him scornfully, rolled up the portrait and stuffed it behind the wardrobe with all the others. Didn't he realize, oaf that he was, that once in a while he blundered into tender territory, threatening to disinter her deepest fear? Having inherited a strong dose of her Aunt Ruth's beauty, Greta stood guard over her own burgeoning mind and body, watching for signs of the more sinister legacy. She found herself drawn to the reflection of her own eyes in the mirror, fixating upon them so long that they glittered, horrifyingly, and seemed to float into space, infused with some malevolent essence all their own. It was as though, beneath the surface-Greta was another far more potent entity, straining to break out.

And she couldn't bring herself, didn't want to stop flirting with this *'thing'* that she recognized as her own peculiar 'madness,' which over the months and years became a secret fetish, an obsession. But then again, there's a certain *'insouciance'* that comes with being mad. It's like traveling to another country. You can always—*almost always*—come back. It's a choice, a life choice. But for how much longer would she be able to move freely in and out, drag herself strenuously, mind and body, back to Kenny's simple surface world, when the hidden, mysterious and dangerous underworld was the one to which she belonged?

Kenny hated it when she sat alone in the dark for hours, staring through the cellar grate at the traveling moon, bedecked in picturesque storm-clouds. It was morbid, he said, gave him the creeps, as did her face, the look in her eyes, as though she were wafting through some invisible nightmare terrain. Greta had always been fascinated, bewitched by the rituals, the symbols, the black theology of Satan. She relished the legends of mediaeval witchcraft, the persecutions, the burnings, the gruesome re-enactments of torture, which preyed on her mind like rat's teeth on live flesh. She felt she was gradually moving closer, and closer, had perhaps already stepped over the threshold of no return. She sensed the invisible presence of the *'Dark Powers'* all around her, just waiting to be harnessed. In her sleep, they were her fearsome companions, flooding her imagination with an intensity that often shook her awake, tossed her, still trembling, onto firm ground again, to the shadowy mound of Kenny's warm back, his almost silky hair, his soft untroubled snore.

"I'm not getting married, I ain't never getting married to no one; marriage is death, Kenny, d'you hear me?"

"Blimey, you ought to go up the doctor's and get your head examined, there's definitely something wrong with you," said Kenny. They had been living together long enough, more two years now, for him to know the easiest way to infuriate her.

"What are you doing here with me then, if I'm mad? I don't need you, I don't want you, get away from me!"

"You won't say that when the baby's born."

"And I don't want this baby, I didn't ask for no baby, I hate babies!"

"Oh, God—"

"I said I hate babies, I really hate them. They want to suck all over you, like little rats. They stink, and they're horrible!"

"God, I've never heard any girl ever say that."

"And d'you know why I'm going to hate this baby, Kenny? 'Cos it's yours! It's going to be fat and ugly and stupid, just like you!"

For the first time, Kenny's hand swung up in the air to hit her. His face was contorted, flushed; his eyes flooded over, darkened, blinking furiously as though he was going to cry. Greta raised her own arm like lightning, forestalled him.

"Don't you *dare* touch me, just try that one more time and you'll never see me, or your bastard baby, ever again!"

The nausea was so debilitating in the early months that Greta had to leave her job at Perkins' Laundry. The reek of turpentine made her so sick, she had to give up oil painting altogether. Imprisoned in the gloomy cellar flat, day after day, she found the strength to do little more than drag her body from bed to armchair, minutely examining the outward manifestations of what was transpiring inside her flesh, her invaded flesh, the hard swell of her abdomen growing steadily larger, the faint kicks gaining in strength until they rippled visibly under the skin, her once-rosebud breasts chafed, thickened and grape-stained around the nipples. It was in her sixth month of pregnancy that Kenny announced he'd been called up to do his military service overseas. That soft-hearted, soft-headed dope! If she hadn't been so furious, she'd have found it funny.

"Oh, no, I ain't going nowhere!"

"Well, you ain't staying here by yourself, we're gonna have to get married now, 'cos the brass, they wants to see that bloody piece of paper—*get it*?"

"D'you think I'm going to go live in that horrible place where they burned Jews. Alive. In the gas ovens! My own grandmother won't even live there no more, and she's German!"

"Oh, Jesus!"

"I'm telling you, they're wicked, them Germans; what makes you think it wouldn't happen again? It could happen again."

"We ain't got no bloody choice, I told you."

"You know my own grandfather was a Kraut too, from Heligoland, and not just a Kraut, but a vicious loony as well! And you think you're taking me to Germany!"

But this, as she later recalled, marked the first of battles lost; the first unwilling twist upon the road. Less than six weeks later, they were traveling together by train through the northern Rhineland of Westphalia. Under assault, that disorienting day, Greta's mind and body were on full-red alert. Defenseless she felt now behind enemy lines, her resistance displaced by fascination and dread. A panoramic vista opened. Gazing beyond the grime of the rushing window-pane and its rattling transom, she absorbed the composite strangeness, the wind-blown essences of the landscape—elixir of wildflower, field manure and mown grass—rising toward the graduated tones of a Teutonic sky. Approaching over-rail, via a towering aqueduct, she saw the cathedral's twin phalluses of stone, fully erect and standing guard over the valley. Random out-croppings of yellowish-beige houses competed for space amongst the trees. Fleetingly, from this height, appeared the townscape's toy-like dimensions, an aggregate of rust-shingled rooftops, aerials, towers and pinnacles, once bombed-out crucifixed spires. A manic, spiraling breeze dispersed the effluvium from factory smokestacks. This was it—her alien yet ancestral homeland, thick with foliage and a rooted, complicit silence, the otherworldly silence imposed by distance and Time.

Hard to imagine how human habitation could co-exist within such a fertile, marauding *'deutsche Wald.'* Even the town *Bahnhof,* the train station, which they swiftly passed without stopping, was banked by fortress-thick walls, overhung with greenery, the pure green breath and pastoral silence of all-forgiving, unrelenting Nature. Not so the military base itself, their last station stop, which was built beyond the fringes of the town. This was a clay-bedded marshland, inlaid in ochre-coloured silt and thrusting weed, anarchic scatterings of pink gneiss and Martian boulder-rock. Melancholy, wind-driven and damp. A no-man's land. Hacked into this landscape like a wound were a cluster of cheap, meandering low-roofed barracks and hangars with pock-marked tin walls rising out of a basin of rust. The mere sight of the military 'married quarters' made Greta almost physically sick. How degrading to have to cohabit in this far-flung military compound, squeezed cheek by jowl between rows of domestic wash-lines, strung with baby nappies and leagues of fluttering khaki.

Even worse, Kenny tried to make their three-roomed cell hospitable. He rattled around, clearing living space, dragging the block furniture from place to place, trying to instill order and comfort into their cramped headquarters. Greta sulked. Suddenly, there he was, *damn him,* thumping around with the unilaterally driven energy of the military man he had become. He irritated her even more than usual as he seized command of their collective destiny, rendering her weakened, disoriented, confused. She knew that she was losing her thrust, her sharp edge, the strategic power of the unpredictable. Forced to share in his military limbo, whilst deferring to almighty orders from above, Greta realized she'd been severed from her own life just as it was germinating. Now she was lock-fastened to his, like the ragged caravan of slave women and children appendaged to Caesar's armies.

CHAPTER 23

Die verlassene Heimat

She watched him polishing his ceremonial buttons. It was not a challenging stare, but covert and cautious, the way you'd approach a starved hound who might turn treacherous, Kenny, now reeking of Lifebuoy soap, pummiced clean and pressed into his khakis. His jaw was razor-nicked, his dull blond hair shorn brutally from the skull. Ruddy blotches over the pallor of his cheeks made him look nervy, tense—*Christ*—why was he pacing around like this? Stroking his dung-coloured lapels. Scrutinizing the mirror-gloss of his boots, compulsive—then, invigilating her as she lumbered about, restoring order to their tiny box quarters. She could feel the taut nerviness of him, the cross-currents of his bridled anger. Something she could understand, at least, and share. But then, why the hell were they even here together? What gave him the right to think he could invade her body, smothering, suffocating her in some sort of never-ending embrace? Surely, he sensed her mild loathing for him, rooted and blossoming like a luxuriant strangle-weed.

And she must have infected him with it, too, surely. He feared her even more now than he loved her, this gigantic child-soldier who slavishly spit-polished his standard-issue hobnailed leather boots of an evening, supposedly trained to treasure his web-kit and bayonet, prepared if need be to dig it into the enemy's gut. This great warrior Oaf King. Of course, he could hardly bear to sit beside her now. To lie beside her. A palpable aura of self-defense had chain-mailed her mind and cloaked her entire misshapen body, barring further intimacy. No need to drive him physically away now, which was a relief; he crept around the walls, as far away from her as possible, battered and coerced on all sides.

She even pitied him at times, though, subjected to the ritualized abuse, the hoarse-throated bawling of the staff sergeant, as were his twenty or so fellow inmates, freshly inducted, reduced and reducible, systematically broken into particles and reassembled into one great iron-booted platoon. *Look here, you fucking pathetic bastards, other young men—just like you—have died on this land, and not so very long ago. Consider yourselves the lucky ones, you're just stepping over the bodies of your dead comrades, so don't feel so bleedin' sorry for yourselves, you'll be getting out of here one day, won't you, you arse-holes, to your cheap beer and your birds...*

Before her eyes the demonic miracle of the deconstructed psyche, forged from the regimented comradeship of mass coercion. This was soul-conditioning such as Greta had never before witnessed, enshrined in its absurd exaltation of rank, ritualized in every last worthless medal, epaulette, beret and boot sole. Of course, they were the detested army of occupation, whether dubious Saviours or uninvited Triumphalists, sealing an end to the delusive dream, *'der Traum,'* the trauma of a 'Greater Germany.'

But to be sequestered in a country where, nevertheless, the subtleties of its foreign tongue fell upon her ears with the bittersweet resonance of childhood—*Milch, bitte, ein paar Brötchen, Kaffee, ein Stück Käse, zwei Knockwürste und einen kleinen Kuchen*—Memories of *'die deutsche Hexe'* (as Lily called Mitzi) brought with them a sense of nostalgia, of curiosity and disquiet. Her German ancestress, the so-called 'witch.' Her once dazzling irises, now milky blue with age. Her crown of dry crimped curls, gradually thinning, and she, forever powder-scented, like a rash of fading lilac blooms. The sturdy corporality of Mitzi may have declined through Time, angst-sickness and war, yet still it could resurrect itself in sudden outrage, a flash temperstorm, her trembling fingers grasped around the curved handle of her knobbed walking cane, pitched high in accusation: *Hateful, just like your father! Du hässliches Mädchen, Du bist genau wie Dein Vater, weg von mir, geh weg!*

Yet this was a kind of renewed closeness, to Mitzi and to her own pre-history. Here she was, by some freak of misadventure, imbibing the anarchic landscape from which Mitzi originated. Westphalia. True, it had begun to lose its disorienting force, its alien aspect, taste and smell. The curdled sky drained and lost itself in a fissured horizon of green. Trodden solid, the rust-red earth was veined by a labyrinth of furrowed pathways, encrusted with pebbles and spiked with grass which was fragrant, rain-soaked and almost preternaturally green. Cloaked in blond lichens, a gothic footbridge lorded over the crash, froth and hiss, the suicidal rock-tangle of stream—*strange, how this had once seemed an extra-terrestrial journey, a moonscape that might, without warning, dissolve itself out of a dream.*

No longer with the air of a sleepwalker did she make her way to the *'Konditorei,'* the *'Postamt,'* the *'Markt,'* and the *'Museum.'* Nonetheless—she sensed it—there was a gloom, a brooding that hung here still. A universal grimness. Austere and solitary, the steepled churches strove to renew and transcend themselves, seeking redemption amid the ghosts of shattered tree stumps, ravaged crops and burnt out water-meadows. At the town's sole haberdashery, imported silks and furs were rare and costly. Clove-and-cinnamon perfumed bakeshops were fresh with the memory of war-rations. In the jeweller's shop window resided heaps of antique brass, pitted with verdigris. Somber-cast pewterware and anonymous silver plate. Tiered trays of hounds-tooth necklaces, garrot chains and chokers, dark, weighty and ominous, evoking instruments of torture from the Devil's own forge.

Beyond this neat cluster of shop-fronts and flint-faced cottages, the turbulent pathway narrowed, snaking across a sprawl of woods. Here the world receded, taking a deep-green silent breath, allowing a single furrow of wild-grass to sprout unmolested along the centre of the track. Yet, vestiges of *fin de siècle*, a scattering of once-elegant benches, here and there, betrayed the fact that secluded rambles through this heartland were once a favoured pastime of *das deutsche Volk*.

Greta trespassed, by chance, upon a private burial-ground where the mediaeval House of Knechthausen once interred their dead. The last living Baron of this tribe still inhabited the moorish turreted '*Wasserschloß,*' a moated castle of pink stone at the periphery of the wood. It was built on a tiny islet, surrounded by a 'fairy-tale' pond of water lilies, and connected to the willowbank by a stone-arched bridge. For some reason, though, the Knechthausens' disused cemetery was situated a good distance from their earthly home. It languished, deep in the forest glade. At its centre a once-grand pagoda was falling into ruin, domain of dew-glistening cobwebs, couchgrass, wild ivy hurling itself up the sunken slate roof and rot-wood supports. Encircling this pagoda was a scattering of headstones, sloping and derelict, engraved with the ornate old German script, much worn, smudged in gilt and greenish mould; further away, a crescent procession of flat marble tablets were mostly cracked and indecipherable.

It was here that Greta gravitated, day after day, to this neglected sanctuary of dank-smelling earth, shrouded closely by pines, themselves heavy and unpruned, almost black with shadow. Another graveyard, her natural habitat. The presence of gravestones, any collection of gravestones, imparted a sense not of peace, but of mystery, of significance. Of power. For all cemeteries are adorned with their own distinctive iconography, their own '*ambiance*' and mournful artistry. If the dead lingered anywhere, surely they must inhabit their final resting place, locked into a perpetual séance of kindred gathering or kindred enmity. Perhaps this was nothing more than an anonymous collection of old bones resting under a profusion of headstones, yet Greta felt an intense affinity, a strange and morbid, even envious nostalgia for those who had passed over.

By now, this was her own peculiar ritual of escape from the barbed wire prison-house, and from Kenny. To reach the graveyard she had to climb down into a resin-perfumed well of green, where the towering black pine-boughs leapt and soared above her head like wings in flight. Always a swift descent of skipping, tripping downward. Pebbles scattered under her shoes as she struggled to keep her balance, clutching onto the alien, ponderous swelling that was now her body. At the bottom, before the slope rose again like the hewn-out cavity of a gigantic Stone Age urn, she saw a stranger, a man.

Unremarkable he was, of course, hardly worth a second glance. Yet, as Greta came closer, it was his aspect that mesmerized, deathly still, concentrated, portentous and dark-spirited amidst the green-black glittering shadows. He was sitting on one of those rain-worn benches, gazing into *'the nothing.'* A nothingness, which she now intruded upon, doubly intruded, being a foreign-bred Madonna with child. These woods belonged to him in a way that was self-evident, yet mysterious; her simple presence, an invasion of his immense, proprietary aloneness.

Sand and grit crunching under her feet as she approached, Greta wondered whether or not to address him. Acknowledge him at least with a glance, a word? Yet it was Sunday morning when the flint-walled *'evangelische Kirche'* in the village was filling up, no doubt, with worshipers. Surely the deliberate choice of this remote spot meant that the man desired to be alone, as she did, her alter ego, so strange-looking, silent, melancholy and apart. As she passed, ignoring, feigning, anyway, to ignore him, he leaned forward, plucked a single wild-blossom and pressed it into her hand. "*Entschuldigen Sie, bitte,*" he said, with a glance of solemn and profound irony. "Let it be said that in my country we revere all mothers, and mothers-to-be."

My country? Hardly a true-blooded German; the man's accent was slight, yet perceptible. Greta was surprised that she knew this, triumphant that she even recognized the fact. An alien, like myself, she thought, observing his face, which was bony and sun-browned. A young starveling, with delicate wisps of hair grown anarchic and wild. In his eyes—what was there but a hint of stricken and watchful vulnerability? Greta paused, intrigued, arrested by some quiet channel, deep and potent, in the ground, perhaps in the wind around him. With an open palm he indicated the worn forest bench. With neither a word nor smile, she sat down beside him.

"You're not from around here, are you?"

"Not any more, that's obvious, isn't it?"

"Who are you, then?"

"My name's Rudi, and you?"

"Greta."

"O, Greta, Greta, beware Mephisto!"

"What?"

For the first time Rudi smiled. It was less a smile than a transient glimmer of warmth, and of infinite weariness. "Nothing, that's just an old, old story, but tell me, Greta, what are you doing here, so far from home, in this sad country?"

Strangers they were, true, and yet they had talked for hours; it seemed that aeons had already passed between them. That same night, exhausted and exhilarated, Greta slipped down a shaft of sleep, swift-flowing, liquid and black. Tongue bestilled, sight obliterated, she was treading and treading darkness; somehow she'd penetrated even further than the Knechthausen family plot into that place, that melancholy place that Rudi had shown her. Yet she couldn't recall making the journey. All around, the air had turned to mould. Rudi was digging. Despite the darkness she could see, or at least feel, his presence. Furrows appeared in the ground, like tiny bite marks, as Rudi dug with his fingers, ripping sinews of ivy out of the foul squelching clay. His palms were streaked with mud—or was it blood?—enough, anyway, to fling her out of the deepest slumber, a soul-dream to banish sleep.

Greta's eyes opened, absorbing yet another realm of blackness. A transient, prosaic, pre-dawn blackness. Nevertheless, her pillow dripped with sweat. Her entire body seemed to be humming, almost vibrating; an anarchic pulse was rattling inside the shell of her ear. In its warm prison of flesh, the baby heaved. Rock-hardened the walls of her abdomen. Twisted around within its even greater darkness, rippling its shoulders like underwater wings. Perhaps it was sobbing, hiccuping bubbles into its watery enclosure, pushing the crown of its head against the palm of her hand, feline-like, testing its strength. Making her gasp with its sharp rebellious kicks against the cervix.

How long before this overpowering blackness bled to an indistinct dawnlight, revealing the age-old tableau, familial trinity that they were now, bound together in a dark primeval bed? All three of them in absolute deadlock. The Infant Supreme, coiled and twisted under her heart. Kenny, her lawful Keeper, slumbering beside her like a human mound, wrapped loosely in a heap of cloth. At the heart of it all, a dark malaise. A pang of desolation. The familiar taste of bitter, of Myrrh, creeping from gut to gullet, seeping up and over the root of her tongue. Her insides bored hollow, scraped away almost to nothing with the longing for something—for someone—perhaps for Rudi as he gazed into the woods, into *'the nothing,'* in pursuit of the evergreen memoir of 'the disappeared'.

In the winter of 1943—Rudi had said—*my mother and my father were executed in the home of Jehovah's Witnesses. Jews, gypsies, trade unionists, socialists, partisans, Marxists, Russian prisoners of war, what does it matter? Just one more blood sacrifice on the Sabbath Day. Don't waste your bullets, shouted one of the Gestapo. And so my sister, Anke, and I were let loose, allowed to bleed away into the landscape like wild game. It was in these same woods—I remember—two other boys, Peter Klaus and young Werner, both children of Witnesses, stumbled along beside us. Stay together, we must stay together, I shouted. They plunged onward, sobbing, crying out for help. Then fell silent. Captured. Or in fear of capture. I never saw them again.*

On the second night, Anke died. She died in her dream, too blissfully little to understand that she had passed over. That wet freezing night, I also dreamed: I dreamed of my mother, haloed by the anguished diffuse aureole that was my father. Give me the baby now, she said, and lifted her out of my arms.

When I awoke, I felt not exactly warm but invigorated somehow. Anke was peaceful. Fingers clenched, but unresisting. White-blond curls, stiff and damp. Cheeks mottled, wet, milky-blue with cold. A scattering of forest soil, a handful of wet oak leaves lay curled upon her chest.

But then, my mother showed me where to place her, lent me the strength to dig a pit deep enough that it should remain undisturbed. I searched for a hefty footstone of pink gneiss rock and dragged it into the clearing; I left this—In Memoriam—at Anke's feet.

It was then that I began to feel them all pressed against my back, an urgent force, their combined breath lifted and carried me, drove me through the forest, led me to safety. Only much much later came the rage, the unrelenting sadness that they had left me behind.

As Greta pushed open the door of their cell, an angular sheath of sunlight glazed the tiles. The wind, arrogant and intrusive, shivered down the passageway. Beyond the tarmac path, the wild grass flamed. Grains of pearl, flint and sand wind-blustered—fitful, yet determined—eastward to the wood.

"Where are you going?" said Kenny.

"Out, for a walk."

"Wait, I'll come with you."

"No, I'm all right."

In the sudden draught, Greta's dark hair became a haloesque swirl. Sun-gilded. Sun-entangled. She turned her back on Kenny, carefully balancing her cumbersome body. Dog-tired and sulky, he stared at his chosen one, his so-called beloved, this arrogance of over-burdened flesh and light.

"Wait, for Christ's sake, I'm getting up."

Kenny's regimental slumber-jacket slid onto the rumpled bed. His mushroom-pale muscular back and shoulders leaned forward, elongated and statuesque, as he fished in vain for one of his slippers.

"Bollocks!" The rank corpse-taste of morning lingered on his tongue. Eyes bloodshot, murky with sleep and resentment, he stared at her. "Wait for me, I said!"

"No, I'm going—" An abrupt slam of the door and Greta vanished, swift and spectre-like; her rose-silk scarf twisted under her chin, the breast buttons of her grey smock coat refusing to fasten as she marshaled the unruly ball of flesh before her.

Rudi was waiting for her at that same spot in the woods, as he had promised. A kind of furtive sylvan tryst—the notion made her smile, if somewhat wistfully, somewhat bitterly. As always, in his wake, was the smell of sunlight and trodden grass, the fragile incense of resinous wood. He smiled, yet seemed anxious at the sight of her, struggling to descend that final slope. He came clambering up to meet her, offering his strong sunburnt hand.

"Careful, I didn't think you'd come, you shouldn't have come." His schooled English tongue was at times halting, but surprisingly rich and skilled.

"Oh, damn it all, I don't care what happens." Her whole body ached. Even the baby had turned quiet, playing dead, alarmed perhaps by the tumult of the journey. Greta panted, sweating, breathless with anger, exertion and fear.

"Hush, come and sit down!" Rudi touched her coat sleeve, and took her hand. Paternal, quizzical, tender, the sort of alarmed tenderness evoked by the sight of a child in trouble.

"I don't want this baby, I told you!"

"Greta—"

"Don't try to humour me, don't tell me I don't mean it. I don't love Kenny, I don't want him, I wish—*(she had to say it, let him think her a monster)*—I wish one of us was dead."

"Look, things will get better." Greta's swift glance of contempt made him retract. "You might— I'm sure you will feel better once the baby is here."

To anyone else, thought Greta, she would have appeared loathsome, fiendish, grotesque. But somehow Rudi managed to cradle her in his gaze, assuring her without words that she, and her unborn child, were something precious. A twin seduction, born of his unconditional acceptance of her—and his tacit power. But a strange brand of power, surely. His was not Kenny's servile abysmal love; it was something other, and something other-worldly. Rudi seemed to dwell in a state of serene gravitas, connected to some occult certainty. His own privileged lifeline to the numinous. Although his tooled leather jacket—of an indeterminate earthen colour—was shabby, his entire body was alight and alert with the soul-cloak of the refugee. Somehow he managed to inhabit both countries, fabricating his own brand of resilience out of the apparent vacuum of the world.

"Tell me about your Church!" challenged Greta—*and your bastard child-deserter of a God*, she thought, envying Rudi's irradiation of calm, his mild refusal to be heckled.

"You know I don't preach to anyone."

"But I'm asking you—"

"What?"

"I want to know exactly what it is that you worship…"—*and die for.* Even she dared not voice that last thought, those last words.

Rudi raised an eyebrow, half in apology, half in defeat. She noted the intaglio of natural age-lines around the eyes, skin burnished and weathered like shale; he was far too young, yet already there were traces of silver in his hair.

"It can't be explained; it's there for anyone, but it has to be found, and felt."

"And do you—feel it?"

No answer now, but a smile, a child-humouring smile, not condescending exactly but rather in the order of peaceable resistance.

"We'll talk more about this later, when you're not so upset."

"What difference does that make? I'm always upset."

"Here, give me your hand," said Rudi. With an effort, she lowered her over-burdened body onto the bench beside him. As he turned to gaze into the green, into *'the nothing,'* his fingers closed, warm, vibrant and potent around hers. "Now, shut your eyes, Greta, shut your eyes—*shhhh, do you feel it?*"

When Greta got back late that afternoon, Kenny was pacing around their tiny box cell of a lounge, waiting for her.

"Where've *you* been?"

"For a walk."

"Well, you've been gone long enough. No shopping?"

"No."

"There's nothing to eat here, you know."

231

"I'll go tomorrow."

"I already went out and got some bread—"

"Oh."

"— and some soup and cheese."

"Did you?"

"Yeah, but don't buy that poxy German sausage no more, it makes me shit bullets!"

"Leave it then, I like it."

"It's a wonder it don't make you go into labour, that stuff is diabolical."

"What would you know about it?"

"That's my kid, ain't it? I don't want it being poisoned by shit smelling cheese and fat salami."

"*Your kid?* Piss off, will you? Remember, I'm the one who's giving birth to it, but after that—you can have it!"

As Greta pushed past him, she thought she saw his face change for a moment. Radically change. From pallid to flushed. Sharp features turned fluid, distorted, Satyresque. Kenny's habitually vacant eyes, his look of bafflement now stirred, glittered and darkened, like a faulty exposure on a photo plate, then flashed the colour of blood. Funny, she remembered afterward, it was at that same instant the baby's head dropped in her womb with the abruptness of a guillotine. Instinctively she curled her fingers around the great fleshy mound, tried to hoist it upward, but it sagged under its own weight. Shifting just a few steps forward required an effort now, yet here she stood, in pitched battle with Kenny—and with his unborn child. The opening salvo was a sudden wrench at her cervix. Then silence. A muted early warning signal that the tussle had started. Mother Nature in tooth and claw—a fight to the death, if need be, for this new life to break free.

CHAPTER 24

TRAVELING SOLDIER

I came into the world
To the sound of flame and wailing
The hand that held me trembled
My milk was tinged with blood

As she stared at it now, dreaming itself into existence within its martial little box-bed, she could hardly believe that this flesh-and-blood thing, this seemingly human creature that had existed inside her all these months had almost killed her. An electrifying combat, waged in a blurred and muffled space, encircled by sterile torture instruments, blank-faced ministrants and mute spectators. Its 'Imminent Arrival,' heralded by a tepid fountain gush between her thin legs, was further sign of her predestined defeat. Her own flesh and blood pre-empted—gladiatorial—whilst her assailant, bruised and blood-spattered, the thing that was tearing at her, tearing away from her, inch by inch, moment by moment, was destined by Nature to be the victor.

Das ist ein großer Säugling—they whispered, half admiring, half in awe—*für so ein junges Mütterchen.*

Monstrously big, registering over ten pounds in weight, it dangled on the hospital scales, limbs writhing, pink flesh glistening like skinned veal, convex forehead slicked with blood and slime and furred in black, silenced for a split second, then amazed and outraged, its untried lungs inflating like tiny bellows, rehearsing its primal song.

And from that moment, it gave her no peace. For weeks she dragged herself from kitchen to cradle, herself a wounded warrior, outraged by the chastening pain of her grossly unhealed incision. And all this because some life-in-miniature had forged itself from her blood, elected to force its way, unwanted, into the world. For this she was obliged to live, to breathe, to sleep—*if one could call it sleep*—side by side with it, to drag it around with her, tense and wakeful, propped momentarily inside the sinking curve of the armchair, slung up sometimes against her shoulder, a couple of bonded primitives, while with trembling hands she measured tablespoons of powdered milk or sterilized a rack of bottles, striving without success to put a stop to its insatiable wants, herself growing ash-pale, hollowed out and fading in strength. Yet, having imbibed its mother's dissatisfaction, the infant cried itself sick. Its sporadic wailing, its erratic little sob-sucking noises were an unspoken reproach, although she couldn't find it in her heart, or in her body, to give it any comfort, she felt so comfortless herself.

Rudi was gone, perhaps for good, why search for him? Why seek him out? That easy familiarity she remembered and missed, his mild-mannered closeness and aspect of a ministering kinsman. But then, thinking back, what could he have understood of her obvious poverty, draped on her starved shoulders like a coat of mail? Her poverty of spirit—no, but her blind heathen constrainedness in which every impulse was to mock, to taunt, to smash, to destroy. So, it had to happen, of course; she knew it. At this very moment she could hear *him,* her husband Kenny. Breaking his heart because, finally, he had hit her. The square-cut utilitarian looking glass, draped with a sheaf of wildflowers, grasped her image, held it captive. Stunned—*la Duchesse de Glace*—yet all the while assessing the damage; as if this were a planned-risk operation, how well had she got through?

Her cheek and left temple felt numb, livid, before the reflexive life-spring welled back to its flesh surface, branded with three distinct finger strokes, like the vengeance of a crazed artist over his botched sculpture. And now the child, Rafael—*it had a name, didn't it?*—started to whimper; soon it was howling, perhaps in sympathy with its distraught sire. The notion was not devoid of humour. Greta grinned faintly, then winced as the first bruising began to appear on her jaw. A smashed padlock seemed to be creaking open with an eerie shudder. The door to her prison. In the next room, barking and sobbing, was that vicious loony of a husband she now had to escape.

"I'm sorry, I'm sorry," gasped Kenny, appearing in the doorway. Hideously in tears, humiliated.

"Get away from me!"

"Why, why do you get me so fucking angry? I can't even talk to you any more." Silence. Was she calculating her next move, her next crucial response in the dock? "You provoke me, I know you do it on purpose."

"Oh, yeah!" She pointed to her cheek. "I did this, did I?"

"Christ!"

"Go on, blame *me* for it, you shit coward."

"I told you, I'm sorry—"

Still weeping, Kenny lunged forward to embrace her, but she turned on him with a flash of malice, a demonic spasm of her bruised features which affrighted him.

"I warned you—" She moved toward the bedroom and lifted Rafael out of his crib. The child stopped screaming. He appeared to be on guard, his tiny cockleshell ears straining intently, his cries further silenced by the rough, trembling grasp of his mother. "I warned you what would happen if you did that."

"You're not taking my kid away—"

Again silence. They were both already gone, he could feel it, mentally thrashing away from him in this dark current. What was she thinking? What was she planning? You've lost, just try to stop me, he could almost hear her say.

"Oh, you calculating bitch, I hate you!"

"Make sure you tell them that in Court; in the meantime, just keep away from me, or I'll call the military."

He was now in deep shit, and she knew it. Private Howden court-martialed for domestic brutality barely weeks after his flight from boot camp. It was just a matter of time. She would get away, of course, but first she needed to dredge up the strength. What did she care if that monumental Oaf was now clutching onto his tiny flesh-seed, Rafael, whose scruff-lock of black hair and rose-dark skin resembled him not in the slightest. Trying to cling onto the remains, and the remains of her, pathetic, almost maternal, the bastard was actually still crying.

"Oh, you disgust me, *I* should be crying. I can't stand this no more, I want to go home."

Home? thought Kenny. Despite everything, he wanted to laugh. Go home to what? To an insane mother and her barren kinswoman of a sister. Flo, the one with the brutal stone-fist, the fixed look of outrage. *Perish the thought that his kid should be brought up by*—but, then, at last he'd begun to comprehend. Greta was his chastisement and his seduction, his initiation and rite into manhood. Arduous, dangerous, but coveted. She was the live flame, thrown his way, that he'd grasped and thought he had the right to handle.

To handle.

He stared at his trembling hands, the fingers that had touched, stroked, held, warmed, caressed—and beaten her. These weren't his hands, gnarled like claws, calloused and begrimed. All this had somehow happened outside himself. It must have been an error, a mis-step, an aberration. He cradled his head in those same hands, touched his own face which was wet, weak and soft, of a sick-lily pallor and hawk-like profile that appeared to lend him a mystique, a toughness that he did not possess. Despite his massive girth, he felt powerless—was powerless—light and insubstantial, a grotesque ornament pitched from a carnival float. In one predestined stroke he had lost her; he knew full well he had lost her, and his kid. He knew, too, that she had goaded him into it; she had not been satisfied, would not be satisfied until she had broken free.

For Kenny, it was now all deadlock. Whichever way he turned. Dead-end. No way out. The trenches behind him, open cannon-mouths ahead. On his lips the taste of gun-metal, within the fucking fog of war. For what had they been training? To ratchet up the required dose of fury. Of savagery. To bear down blindly, to kill or be killed—*Bollocks!* Mostly he just wanted to sink down to sleep, better still, sink his head permanently in the nearby bloody 'Fluß.'

"What's wrong with you, Private? You're late for duty, and it's not the first time, is it? *IS IT?*" shouted the staff sergeant, when Kenny shambled into ranks about an hour later.

"No, Sergeant."

"And what sort of state do you turn up in—*eh*—what do you call this?" The sergeant kicked the scuffed leather tip of Kenny's boot, flecking it with mud. "Didn't you get your beauty sleep last night, soldier?"

"No, Sergeant, I was on picket duty."

"Well, no one gives a bollocks whether you slept one hour or ten. You're not supposed to be on a bleedin' holiday, you are here to do your duty—!"

"Yes, Sergeant."

"—and the rest of you lot, how long have you been practising this routine drill? You're pathetic! I said, how much longer do I have to keep you out here in the pissing rain?" He turned back to Kenny, eyes veined, rheumy and flickering with simulated malevolence, almost transparent in the raw morning light. "What's your name, soldier?"

"Private Howden."

"Well, it's thanks to you that we'll be here another half-hour. *YOU'RE A FUCKING DISGRACE TO YOUR REGIMENT!*"

That weekend it was a relief to be relegated to extra kitchen duty. Penalty for the morning's abysmal performance on drill parade. It meant not having to be around *'her'* for a while.

Time out from having to confront her underground hostility. It was safer for them both, especially these days, that he should be sequestered here with a butcher's array of blades, long open razors—"Watch out, soldier, can't you even handle them right?"

Already his life-blood streamed between the spuds, mingled with a jet of ice cold water from the tap. He resumed his work preparing mounds of diced swedes, hacked greens and carrots. His hands shook, his shoulders tensed, the entire surface of his skin was alive with pins and needles. It was steamy in here, as well. Sweat glittered above his lip, lent a greasy shine to his jaw, formed a club-shaped imprint down the back of his shirt. Still, he thought, his sentence was relatively mild. He could serve time here, see out his whole damned military service quite gratefully here, imbibing the rank scent of yesterday's boiled cabbage, vanilla custard, corned beef. It was quiet, dull, mostly uneventful. The butchery and carvery he could turn his hand to in this old army kitchen of high ceilings, stove-pipe vents, barracks store cupboards, and blistered walls the colour of old cream. Here, at least, you could scrounge a mug of lukewarm tea, a couple of rock raisin scones, you could puff at a Woodbine fag in between shifts, gossip with the pot-bellied old Tomcat who managed the kitchens and the Officers' Mess. You had to be grateful that you weren't dipped up to your arse and bollocks in rain and muck, forced to climb over barbed wire or wade ankle-deep in diesel fuel.

Kenny was just barely old enough to have witnessed the beginning of London's Blitz. The indelible dream recollection of sirens wailing, sky, cloud and wind on fire. Thunderbolts that seemed to explode from underground. Flying roof shingles, tenement walls that crumpled and sank like doll-houses. Then, abruptly, he was being spirited away on board a train, clutching hands with his cousin, Rosemary, on route to a remote Welsh farmstead—its name had already vanished from memory—a newly discovered planet, spinning within a pure, green and tranquil space, almost eerily spellbound in the way it seemed to deny that war existed or could ever invade its bucolic normality—*normality.*

His own father numbered among those who had vanished aboard a mine sweeper in the North Atlantic, somewhere along the dreary, unchronicled 'progress' of the war. Perhaps born outside of holy wedlock and, if so, Kenny himself originated from the one lapse from grace—only one, he had no other siblings—that his mother had ever made. Her wedding ring, if it ever existed, was long since pawned. No photograph survived of the ill-fated mariner who had tempted her into thoughtless maternity. Annie Howden seemed almost devoid of sentimentality. Sullen and taciturn by nature, what had she tried, as a point of honour, to teach him? Never to confide and never to depend. 'Harsh-mannered, yet a tower of strength,' whispered her admirers; 'tough bleedin' bitch,' said the others. At any rate, her spinal vertebrae seemed to be fused in an unyielding line, inherited from her own Originator, perhaps. Even now, growing older, not mellower, her aspect was thunder-stern, all bone and shadow, so unlike his own, he thought, his own tremulous moon-sallow flesh.

"Do I look like my dad?" he once asked, wondering why she stared back at him, surprised, perturbed, perhaps even remorseful. '*You look like no one but yourself, little Sunshine, you have fashioned yourself out of nought,*' she replied, a little too tartly for his liking. How bizarre, how eccentric even, to tell a small child not to inquire after his own paternity. Kenny was her progeny—indisputably—any more she declined to say.

Meanwhile, Tom, the veteran army cook was bashing about in front of the massive ovens, his pile of tin saucepans and industrial bake trays rattling like arsenal in his deft, efficient grasp. He gave Kenny a mild clout on the shoulder.

"Get a move on, mate, enough of that day-dreaming, what's the matter with you today?"

"Nothing."

"You're acting pretty dopey these days, I suppose the baby's keeping you up at night?"

"How d'you guess?"

"Well, that's family life, it don't mix too well, does it? Just you hang on a bit, you'll soon be in the clear. Come work here in the kitchen with me, permanent, you'll be set for life."

"No, thanks."

"Eh?"

"You already told me, didn't ya, I ain't worth shit in here."

"No, no, I never! When did I ever tell you that? You're doing all right, son. The only thing you've got to watch out for now is handling them explosives, that can be nasty, but once you're through that, that's the worst of it over."

"Is it?"

"Yeah, then you choose yourself a good trade, and you're in for life."

In for life! Kenny had already stopped listening. His whole life was already one bleedin' mess—drafted into the Forces at the age of 20, the father of a kid and with a marriage (some poxy joke that was) already in ruins. When *'she'* went her way, what might she tell it in ten or twenty years from now—*You look like no one but yourself, little bastard, you have fashioned yourself out of nought.* Another poxy Immaculate Conception fable! Characteristically, it looked nothing like him. Could he be certain he was the father? How could he be sure?

Tom's vat-sized soup kettle held a confection of shredded cabbage, onion, potato and bacon fat, agitating in a muddy looking Oxo broth and steadily permeating the space with the odour of impoverished school kitchens.

"Keep an eye on that, will you, make sure it don't boil over," he said, disappearing on some errand or other and leaving Kenny the freedom of the kitchen, a rare indulgence. There might just be some leftover fruitcake, or half a packet of biscuits to nick. Kenny dragged a chair across the floor and settled himself into a corner; given the chance, he'd willingly spin out his whole tour of duty right here.

Rudi's long-awaited postcard, meanwhile, when it arrived, bore a postmark and temporary address from Madrid, his fugitive home. '*Pardon the long silence, Greta, please tell me how you are. The baby—was it a girl or a boy? Unfortunately, I won't be staying here long, but I will try to keep in touch. I remember how distressed you were. Have been thinking of you ever since I left.*'

Oh, have you, thought Greta disconsolately, then just how will you manage to keep in touch, once I go back? To London, *London*. Whoever would believe she could miss that dead city? Not the city itself, and certainly not the indigenous tribe of her living ancestors, but the familiarity, the comforting and shabby predictability of the place. Walden Street would forever run at right angles to Philpot. Perkins' Laundry clanked, sweated and groaned in the space between the cornerhouse Chemist and the Post Office. Commercial Road, damped in coal-dust, trundled its way east to the Limehouse railway arches or crept ignominiously westward as far as Aldgate, halting at the frontiers of the 'Great City.'

What would they do, how would they react when she finally managed to return to the East End with her first-born? She'd begin by flaunting it in Aunt Flo's face, although she was sure Lily couldn't be trusted to handle it; she'd probably take fright and drop the thing into a coal-bucket. The child was heavy and solid enough by now, gaining in presence and in strength, a drain on her reserves of body and mind. Rafael, her work of art—her masterpiece—hardly anything to do with Kenny; whether he knew it or not, whether he intended it or not, he was shifting toward that universal destiny intended by Nature for biological fathers, he was moving toward oblivion.

Rafael responded only to *her* movements, to her touch, to her voice. When she picked it up to examine it, sometimes even deliberately rousing it from sleep, it would shudder and bristle, warm, powder-fragrant and feline, stretching itself full length in her arms, its pool dark eyes straining to focus, alert, suspicious and scrutinizing, a cross-hatch between released convict and dwarf-athlete required to perform great feats.

She willed Kenny to disappear, if need be, she willed him dead. Filling out his massive coffin, inert and powerless, permanently stripped of his capacity to imprison, to hamper, to abuse. It may not be necessary, she might still fight her way out of this cul-de-sac of a marriage. She may be smaller, but she was fiercer, meaner, more determined than him. If she could just manage to get herself back to home ground, where even the abandoned detritus of Walden Street took on the improbable nostalgic air of safe haven, lodged within a bedrock of soot-caked tenement walls, gaping bomb-sites and fluttering plague-pigeons. In the mind's eye, its essence flourished falsely, magnifying itself through the force and conviction of her fevered mind. Deserted homeland of the living dead it may well be, but Greta was now strong—perhaps desperate enough to infuse it with new spirit, enkindled by fear, confused desire and ennui. As for the child, it was now hers, her appendage. She had not wanted it, but there it was, living and breathing in the world. Outside of herself, yet forever part of her, a natural succession, her own ingrained evil, she well knew, transmitted through the blood like an indelible birthright, a malign bequest.

The explosives training ground was located in a ringed 'purdah,' far enough away from the main barracks, the outbuildings and the Mess. On Friday morning at 08:45 hours, a military jeep rounded up Kenny and his comrades, all briefly trained to perform routine acts of calculated barbarity. It was scaringly funny to think that they expected him to carry out this rite after only a few hours of instruction and a series of demonstrations that were less than flawless.

Like the premonition of autumn, a mud-soaked field awaited them. An open-air theatre of bleak and chilling stillness. The sun made its stark dazzling appearance, then slunk behind a mask of cloud. A keen breeze ruffled the sleeves of Kenny's combat fatigues, creating a rash of goose bumps along his upper arms. Why of all mornings did his fingers and thumbs feel slack and nerveless? They were unbearably raw, as well, and reeked of government-issue carbolic. A mess of clipped wires and coded tags slipped from his grip and snaked across the pebbly tarmac.

"Clumsy ass-hole," shouted the Ammunition Technical Officer from twenty feet away.

Kenny's eyes burned and simmered inside their sockets, his back and shoulder muscles, especially the front of his thighs ached, perhaps the ominous sign of some plaguelet, dubbed the flu; who knew whether that mediaeval pestilence known as the 'Black Death' might also have had such innocent beginnings. It cost him an unusual effort to walk, even to stand to attention, but he knew by now the futility of trying to beg off a couple of days on sick parade. You had to be literally crawling on your hands and knees before a company medic would sign you off a sick note, and even then they managed to rough you up in a series of harsh, barking interrogation sessions, designed to weed out the fakes and the faint-of-heart, and drive them back to duty.

"Quick, Howden, you're holding up the team!" shouted the ATO.

Bollocks the team—Kenny was starting to shiver, a muted febrile shiver; the heat drained from his body as though at the press of a button. His lower jaw shuddered in an uncontrollable spasm.

"Howden, get your ass over here, and *schnell!*"

"Yessir."

He moved waywardly toward the group and ranged himself between the flapping combat fatigues of his comrades. The air around them bristled with malaise, fresh male-sweat and fear. Even the poxy birds sounded hysterical, clamouring for survival, for dominance in the nearby woods.

"We're not playing games here, lads, I repeat, this is live ammunition; if you're not careful, it can blow your bloody balls off!"

Fuckin' ell, thought Kenny. He bent forward, dropped to his knees, and tried to focus his attention on the snake-tangle of wires at his feet. It was the last thing he remembered except, for some reason, in his mind's eye, came the flash-image of newborn Rafael, purblind and blood-spattered, like a live offering on the altar.

CHAPTER 25

ON LETHE'S BANK

Greta steered the pram between the jam-packed market stalls of Watney Street. On her right arm she balanced a couple of carrier bags filled with Nestle's tinned milk, mätzos crackers, eggs, potatoes, cheese, bagels, fruit, spiced sausage and a blood-stained package of mince. Along this tumultuous stretch, the air was filled with the hawking, baiting and cursing of street vendors, some with guard dogs, off Commercial Road all the way to Cable Street. A gauntlet of open shopfronts and market barrows, gutter drains and rainsoaked awnings alive with the mild breath of morning, sunbeams eroding the island damp in an infinitude of surprise.

Boat-necked summer dresses, floral sleeveless blouses and narrow-pleated skirts were out fluttering on the racks. Greta picked over the shoes and sandals, dangling from ropes or piled in cartons along the pavement. There was narrow black plastic footwear with heels of cork, brushed suede, rubber-soled canvas plimsolls and glossy patent leather; cheap, yes, but not cheap enough. Next week, perhaps, when she received her 'Assistance'—*O Christ,* she never believed she'd have to lower herself to this degree, compelled to reveal her entire life story, which was duly recorded on file with the 'authorities,' a retinue of snotty bitches and bastards working in fine Council offices, well dressed they—able to afford to buy whatever they pleased—who, somehow, managed to appoint themselves guardians of the public purse, doling out a pitiful stream of charity to resentful beggars like herself, a few quid a week just to keep her from starving, but not enough to crawl out of the shit-hole she found herself in.

Greta stepped through trails of spoiled fruit, crushed eggshells, vagrant paper bags, the spilled remnants of a fish and chip dinner in the cobblestoned gutter, attracting a constellation of ravenous inland gulls, town pigeons and dainty hopping sparrows. Once they were clear of the marketplace, the pram clattered under the railway arches then, as always, came the long trek 'home' between the immense wharf-like walls of Wapping Lane. They frightened Rafael, pressing close together, they all but shut out the light like a cliff face or sheer tower of blank brick, massive to his gaze and tiny girth, heralding the steep downward passage across the jutting swing bridge into the 'Underworld.' A predatory swoop of screeching river gulls circled and pursued them. Rafael tugged at his frayed leather harness strap, tearful and howling, battling to climb out. Greta had to stop the pram, shove her shopping bags into it and drag the kid home in her arms.

The emergency housing nearby St. Patrick's Church, granted due to her obvious plight as a single, domestically abused mother of a young child, was a forlorn looking rowhouse with a solitary front door on the shadow-side of the building and a single box-like window which attempted vainly to peer outward onto the world. Grateful though she was to find a refuge—two minimalist rooms, facing north and east, with a few oddments of abandoned furniture nested like stage props against the walls, the rounded iron bedframe and broken spring under its stuffed slab of a buttoned mattress, the yellowing muslin hanging askew across her only window, the draughty nook under the sink where she stored her milk, the grease-baked cooker with its scent of escaping gas—all this smothered and depressed her. What was worse, within a few weeks of her arrival, two elderly ladies from the Catholic Mission knocked at the door, carrying a pillowcase full of clean, although used, baby clothes and nappies and a shiny red wooden cot for eight-month-old Rafael.

The notoriety of her poverty made Greta flinch with resentment and shame. She frowned at this gormless intrusion into her admittedly slummish domain, gazed upon the gifts with the affronted air of a countess, fallen on hard times. She considered, just for a moment, emptying the pillow bag all over the dusty steps, and hurling the painted cot after them as they walked away; but she knew only too well that this was a vindictive satisfaction she couldn't afford. Her kid was desperately bursting out of his clothes, her dwindling pile of baby nappies mostly threadbare, stained and rent with holes.

"That's all right, love, we understand," whispered the taller of the pair, with a gesture of benevolent conspiracy. She resembled grandmother Mitzi in the way that all old people resemble one another, genuinely kind-looking, with frail flickering eyes, a thinning halo of wavelets, sagging cheeks crisscrossed by rose-purplish veins, a pair of ill-fitting dentures held together by a tremulous smile. "We just wanted to make sure you was all right, and the baby an' all; he's a beautiful child, isn't he, Gladys?" she said, addressing the aging clone beside her.

As Rafael struggled to leap out of her arms, Greta swayed like an over-burdened flower stem. She steadied herself against the passage wall to keep her balance and, irritated, she smacked him sharply, a little too sharply perhaps, on the rosy mottling flesh of his arm. It's always the same, she thought, total strangers accosting her on the street to fawn over her baby. It enraged, even alarmed her. Her baby, Rafael, was hers and hers alone. She abhorred this exhibitionist, this false adulation of other women's babies. The idiotic finger-poking and high-pitched clucking noises, the stream of repetitious nonsense talk invented solely for babies, for idiots rather. She did not want Rafael contaminated by it. He wasn't a child anyway; just like her he was potent, intractable and headstrong, swiftly transforming into a stoneweight of brain, flexed muscle and bone. Having somehow imbibed the military ethos of his birthplace, wasn't he already a burgeoning 'life warrior!'

He was too strong, though, too wily, mostly getting the upper hand in the battle of wills. Small though he was, he'd learned to beat his head upon the floor, certain that she would rush to pick him up before he knocked himself senseless. If he awoke, imprisoned in his cot between feeding times, he screamed as

247

though he were being murdered. The neighbours are going to think I'm doing him in, the little bastard, thought Greta, I feel like throttling him, an' all. Already crawling, he'd begun to invade her stash of books and magazines, her letters, postcards and souvenirs, her rack of mixing bowls, pots and pans, her tubes of oil paint, turpentine, charcoals and sketchpad. It was no use. She had to hide everything away until he was sleeping, moving around her darkroom of a refuge, eventually cobbling together a makeshift easel at the narrow window. Why even bother, she wondered, he'll be awake before I begin. Nevertheless, Rafael invaded her drawings as well, materializing upon her sketchpad—floating, flying, crawling—both cherub and demon; with her pencil she studied, strived to take the measure of him. Who was he? What was he going to be?

He was half Kenny's, as well, Kenny whom she had succeeded in driving away by the force of her will. She knew, without doubt, that it was *she* who was responsible for Kenny's accident and the horror of knowing made her feel guilty, and sometimes elated. She'd wished powerfully for her freedom, and here it was. Visiting him months ago in military hospital, she witnessed him stilled, immobilized, obviously in great pain, the right side of his face and both hands burnt, his eyes bandaged. *We are trying hard to save the left eye*, said the military surgeon, gazing upon her with a serious, perhaps even an accusing air; meanwhile she, clutching their infant Rafael, wondered whether to confess her guilt or dissemble the grieving young wife. Kenny flinched at the sound of her voice, the trembling pressure of her cold fingers on his arm.

"Where's the baby? When I get out of here, I'm taking him home with me."

She didn't answer.

"Don't pretend, I know you don't want him," he'd said.

Now, back in East London, Greta requested to be housed as far away as possible from Kenny and his kith and kin. She fled to the unfamiliar territory of Wapping, a moated enclave of brick tenements, canals and hump bridges where the dockers, the Irish 'wharf rats,' and their families lived. It was a peculiar confluence of Catholicism staunchly bonded in poverty, proliferating church missions and an even greater number of brothels, Chinese coastal migrants and Lascars, opium caves and dockside liquor vaults erected from damp black stone. Due north east, as the crow flies, was the origin of it all, at least for her, the celebrated Sailor's Palace or seaman's refuge at Limehouse where Taddeusz had disembarked briefly on his life's journey from Lord knows where, stopping just long enough to spawn then project her, defenseless, into the world. As she had unwillingly done to Rafael. It was no comfort to contemplate her own complicity with his, or another's evil design.

For the child was evil, or destined to be evil. How could it be otherwise? Directly sharing the gene-line, hers and that of Taddeusz, his legacy was guaranteed. Perhaps that was why she sometimes felt such a hatred for him; her 'de facto' dictator, his screams determined her waking and sleeping hours. His demands to be washed, clothed and fed persisted through the day and often into the night as well. Like her, he enjoyed a perverse wakefulness during moonlit hours. Perhaps he feared the remote corners of the ceilings, shrunken and flushed with dusk, the diurnal round of seemingly endless night. As the surrounding dockside streets settled into their darkness of dream, Rafael awoke to a malaise of quiet. Petulant, kicking off his blankets, restlessly knocking a crib toy to the ground, giving forth a rattling wail, then a piercing cry of distress from the bowels of his solitude.

The transparent ceiling bulb with its thin yellowish glare was unbearable, anyway. Greta preferred to sit cross-legged on the mattress beneath her only window, a kind of blurry moonlit crevasse, while she read by torchlight anything she could borrow from the library, Victorian novels, fables and legends, historic records of mediaeval witchcraft, anything to release her from this life sentence, to stave off the boredom, the slow-motion isolation and inward-drawing silence that gradually sapped even the power of speech, the prolonged uneventfulness of the present tense.

This was disturbed one morning, though, by the abrupt brassy clang of the doorknocker. Who was it, not those two creeping Charities, again! Well, she wouldn't answer; let them mind their business and steer well away from her from now on. Yet her heart thumped powerfully as if an armed enemy were standing outside. She hesitated, clinging on to Rafael, and even the brief interval she waited seemed portentous, sinister. Transfixed and alert, like an embalmed human sculpture from Pompeii, she stood there, hardly breathing, her bedjacket wrapped around her body, her shoulders cramped, her head slightly upturned, her eyes glittering with suspicion, curiosity and fear. In the tension of that silence, she sensed the presence of a shadow—no, twin shadows—standing in judgement on the other side of the door.

Could it be that someone already knew about Rafael, that he was evil? Were they going to try to take him away? Certainly she mustn't open the door, she needn't open the door, yet the stark panic she felt was unaccountable, illogical, idiotic, weak, characteristic of Lily, she told herself later yet, at that moment, the arrogant intrusion had terrified her.

Whoever they were, there were two of them; of that she felt certain. Perhaps they were watching the house, her temporary refuge. Perhaps they already knew of her comings and goings with Rafael to Watney Market, to the medical clinic, to the library, to Shadwell Park. Trundling under the blackened brick railway arches, with the wheels of her tin pram bouncing in the ruts and crevasses of the pavement, Greta tried to shield her kid with the defensive shade of her own slight body. When strangers wandered near, eyeing her and her infant son with idle or benevolent curiosity, she retreated a safe distance away to the railed embankment overlooking the indolent waters of Shadwell Basin. Here she stood for a time, breathing in the sodden wind, holding Rafael high enough so that he could look down onto the river, but not high enough for the evil little bastard to be able to pitch himself in. The River Thames, *La Tameez,* as they pronounced it in France, flowing sluggish, the colour of mud, alongside the rust-eaten shell-shocked margin of Wapping Docks. Alive and afloat with refuse tossed in by marauding kids: stolen cigarette packages, paper boats, half drowned matchboxes, drunken bottles, splinters of wood and cork, the myriad flotsam clogging the veins of this great, wounded city.

And then again, perhaps it was Kenny who pursued her, or Kenny's mother, that towering rasp of a woman who happened to be Rafael's natural grandmother. Grimheart o' Gold they called her, didn't they? Would she have the *chutzpah* to try to reclaim her grandchild? To wreak vengeance on Greta for the damage inflicted on her son. An eye for an eye—just let her bloody well try! It wouldn't be too long, though, before she tracked Greta down, if that was her intent. For East is East, and the illusion of Wapping's remoteness was simply that, an illusion. She was certain to bump into Annie Howden one day along the sunstreaked littered pavements of Watney Market. It was, she knew, just a matter of time.

And so, despite her vaunted bravado, rehearsed arguments and defiant rhetoric, (even while castigating herself for her own cowardice) Greta began to avoid Watney Street except very early in the morning before Annie could be expected to be out and about. Often she shopped on Sundays in Hessel Street, the Jewish quarter, where she felt safer. Wasn't there some rumour that they were Jewish, anyway, that Taddeusz owed his genesis to that fabled, that tragic race? If so, she ought to feel at home among the stalls overladen with packaged mätzoth, tubs of olives, smoked salmon, pickles and cream cheese, cooked sweets, blintzes, gefilte fish, chopped liver and giblets—*bollocks*—was this to be her life from now on? Was she going to remain both fugitive and prisoner? Padlocked night and day to this kid who might nevertheless be stolen from her if ever she ceased her vigil, if ever for one moment she lowered her guard?

CHAPTER 26

SEA CHANGE

The letter from the housing agency said that permanent accommodation was now available. Greta was advised to view the flat and respond within two weeks of receipt of the notice. Her case had been granted priority but, in view of the number of applicants on the waiting list, this offer would not normally be extended beyond fourteen days.

Ryeworth House was a relatively new Council-owned dwelling in the centre of Wapping. It was faced in clean sand-coloured brick, solidly built around a paved courtyard and rising three storeys beneath a sloping red tiled roof. In this communal courtyard, milk-skinned wire-thin children played at Tag or Blindman's Buff or sat around in little clutches, arranging cards or rolling exquisite glass marbles across the cement paving. Greta followed the caretaker's wife upstairs, pausing behind her at each landing as the woman stopped to catch her breath, a soft pneumatic wheeze. Angina, she whispered to Greta, she shouldn't be having to mount these stairs so often, but what can you do? Her moist, pale green eyes appeared half-blind as she peered, painfully, it would seem, through the raw purplish slits of her eyelids. Yet she missed nothing, absorbing in just a few moments the sight of this thin—a little too thin—young single mother wearing scuffed black shoes with one broken strap held together by a safety pin, a narrow black skirt and fleecy grey jacket, much washed and much worn. Her pram was folded under one arm, while perched on the other, practically splitting the seams of his dungarees, was her baby, a boy not much older than a year. He had an unusual miniature widow's peak of stiff black hair and rough crimson patches on his cheek, dribbling, obviously teething, he was straining to be put down.

"On your own, are you, your husband not with you no more?" said the caretaker's wife, with a tender conspiratorial glance of understanding.

"I just came over 'ere to see the flat—" *Mind your own bleedin' business,* was what she thought.

When they reached the second storey, they had to fend their way past a line of domestic laundry, so Greta put Rafael back into his pram and pushed it along the exterior passageway to the front door. This flat was somewhat bigger than her present quarters, with even an extra room for the kid. It contained a few relics of furniture, abandoned seemingly in haste, and it breathed the atmospheric emptiness of a space fallen abruptly silent, its myriad sounds, curses, laughter, arguments and screams having died away. The Council must have arranged for the premises to be cleaned after the departure of its latest occupants, for it smelled of carbolic and freshly thrown sawdust—*what for, to soak up spilt blood?*

That's your wild bloody imagination again, just stop it—! she told herself. "So who was it that was living here before, then?"

"It was a couple—well, they was not married, not really, they just moved in together. Caused a lot of disturbance, they did. I wasn't surprised when it happened."

"When what happened?"

"Never mind, love, I shouldn't be gossiping; these walls have ears."

Mean ugly cow, thought Greta, fingering her own wedding ring, which she wore out of convenience and to muzzle idle talk. 'My husband's in the Forces,' she sometimes told strangers, 'he's a traveling soldier, *(this was a private joke of hers, eliciting an enigmatic grin)* only I came home on my own because I didn't want to live overseas no more.'

Yet this Council flat was hers for the asking; it was her first real flat to invade and settle, to adorn and possess. It was hers to share with no one except, of course, the kid—Rafael, whose eyes

254

at birth seemed as large as saucers, proportionately smaller now that the rest of his body had evolved its balancing act of brain, torso and limb. It was a solo feat which Nature seemed able to perform blindfolded, for Rafael continued to sprout like a malignant seed, all bristles and burrs, rough-skinned, prone to allergic flashes and flares, his long heavy bones encased in a powerful torque of joint, muscle and tendon. Irritable in his frayed loincloth of piddle, he had trained himself to the chamber pot early, having taken his own guardianship resolutely in hand. Trailing behind Greta, he was now a robust walker who no longer swayed and gripped his way between the distant stick furniture of their living-room. Warily, quizzically, he observed her inspired fits of scrubbing and tidying, her restless ordering and reordering of their dwelling in this elevated riverside kingdom of Wapping.

And it was true that she kept it defiantly spotless at first, but then the static days of irredeemable sameness, the present boredom of time and place gradually leached her of energy and will. Her sense of novelty yielded to discontent, to the lounging beast of apathy. This shelter-prison, with its dual energies reversed, became an antagonist with which to grapple. It assumed a force of identity in which she lost hers; her all-too-familiar surroundings degenerated in tandem with her mood.

Neglected for days on end, the slow-leaking base of the toilet bowl grew permanent spores of mould; the washbasin and bathtub sank beneath a patina of grime. Rafael's cradle room was shaded, cluttered, and reeked of baby sick and piss. Windowless and dark, the galley kitchen concealed a further multitude of sins. Dust clung to the ivory-painted mantelpiece. It cleaved to her fossil starfish that had traveled all the way from Margate, to her bereft and denuded cockleshells and smooth iridescent pebbles, to the huge, almost perfect split-shell mother of pearl. The stiff linen sails and copper mast of a miniature 'Cutty Sark' lay imprisoned, without even a breath-wind, in a begrimed, cloudy bottle; the hemp-smelling fishnet, pregnant with grime, languished upon the wall. Meanwhile, Rafael claimed as his own the square fringe of rug, encircled by a fountain of toys, toys that leaked and traveled through every room. Wherever Greta stepped, she trod on his painted wooden blocks, rubber mallets, bath toys or old plastic rattles; throughout the day, every day, she stumbled upon them and swore.

There was a morbidity in the walls, as well, she could feel it. It wasn't due to a trick of shadow or the pall of night; even in broad daylight these walls and ceilings harboured—*something*. Although the shade-curtains of her bedroom hung as still as ropes—she refused to open those windows—whenever she walked in there she picked up a sort of febrile shiver, an almost audible humming. Coming from where? Sometimes from behind the ornate swing-mirror of her dressing table—*an indulgence of second-hand Victoriana she'd not truly been able to afford*—or else sometimes from directly above her bed. Was it in her head? Once Rafael was asleep, she drove herself through the yawning hours, pacing the flat like a besieged commander, plotting her deliverance, furiously thinking and dreaming, reading and scribbling, fending off that moment when her eyes closed of their own accord and her brain cut out, like a battery gone dead.

Early on, she was accosted in the passageway by a kid from the downstairs flat named Genevieve. "Ain't you scared livin' in that flat?" the girl asked. She had a freckly milk-white face and glow-in-the-dark hair, all twisted bronze and orangy gold. Genevieve paused, breathless, her bulging cheeks and mauve-stained lips clamped firmly around a 'gobstopper.' Whirring her skipping-rope in orbit around her like a humming bird, she resembled a flyaway Celtic princess with scabs on her knees.

"Why scared?" said Greta, with a hostile glare. *Get out of my way,* she thought. She detested kids of that age; she hated their arrogance, their oblivious capacity for making noise, their frank nosiness. Long-boned, loose-haired and leaping toward pubescence, this girl gazed at Greta in an inquisitive adoring way—*Anyone would think I was a visiting celebrity, for God's sake*—as if tempted to touch Greta's sleeve or the hem of her skirt, to reassure herself she was real.

"Well, 'cos that horrible bloke who used to live up there, he got done in; my mum read about it in the newspaper."

Greta pushed by her without answering. She shivered inwardly, yielding to a sudden fearful and malignant pleasure, her hunger for high-flown drama. Proof, yet again, that she was a magnet for evil, attracting it naturally as a root divines water. Just my bleedin' luck, she thought, of all the poxy Council flats in Wapping, I get the one that needs an exorcism. So it was a *man* who got done in this time, that makes a bleedin' change, don't it?

Of course, the *News of the World* kept up its hounding commentary on the tragedy, serving up spine-chilling details and prurient glimpses into the lives of the ill-starred couple. A man by the name of Ferguson, a docker, a tough and a braggart, fatally stabbed by his co-habiting partner, Aline. In self-defense, she pleaded, breaking down under the glare of the photographer's bulb, the trauma of fingerprinting, the days spent in police custody following formal charges whilst awaiting trial. Greta began to pore over the news reports with a mingling of fascination and revulsion. This seemingly uneventful backwater cave of hers was the very spot in which the incident had happened—well, not quite, the victim had expired in the ambulance—but how ironic to discover, through some neighbour's bratty kid, the macabre history of her borrowed dwelling place. Now, at least, she had a corporeal face to link to her haunting.

"You're dead, you bastard, and you deserved it, now fuck off out of here!" she said to the glimmering, humming space above her bed.

Still, there were moments when she trembled at the thought of sharing her bedroom with a visiting corpse. Don't be stupid, she told herself, what can it do to you? Followed by the thought, but what about Rafael? And then—who knows why?—came the thought of Rudi, his face a watermark, his spirit-essence rematerializing in a bittersweet gust of memory, the sensation of his absent presence falling swiftly away again, like disintegrating fragments of paper. What was it that he once said? Something that read like a verse from a holy book: *All mothers, all mothers-to-be are revered in my country.* Yet it was so long since she'd heard anything from him, his last postcard having reached her before she left Germany. Since then, their respective worlds had twisted themselves inside out, flinging them apart with no stronger bond than the uncanny force of recollection, regret and sentimental desire.

But Rudi was gone; he would never come back. How could he find her again, even if he tried, on this dark pinprick of the globe—despite the peripheral crash-and-tumble of the docks—a remote narrow inlet resembling Lethe's Wharf? Here her days and nights poured into one another, twinning vessels of light and dark, a stream of calendar days and hours that beat slowly, anonymously, like rain on the roof. Only Rafael existed to hoist her mind and body back into the present tense; she awoke abruptly like a resuscitated corpse, whether morning or evening, sometimes she could hardly tell them apart. A surreal white light flooded the windowpanes, piercing her charmed spiral of sleep and waking. Although she strived to move, she felt rooted to the spot. Yet her hearing was sharp, she could see through walls; she knew that Rafael was feverish hot, wailing passionately and rocking the rungs of his crib. Why couldn't she go to him? Was she still locked into her dream? Meanwhile, they were all there, a rogue's gallery wandering through this hollow space—there was Ferguson, Taddeusz, Luc de Peyrac. They traversed the neglected fireplace, the crumb-strewn mat, the stiff wooden swing-mirror of her dressing table, vanishing, then reappearing. Taddeusz stared at her solemnly, surveyed the lamentable débris that was her dwelling; his gaze sufficient—trollop, slut, fishmonger—it said.

Who invited you in here? This is my flat, get out, get out!

Wrenching herself free from this mind-dark pool, she chased them all down and they vanished, only to hide—Luc, grinning at her from the lid of Rafael's toybox, Taddeusz, behind the hinged door of the airing cupboard, Ferguson, the filthy brute, armed with a blade, sliding unnoticed into her bed. And all these noises inside her head, the grinding, the shrieking! She felt unsteady, falling, falling endlessly into nowhere. Even the ground was gone—there was nowhere to put her feet—nothing but a stream of malignant images, searing, bleeding through her mind. She felt giddy and sick. Meanwhile Rafael continued to cry for what seemed like hours, his screams pouring through her dreams. What was wrong with the kid, why wasn't he sleeping? What time was it? Now that—*Oh, God, finally*—the intruders were gone, this space was a battleground littered with corpses. The brief respite was only a silence-in-waiting. Gone was the preternatural light, the intensely white flooding of glass; Greta parted the rope-like drapes onto a moonless world outside, disconnected, morose and sunken, a drowned Atlantis of the night.

CHAPTER 27

WITNESS

Genevieve, pronounced *Geneveeve* around these parts, the mouthy one with the freckly milk-skin and glow-orange hair, often came crawling around the second storey landing, usually disappearing through someone's front door. I suppose that's her family, thought Greta; she herself hadn't yet made the acquaintance of anyone in the building. She resisted socializing with the neighbourly commune of Ryeworth House, for that—she well knew—was when all the bother started. Virtual strangers rattling at your door, day in, day out, poking their way into your kitchen to beguile their loneliness and boredom, extorting endless cups of strong sweet tea and biscuits, and feasting on the latest gossip.

"Are you getting on all right, luv?" asked her next-door neighbour, Nell. "The baby was crying a lot last night, weren't he? Is he teething again, poor little tyke?"

Nell and her granddaughter, Genevieve, stood close together on the balcony passage, two doors down. Nell's grey-white hair was scrolled tightly around wire-bristle curlers under a flounced headcap. Pastoral looking, she was swaddled in her housewifely garb, a trunk-shaped frock the colour of wrinkled cream bespattered with roses, a pair of beaten-down house slippers, a wide-bellied apron, shiny with flour and pork drippings. From her dwelling issued the airborne scents of potatoes and greens, 'Yorkies' and loin roast, the simmering hubbub of 'kinder' voices. She hovered, looking directly across at Greta, for all the world resembling the archetypal mother of poverty, self-assured in her shabbiness, deep-wrinkled and unhealthily pale, a reeking aureole of fag-smoke, soapflakes and passive benevolence. Young Genevieve skittered about, tugging at Nell's flabby arms like a possessive genie, a clingfilm of shadow. Unexpectedly, her guard lowered for just a moment, Greta felt a pang of—what was it? Nostalgia, desolation, regret?

"Later on, when this noisy lot's all gone home, come and eat a bit of dinner with me, I'll keep a plate warm in the oven for you," said Nell.

I wouldn't be caught dead eating off one of your plates, thought Greta, retreating to her cloistered domain without a word, let alone a smile. But the promised hot plate arrived shortly thereafter via Genevieve; there was also a dish of red currants and custard for Rafael tucked flat inside a brown paper bag. A traditional Sunday dinner. Soft watery brussel sprouts, lard-baked potatoes, Yorkshire pudding and crackling pork roast under a leaking canopy of pale onion rings and brown gravy. Still, it smelled appetizing and Greta, gazing at it suspiciously, couldn't remember when she had last sat down to such a feast. But all too soon, she regretted her famishing gluttony; this food offering must surely be a bribe, the first stone dislodged from her siege castle. From now on, she might be beholden to Nell, Nelly, or whatever her name was, having traded her anonymity and stone-walled independence for a seductive 'mess of pottage.'

Shamed and resentful, she avoided being seen at all the next day; but then, early Tuesday morning, came the first post. An official letter, despite its fusty cheap brown envelope, from the Borough Council. Specifically, from the Social Services Department. Greta's fingers trembled—*What's the matter with you, it's only a bleedin' letter!* But she guessed, she'd been expecting it all along, this polite advice from her social worker, Mrs. *High-and-Mighty* Mildred Margolis; her ex-spouse, Mr. Kenneth Howden, had requested to see his son.

And surprisingly, she wouldn't have believed it herself, a few hours later she was sitting face to face with her neighbour, uncorking her anger and her angst, surrounded by the domestic claptrap of Nell's kitchen table.

"What d'you think of that, she wants to come over here and talk to me about it!" cried Greta, and Nell gazed back at her, a pale, engraven, flesh-mound of sympathy, trying vainly to restrain her drifting fag-smoke so as not to clog little Rafael's lungs, and sounding the occasional *Oh!* and *How can they do that to you!* and *Ain't it wicked?*

Born on the cusp of the centuries, Nell had traveled through almost six decades of irony and sorrow. Abutted by her six grown-up children (three others had died in infancy) and their mushrooming descendants, she had sampled much of what this life had to offer—bomb-damage and motherhood, hunger and homelessness, the imprisoning security of a rent-controlled Council house shelter. Mind-rooted to her own time and place, Nell gazed down from the living crown of her familial tree, placid and fatalistic, observing the many thrusting or sinuous branches to which she had given life, their eager sprouting buds, their occasional leaves pitted and scarred with rot. Predictably, she tended her ailing husband, nourished the spirits of her ever-pregnant daughters and stuffed care-packages for young Danny, her delinquent grandson, walled up for the moment at Wormwood Scrubs. Wild young 'Dannyo' had survived a fall from the second floor balcony when he was five. He had suckled paraffin from a tin drum under the sink at the age of two. During his teens, he set fire to the net curtains of their Council flat with a handful of Swan Vesta matches. As long as he was being forcibly contained for his own protection, his family shamed and sorrowed on his behalf, breathing a momentary sigh of relief until he was released back into their world again.

"Poor little Dannyo," said Nell, with a throaty, almost soundless laugh that had the quality of a dirge. Of necessity she had attained that pinnacle of familial devotion, tempered by detachment, without which no human creature could survive its life sentence on this earth. She fashioned her little day-to-day supports, mind-forged and time-weathered, fostering her modest pleasures here and there, a small glass of port on Sundays, sometimes even on Mondays, her twist-wrapped

263

caramel sweets, her faithful packet of Woodbine fags; somehow they helped her plough through the hours, drag herself over the intractable humps of time. Nell fished into the glazed drinks cupboard and replaced the dregs of their lukewarm tea with two diamond-cut glasses of gilded Irish brandy. "That's the only good glasses I've got left from my wedding anniversary," she said, "would you believe, the rest all got smashed by the kids, *my life!*" She then hoisted herself to the kitchen counter and, with the reluctant air of the hired help anticipating the master's early return, began soaking potatoes, breading veal cutlets and opening tins of mint-flavoured peas.

Greta was stirred with envy again. With my luck, I had to get Lily for a mother, indolent, self-pitying, good-for-nothing, bomb-damaged Lily, that's who I had to get. As for Taddeusz, rooted to his own endemic rootlessness, all he had engendered—carelessly—was a lineage of deprivation, crossed by the occasional token of largesse. She felt petulant, irrationally possessive and sour. It wasn't long before Nell's layered brood started traipsing through the dwelling, dragging with them their satchels and oily bikes, their clattering tricycles and prams. The place filled up with yelping grandkids, just released from school, followed by a clutch of worldly-wise teenagers, all pimples, body hair, earrings and tattoos. Greta couldn't face it. She mumbled her good-byes, collected little Rafael from under the kitchen table and fled.

"Why do I have to let him see Rafael?" she demanded a few days later, when her social worker, Mildred Margolis, a brash flame-headed hatchet-face, paid a special visit to see her. "I told you he used to beat me up, he's violent and he's treacherous, I don't want him coming anywhere near my kid."

"I'm sorry, but that's not for you to decide, Greta," replied Mrs. Margolis. A defensive flush stained her excessively white cheeks; she seemed mildly perturbed, yet essentially unmoved. "As it stands, the law is the law; Mr. Howden is Rafael's father and he is entitled to see his son."

"So what am I supposed to do?" said Greta, taking refuge at Nell's again, the next day. "That bitch, Margolis, as long as she's getting her wages from the Council, what does she care if Kenny comes down here, *all legal like*, and starts bashing me around; he's got a right to see his kid!"

"Don't you worry, darlin', I'm just down the landing, and these feckin' walls are made of rice paper; if anything happens, just give me a holler and I'll send my Bernie over there to sort him out."

Bernie, her invalid spouse, her worse-half, rendered useless and breathless by heart-lung disease! *Fat chance,* thought Greta, although the thought comforted her. So, oddly enough, did the accoutrements of settled domesticity all around her. Nell's framed wedding photos on the oaken sideboard—*exhibit-A*—proof of the original hope and beauty of her face, once fresh, firm and heart-shaped, now little more than flab and wastage, witness to her turbulent steerage on the prison ship of Time.

Greta felt flattered to receive Nell's confidences, although uncomfortably obligated by her trust. If life could be divined in one's palm, the significant breakdown in Nell's middle, her mediaeval years, would have been marked by a lined schism from ring-finger to wrist. After a succession of live births and two stillborn (another infant was born without a 'back passage' and lived only a few hours) the children sprouted like mushrooms all around her. With them they brought confusion and conflict, the familial crash and clatter that drugged her days—*for years I went around with cotton wool in my ears*—until the moment when Nell roused herself from her inertia, surveyed the tumultuous débris of her existence, and left.

"I was motherless myself, brought up in a children's home," said Nell, "my own mother, God bless and rest her soul, was widowed young with five children, how could she have coped?"

Bernie, of the legendary Irish temper, (who during his married life restrained neither fist nor tongue) roared and blasphemed, learned how to work the old wringer-washer, opened tins of corned beef, chopped slab loaves into sandwiches for the kids and wept. It was rightly called abandonment, the youngest being only two years old. Nell disappeared for more than six months and, to this day, declined to say where she had gone. She had a dark seaman friend, a Lascar, who offered to put her up for a time in his rusting houseboat on the canal. Along the docks was a profusion of taverns, brothels and rooming-houses which traded bed and board for service. Months went by. Nell seemed to have no intention of going back, but eventually the older kids found her. One after the other, they showed up like homing pigeons, navigating back to their source; and it must be said, it was the Church—Nell was currently a lapsed Witness—that salvaged her in those years, her restoration years. Jehovah's Witness ministering Elders, recruiting the faith-less and the hope-less in their midst, helped her to stop smoking and drinking. They steered her back to her senses, and her duties. Nevertheless, she'd forever be a hybrid Catholic with a touch of the wild Irish, retaining both her pagan and whore-of-Babylon ways, stubbornly celebrating Xmas and birthdays in defiance of Kingdom Hall, crossing her forehead with holy water, surreptitiously sprinkling it on her breasts, between her legs, and on the outside doormat.

"I'm trying to get back into the Church," said Nell, "but first I've got to give up my fags."

Greta was there one day when two Elders of the Witness Church came to visit. A pair of darklings, they stood at the door, steadfast and deferential, wrapped in their placid aura of millenarian gloom. Mildly flustered, Nell welcomed them inside. It was rare to receive a visit from the senior chieftain Johannes—*just call me John*—Erskine, shadowed by his obsequious callow-looking disciple, Simon Freed. John smiled obscurely, a gesture of reassurance to his confrère-in-training, who dragged around their treasured briefcase of Bibles, leaflets and printed tracts. Greta glared at them both, particularly John Erskine, feeling both piqued and combative. Just who did they

266

think they were, these well-coiffed shining prats, these bleedin' self-styled archangels who, without warning or permission, came breaking into their shared confidences, descending on Nell in the rank poverty of her domesticity—Nell, who was, by the way, dressed in her absolute shabbiest, all were aware of that.

Erskine addressed Nell with the elaborate concern he might show to a dying child. He inquired about her health, questioned her about her present circumstances, then invited her to rejoin their Bible study class, bringing along her friend, if she wished. That was when he glanced at Greta, smiling mildly, well-practised in deflecting what he usually encountered—at best, someone's baffled expression of amused contempt—with a refractory gleam of serene unconcern; she noted his slight immigrant clip, the tongue that lingered as it pronounced the ends of words, like an after-taste of Italian, perhaps transplanted Slav—*Although some may not believe, we are simply doing our duty, as required by Jehovah, we are spreading His Word throughout the world,* was what he said.

Greta was still a young girl. The excesses of motherhood had hardly touched her. She was beautiful, she knew it, she was unique, a gypsy and an artist, the embodiment of Aunt Ruth's beauty, Taddeusz's brain and also his cruelty, their mystic offspring, the daughter they were destined never to have. John Erskine, too, despite his cloak of unruffled spirituality, may have been struck and aroused by it. Or was she imagining this? She saw his defenses raised then, reluctantly, lowered again. In his covert glance was a spark of curiosity, or was it half-smothered lust? Perhaps he was intrigued by her intense dark looks, somehow resonant, somehow familiar, her moth-like waist and fulsome breasts, so unlike the chaste button-breasts and ample life-giving hips beloved of the Renaissance Masters.

I can get something out of him, thought Greta, *maybe he can at least tell me where to start to look.*

"Certainly, we might be able to locate your Witness friend, Rudi," replied Erskine. "We could try the overseas register, or the branch office in Madrid." He stood up, looking mildly triumphant, pressing Greta's hand with a fierce, unexpected softness and warmth. Simon, too, closed his briefcase and resurrected himself to his feet. He handed them each the latest copy of *The Watchtower,* all freshly printed and glowing with hope and colour. "We'll be in touch again then," said Erskine, gazing significantly at Greta, and only at Greta, "I promise I will do my best."

CHAPTER 28

Apocalypse-in-waiting

Greta was mildly surprised to recognize a number of these millenarian church worshipers. She knew them from her occasional trips to Watney Market and back. Like most, they did not identify themselves by symbol or icon stitched to the breast, a rose, a fleur-de-lis, a golden orb or purple star. Instead they massed themselves silently and anonymously into Kingdom Hall, taking up their customary seats, not pews, like a scattered family returning gratefully to the meal table. Their pastor, Johannes Erskine, caught Greta's eye the moment she entered. To her soul-imagination, his mere presence permeated the hall with an abstract light of somber ethereal force. But then, she glanced covertly around for Mrs. Johannes Erskine; where was she? Most Witness families seemed to arrive intact, propped up by their many children, some fretful and whining whilst parents attempted to settle into their seats, juggling a heap of prayer books, hymnals and tracts. Yet there seemed to be no miniature Erskines gamboling about or agitating on the plain wooden seats nearby. *Curiouser and curiouser,* thought Greta, and smiled.

Nell stood beside her, appearing a little self-conscious but grateful to be back in the fold. Quite a number of her Witness friends came over to grip her by the hand in soulful welcome. Greta, too, was greeted as a daughter of the house, this house of communal worship, a reclaimed, refurbished former dockside warehouse with an exterior façade of white-washed cement. KINGDOM HALL was spelled in ornate gold-lettering above the lintel of its double front doors. Subtly painted on the inside, waxed, furnished and lamp-lit, it rattled and sighed, echoed and sang with the scraping of chairs, murmurs and whispers, rumbling coughs, erratic shrieks and blubbering sounds of infants and babes-in-arms.

Erskine stepped to the raised dais, which was ornamented with lily-blossoms and candles in glimmering brass. His corpus, of heavy powerful stock from an ancestral bloodline of Polish forefathers, was thick with muscle and flesh. That glossy ash-pale face of his, which tanned deeply no doubt in summer, was truncated by a pinched and wizened chin. Surveying what might be called his flock, Erskine's gaze traveled pensively from head to head, pausing a fraction longer, or so it seemed, at the sight of Greta, dark, smooth-skinned and Madonna-like, with Rafael planted heavily on her knee. Greta noticed—*at least so she believed*—that his gaze returned to her more and more frequently throughout this hour of Sunday worship. To her it was little more than a universal glossolalia of abstractions, private codes and axioms commonly shared, especially that 'fairy tale' of imminent apocalyptic redemption, the expropriation of Evil by a divine army of occupation, the promise of a renewed City of God—*in our lifetime*—upon this earth.

How can they just sit there and listen to that poxy pious drivel, how the hell can they believe one effing word he says?

With an obscure glance cast in her direction, Erskine spoke somberly of some unknown former member, disfellowshipped for 'independent thought,' at variance with the teachings of their Church, a danger to be shunned for mankind errs gravely when it rejects the Scriptures, exalts itself, and apes God. Another of his unfathomable glances, and Greta knew the remark was intended for her.

"Peace be with you; let us all pray that these errant souls may be reclaimed." At his signal the entire congregation, Elders, parents, infants and children, all rose up with the clatter and crash of an army called into battle. Erskine, serene and towering above them all, remained the human magnet drawing them into one bonding force, forging their disparate egos into a single power that flowed backward to its source, rendering *him* recharged and buoyant, he, Jehovah's organizing principle, firing their universal will toward salvation.

A few days later, Johannes Erskine appeared at Greta's door. He happened to be passing by after work, he said, his day job being foreman-bookkeeper for a large warehousing concern on the wharf. Fellow Witness, Simon Freed, was not present; therefore, he hung on the threshold, not entering. The international Church Office had found no record of her friend Rudi, despite their best attempts; he just wanted her to know he had not forgotten about her, and her request. Was she interested, meanwhile, in knowing more about the faith of Jehovah's Witness, would she like him—and Simon, too, of course—to pay her a visit one evening, just to talk?

Not really, thought Greta, unable to disguise the trace of a sneer. Erskine drew back slightly, accustomed, through years of practice, in dealing with this typical derision of the public response. He did not smile. Instead, it was a gesture of mild resignation and detachment; his gaze of somber grey light flickered and blazed, reflectively, as if he had encountered such disdain a thousand and one times and shored up sufficient arsenal to counter it. His mind a fortress, stalwart and sure, he turned away and departed, the potent shade of his wide shoulders further darkening the street. It was then that Greta sensed an unexpected pang, a feeling of sharp pathos which she stifled at once—it being far too Lily-like—it felt almost as though Rudi himself had returned and she'd repudiated him.

Erskine was gone, and immediately afterward she regretted his leave-taking. Should she have said yes? Would he even bother calling on her again? In retrospect, he seemed indifferent to her, to her '*yes*' or to her '*no*.' Why should he care, after all? He had his work, his life's mission, his personal acolytes and church family of souls. Did he have a wife and children too? The thought intrigued and disturbed her unreasonably.

"What's the matter with you, bleedin' silly fool?"—for no reason, Greta paced back into her bedroom and languished for a time like a fretful glittering creature of shadow, a dark Narcissus in her Victorian cheval glass.

"How old do you think he is, is he married?" she said to Nell next day, trying to assume an air of disinterested curiosity. Nell seemed unsurprised by the question.

"He used to be, but his wife ran away and left him; she went back to Poland, I think it was, took the kid with her, a little girl of about two or three. Poor woman, I felt sorry for her, she was so far away from her own kith and kin, and *he* can't be easy to live with, I shouldn't imagine. She couldn't stand it here, she just weren't the type that grafts easily. I remember when it happened, it caused quite a commotion in the Church at the time."

"Did it?" said Greta lightly, flippantly.

"If you want to, come to Church with me again next time; none of my lot are interested and I don't really want to go on me'own."

At Kingdom Hall on Sunday, Erskine made no attempt to speak to Greta. She appeared to be a closed and defunct file, a settled question. If he was surprised or even mildly pleased to see her ensconced on the bench next to Nell, he gave no sign; on the contrary, flanked by his fellow Elders, he held himself aloof with a seemingly cool determination that dismayed and disappointed her. Greta sat tensely in her seat, paying strict attention to the homily. What gibberish they were all talking and praying. She felt a distinct embarrassment, a revulsion, hearing and even uttering the word Jehovah, it sounded too devout, poetic, Old-Testament-like, primitive and fey. And to think that Rudi set his transcendent faith in this elevated hodge-podge of invention and myth, that his entire family were made to sacrifice their lives for it! Not that this earthly life was the great bleedin' gift so many people made it out to be. She personally could have done without it—would have preferred to have done without it—had Taddeusz, fired by Olympian lust, not chosen a frail mortal named Lily by which to beget her. *God damn him eternally for that!*

Meanwhile, like an axe tooling itself on God's whetstone, with repeated strokes Erskine became more empowered, more

272

precise. With energy and unmistakable fervour he irradiated his spirit flock, simultaneously drawing on their latent energies for his own storehouse of power. Toward the close of the service, true to his own preachings, he shifted himself out of the limelight, inviting members of the Church to come forward and bear testimony to Jehovah's Truth. Here again was something Greta had never witnessed before, people standing up one by one, sharing their confidences and their doubts, asking others for help to buttress and support their wayward faith. Once started, it seemed to go on forever, fraught by obscure questions of doctrine, public self-castigations and examinations of conscience. She fidgeted and flushed, shifted rebellious Rafael from lap to shoulder, then handed him over, squirming, to Nell who opened wide her arms, the embodiment of sacrificial motherhood and passive contentment. Glancing toward Erskine again, Greta felt a sense of breath-catching trepidation that alarmed her. What was it about this man? And he was *just a man* after all, although raised up for the moment, transiently magnified by the potency of this hundred-strong congregation.

Well then, why this paining sense of regret?

She knew she had once detected the smothered gleam of covetousness in his gaze. Or had she? At this moment all she witnessed was his detachment, his cautionary and well-oiled stance of neutrality. Had she offended him? Probably, almost certainly. She knew that her looks were by nature sullen, sneering, even in repose. She couldn't help that, she thought defiantly; neither could she reverse the contempt she felt for the world, that splintered and stung out of her eyes. At the close of the service, as church members were shuffling their way out through the main doors, Erskine came directly toward her, flushed and heavy with the stillness of power. He nodded affably to Nell, then took Greta's hand in an emphatic gesture of greeting; he looked at her in a mild and questioning way, then placed some pamphlets into her hands.

"Greta, I'm very glad you came," he said.

Next day, of course, Rafael ripped the pages to ribbons. Greta swore as she sellotaped them back together. If anyone, if Erskine should ask, she wanted to be able to say that she'd read the literature, but could make neither head nor tail of it. By nature she was disinclined to religion anyway, whether from almighty Rome or any of its baroque and far-flung satellites. Did it mean that there was something essentially wrong with her head, or with her heart that she should feel this way? All she remembered was the brief touch of Erskine's fingers, electric and warm; she kept these pages intact solely because his hand had first touched and offered them, because he had deliberately crossed that breezy hall, with the doors re-opened to admit the damp autumnal sunlight, and placed the collection of printed tracts into her hand: *Since our emergence from the coven of history all we have witnessed is an unbroken chain of terror, hatred, bloodshed and atrocity. The time is nigh, dear friends and fellow worshipers of Jehovah. It is absolutely certain—the very date has long been written into the Scriptures—that the Government of Heaven is about to bring an end to almost two millennia of misrule by the proud and evil men of this earth.*

Greta flung the crippled pages against the wall; then feeling remorseful, she picked them up again. "Oh, hell, what's the use?" she muttered, and began to read.

CHAPTER 29
February, 1961

YOUR BOY HAS SPOKEN

Eleven-year-old Peter felt as though he were on the verge of drowning, his lungs gradually filling up like a ship's hold that has struck rock. The nocturnal hacking, the burning, the meltdown in his lungs, bringing Lily's angst-ridden shade looming into view.

"Oh, my God, my poor darling—!" Then she began pounding his back with her thin unsteady hand, as if that helped. The unmistakable glitter of fear in her eyes unnerved him; she came hovering around like a moth with grimy wings, wearing that look of guilt as though, somehow, it was her fault he was coughing. Lily made everything worse; he pushed her away, cursed her, called out for his Aunt Flo whose granite-calm presence reassured him, made him secure. Why was Lily always trembling whenever they approached the hospital, his second home, as though she feared this time, either one of them might not exit alive? It was always the same, he knew the story by heart; his white flannel vest was rolled up, the doctor's ice-cold stethoscope traveled up and down his back, his chest.

"Breathe slowly, breathe deeply, that's a good boy, Peter, all right then, let's wait a few minutes till you stop coughing."

Then came time to stretch out his thin white arm for the blood test, collect a stream of dark cloudy urine in a sterile cup, regularly deliver up voluminous samples from his bowels to be examined in the hospital Lab. He was resigned even to swallowing mounds of whitish choke-powder, whose smell alone made him retch before each meal, as well as special doses of canary-yellow cough syrup, nightly, to pacify his damaged lungs.

Sometimes, while Peter was lying on the hospital bed, waiting for the endless wreath of doctors and interns to make their rounds, to probe the unseen cave of his innards with their warm, cold or tepid fingers, seeking to divine or prophesy the mysterious inner workings of his secret life-spring, he allowed his mind to spin backwards like a top, floating out there into the universe, visualizing the darkness that must have existed before the world was born—and what must have been there before that, and before that, and before that? It was a riddle to which there was no answer, but which gave him the intriguing sensation that his mind was spinning backwards in time, before Time, darkening like the immense spaces of the universe, and sometimes, if he concentrated hard enough, grasped onto the retreating riddle long enough, not only did his mind spin backward into peaceful chaos, but his whole body was pulled along into a tranquil sea of nothingness, *the great escape!* Suddenly, there was a commotion of sorts, an elderly man was being wheeled in, then hauled onto the bed beside Peter.

"It's something deep in my gut," he gasped, his fairy-tale wisps of white hair streaking his damp forehead; he held onto his flabby old belly and tried to sit up. "They still don't know what it is—*my life, such pain!*—but what's the matter with you, son?"

"I can't breathe properly, got a hole in my lung, the doctor says."

Grimacing, the old man stared at Peter more closely. "*Oy vey,* God is cruel sometimes. Me, I'm an old man, I get sick, this is normal, but you're just a little child." Peter gazed at him wanly, then closed his eyes. "Look here, I promise you, son, as soon as we both get out of here I'm going to bring you down to my little shop in Hessel Street. It's a long time I needed a clever little helper like you. I'm going to teach you everything about repairing watches, would you like?"

But even before the old man stopped talking, Peter was asleep again, navigating his own bestilled universe of darkness and light. How long before he sensed something? The presence of darkness within a greater darkness, although it was now silent in the ward. He opened his eyes, squinted, didn't recognize her at once. True, he hadn't seen her for at least a year, maybe two. And she was so changed. As she held Rafael over her shoulder, she seemed to draw all the shadows in the room toward her. The look in her eyes, it frightened him, as did her aura of suppressed excitement, of agitation.

"Greta!"

"I heard you was here, Peter, I had to come and tell you something."

"What is it, what's the matter?"

The baby started to cry. Greta hushed it quiet. She bent closer to her brother, hissed into his ear. "Peter, you're living on borrowed time."

"*What?*"

"It's important, you've got to prepare yourself, you're going to die—"

"Hey—!" It was a brassy jarring tone, indignant, scared. "Who said you could come here, anyway? I don't want to see you no more, go away—*Nurse! Nurse!*"

Greta glanced over her shoulder; she continued to rock the fidgety toddler, erratically tapping his small back and padded dungarees. "I only wanted you to know we're not going to see each other for a long, long time."

"Go tell the nurse I want her, just go—" Fearfully he noted his sister's flushed cheek, her glittering eye, her final testament imparted in such a desperate whisper. She tried to kiss him, but he pushed her away.

"You're going on the other side, Peter, very soon, but I don't want you to be scared, it's all right, I only came to say good-bye."

Later in the day, Lily and Flo stepped out of the lift into the hospital lobby. To their right, through the corridor window, they could see a labyrinth of connecting rooftops, a forest of vents and smokestacks, an oblique steady crossfire of snow.

"Wait here for a bit, Lil, for God's sake, don't let the poor child see you like that. You'll frighten him to death!"

But the air was thick with her own phantoms, her own terrors chasing her hither and thither. An amorphous mass of groans and whimpers, Lily was out of control, jaws, eyelids, lips, everything twitching and convulsing.

"I'm so scared," she mumbled over and over to herself, "I'm so scared he's not going to come back."

She was no longer walking this earth; she'd been transported to another planet, perhaps another galaxy. And the acuteness of her agony only intensified as the moments passed—she, pacing back and forth over the grooved rubber mat, thumbnails clenched into palms, eyes starry, lips mumbling an endless rosary of angst. After a while, Flo came looking for her. She dragged Lily by the arm into Peter's room, and made her sit down while she herself washed the boy from head to toe in antiseptic liquid soap. The nurse then brought a basin of red liquid to drizzle on Peter's fine, almost transparent body. It left a yellowish stain from neck to waist. Seventy-two hours of relentless fasting had transformed his glossy cherub's stomach into a hollow wrinkled cave. Drooping against the pillow, swaddled in a cheesecloth gown, the boy was weakened, listless, and the colour of old alabaster.

"What's the matter, darling, why're you crying?" said Flo.

"Don't let that bitch, Greta, come in here no more, I hate her."

Then, trailed by his squadron of medical assistants, Dr. Isaacson marched in. Clad in a loose lab coat, he was short, slight, hirsute, but youthful looking, despite his sprawl of moustache, white-flecked hair and beard. Behind him appeared the theatre nurse, face and head shrouded in white fishnet, like a masked thief, as she grasped the metallic spokes of Peter's bedframe.

"Doctor—?"

"All right, Peter?" It was a gentle, perfunctory question; a necessary gesture. As though he had all the time in the world to spare, Isaacson sat down close beside the boy. Peter smiled faintly, stretched out his hand, slung his arm around Dr. Isaacson's shoulder, peered intently into his eyes.

"You'll take care of me, won't you, Doctor?"

"Say good-bye to Mummy and Auntie," said the theatre nurse, glancing surreptitiously at her watch.

"Doctor, promise I'll be all right, you're not going to let me—die?"

Dr. Isaacson stroked Peter's thin shoulder, briefly, murmured something inaudible, got up, then hunched away as though shielding something private of his own, a sudden cough, perhaps. The tips of his fingers brushed across his cheek. His eyes reddened, glittered unnaturally as he stifled another cough, perhaps the treacherous uprising of—*but no, no*—tense and attentive, his squadron of interns gaped and stirred uneasily as they shuffled around him, seeming perplexed or disturbed. Into the breach loomed the theatre nurse; she glanced down at Peter, flexed her shoulders in the guise of a hired henchman, resolute and tough; her voice was too harsh, too strident, almost horrifying in its enforced joviality.

"All right, it's time to go now, Peter, *we-are-on-our-way to Bimbombay—*"

I'll *effing* kill her, thought Lily, is that stupid nurse bitch actually singing?

Propelled by the nurse's determined grasp, Peter's bed began tilting toward the door. He lifted his head from the pillow and raised his gnomish little fist in a helpless gesture toward Flo. She flashed him a twisted smile, then he was gone.

"Cm'on, come into the waiting lounge, Lil," said Flo.

But Lily sat very still, head bowed, like a bird brooding. Her innards heaved and plunged. A lump kept rising in her throat, tasting of salt and phlegm. She stared at her long bony fingers trembling on her knees; it was a trance-like stare. Flo said no more. A pang rippled through her own injured leg. Like a flash of ancient history, it radiated outward along screaming nerve ends from somewhere deep inside the bone. It throbbed fitfully, on and off, until an overpowering weariness felled her. She heaved herself onto an empty hospital bed, propped her fleshy back against the pillow. Silence. Her eyes closed; soon she lapsed into her usual gentle snoring. It was Lily, unusually alert and starry-eyed, who steadfastly kept the wake.

Nurses were pacing the corridors, wielding flashlights or carrying wire trays nested with blood samples. Here, in this dreaded place, came the night-sounds of sickness, the whimpering of babies, the rumble of machinery, the squeak and clatter of intravenous tubes dangling from their poles. And all around was the noiseless drip drip, drip of the saline; so many little sicklings hooked up and floating in their beds like dying fish upon the Dead Sea. No true day or night, no real waking or sleeping. Here was always the steel-blossomed glare of lamplight over the beds, the eternal hum of the ventilator, the creaking in a nest of wheelchairs. To be sick in this wretched place, this hell on earth, was to conform to the norm. Here, on this planet of sicklings, pain was an abiding presence, forever hovering inside the point of a hypodermic needle, or along the surgical rim of a blade.

Chopping by, dropping by, the long red finger inside the wall clock snapped inexorably closer to ten, eleven, twelve—and now the walls became metaphysical and dissolved; they were all here in the room with her. Lily could actually see the surgeon's scalpel-blade slicing through her baby's chest cavity, through his rib-bone, probing deep inside his lung, and now his life-blood was gushing like a fountain, too much blood—*Oh, God, too much blood!* An intern kept glancing at a neat row of gauges. Pressure too high, he called, as the nurse frantically soaked up the blood-tide with a handful of towels. Lily fixated on this phantasmagoric theatre glimmering before her eyes. She thought she could hear her baby's slow and muffled heartbeats, the metallic clatter of scissor, wire and blade, the starched bedsheets rustling, the occasional thud of foot-soles around the operating table, the collective angst, the whispers, murmurs and sighs. By now, her own rib cage felt as taut as a rubber band. Her lungs were on fire. Each shallow breath was a rasp, a strip of gauze ripped apart on a nail. She didn't hear the surgeon coming; before she noticed, there was Dr. Isaacson already standing at the open door.

"It's over, Mrs. Morvaye, your boy's alert, he's awake," said the doctor matter-of-factly, as though he weren't announcing a miracle. "Your boy has spoken."

"What?"

Lily stared in astonishment. She tried to pull herself together and rise from the rocking chair. She smiled, tears leaking down her cheeks, like the village idiot; when she laughed, it sounded like a violent hiccup or a sob. All at once, the deadly intravenous air bubbles sparkled, bubbled over like champagne. Coloured balloons seemed to ripple slowly toward the ceiling. The walls were splashed in celebration colours. Clear plastic tubing twirled and twisted through the air like party serpentines.

Your boy has spoken—was it possible, merciful God? Peter's bed was already tilting toward the door. The orderly made a wide-angled curve and eased it into the room, almost scraping off one of the door-hinges as it passed. Lily stared at her son, his cheeks of tallow-wax, his dark straw-like hair against the regulation pillow. Below his shoulder, barely dry, were tossed-off flecks of blood.

"Peter, Peter—" The theatre nurse bent her white-shrouded head close to his cheek. "Are you awake?"

Peter lifted one hand, then let it fall. His clubbed fingers, deformed and mangled by disease, seemed half gnawed away at the joints. His eyes remained closed, his limbs held in thrall by a deep faraway stillness. Just like a corpse, thought Lily, torturing herself with dreadful visions, the satin lining of his casket, the crucifix on his chest, the wreath of lilies.

"Peter—"

"Don't—" mumbled Peter, with a great effort raising his hand again, as though in warning, "don't talk."

Where were the words she needed now to thank the doctor, to thank his cloud of white-shrouded assistants, his team of nurses, orderlies and interns who were already dribbling away through hospital corridors, dispersing far and wide to embrace their own hungers, fears and joys; blessed saviours, they were, angels whom Lily would never meet. She wanted to thank even the surgeon's instruments, to reverently kiss the scalpel blade, the clamp, the scissors, revere them for being so deadly accurate, yet merciful. *Thank you, thank you, thank you,* Almighty God and Jesus, Mother Mary, the Holy Ghost and all the merciful Saints. *Thank you,* Fate or Indifferent Chance, should such deities exist. Lily would gladly have knelt at their chilly altar-slab to whisper her gratitude, if only she could find the words.

CHAPTER 30

PARADISE-IN-WAITING

How does one prepare to receive God or, at least, the fleshly emissary of God, into one's grungy sitting-room? Greta scrubbed the floors, daubed imitation frescoes across the walls, lit spice candles and decorated the kitchen table with fresh-cut lilies and antique silver; Erskine's presence, his essence streamed into every shade-corner of her dwelling, pulsated inside her brain, her heart and every cell of her body. Each time he left, unknowingly he wrenched half of her *Self* away with him; meanwhile she, resisting, hankered after her missing *'Self'* the instant he was gone.

Erskine no longer visited her in the company of his apostle, Simon; he now came to Greta late at night, under cover of night, when her borrowed shelter was transformed into a chiaroscuro of mystery, a throbbing microcosm of the world at large—*Just imagine, my love, a renewed world in which God's goodness, peace and mercy reigns supreme; where sickness, death and sorrow perish, and Evil is forever banished by a single stroke of the Divine brush.* Erskine's powerful arms, winter pale, his chest mantle of dark swansdown, his warmth seemed to enclose and seal her in a duvet of angel feathers. With soul kisses he pledged to love her always, both as chosen female of his desire and fellow creature of God.

Baby Rafael stirred and sighed, dream-tossing in his nearby crib, stewing in his own pool of darkness. Erskine sat bolt upright, bare chest heaving, listening intently to the sounds. He must know that the kid's evil, thought Greta, and felt afraid. When she offered to feed her lover, the larder being so often bare, it was like scattering a handful of seeds or crumbs upon the altar. I don't need anything, said Erskine, appearing ashamed to deprive her of what little she had. Soon afterward he came bearing gifts, more food than either of them could eat in a week. Greta protested. He answered her with a kiss.

On Sundays when she sat in his church, his kingdom of Kingdom Halls, she observed that he avoided her eyes, focusing his mind on the sermon and he succeeded—*damn him*—in displacing all trace of her by the urgent constraints of the public regard. She did feel resentful that he could so easily rivet his mind to his self-appointed duties whereas she, transformed into hostage, could not displace him by thoughts celestial. If he could fire her senses, causing her heart to lurch overboard until she squirmed and gasped for air, she demanded no less from him. Who ordained that he should hold the scales of erotic power? If he was King of Kingdom Hall, so be it, she would be Queen! When Erskine raised his hand, soberly addressing the congregation, in her visions he was naked as a cherub, disarmed and vulnerable to assault. Resentful that he seemed so blithely to be able to disown her, she felt the perverse desire to stride up to the front of the hall and disrobe him publicly; like Salome, in her wicked moments, she wanted his head.

And then afterward, there she was, walking home with his gift of a Bible. A Bible, *for fuck's sake*, hadn't she had enough of Bibles in her brief life? Hadn't she bolted out of holy holy St. Victoire's Convent as though her backside were on fire? What was she doing then with this bland, modern-looking volume, re-labeled, re-interpreted and re-explained, Jehovah's mouthpiece, or so it was claimed, crystal clear and unequivocal. *Bollocks,* it was all bollocks, most of it anyway, specially those Old Testament chronicles of grand-scale disaster that seemed to go on forever, nothing but war after plague after drought after famine, tedious and boring as hell. Who gave a tinker's damn whether it was the poxy Israelites, Hittites, Jebusites or Canaanites that were slain by an enemy claiming direct intervention by its favouritist God? Whatever else the Bible taught, it proved the present century had no monopoly on slaughter.

Upon reflection, Erskine, too, was pathetic, even ludicrous when he insisted on prefacing their passion hours with prayers for forgiveness and healing. Was this his insurance policy against sin? He must know, deep in his heart, that she was bad, and bad for him, that he had less chance of abducting her over to his side of heaven than she had of degrading and corrupting him. The great Erskine, spirit-ambassador and leader among men, ensnared in her bedroom despite the whole array of his God-like armour, token hostage to the seduction of the flesh.

Then again, on certain days, it felt reassuring just to be seated next to Nell within this declared family of God. *Good to see you again, Greta, how's the baby getting along?* ventured Margie, a tall, florid chunky woman, one of Nell's long-time friends. In former days, Greta would have spat in the old crone's eye, but these were fast becoming familiar faces, this tribe of gentle friendly Witnesses who all seemed to know one another and weren't too proud to emote, hug and kiss, demonstrating a sentimental familiarity that Greta had always regarded with suspicion and disdain. Here, in this riverside backwash, though, it seemed not so very out of place. On the surface, at least, this otherworldly gathering, these souls of Jehovah were united by a fervent communal glue; she was still the outsider to whom they extended welcome, hastening almost obsequiously to clear a space for her in their midst.

Nevertheless, her dominant impulse was to shun and mock them. She knew that spending too long virtually alone, deep in her winter darkness, made her soul-sunken and morose, but then this was natural to her. If it was an affliction, it was one that she relished. Her mind was forever stamped into a theatre of war, a daily battleground and nightly eruption of fright-visions, voices merging, competing for space, for attention. It was difficult to concentrate on anything, especially this ancient book of admonitions, lamentations and odd lyrical psalms—*O Lord, thou hast brought up my soul out of the grave; the dark places of the earth are full of habitations of cruelty. Remember not the sins of my youth, remember thou me for thy goodness's sake;*

when my father and my mother forsake me, thou O Lord will take me up—What utter nonsense. It was their aura of calm certainty that amazed, intrigued and infuriated her. How was it possible to find solutions to life's dilemmas in what they called the *'Holy Book'*? Had any of these simpleton-saints been born under a raging firestorm, then abandoned by their Maker to Lily's stinking crockpot of poverty and madness? That, in itself, should be enough to snuff out their faith for Eternity. Greta opened the pages at random, searching for a passage to curse and mock and heap with scorn—*Wait on the Lord, be of good courage, and He shall strengthen your heart*—What lies, what bleedin' lies, and he's the worst of the lying bastards, she whispered to herself that saturnine winter night as she waited longingly for Erskine, and he failed to come.

"What have you done to yourself, Greta—Oh, God!"

She had timed it perfectly, she thought later, and it was worth it—once the pain was less—to witness Erskine, when he finally did appear that night, flushed out of his angelic composure; at the time, strangely enough, she hardly felt it. Remorseful, his eyes full of fear, he tore open an old pillowcase and bandaged her wrist. The blood was on her handkerchief, on her skirt, on the pages of her Bible, all over her yellow-and-white striped apron. Baby Rafael in his solitary crib was screaming too, as though he were dying.

"If you hadn'tve come tonight, like you promised, I would have bled to death, that's what I wanted—"

"My God, *my God,* how could you do this?"

She smiled, faintly, as she closed her eyes. *What's the matter, where's your bleedin' faith now?* she thought, with a touch of malice. Stunned, Erskine held her in his arms, his chilled trembling arms; all she felt was the fierce erratic thumping of his heart.

CHAPTER 31

THE LORD GIVETH...

What a betrayal, thought Lily, how could this happen?

"We wish to carve up your son's body for the enlightenment of Science, Mrs. Morvaye." True, this was not what the doctor said, but this was what Lily understood.

"No—!" It was a little shriek. "No, doctor."

"Mrs. Morvaye, I know how difficult this must be for you, but would you please sign this permission form?"

"Doctor, I just can't—" Lily's face was contorted beyond recognition as she struggled to control herself in this consecrated Holy of Holies, the doctor's Surgery.

"You understand (he sighed) that we do legally require your signature."

"Yes, doctor, but—"

"And by simply putting your name to this authorization, you will be helping hundreds, possibly thousands of children, just like Peter."

Lily started to cry.

"We lavished the utmost care on your son, Mrs. Morvaye, until the very end—" (another martyr's sigh)

"Please, Doctor, don't think—don't think I'm not grateful."

"We succeeded in keeping him alive longer than most—" Lily was now sobbing uncontrollably. The doctor waited for her to pause, then he tried again, probing for a responsive chord, any sign of weakening in her resolve. "Just think of all those children, those children yet to be born; you have it in your power to help them."

"Doctor, I just couldn't bear the thought of it, I couldn't."

"Please, Mrs. Morvaye—" (releasing a loud inbreath of frustration) "—won't you reconsider?"

"I—I just can't do it!" The timbre of Lily's high-pitched, tremulous voice riddled his ears. *"No, doctor, no!"*

"Perhaps I have no right to say this, but I feel it is your moral duty to help us, just one last sacrifice, after all we have done."

"No, doctor."

"Please."

"No, I said I can't!" cried Lily as she crept, sobbing, from the room.

For who could explain it? During the last few days, Peter had definitely seemed to be getting stronger. He was last seen walking out of the ward toward the public telephone stand, dragging his intravenous tube and pole behind him. Flo received his last phone call; he was coughing and crying and begging her to come. She hobbled to his bedside on her crippled thighs; Lily, impaled on her own fear, wailing like a Banshee, executing a paralytic dance of terror and fatigue, failed to arrive on time.

It mattered not. Peter had already begun his abrupt descent and was drowning in his own phlegm. Waves of spume crashed through his lungs and bronchial tree. Salt beaded his hairline, deep-christened every pore of his body as it plunged into shock. First the blood pressure, then his temperature dropped. Under grave assault, both lungs collapsed—then there was no more movement in the chest. For the boy's own sake it must be done, a swift injection from the doctor's hand. Peter scarcely seemed to realize where he was going as he rushed to meet his death.

"It's what we've always feared, Mrs. Morvaye, I'm sorry, it's almost over now, we can't risk it, we don't want him to wake up."

In the hushed ward, standing just inside the sealed white curtains, Flo and Lily gazed down at Peter's inert body. Strapped to his wrist was Flo's Xmas gift watch, still ticking. His clubbed misshapen fingers, which she hid beneath the coverlet, contrasted strangely with his chopped dark fringe, winter pale cheeks and bestilled cherub's lips. By nightfall, dressed in black and weeping like mourners from Calvary, she and Lily made their way back to collect his body. Peter slept on, meanwhile, as they kept the wake; for three days and three nights he slumbered within Flo's ice-cold altar of a sitting-room, until his body turned blue.

On the funeral eve, late in the afternoon, Lily lay shoulder deep in the bathtub, limbs like driftwood, palms like milky prunes. She gazed around at the blank wall partitions of the public stall where there was hardly a niche in which to place her bar of soap; it kept slipping and melting in the bathwater, which was growing steadily colder. Sheer agony it was, lying in almost ice-cold water, unable to move.

"Are you ready, Lil?" called Flo from outside, her hoarse voice almost breaking. "You've been in there for hours. It's always the same, we can never get you in the bath and we can never get you out!"

"Oh, I can't bear this life no more," whispered Lily, "why can't I just die!"

There was a rattling sound at the lock. The matron of the York Public Bath House unlocked the stall door. Lily didn't move. Her eyes were closed. Her hair, plastered in damp threads around her skull, seemed to have greyed overnight from grief. Soap scum marbled the surface of the bathwater, revealing—like the drowned remnants of a shipwreck—the dark waving mass, guarding the entrance to her womb. Lily's arms were crossed stoically over her flaccid breasts.

"It would've been better if I'd never had no kids—like Ruth, O God, help me—now two of them gone, O God!"

At St. Mary's and St. Michael's Church the next morning, the coffin was rolled up to the altar rail. It was buried under a white embroidered cloth and a chaos of flowers. The air was thick with incense and tears. Father Willard, in his lacy white cassock and altar gown, raised his arms in some obscure solemn gesture as he turned to face the mourners. To the left of the altar was Lily, seated between Flo and Albert. Beside them, Angie, Greta and baby Rafael, Ruth and Stanley. In the pew behind were Great Uncle Henry, old Bridgie, Beattie and Georgie and their four sons. Raymond and his family from Dover, were also huddled together nearby. On the right hand side were a handful of uniformed hospital staff and a couple of Peter's chums from school.

"Dear brothers and sisters in Christ," said the priest, *"today we say farewell to Peter, a boy whom we all loved, who was chosen by our Lord to share, and to bear, a very special cross. We do not know why Peter was taken from us so early; yet we recognize that, in His infinite wisdom, the Lord giveth and the Lord also taketh away. This mystery of faith, beyond ordinary human understanding, is bitter, truly bitter for us to accept. But let us also remember this as a time of comfort. Peter has entered Eternity, to be reunited with our loving Saviour, where mortal pain and suffering are no more."*

It was Greta who first noticed the church door slowly opening, the plaintive creak and whine of the hinge, the draughty well of light sweeping the length of the aisle, the unfamiliar footsteps which, in the silence following the communion bell, seemed to pound their way to the altar rail. She was the first to witness the latecomer, this sort of corporeal apparition with a crown of blazing white hair, sunwashed skin, and eyes like tarnished silver. Would Almighty God now hurl down the church pillars upon the heads of the assembled mourners? Upon this abomination? There was the Great Goddamned Taddeusz himself, standing amongst the communicants. Only he would have the audacity to receive the consecrated wafer-Host—almost certainly without due Penance, and innocent of any Confession.

Lily was so shocked when she saw Taddeusz that she sank down in her pew and couldn't get up. Sister-in-law, Beattie, kept glancing at him furtively, sizing up this virtual stranger, this foreign bastard whom she had so oft maligned. Flo, who'd sent the overseas telegram, never dreaming that Taddeusz would appear at the funeral, felt an instantaneous blend of angst, relief, surprise. Anything might happen. What she feared most was an outbreak of hysteria from Lily, a public scene. Greta, who'd instinctually committed every nuance of the situation to memory, held Rafael tighter, shrouding him under his blanket as if a mere glance from Taddeusz could somehow do him harm.

Taddeusz moved cautiously, as though girding himself in invisible armour. He hadn't expected his 'Second Coming' to elicit any great outpouring of joy amongst the family, and he was prepared to defend himself against attack. What he wasn't prepared for, what shocked him most, was Lily. Anywhere else, drifting along the streets perhaps, how would he have recognized her? Barely forty, and she was already an old woman, as though their elapsed years had exacted double toll on her mind and body. A black crêpe scarf half concealed her mottled grey hair, which was wispy around the ears and trimmed bluntly, without the least pretense to fashion. The bottle-thick eyeglasses only magnified her raw swollen eyes, her ghastly washed-out skin. Around her shoulders was a mouldy rag of a winter coat, olive-green, that looked as though it might fall to pieces in a gust of wind.

Later, to the wax-fragrant sanctuary of Flo's sitting-room, came a procession of friends and family, seeking pretexts to gape at this 'bloody foreigner' who, in response, scarcely deigned to acknowledge their presence. Ill at ease, dumbstruck, one by one they retreated to the shelter of their own dwellings, unusually shamed, now, by the familiar ingrained grime of their world. Perhaps they perceived it clearly for the first time; Taddeusz's presence, polished and somber, threw all into stark relief. Well groomed, well dressed and self-assured, he appeared to move comfortably through many a foreign world, above and far far beyond the shabby precincts of Walden.

His tailored suit of grey-pearl, smooth and silken, was slightly rumpled like a sky in winter. With clenched fists, glittering in gold and cosmic gemstones, his aura was of gloom, his eyes saturnine; they harboured retribution. Together he and Angie crossed Commercial Road into Watney Market and passersby stopped to gape at them; the pair were unmistakably father and daughter, despite the disparity of his princely and her pauper attire. And, unaccountably, despite her world of famishing, fourteen-year-old Angie had sprouted from his genes into a tall blonde resembling weed of pale bony limbs and thick witch's tresses. He, on the other hand, was not tall, and this surprised her. His wavy hair was prematurely white. He carried his corpulence with pride. Red-eyed from crying, stricken speechless in his presence as though he were a stranger, Angie—like a blindman's faithful guide-dog—led her father across the canal-bridge toward the docklands.

Taddeusz stepped into Wapping, piercing the mildness of the English mist as the stark wind rose and the sun descended through billows of twilight. Together, they crossed Cable Street and he paused as though sniffing the air, aroused, curious yet cautious. If he harboured deep memories of this place—of wartime brothels, assignations and bombing raids—of course, these could mean nothing to Angie. He knew that Wapping Underground Station, near the Dock Stairs, had received a direct hit by the Luftwaffe; even now, it languished in its forgotten state of disrepair. Nothing more than a tower-deep débris of dark gaping spaces, torn out brick and mangled metal. Few travelers descended into its bowels and the few that dared were fleet of foot, adventuresome or foolhardy. Angie had, only once, ascended its perilous stairwell from the damaged platform to the street-level exit; she refused ever to go there again.

When they arrived at Greta's front door, an overwhelming silence greeted them. Taddeusz paced irritably, staring at the makeshift laundry lines fluttering the length of the balconies. There was a slight trembling of curtain nets at the neighbouring window, but no response from within.

"Where is she?" demanded Taddeusz.

Angie tapped on the door knocker again, then rapped against the wide pane of grimy glass. The impact reverberated through Greta's beshrouded windowpanes. They heard a baby crying. Taddeusz, flushed and furious looking, hammered with his plump bejewelled hand against the door; he resembled a siege commander or strikebreaker, rallying his men.

"Greta, I said *OPEN* the door!"

They heard Rafael's whimpers growing louder, then a grinding creaking sound along the corridor, before the door opened. Taddeusz retreated slightly at the sight of Greta barring his path, a flesh-and-blood obstacle, seething with hostility. He recognized, only too well, the inherited 'rebel-gleam' of Romany in her eye.

"Who said you two could come here? I didn't invite you. On top of that, you just blasted well woke up the kid—"

Coldly, she spurned his embrace, then allowed them both, grudgingly, sulkily, perhaps as a calculated rear guard move, into her solitary sitting-room. Provocative and taunting, pointedly ignoring Angie, she continued to stare *him* down, Taddeusz, her so-called father, refusing even to let him touch Rafael, the first of his grandchildren.

Taddeusz was mortally offended. He gazed around him somberly, baffled and incensed; this was hardly the ancestral tribute to which he was due, and from a foul-mouthed gypsy, no less, albeit his own natural daughter. There followed a long malaise, a tense war-like standoff, before Greta vanished into the kitchen and reappeared with an elegant, though soiled porcelain teapot, three chip-stained mugs and a plate of tea biscuits on a tray.

"'Ere, what's that you're doing?" she said to Angie, who was opening up a bagful of green apples from the Watney Market. "Don't you dare give my kid anything without asking me first!"

Rafael screamed, indignant at being denied the offered gift. Greta put down the tray and smacked him. "From now on, you'll eat what I give you, when I give it to you; you eat what you're told," she said.

Taddeusz looked pained. He was gradually absorbing the desolation of this dwelling place. The darkness, the heaviness, the reek of decay. What little she had she'd cobbled, lumped and arranged carefully together, hand-woven paper card inlaid with pressed petals and dried flowers, treasured acorns and conkers, dusty seashells, starfish, stones, pebbles and bones. A couple of wall mirrors, framed in wood, smeared, speckled with age and inhabited by shadows. A grainy-looking settee, stiff-backed and salvaged probably from some poverty-street dump. A mahogany coffin of a coffee table; a scattering of hand-painted frescoes along the walls and live cobwebs on the ceiling. Stacks of books, Bibles and church pamphlets were on the bookshelves, mostly buried under a sheet-layer of dust. Observing the inside of her left wrist, Taddeusz flinched at the sight of a raised raw welt, a healing flesh wound, the unmistakable tracing of a crucifix.

"So, you've behaved exactly as you pleased—" he gestured toward Rafael— "and this is the result."

Greta stared back at him, murder in her eyes.

"I came to offer you one last chance, you can come with me to America, get out of this—hovel you're living in, and make a new start for yourself and the baby."

"No!" said Greta ferociously, without thought and without reflection. "No!"

"What do you mean—*no*?"

"I said no. I don't want nothing from you, you bastard, it's too late for that!"

Taddeusz flinched again; he turned pale. The lines on his forehead became completely smooth—*always a terrorizing sign*—lending him the air of a divinity witnessing blasphemy in its own temple.

"All right, then—"

He stood up and gestured sternly to Angie; together, they moved toward the door and Greta, in a delirium of fury, smashed it shut behind them. They had hardly reached the ground floor of the building before Greta came raging out of her flat, tossing a fountain of bank-notes (which Taddeusz had moments beforehand covertly stuffed inside her Bible) down the brick stairwell.

"I told you, didn't I—we don't need your bleedin' charity!" Her words reverberated round and around the darkening courtyard like the peel of a tocsin bell, an outraged echo. *"Bastard! You Bastard! Don't you dare ever come back!"*

Later, came the final showdown.

Taddeusz steeled himself to face Lily, who was huddled in black, petrified and weeping, in Flo's ornate sitting-room.

"Listen, forget Greta, she's utterly lost. But I've made up my mind, I'm taking Angie—"

"No, you can't, you can't take her! Flo, tell him he can't—!"

God, O God, not again—and specially not now—not a replay of that devious Court-room scene, that custodial tug-of-war played out between them so many years before.

"It's no use, Lily, don't make a scene, and don't try to stop me. Understand, I'm going to give the kid a fighting chance—God knows, a few more years in this stinking sump hole, she might well be underground."

As is recorded in the Holy Scriptures: *The Lord Giveth and the Lord Taketh Away*

PART THREE
CHAPTER 32
March 1961

Bʀᴀᴠᴇ ɴᴇᴡ ᴡᴏʀʟᴅ

At first, America declined to open its arms to Taddeusz; nevertheless, he and his new entourage soared across the 'Great Swamp' on the magic carpet of credit. He touched down at Dorval Airport, fuelled by desperation, curiosity and hope. Why the vulcan citadel of Montréal in *la belle province de Québec*? Well, simply because this northern refuge was the first to process his immigration papers, he was legally bankrupt—therefore, just a nimble shade ahead of his creditors—and no one had whispered to him about the saturnine nature of its winters. It was suitable, too, for his third wife, Suraiya, beloved niece of arch nemesis, Ranjit Ghosh. Born to a French mother and a Hindu father, given the nature of the times, Suraiya's complex genesis may possibly have engendered a level of exclusion at home, but abroad would be welcomed as a *métissage* of rarefied exotica. Stepping delicately as though from amongst the plate gloss illustrations of the god-legends, the Bhagavad-Gita, or resembling a masterwork of preservation from a museum antechamber, Suraiya shunned all excess of light and sun.

And so to wintry Montreal, one of the world's best kept secrets and also, without doubt, one of the most beautiful places in North America; but, due to his precarious finances, Taddeusz was obliged, at first, to lodge his family in an unrelentingly grim and ugly pocket-fold of that city. Their first rented apartment was situated somewhere vaguely north-east, cut off from the glamorous '*Centreville*' by raised concrete viaducts, motorways, lamentable stretches of wind-driven firs, narrow sloughs and unpaved slush-rutted roads. From their front lounge they could see and hear an open highway, pocked with truculent slow-moving cars and ice-coated city buses, traversing an urban wilderness of packed snow. Angie's grey woollen school coat might just as well have been spun from cotton; Suraiya's resplendent mirror-sequined saris and Taddeusz's floating white tropical garb remained buried at the bottom of their unpacked trunk. None of them was properly clothed or sufficiently prepared for this welcoming tail-end of the Canadian winter-beaste. Already the middle of March, supposedly the approach of Spring, yet the morning air stung colder than death; the wind was a gauntlet of knife-thrusts concealed in a cloak of mist.

Feeling as disoriented as if she had been set down on the dark side of the moon, Suraiya retreated, shivering, to the depths of her newfound land-shelter, surveying the state of their furnished apartment—the fake pine paneling which curled, split and came apart like parchment in her hand, the unbelievably antique gas stove, the smoke-somber ceilings and hoar-frosted windowpanes—with a mixture of bafflement and disbelief. Apparently, although who would have believed it, the New World also harboured old dwellings, unloved dwellings, dwellings encrusted and swirling with refuse, home to secret piles of maggots and the occasional roach. Suraiya wept, but her tears flowed from anger. They were silent and short-lived. She summoned Angie into her presence and spoke to her in a rage of quietness.

"You must now attempt to make yourself useful," she said. "I cannot put even my foot into this stinking cave of old tiles that is supposed to be our bathroom."

Thirteen domestic trunks had been shipped by a forwarding agency in Calcutta. It had cost a small fortune. Taddeusz heaved a few crates of Astrology textbooks around the ten-foot-high dust alcove destined to serve as his temporary office. He looked around irritably, as though in pursuit of a fleeing Hindu servant boy, and swore in three languages.

"What did I tell you, Taddeusz, she can't even perform the simplest of tasks; she will have to be trained," said Suraiya, in her softly polished, ceremonial 'Colonial Raj' tones.

Angie protested.

Taddeusz, fatigued, dispirited and hovering at the raw edge of his nerves, turned to glare at this ash-blonde tumbleweed, this virtual stranger—despite their blood ties—whom he had chosen to salvage from the dump. His features were twisted in rage and disgust; his eyes flickered and burned like coals.

"Oh, you blasted Cockney fishmonger, just shut up until you learn to speak properly. I can't tolerate it, Suraiya, it breaks my ears just to listen to her!"

"This is what I have been saying as well, you know. The child has no manners at all. She knows nothing, she understands nothing, she arrived here from London half starving and yet still she picks at her food, she eats nothing, she is a wild animal."

"This is all going to change, believe me. What have they been teaching her in school? My own natural daughter, an idiot fishmonger? I can't believe it!"

Suraiya examined the somber high-ceilinged kitchen to see how it could be reclaimed. Someone would need to disinfect the walls, the cracked grungy tiles and counters, the insides of cupboards, the harsh-splintered hardwood floors.

"I'm hungry," scowled Taddeusz, "make me some of that Chicken Madras, I can't survive on just bloody vegetables, damn it!"

"Yes, yes, but you can wait half an hour, can't you?"

"No, I can't, make it now."

"Angie, leave the bathroom, I need you," said Suraiya, disappearing into her bedroom, which was a pandemonium of unopened boxes. Delivered from her wrapped shroud, the bronze statuette of Goddess Kali had a terrifying aspect, black-faced, luminescent evil-eyed, bloodthirsty and grinning. Suraiya placed Kali up against the mirror of the ratty pressed-wood bureau; this was her treasured talisman, purchased long ago from a stall near the Dakineshwar Temple in Calcutta.

"It's the warrior goddess, she gives me strength," she said, lighting an incense stick which gradually infiltrated the entire dwelling, masking although not driving away the winter-enclosed reek of old cigarette smoke, bacon fat and fetid human waste.

In those saturnine days Taddeusz was steeped in a grave of gloom. It was clear that the family weighed heavily upon him. He looked bloated, puffy-eyed and nervy. His stark white hair grew untended and wild. With fingers stained in nicotine and ink, shirt flecked with coffee stains and singed with ash, he spent his days astral traveling through the 'Classified' pages of the *Montreal Star* and the *Gazette*, researching local businesses at the public library and monopolizing the public telephone in the lobby downstairs. During those first fruitless days he returned, violently flinging off his suit and tie and ghosting bare-chested through the rooms of their apartment in his droopy white Ghandiesque loin-shorts, glowing defiance at Suraiya, the maiden, who responded in a dusk of resentment at this public display of his flabby varicose-veined legs, his tub of opulent chest-rolls, seeded with gingery-white curls.

"Taddeusz! Really—"

"So what, who cares? I'm comfortable like this."

"Don't you have any respect?"

"Put up the thermostat, will you! What do I care about gas bills? We won't be in this dump much longer, I promise you that!"

So where was the God-figure that had haunted the nether realms of Angie's imagination for all those years? Here He was, directly before her; a flesh-and-blood visitation that unabashedly swore, belched, broke wind and snored.

"He keeps me awake half the night, it's unbearable," said Suraiya. Four months into her pregnancy yet still she felt nauseous both night and day. Just the smell of red meat was enough to drive her, retching and moaning, into their miserable bathroom. "Come here, Angie, didn't you hear me calling? Chop these onions and carrots. I've just got to lie down now, I feel as though I'm going to faint!"

"I'm going to send the little good-for-nothing out to work," said Taddeusz, ever wild-haired, chain-smoking and belligerent. "She's going to miss half her damned school year, for the little she was learning there anyway; for the next few months she's going to have to help out, at least till we get back on our feet."

Taddeusz relented a few days later and sent Angie out on a quest through the Arctic streets in search of the nearest high school, St. Isidore. A plump motherly looking secretary came hurrying out of her office, shivering and tugging down the sleeves of her frosted pink twin-set, ornamented with a double string of cultured pearls. 'Yes, dear—?' she frowned, striving to make sense of Angie's crumpled hieroglyphics of identification: *Angelina Domenica Morvaye, Status: Landed Immigrant to Canada, Minor, Aged 14 years.* And so it was; by mid-morning, these immigration papers were declared irregular if not invalid, her proficiency in Mathematics abysmal and in Canadian History non-existent, her schoolbook Parisian French, of limited value beside the Molièresque archaisms of French Canada, her skill in Latin Grammar and Translation commendable, but of what use was a dead language? Taddeusz was right, Angie was ranked with the other village idiots and dumped into the lowest stream.

"Oh, it's so cute, I love your accent, we all think you're a swell kid," said Vera, a blooming, earthy looking Ukrainian girl, who stood in line beside her in the schoolyard.

"Settle down everyone, please; take your seats," said Miss Kane. She waited ultra solemnly for Angie to cease her illicit whispering with Vera. In mid-career, Miss Kane appeared lean, roughed up and battle-hardened. A rash of nervy 'itch' blemishes covered her chalky palms and sprinkled her wide forehead and jaw. Fatigue and cynicism gleamed from her swamp-circled half-shut eyes. Mildly wheezing, and with great effort, her voice summoned itself from the cave of her throat. "By the way, I have been observing you, Angie, since you first arrived in my class and—*as I expected*—like a stone that finds its level, you have sunk to the very bottom of the sludge."

Taddeusz accosted Angie as soon as she arrived home that day.

"There's a *'Help Wanted'* sign on the plaza across the road. A shoe shop. They're looking for a part-time student, evenings and Saturdays. You've got a good chance, go over and apply for the job right now. Your school French must be good enough; what do you need to know—*Quelle pointure chaussez-vous? Est-ce trop grand? Trop petit? Voulez-vous essayer une pointure 6, 7, 81/2 ?* Ask Suraiya, she'll coach you. And before you go, get her to fix your hair and put some make-up on you, or something. You've got to be at least sixteen for that job."

Amazingly, the young shop manager, Charmaine, must have taken pity on her. Somehow she was hired, on a trial basis, with nothing to recommend her other than her tall bespectacled bluestocking guise, her silent chastened air of a malleable slave. The job provided no wage slips, just a tiny sum, cash in hand, every other Friday. Taddeusz was elated, but Suraiya resentful. Once her chronic nausea abated, she was trying to gather up her strength, determined somehow to manage the household without a servant in sight.

"Angie, today after school you've got to take the washing to the launderette; on the way back, get me some patna rice and fresh ginger, and don't forget after that to iron your father's new shirt and tie; finally he's managed to get a job interview for tomorrow."

By the next evening, Taddeusz was seething with resentment despite his good fortune and what he regarded as a 'paltry' success. His overdraught credit line was nearing exhaustion,

304

and cash was in short supply. Of course, he'd swallowed his pride and accepted the first job that was offered, book-keeper accountant and office manager for a sewerage pipe construction company in the grimmest north end of the city.

"The old Shylock, he told me himself how he was salvaged, miraculously, from a concentration camp in Poland at the end of the war. Somehow he managed to emigrate to the New World. Can you believe it? He started a tiny construction business and now he calls himself President of Shit-Pipe Enterprises. Ninety-five dollars a week! He thinks he can con me but I know he's getting me dirt cheap for twelve hours a day. Now *he's* exploiting the 'Immigrant!'"

Like a species in process of radical change, Angie froze and fell silent, shape-shifting to the demands of camouflage, absorbing the surrounding novelty of sight and sound. Gone was beloved London, a place she never realized was so beloved until now: her vanished birthplace—this *'scepter'd isle, ...this precious stone set in the silver sea.'* As she'd stepped from the great-bellied aircraft, Britannia, the gale on the Arctic runway pierced her charcoal-grey school coat like a forest of knives. An ice-water dip. Soaring literally overnight from her Old-World metropolis of forged-iron Victorian gate, gaping bomb-site and mist-terraces, of white-wimpled Nunnery, Communion Fast, Confessional Box and flute-like dawn choir of adolescent voices—*Do you ken John Peel at the break of day?*—to non-stop radio 'rock' musak, bobbie socks, Barbie dolls, multi-coloured triangular flags flapping atop gas stations and car lots, the pervasive reek of liquid dish detergent, pizza 'joints', and freezers large enough to store whole quarts of ice cream.

Was it the Judas in her that made Angie slam the door, thoughtlessly and without introspection, on her past? It had elapsed as naturally as a season or a dream. It simply was, and was beyond questioning, her fate in microcosm of a far vaster global migration. Apt to the flux of change, she had inherited a porous ear, if not the gift of mimicry from her mother, Lily. After weeks of diligent practice, she managed to blend herself

305

and her offending speech unnoticed into her brave new Arctic world. Suraiya, on the other hand, responded in the several guises of her soul-patroness, Kali. Often she was portentously silent, otherwise raging and railing, commanding or beguiling, making passionate love or war with Taddeusz, not always behind closed doors.

"It's a desert of ice and snow out there, I can hardly see through the window, I can't find my way around. I can't even walk safely on the pavement outside! I refuse to stay in this place, I'm warning you, I shall leave!"

"Damn it, just stay indoors then until the weather clears. Angie will get the shopping."

"But what on earth were you thinking about? I thought we were going to America or Australia and you've brought me to the middle of the 'Arctic Nowhere.' Why didn't we go to Paris, instead, as my grandmother said we should?"

But it fell to Angie to listen to her litany of lamentations, since Taddeusz was more and more absent from home. Coerced into twelve-hour days at the office, he spent his remaining free hours seeking ways to escape the cul-de-sac he found himself in. The house descended in a shroud of gloom that the approach of the Spring equinox did nothing to clear. The sooty crust-ridges of snow, the icy whippet gales were banished by a transient lukewarm wash, then a feverish blaze of sunshine, gradually revealing the sere moribund tufts of last year's grass, whole swaths of it languishing alongside the dust-glittering highway and concrete overpass.

Suraiya took her first faltering steps outside as if she were an invalid. What she saw depressed and demoralized her. A wide intensely blue sky, a desert of tar and concrete, an outcropping of factory shops, a dual stream of moving vehicles, a brightly painted plaza fringed by starving firs. As Taddeusz remarked, a car is more useful than a pair of legs in this country. Suraiya did not drive and she didn't care to walk. Swelling heavier and rounder into her maternity, she soon retreated 'home.'

CHAPTER 33

HOUSE OF SHADE

There was a tightness, a closeness in the house, an underground assault upon the mind and senses, the still dark energy of malaise. It emanated from Suraiya, seeping from her pores like an incense of darkness, breathing discontent into the shade corners of their dwelling as she clutched onto the life-to-be in her womb like some fertile goddess of the night.

"Come here," she said to Angie one evening while Taddeusz was away, pursuing whatever business or pleasure could be found. "I want to explain something to you; you will not find it very pleasant but you are British born and so, whether you like it or not, you are partly responsible for the many evils in my country."

"What? *Me?* I don't understand, what do you mean?"

"No, you are still very ignorant of the world, and of history in general, but let me tell you that before ever the accursèd white British invaders came, raping and pillaging and fomenting discontent in our land, we Hindus and Sikhs and our Moslem countrymen were living very peacefully together."

Angie stared at Suraiya's precious statue-icon, the Goddess Kali, and felt uneasy. She felt herself, in some ironic way, to be Suraiya's prisoner, or prisoner of conscience. Suraiya's glance, like that of Goddess Kali, was potent and full of malice, as if she thrived on the force of fear she instilled in whoever should gaze upon her.

"The British upper classes—*the toffs*—it is well known that most of them are centuries-long inbred in their insanity, they conceived this notion simply to carve up the map of our territory, whether in equal or unequal slices, and then as if that weren't enough, they forced millions of people to leave their homes, killing and maiming one another in brutal collisions, on route, as they headed either south to Mother India or north to Pakistan. I was sixteen years old, about your age, at the time. We were living in Calcutta then and we witnessed the most terrible slaughter. Have you even the slightest idea how many people lost their lives in this lunatic escapade?"

Angie shook her head. Was she supposed to feel culpable for something that had happened, without her knowledge or consent, barely a year after her birth? A megadose of *Original Sin* to be heaped on her pre-tainted soul! She stared at Suraiya with the air of a disgraced and sulky combatant, but could think of nothing to say.

Suraiya then produced an airmail envelope that was hidden beneath her jewel-box. Postmarked from London and already opened, it was penned in Greta's unformed script, a chaos of curves, letters and sloping lines.

"By the way, what sorts of lies have you been telling your sister, Greta? It seems to me that you are very ungrateful to us, your parents, and also very disloyal!"

Apprehensive, feeling guilty for what, she did not know, Angie unfolded the letter.

So you're homesick, now, well, I don't pity you, wrote Greta. *You're a turncoat, a traitor, remember? You deserted your own country and your own kind. Never mind, when I've got a bit extra for stamps, I'm going to send you our special Watchtower book. It explains exactly what Jehovah wants us to do. See if you can find a Kingdom Hall near you. It's important for you to join the Witness Church. I didn't believe it at first, either, and now I do, but somehow I just don't think you are going to understand. Next Monday, my friend Nell and me and the baby, and Margie and Jean and their kids, we're all going down on the bus to a holiday camp in Margate. See, I know this is the true Church, not like that Catholic whore we were brought up with. I know this is the true Church because here they really take care of you like a family.*

"A family," said Suraiya, "a real family, you have no idea what that is! Just how have you been raised, my God, to be so selfish and cold-hearted, you think and act only for yourself! Even if I call and call, you never seem to hear. You pretend to be absorbed in some book, a schoolbook, you tell me, but I know you're just amusing yourself with stupid love stories and gothic tales."

"I was doing my homework."

"Well, that can wait. You must help out more, remember the doctor's warning. Toxemia can be very dangerous for me, and for the baby."

Angie flushed under Suraiya's accusing stare, wishing vehemently for escape. Suraiya's mood was charged and desperate. Her eyes kindled, her skin paled and raged in an unnatural alliance of malice and beauty.

"And now he's kicking me so fiercely, I can hardly breathe; I'm sure it's going to be a boy. Oh, God, my life with your father isn't worth a candle. I only wish I'd been born a man! I swear I would have been a military commander like my father, I'd have fought like a demon in defense of my country, I would have slaughtered the murderous British, yes, I can promise you I would."

The next day at St. Isidore Secondary High, Sister Hélène was absent. Miss Kane was asked to cover her Canadian History lesson. She looked harassed and fatigued, this extra burden cut into her lunch hour. At all costs, the students had to be kept busy, she had such a horrific pile of marking already overdue. Rifling through her colleague's textbook, interleaved with a flurry of notes and little markers, she tried to divine exactly what she was required to do.

"What section did you cover yesterday? Did you get as far as Lord Durham's report? Oh, here, I've found them; these are the review questions for your test. Everybody just take out your copybooks—no, don't use loose-leaf—I don't want this getting lost and flying around the classroom, you have to learn to keep your notes in proper order." With the air of a disgruntled martyr, she began copying sentences on the chalk-smeared blackboard.

Describe the significant events that led up to the rebellion of 1837 in Lower Canada.
What were the most important grievances of the French settlers?
How many French Canadian patriots lost their lives in the uprising and battle of Saint-Eustache?
Name the British general who was sent by the authorities to put down the revolt.
Explain why Sir Durham was dispatched to the colonies by the British Crown.
List and explain three main recommendations of the Durham Report.
Explain the significance of Lord Durham's recommendations for the colony of Lower Canada.
How did these recommendations affect the future development of Canada as a nation?

Miss Kane could sense the unrest developing at the back of the classroom. By now she knew the troublemakers, the innocent, the devious, the leaders and the followers, the serious misfits and the self-conscious clowns. During the course of her seemingly interminable career, she had forged a battle-tested and, by now, instinctual strategy on how to deal with the students in her charge. Somehow, she managed to rise taller than she was, her body empowered itself with a flush of adrenaline, her eyes blazed in the necessary guise of intimidation, her lungs expanded to project her frail voice to the outer fringes of the classroom where the identified rebels were entrenched. She steeled herself, once again, to quell the all-agitating-together voices of emerging revolt.

"Miss, it's not fair, the answers are not all in our book."

"We can't finish all that today, Miss!"

"I don't have my notes, I forgot my binder on the desk yesterday and someone stole it."

"I left my history book at home, can I sit and work with Linda?" said one girl, half-rising out of her seat without permission, poised to skitter across the room.

Again, Miss Kane's preternaturally forceful voice struck order into chaos with a verbal imperative, backed by the entire arsenal of institutional coercion. "Now *LISTEN* carefully, class, because I will say this once, and only once: This review exercise must be finished by Friday and it counts for marks, so check your notes from Sister Hélène or go to the school library or else your public library and find whatever information you need. You're no longer in elementary school and we can't spoon-feed you any more. You must start to take responsibility for your own learning; is that understood?" She hung tough, bristling with intimidation, for the umpteenth time facing down their familiar blue fug of not-so-silent resentment, their united front. "Are there any more questions? Good—now I want perfect concentration for the next hour, and perfect silence, so get to work!"

Back at home, Taddeusz was also in revolt.

"Does Almighty Shylock think I'm going to labour in his sweatshop for more than a few weeks? Angie, run out and get the papers, quick—yes, of course, the *Star* and the *Gazette*, I need to check the 'Classifieds'—but first, bring me my coffee. Suraiya, have you made my eggs yet?"

"How do you expect me to cook for the whole family, on what you give me, I couldn't keep a fly alive! And you, Angie, keep out of the fridge unless I give you permission."

"I'm making dad's coffee."

"I don't know what we are going to do, once the baby is born—*Ô mon Dieu!* why ever did I agree to come to this dreadful place?"

By July of that year, the entire metropolis and its environs were ablaze in the fever of summer. The suburban homestead on Île Jésus belonging to Jacques Viger, the company president of *Imperial Mansions*, was hacked out of a mosquito-ridden swampland, dredged, leveled, earth-filled, then designed by a European *'paysagiste'* of neo-gothic sensibility. Viger's guests wandered along the stone pathways and romantic wild-rose arbours. In their hands they cradled little cut glasses of frosted sherbet and crème de menthe. Fleeing the excesses of the Canadian tropics, they took refuge beneath a trellised wilderness of crawling grape-leaf and Virginia creeper.

This was a rare 'perk' afforded to Taddeusz through the good graces of his present job at *'Shit-Pipe' Enterprises*. A convivial business associate, Jacques Viger, was hosting a garden barbecue lunch to which only the most 'significant people' were invited. Taddeusz's deep rumbling voice could be heard amongst the waterfall of chatter below the greystone patio deck. An attractive young female, Céline, Jacques Viger's sister-in-law, all chestnut flowing hair, bare midriff and glistening soulful eyes, held out her hand and Taddeusz grasped it in his own vibrantly fleshy palm. With his lingering forefinger he pointed to the destiny lines, the whorls and fissures that crossed her palm, pronouncing upon her occult character-fate with an air of reflective good-natured gravity.

"Just look, your father's showing off again, that's typical," said Suraiya, contemptuous and frankly bitter.

Grossly distended and deformed by her pregnancy, she sat on the ornate verdigris bench beneath the shade of the grape leaves, laden with ancestral gold, a cluster of snake-banglets on her wrists. The embodiment of nobility, of Old World-oriental beauty. Shrouded within her pale mauve sari and veil, a phantasm of embroidered silk, she exuded the aura of the costliest French perfume; it was the trademark of class which, she knew, distinguished her from the trifling little tarts of whom Taddeusz seemed all too fond.

"Always an audience, always he needs an audience," she whispered, "just look at him now performing for the crowd like a trained mongoose—*or a snake charmer, rather*—while everyone imagines how brilliant he is. They don't know what it's like for me, putting up with him at home."

"Are you feeling all right, you look hot," said Angie. She wished she were wearing a sun hat. Her own nordic body rebelled against the heat, suffered under the unbearable glare and weight of the sun.

Yet Taddeusz, by contrast, was transformed, he seemed to thrive in a sunburst of energy. His gathering of fans and followers listened, amused and fascinated by the striking accuracy of his palm readings, his wryly penetrating personal comments, his teasing glances of overt seduction. An invisible flame-aura sparked from his brain, issued fluently on his tongue. Presiding over the soft carpet-lawn like a magician Father Confessor, his sun-glowing, impressive and finely aging features, his float of wild white hair and loose garb of flesh was carelessly sexual; a kind of tangible electric charge flowed from his quick mind and aroused body, always at ease, always compelling, he glowed white-hot in the adulation of the public eye.

He must have sensed that the hour was nigh.

Like the simultaneous grandeur-desolation of East Berlin, on either cusp of the Brandenburg Gate, there was Taddeusz, poised to blaze forth as luminous figurehead from a House of Shade.

You were not in your place
someone had dropped you; smashed
your glass
and left you lying
helpless
on your side
It's true I always dust you off
each Thursday,
but for many Thursdays now
I've scarcely seen you
propped upright
between my combs and bottles
of cologne, my dried-out
flowers stemming
from their vase
of ivory bone
and yet—today—you catch my eye
you smile at me inside your
naked silver frame
as though you might just
brush that fringe of chopped unruly hair
out of your eyes
and break into a laugh;
like peter pan
you've dodged the hook again
and vanished
through the stardust sky
It's true I have not truly
looked at you
for many Thursdays; simply
picked you up to dust and
set you down again
between the rising moon
and setting sun
I half confess
(it hurts me now)
I'd half forgotten you
Yet you must stay
forever fresh
preserved in glass
and grimy silver; I
must stumble on
grown coarse
and dry
and brittle
with the seasons; who's responsible?
Who is it that decides
your name is peter...
mine is wendy

CHAPTER 34

FLESH AND BLOOD

An airmail letter arrived from London and Angie seized it before anyone else could. Lily's tombstone-engraved letters addressed themselves solely to her, the daughter of the house.

My darling Angie, your Aunt Flo is standing over me with the broom handle, she said I must write to you today since it's been more than 7 months since you went away. It's not that I don't want to write—you know how much I love you—it's just that I can't seem to be able to get myself to do anything at all. I don't know where the time goes, the hours, days and weeks pass in a continuous blur. I've not been eating much either, though Flo brings back these invalid dinners for me from the hospital canteen. I don't want to upset her but I detest them, they smell of death, and anyway I can hardly keep anything down. Since Peter died, I just couldn't—didn't want—to pull myself out of my hole of desolation. Greta never comes here any more, we never see the baby, you were the only one I had—and now you've left me as well.

Aunt Flo was very bad with grief, but she takes care of me now and I'm grateful. She won't stop talking about the angel she saw cradling Peter as he slept with his head high up on the pillow; she woke up in the middle of the night and witnessed this blinding radiance around him, it was so fierce she had to keep blinking and closing her eyes. It happened just a few weeks before he died, but she was too amazed and too frightened to say anything at the time.

Your godmother, poor Aunt Tweetie, before she died, used to say how miraculous it was that, somehow, we all lived and breathed one another. Do you remember—no, of course not, you weren't even born—those two days in Bayswater when I was so

315

ill I couldn't even get up off the mattress. Your father was gone, only the Devil knows where. Greta was wandering around the flat, a three-year-old baby scavenging for food and milk, and suddenly there was my sister, Tweetie, banging down the front door, carrying two full bags from the market all the way from the East End, because she said that something—some powerful feeling she couldn't understand, ignore or deny—had literally forced her to come.

Meanwhile, I'll never be able to understand what's happening to Greta. She's joined some Church, the Witnesses, they call themselves and, all of a sudden, it looks like she belongs completely to them. She's cut herself off from us, like we're the Devil or something, her own flesh and blood. The last time after she left, I cried and cried; she's so harsh with little Rafael, it worries me sick. Your Uncle Albert stormed out of the house when he saw she'd brought over another load of tracts and pamphlets to try to convert the lot of us. Your Aunt Flo fed the boy and gave Greta a bit of money and tried to talk sense to her, but when she saw we wouldn't have none of her proselytizing she declared that she wasn't ever coming back to Walden because we were unbelievers and apostates and destined to be damned. Then she started preaching, all lofty-like, about chastising Rafael for his sins—a small innocent child with sins—can you believe it? I can't help thinking about it, I brood and brood. I hope I'm not making you too depressed by all the news. I can't imagine what your life must be like so far away. Don't you miss your own country? Don't you want to come home?

It was a startling question, seditious, with an aftertaste of treason. To come home? Well, just what was home? Home was a passionate wrench in the gut, the stark undeniable remnants of starvation. Home was a blithe, ravenous, free-wandering sojourn through the mist of her mythic days, the boundless and boundary-less home territory of total freedom and benign neglect. Home was Lily and her keepers, her demons and her fears. It was also the blue-lipped taste of fog, of soul-levitation during the early morning 'rush hour' crawl through the mist-invisibility of the number 253 double-decker bus route from Whitechapel to Hackney, from the bestilled brick terraces of Walden to the forged-iron gates of St. Victoire's Convent Grammar School, the bipolar journey between land-locked mother, Lily, and the alien reaches of Angie's out-flung world.

And did you know that your Aunt Beattie, the Death Eater, is pregnant again? She's relentless, so soon there'll be seven of them packed into two tiny rooms. The kids are forever getting under our feet, crawling or swinging up and down the staircase, into the filthy bicycle locker, around the outdoor water pipes, under the pigeon shed or over the brick wall into that stinking débris. We all try to keep an eye on them and help out but Beattie is so fearfully wicked to your Aunt Ruth! She won't let her anywhere near the kids—all of them mute, pale and poorly looking. She doesn't trust her, so she says, as if poor Ruth, who's got a heart of gold, would ever do any harm to anyone, let alone the little children in her own family, but Beattie is adamant, she causes no end of grief and rows and she will not stop.

Meanwhile, would you believe that your grandmother, the German Traitoress, came tottering around the corner of Walden on her wooden cane last week, on the pretense of bringing us news. I know how much you love her, and that cuts me to the heart, but she's my sworn enemy, and always has been. What she wants from me now, I do not know. I have nothing left to lose or steal, and neither does she! In fact, she wanted to know where Greta was living, so she could visit her and the little boy in Wapping. Well, a pox on all their houses! Mitzi's in for a shock because Greta is sure to start quoting 'Chapter and Verse' at her and stuffing her handbag with Watchtower pamphlets—that is, if she deigns even to let her in the front door.

A little while ago Jezz came down here, looking for Flo. He arrived in a polished grey-silver taxi, like he was delivering the crown jewels or something. I was having a cup of tea downstairs with Flo and suddenly there was this knock, and what a shock we got. It was Jezz standing outside the front door, arm in arm with these two swish blokes that—my life—looked like a couple of pimps, what do you suppose the neighbours were thinking? Jezz was still half made up, with traces of eye-shadow and rouge left over from the show he was doing the night before, up the West End; he says he's pulling in hundreds of quid every week just for tap dancing on stage, wearing not much more than a fuzz of garlands and plumes. He brought some glossy stage photos of himself, signed, and a great bouquet of roses from Kelly's and Swiss chocolates and an envelope full of dosh, then he gave Aunt Flo a big hug and a kiss—the little devil—it broke my heart when he shouted as loud as he could down the passage, sort of joking, but resentful really, cheeky-like but half tearful. He said his new stage name's Candy now; he reckoned she'd always wanted to have a girl.

Things have gone quiet now, we haven't seen either of them for months and we've lost our darling son, Peter, and you're gone, too, now—all of you gone—I don't know what I'm still doing creeping around here; this old house creaks and smells and yawns like an open grave. No need for me to sleep or wake or eat or breathe any more. I'm all used up, every last precious shred of me, so why go on? Where to? What for?

Lily's heroic, although meager script came to a close; so did her feeble attempt to bear witness to all she thought and felt, feared and dreamed. It fell to Angie to populate the hollow spaces; by now, she was well versed in reading—and writing between the lines.

CHAPTER 35

House of prophecy

Gradually Suraiya adopted the North American pastime of stock-piling food against the anticipated lean years although, by the end of that summer, Taddeusz's situation had marginally improved. He'd joined the staff ranks of Imperial Gardens. He also installed a private telephone in the flat and purchased a second-hand burgundy and silver Rolls, courtesy of his friend and new boss, Jacques Viger. Once he ceased blaspheming against the accursèd right-versus-left-side conventions on Montreal's roads and until he got bored with the novel conveniences of domesticity, he escorted Suraiya to the parking lot of a great cathedral-like Steinberg Supermarket some distance away. As a linked couple the very sight of them stopped traffic, eliciting grins and curious stares, no doubt due to their physical *mésalliance,* compounded by the sight of their appendage, the teenaged ash-weed who trailed sullenly, reluctantly in their wake.

Suraiya was beautiful, astonishingly so. Delicate-boned and regal-looking in her narrow headdress of chain-gold, her bejeweled kid sandals and diaphanous mauve sari—so convenient in advanced maternity—she trod slowly across the asphalt tarmac in the intense and blinding heat beside her husband, Taddeusz. In his own way he was also picturesque, robust and powerful, sweating into his old white cotton T-shirt and khaki shorts with the arrogant carelessness of a brigand-at-large. Given his belligerent swirl of premature white hair and her dark stylish oil-shimmering coiffure, there appeared far more than a decade in age between them.

Often contemptuous of all that fell under his gaze, even Taddeusz could hardly fault the quality of the food and drink, stock-piled along these sloping aisles at Steinberg's, their overwhelming abundance and freshness defied even his raspish tongue. "No, that's too expensive—I won't pay for that," he said, scowling, his deep resonant voice carrying far enough through the store to humiliate Suraiya as, pensively, she stroked the cool flesh of the courgettes, the leafy endives, the massed colony of artichokes, gleaming with dew and arranged temptingly in their baize-carpeted tray beneath a concealed row of neon beams.

Although he wouldn't admit it, Taddeusz also couldn't help but be impressed by the supermarket's assembly-line efficiency, never to be found in Europe, from the fleet-fingered cashier to the uniformed packing boy who sped their glow-orange tagged grocery bags, filled with feathery fresh produce and a gaudy tonnage of cans, onto a transport of sliding ramps from which they emerged ten minutes later at the warehouse depot, to be loaded into the open trunk of their car.

"No, don't tip him, he's well paid for that job," he growled, "and next time make sure that you check the prices as they go through the cash. I don't want to get cheated. Angie, that's going to be your job from now on—(he paused, twisting his head around from the steering wheel to inflict his awesome *Götterdämmerung* glare)—and I mean it, girl, God help you if ever you forget from now on!"

Once back on the highway, Taddeusz stamped on the horn like a crazed commander of the Light Brigade.

"*Hey,* what are you doing, you just cut me off, you hag, you're a menace, you ought to be taken off the road!" he roared over the din of the engine, poking his wild hoary head out of the open car window and brandishing his plump fist, sparkling with crystals and gold, at the woman driver as she eased her vehicle into the swift-moving flow of traffic from the feeder lane on the left. Angie flushed, her ashen cheeks braised as much by embarrassment as by wind and sun. Suraiya draped her transparent veil over her eyes, silently outraged, for a few moments seeming to hang her head in shame.

As they breezed along, Taddeusz glanced back at Angie. His voice became teasing and playful; his glowing amber rage morphed into a wily grin. "What's that face for? Stop sulking, damn it, as soon as we get home, you'll need to sort out the monthly invoices for me and prepare the cheques for signing. After that I've got hundreds of Rolodex cards for you to fill in, with your nice neat handwriting, remember? From now on, I'm training you to be my second-in-command!"

Suraiya resembled an affronted deity. Her enigmatic expression, her silence spoke volumes. Angie, wedged in the back seat—a veritable bounce-caravan of supplies—interpreted that stiff, deliberate turning away of her head, stirred up that familiar potent silence in her own mind until it spread and suffocated, grew eyes and claws. *She's angry with me again, and I don't know what I've done. I know she hates me, she hates herself, she hates all women, she hates all womanhood.* Nature erred gravely when it fashioned Suraiya, or else perhaps this was her penitential karma, she had so much wanted to be born a man.

"Hurry up with those bags," said Taddeusz, as soon as they arrived home. "I've been waiting all week for an important phone call. That damned Viger was supposed to have called me back by now!"

Suraiya hoisted herself out of the car, the stone-embodiment of hostility, carrying a small grocery bag, the only one she could manage, into the house. She installed herself and her unborn child at the kitchen table; once the bags and boxes were lugged inside, she began directing Angie on where to stock the food. Wiping perspiration from her neck and forehead, she motioned here and there, panting slightly and stroking her enormous abdomen with a gesture of discomfort, even of pain.

"Oh, this debilitating heat, I can't bear it any longer, the baby used to move like a tiger but now it's gone quiet. I just know it will be born premature."

"Was that the phone ringing?" shouted Taddeusz, as he dragged in a carton of office supplies. He dumped the boxes onto the sofa and lunged down the hall.

Suraiya shifted in her chair, closed her eyes infinitely slowly, then roused herself. "Start chopping some parsley and onions for dinner," she said, fixing Angie with an aggrieved, somber stare.

A minute later Taddeusz crashed into the kitchen, kicking an empty box-carton out of his path. "Guess what, Viger finally got back to me, his contact down at Radio CKGM wants me to do an early morning radio interview. A phone-in horoscope consultation for the public, live, next Thursday. Finally, a breakthrough, and it's about time!"

"An interview on the radio?"

"Be quiet, Angie, your father is speaking to me, not to you!"

Suraiya did not appear impressed; she looked grave and judgmental, but Taddeusz was beside himself, enervated with excitement, as though impelled to the ends of the earth by his own *'heavenly hound.'* Here was his big break! Here it was at last, his manifest destiny—he knew it, he sensed it; even here in exile, on this bleak saturnine planet, his fate surely was to transcend the illusion of obscurity till he glowed white-hot in the public eye.

"Angie, finish up in the kitchen, quick," he said, "I'll need all my astrology notes at hand, so start transcribing them onto cards right away."

Avoiding Suraiya's raging glance, Angie rinsed her parsley-and-onion-stained fingers and followed Taddeusz into the office. From his desk drawer he produced a sheaf of loose typescripts, their corners well thumbed, slightly coffee-coloured and shiny with age. Angie began copying from a list of prophetic vignettes onto individual drill-punched index cards in her childlike, slightly up-angling script. *Venus in the First House: Beauty, grace, good reasoning, but poor judgment of character leading to deception, esthetic refinement, generosity, capacity for affection, appreciation of the arts and beauty. Venus in the Second House: Riches gained through the opposite sex, talent for trades beautifying the body or entertaining the mind; money spent on luxury, adornment and pleasure. Venus in the Third House: Perfect harmony in the family, good mental aptitudes, many social acquaintances, love of peace, pleasure, trips, and gains through travel. Venus in the Fourth House: Prone to excesses and lack of constancy, happiness through parents and favourable domestic affairs, ease and comfort in later life.*

This sounds nuts, thought Angie. She was now a North-American changeling, so the word was no longer: crazy, insane, or mad, but nuts. "Who typed this?" she said.

"I did, from the translations of Hindu textbooks, now get on with it, will you?"

Oh, damn, this is going to take forever, she thought, once she reached halfway down the page; her attention wavered, then returned to its task. Where was she when those birthday gifts were being dispensed from the furthest reaches of the solar system? She scanned the list for any Venusian attributes she might conceivably claim as her own: *Poverty in early life, separation from parents, domestic battleground and famine field, enforced long journeys, obstacles, death of siblings, a life of exile, secret enemies and self-undoing*—could there be anything else?

"Once you've finished transcribing Venus in the Twelve Houses," said Taddeusz, "you do exactly the same for the Moon."

Moon in the First House: Queer tastes—(queer? echoed Angie)—Okay, change that to *'peculiar' tastes and constant changes. Moon in the Second House: A number of successive occupations and lack of stability in pursuits. Moon in the Third House: Twin siblings, early death of mother, many short journeys. Moon in the Fourth House: Accidents on the water and danger of drowning, possible insanity, many changes in situation. Moon in the Fifth House: Childish disposition. Moon in the Sixth House: Persistent delusions of wealth, often living in the train of some wealthy protector. Moon in the Seventh House: Unlucky in love. Moon in the Eighth House: Fatal ending of life on water due to the hatred of persons of the opposite sex. Moon in the Ninth House: Travel to foreign countries, life of exile, death in a foreign land. Moon in the Tenth House: Upsetting of good prospects due to wicked conduct. Wretched and restless life, and tarnished reputation. Moon in the Eleventh House: Undesirable associations and ruined chances. Moon in the Twelfth House: The worst position—criminal tendencies leading to a life of dissipation and corruption amidst the lowest surroundings.*

So was nothing blessèd to be found from lunar fortune? Was Mother Moon a malicious and unstable heavenly body, a frigid spyglass and planet of negation, engendering a martial crusade of mothers, lovers and surrogate motherers—Renie, Mitzi, Lily, Lena, and now Suraiya—each of them waxing and waning through her life, an unquenchable procession of beheaded castle ghosts, fleet-following one after the other, grinding their own personal legend, their defeated insignia, into Angie's nascent years?

Taddeusz declined to comment or explain. Though he enjoyed nothing better than setting his household retinue to work, today he was also applying his own manic energy to reorganizing his cramped and overflowing office space. He unpacked the crates of limp-tattered Astrology books. He resurrected three ancient wall charts, Raphael's thin dust-blue Ephemeris Tables, Conversion Tables, Tables of Houses, Latitudes, Ascendants and Descendants, as well as blank templates of celestial charts. Despite their miserable circumstances, this one phone call on behalf of the radio station, so unexpected, so miraculous, had electrified him with hope.

"I'll need to design a new business card and letterhead, T. Morvaye Astrological Consultancy. It'll cost a bit, but it'll be worth it. There's a great hunger out there for what I have to offer. So many people are lost, confused and misguided, despite the government, despite the schools, despite even the so-called churches, people still need to be instructed, to be guided and encouraged, to be enlightened. They need to be able to contemplate their own past, present and future, to take cognizance and to take control. There's a universal dissatisfaction, a profound malaise within the human soul that needs to be assuaged. I can promise you, girl, that paltry little task that you're doing for me now will one day reap fantastic rewards."

Taddeusz had spoken, and his words required no response. Angie's inscrutable gaze returned to her note-copying. Her lips, which so much resembled his, remained closed; her mind resumed its murky fishbowl of thoughts. Despite the fleeting respite from domestic warfare *à la Suraiya,* she re-entrenched herself, conditioned more than ever now to silence and to circumspection, standing guard behind a permanent shield-work of self-defense. Virtually that whole weekend was spent cloistered, like a mediaeval copyist-scribe, in her father's must-scented '*Inner Sanctum.*' On Sunday evening Taddeusz placed in front of her a blank celestial chart.

"All right, now that you know the principles of casting a chart, let's practise with yours," he said. "What's your exact time of birth?"

"I don't know, Mum told us she had to get to the hospital on her own; you were broadcasting the evening news on *B.B.C.*—so it could have been anytime between 9 o'clock and midnight."

Taddeusz scanned Raphael's Ephemeris Tables for 1946, the Chinese year of the Dog. "*Ach,* no good, that's not accurate enough; I'm just checking whether there was single or double summertime that year. We can cast your planetary positions but, as for your Ascendant, it could either be Aries, Taurus or Gemini; you'll need to make an educated guess, based on—"

"On what?"

"On objective self-knowledge and empirical observation of your own character." His grin was wizard-like, as he dutifully dispensed a dose of mediaeval physick unpalatable to himself. "So my advice to you, in this instance, is—don't rationalize or ignore your flaws or weaknesses, face up to the truth about yourself or you'll be led astray."

Advice to sublimely ignore. Angie amused herself for a time by creating separate celestial charts and puzzling over her three potential destinies. She wanted, she willed for herself a glorious fate; it was a desire transmitted to her, gene to gene, via her father, Taddeusz. Yet the task before her required careful concentration and the patience and skill to juggle a host of planetary bodies, and their alleged consequences, in the air. She considered the option of Taurus Rising, lining up all its planetary aspects and astral implications. Then she adjusted her Ascendant from Taurus to Gemini, but decided that wouldn't do. What if she placed her Moon in Aries into the First House? No, that was no good, either. This pastime was entertaining, and worrisome. None of the three cosmic arrangements was completely satisfactory and certain permutations amongst them appeared disastrous. Angie visualized herself hovering at the 'Gates of Heaven' before her ill-advised descent onto earth, having last-minute talks with God.

"Well," He might say, "make up your mind, I can give you a poetic tongue, a legacy toward the middle of your life, a good strong energetic constitution, but death to one of your children—

"Or how about an eccentric, bordering on schizophrenic personality, deaths among brothers and sisters, a long life and many children, but restrictions and confinements and a lacklustre career—?

"Or else, and this is definitely my last offer, a mediocre career which you'll beat out with the utmost of hardship, a blissful marriage, brilliant children, a battlefield for an early home, and an untimely death by drowning."

It was Suraiya herself who offered to settle the question.

"Almost anyone in India can do that just as well or better than your father; for example, palmistry is an ancient skill that is widely practised in our country," she said, peering into Angie's palm, her eyes darkening, her magnificent head perched solemnly to one side like a physician with dire news to impart. "I can see that most of your lines are unformed, just look at both your life line and your destiny line; they definitely indicate an undecided, vacillating type of character. Your hand shows no direction, no conviction—(Angie noted that Suraiya's own leathery cross-hatched palm appeared hacked into being by some raving mystic-machete)—a very ordinary life you're going to have, Angie, very safe, uneventful, and ordinary."

Suraiya's gloating pronouncement was received in meek and silent acquiescence. This was now a marked characteristic of Angie's, perhaps of them both, although, for that reason, so difficult to detect, this hybrid vice-virtue of deceitful inscrutability and buried resolve: *All right, so she's out to kill,* thought Angie, careful neither to respond nor to react, *why not just whip out that kitchen blade and slit my throat at once!*

CHAPTER 36

MAGUS

Suraiya's son, Amarendra, was born in September, two weeks premature as she had predicted and, in keeping with tradition, Taddeusz was broadcasting live on the air at the very moment her first-born was being ushered into the world.

It was such a monumental transgression, such a hurling-to-the-sky grievance that it became legend and was never allowed to be forgotten by anyone. It mattered not that Taddeusz's interview and open-line radio broadcast was a 'raving success,' these literally being the words of the station manager who claimed that CKGM's network of phone lines were jammed almost from the instant that Taddeusz's deep Dracularesque voice, with the hint of a ghost-echo from Bran Castle, invited ordinary members of the public to phone in for an instantaneous horoscope forecast.

"They were mostly young or middle-aged housewives," recalled Taddeusz, brimming with elation, hoisting a coffee cup in one hand and breathing new life into an almost-extinguished cigarette in the other. "There were a few young people, students, I suppose, and the occasional stay-at-home, unemployed or shift-working male. I impressed and astounded all of them, I took them all on, both the sweeties and the belligerent cynics; one or two of them tried to set traps for me, they tried to bait me, but it was child's play, especially when they started bringing the Church into it and I responded by quoting Kepler and Jung; besides, since I was dead right ninety-five percent of the time in my natal-chart analyses, I won every argument, hands down!"

Suraiya soon tired of hearing all this. She was aggrieved that Taddeusz had left her to the mercy of the world at her most vulnerable and celebrated moment. "A first baby, the most extraordinary event for any woman, like traveling to another planet, it's indescribable, and the labour was so harsh at the very end, I thought I was going to die. Can you imagine, Angie, the man barely even glanced at his newborn son and he hardly had a moment to spare for me, either! Of course, he's so wrapped up in his own Super-Ego, his own brilliant success, we could both have perished, I and the baby; he simply left me here to fend for myself although, thank goodness, you were able to come with me in the taxi. I swear by the Goddess, I swear, I shall never never forgive him for this, not till my dying day."

Nevertheless, to his public, Taddeusz was a sought-after novelty, a breath of exotica, erudition, entertainment and intrigue. His notoriety spread and a rival radio station soon offered him a lucrative 12-week 'experimental' slot. Press releases were fed to the English, then even the French media. Newspaper interviews, book contracts, even the occasional TV guest appearance followed, as did his private consultation service and media requests for biographical blurbs, which Taddeusz composed with lively inventiveness. The Morvaye family moved out of their miserable hovel in no-man's land, for Amarendra needed a nursery-room, and Taddeusz a suite of office space in which to receive a procession of client-guests. Their private library grew more voluminous, impressive and inspiring. By the end of that year, Taddeusz was routinely inundated with piles of fan letters and official correspondence. He was also encircled by women, of every age and genre.

Like Jesus, Taddeusz had been born onto the earth, the son of a mixed race, a *'Mischehe'*; like Jesus, he, too, believed himself to be part Jewish, part Divine. From his earliest coming to consciousness he felt powerful, even invincible, as though he walked the earth with 'the force' behind him. During his darkest days, somehow he managed to retain a belligerent belief in his own genius, his own destiny. Although bankrupted more than once in the course of his tumultuous life, Taddeusz rarely felt poor. His personal legend renounced the very concept, the debilitating notion of poverty. So Christ's famed miracle of the *'Loaves and Fishes'* held a profound and particular significance

for him, as did His stuntman-like feat of '*Walking on Water.*'
At the height of his new fame, incongruously, or so it might
seem, Taddeusz took to studying the Gospels: *In the days of
Herod the king, behold, there came three wise men from the East
to Jerusalem, saying, Where is He that is born King of the Jews?
for we have seen His star in the East and are come to worship
him.* Arriving home from school one day around mid-December,
Angie found her father hard at work amidst a heaped chaos of
books and unfurled charts, scribbling, humming and frowning,
painstakingly correlating the movements of the heavenly
spheres with the Messiah's risen, and fallen Star, casting a
posthumous celestial chart for Jesus.

He dabbled in oils, producing amongst other works a pug-
nosed, modernist Christ which Suraiya hid behind the credenza.
Taddeusz detested the symbol of the crucifix, the dark side
of Christ. The Messiah was not merely a symbol of suffering,
He was also the incarnation of power, of glory, of ultimate
charisma. Why then was the crucifix so ubiquitous, why was
it chosen as the supreme symbol of Christendom? Taddeusz
rejected its morbid message of abasement and self-immolation.
It made him feel resentful, even angry, and he refused to keep
one in the house. Instead, he favoured the vision of his Christ
ablaze in glory, gazing out over His conquered world. Given his
own rise in popularity on the airwaves and his remarkable spike
in growth on the ratings charts, Taddeusz was now being given
free rein. On one radio show he discussed, or rather monologued
on his personal interpretation of Christ's *'Hidden Years.'* Angie
caught snippets of the morning broadcast on her tinny little
transistor radio during a brief recess period at school.

*Now who was the real Jesus Christ, the human flesh-and-
blood, as well as the astrological Christ?"* she heard Taddeusz
demand rhetorically of the unseen multitudes, his million-fold
audience spread out anonymously across the city. "We know
from the Scriptures that He was a rising Superstar, a minefield
of healing power, ferocious energy and charisma. There has
always been speculation about whether Jesus did, in fact, marry,

331

whether He had consorts, or even concubines. Everyone has heard, of course, of His celebrated acolyte, Mary Magdalene, (*forgive me if I get personal and inject a note of humour, but my own former wife Lena used to detest it when I teasingly called her Magda Lena*). Anyway, my own belief is that if Christ acted according to the cultural traditions and mores of His times, He may well have had, granted, not a harem but, at the very least, (*sorry to spout such 20th century platitudes over the airwaves*) a normal stable relationship with a chosen partner."

As might be expected, within hours, the radio station was inundated with complaints from this, the great city of Churches

"Can you tone it down a bit, Tad?" said Joel, the assistant Manager. "I don't know what it's like in Europe, but here the Church establishments are heavy-duty powerhouses, especially the French."

"But I don't understand!" said Taddeusz, wolfing down his smoked meat bagel, which he knew was going to give him heartburn. "Why do they get so touchy whenever the word Christ is mentioned? The Churches have had a two-thousand-year monopoly on serving up their Messiah, according to their dictates, but the historic Jesus means many things to many people and, besides, what about freedom of speech? I thought this was a democracy?"

"Well, I guess you thought so, until proven otherwise." Manofski grinned faintly, but he looked worried. He wasn't going to be able to digest his smoked meat, either. Consulting a teleprinter in the mailroom office, he called over to Taddeusz. "Listen to this one—'*Your recent comments on the air are offensive to many Christians and distort the facts and pervert the spirit of the Scriptures*'."

"Exactly how did I do that? Let the priestly complainers explain—why not invite the '*Holy Guns*' here onto the air for a debate!"

"Oh, Christ!" said Joel.

"Well, why not?"

"The show's classified as light entertainment, no need to get confrontational."

Taddeusz shook his head, clearly angry and upset. This was not the first time that his impulse toward histrionics defied all reason and caution. But there was more. Hadn't he already blazed his way through the most devastating war of the century and, against all odds, survived unscathed? Was it not a flood of naked race-hatred that had first driven him from home, robbing him of family, freedom, security and ancestral legacy? Fascist intolerance, even when cloaked beneath a Christian surplice, came essentially from the same bestiary and must be opposed, on principle. His cheeks flamed, his entire body bristled with holy steaming anger. "Let them do their worst, I won't recant," he said.

"If this keeps up," replied Joel, gesturing toward the overflowing mailbox, "I'm sorry, Tad, but you may have to."

Suraiya (between sessions of feeding, burping and diaper-changing Amarendra) had 'eavesdropped' for a few moments on the morning radio show; she added her own voice of assent.

"Of course, he cannot hold his tongue, *il ne peut pas se la fermer, non!*" she remarked, sliding more and more into her inherited native Frenchness. She spoke of Taddeusz in the third person as if he were deaf, or an absent deity. "He *must* make enemies wherever he goes; mark my words, this will be his downfall yet again."

"*Rubbisshh,* what are you talking about?" Taddeusz was plainly irritable and exasperated at Suraiya's little half-dose of truth; it was distinctly uncomfortable.

"Whenever your father finds a good situation he has to ruin it for himself—*il n'agit jamais autrement*—it's a sick compulsion of his. People say he is a genius but, in reality, he has a strong touch of madness, as well."

333

Her child, Amarendra, and she remained connected to one another, as though still in the flesh. Plaintive and disoriented, whenever she put him down, he maintained his guard-vigil, searching always for his true protectress, Suraiya, detecting her fragrant presence in the room, twisting his feathery dark elongated little head, calling out to his *'Other Self'* with his habitual little choking noises, those well-practiced sounds detectable only to her ear, which routinely drew her back into his orbit, he, having perhaps regurgitated a tiny avalanche of curdled milk onto his miniature bib and velveteen sleeper.

For his part, Taddeusz, although once again a new father, remained disconnected, uninvolved, moving invisibly around the nether reaches of their familial universe. Cooking, cleaning, child-bearing and child-rearing, this was women's world and women's work. It was the accidental fallout from real life, having little or nothing to do with him. By now, he had shifted his professional consulting office to the second storey of a nearby shopping plaza. Of necessity, Suraiya depended more and more upon Angie.

Her confinement persisted and deepened, for her emptied gut had been re-filled with earth from which flourished a bloom of passion for her infant jailor, Amarendra. He was now her Sun and her god-legend. She blossomed within his infant radiance, his prowess and his beauty. She fed him the costliest, most exquisite infant platters, flakes of cereal, honey and warm milk, blended spinach, zucchini, carrots and sweet potatoes, mixed with a half-spoonful of raw egg yolk.

"It's so important, the early nourishment of babies," she said, protective and proud, then hesitating in a mildly pained manner before continuing. "You're always so pale, Angie, so dreadfully weak-looking and pale; your father told me all about your lazy, half-mad mother who never took care of you properly and never fed you. It's such a tragedy, when you realize that a baby's brain cells develop from the moment of birth; this is such a crucial time for an infant to be fed properly, and goodness only knows what you survived on, it's irreparable, one can never reclaim that time, nor make good the damage!"

Angie fell silent, ruefully contemplating the starved and stunted condition of her brain.

Taddeusz, meanwhile, was a man with a brain on fire. Before breakfast the next day, he was already scribbling the first draft of his rebuttal against the united Churchmen of Montreal. In particular, their figurehead, le Père Boucher.

'I do not speak and have never spoken blasphemously against the Person or the Godhead of Jesus Christ, I have nothing but the greatest reverence and esteem for Him. I do not attack Him, rather I seek to shed some small light on His miraculous Being. I seek to put myself into His shoes, identify with His Flesh and Blood at that crucial moment of historic Time; I seek to understand the dangers and challenges of embodying an exalted spiritual mission such as His in a world of Imperial Slave Masters, Disbelievers, Apostates and Pharisees.'

"Let's hope that these miserable little Churchmen recognize themselves amongst that motley crowd," said Taddeusz, half to himself, impatiently hoisting up his flagging pajama bottoms, the tip of his ballpoint pen poised in the air like a tiny spearhead. "Angie, where's my coffee, for Christ's sake!"

"The water's boiling."

"Suraiya, my shoes, I need them polished, and a couple of new shirts and socks and my shaving gear—Oh, and also some underwear and my winter jacket. No, not that one, the new one. I'm going down to Vermont for the weekend, I've got a station manager down there interested in broadcasting a show!"

Then finally, he was gone, along with his crushing footstep, gravelstone voice and windy coat-tails. The echoes of his fierce rush and bluster drifted away; the household inhaled a deep meditative breath, restoring itself to the centrifugal gravity of its bond-Mistress, Suraiya.

As though retreating to the hushed ruins of a temple, she re-assumed her yogi-like position, seated cross-legged and barefoot upon the sofa. In her white silk lounging suit, she seemed little more than bone and shadow. Scarce of flesh, although soul-heavy, pensive and brooding, she calculated the improbable chances of her escape, she, a condemned prisoner, an enchained and ravished power. In the saturnine dimness of her son's second winter on earth, Suraiya gazed tragically out from her living sarcophagus, mesmerizing Angie in the solemnity of her stare.

"You don't suppose I believe one word your father says, do you? He's got another woman *again.* Oh, yes, I know him too well, he can't deceive me although he tries, I feel it in every pore of my body. That's where he's going, you can be sure; he's planning a sordid weekend with his supposedly secret paramour."

Angie felt herself seizing up, yet again, in a kind of rigor mortis of the mind and body. She was agitated and resentful that Suraiya should compel her to listen, in impotent silence, *surely for the hundredth time* to her eternal fury and her ceaseless lament. At the same time, she raged against Taddeusz, the alleged, larger-than-life source of Suraiya's misery; she wanted to get up and run screaming from the room—*Oh, no, no, not again*—*!* She's going to rehearse and relive all her dramas from the very beginning, about his cruelty, his carelessness, about the stream of illicit lovers he's flaunted in front of her eyes during the whole of their ill-fated alliance; she needs to proclaim it, she thrives and flourishes on it, but I can't bear it!

It's one thing for mortals to hear tales of murder, pitched warfare, fornication, deceit and betrayal amongst the Olympian gods—Jupiter and Juno, Leda, Apollo, Dido and Aphrodite—but when the alleged exploits of such pleasure-seeking deities came ravaging the very corners of this prosaic living room, it, too, became transformed to lit stage and proscenium, dominated by its lone statuesque figurine, incandescent and trembling, semi-molten with rage, Suraiya.

. In the encircling silence, as if the whole of the ancient world looked on, petrified and sighing in their cracked stone bleachers, she performed and performed and performed, unceasingly, for an audience of one.

CHAPTER 37

Nativity Play

Suraiya gradually lost her subtle darkness, washing paler and paler with each successive winter. It was inevitable that her migration of mind and body should veer more and more toward the European. Before Amarendra entered nursery school, she found herself a talented French Canadian *'coiffeuse'* and traded her sandals, beaded veil and sari for the chic little designer dresses, petite tops, slacks and skirts of *'La boutique centreville.'* At the same time, she retaliated against Taddeusz and his blatant womanizing by taking a lover. Who precisely this might be was shrouded in mystery, for Suraiya's blossoming history of garden parties in old Calcutta had instilled in her the proper sense of discretion. She depended on Angie to stand guard over Amarendra on certain evenings during the week and also to be her necessary mouthpiece, prevaricator—if need be—and more or less willing conspirator.

'I have a friend now, a man friend,' she said. *'He takes me out once in a while, but it's purely platonic. I need some diversion, some harmless recreation, I need to get out of the house—for a few hours at least. I've been locked up here for years now with nothing but the children and the household in my charge and your father, as you know, is never at home, well, hardly ever!'*

Surely Angie must have lied before, white lies, fibs, secrets and silences of commission or omission, but the evening Taddeusz came home from a business trip two days earlier than expected, she told the first serious lie she could ever remember.

"Where's Suraiya?" growled Taddeusz, smelling a rat.

"I don't know."

"You don't know, *you don't know*? She didn't tell you where she was going?"

Silence. Angie held her breath, appearing flushed, furtive and guilty. Taddeusz must have understood. He paced around the apartment in a consternation of unrest. He consumed Camel cigarettes until the tumultuous living room was a fug of blue smoke and littered ash, its 'ambiance' and proscenium props transforming themselves in readiness for whatever fresh drama was about to unfold. Angie vanished to the temporary safety of the 'shade-wings,' feeling anxious and worried. Petrified, actually. She knew she was somehow responsible, even though she'd been propelled into this ghastly incriminating situation against her will. At around one o'clock, Taddeusz chain-bolted the front door. He retired upstairs to the master bedroom. But no one slept much that night; as the oppressive nocturne sky faded to a pinkish azure-grey, came the tinkling crash of '*la châtelaine's*' house-keys against the windowpane.

"Angie, Angie, wake up—I can't get in."

Taddeusz was wide awake too, listening out for Suraiya's arrival. His heavy step was heard crunching along the unlit passageway. Amarendra stirred in his bed and began to cry.

"Don't you dare open the door," shouted Taddeusz from the kitchen; then came a smash of porcelain china—"*Verdammte Scheiße!*"—as he attempted to make himself a cup of coffee.

"Angie, Angie—" Suraiya sounded giddy and unusually light-hearted. She giggled, as though still floating on the effects of last evening's champagne. "The milkman will be passing soon; does your father want to scandalize the neighbours?"

"She's not coming back into this house!" shouted Taddeusz. Amarendra, in instinctive sympathy with his beloved progenitor, hurtled toward them along the passageway, screaming at the top of his lungs.

"*Angie, Angie, viens, je te répète, viens ouvrir la porte!*"

"I said don't let her in!"

"Angie, *Angie*—" Suraiya was now calling out to her through the slit letterbox.

340

"Oh, Jesus!" Tense, angry and disturbed, Angie threw on her dressing gown and ran barefoot to unbolt the front door.

How much longer, *Christ O Christ!* Already four years, four stinking years since her incarceration in this quasi-familial Gulag, not of her choosing; it felt like four hundred. Almost from the start, Suraiya had pushed forth her tough burgeoning little shoots until they pierced, took root and lodged inside Angie's inner core—fertile ground, indeed—for the practice of Soul-Control. Over time, Angie soaked up each subtle nuance of her adoptive Keeper, the myriad faces of surrogate Earth Mother, Mentor and Tormentor, Captive and Jailor, Oppressed and Oppressor, Ally and Foe. When Suraiya spoke, Angie sprang to attention. If Suraiya frowned, if the 'iron curtain' of her silence fell for days on end, Angie searched, sick with malaise, until she detected or invented whatever secret act of guilt might have caused Suraiya's disapproval or distress. At the age of eighteen she was now thoroughly brained into a mother-cult, herself, a lone membership of one. She could hardly remember ever having pursued her own thoughts or wishes unmolested. Where was her wild, ragged and starving gypsy Self, her blithe and carefree 'Self,' benignly loved and neglected by mother, Lily, in their tribal backwater-dwelling on Walden? Angie was now clothed, fed and fattened; it was a pact that carried a price. For the last four years, the simplest act of eating, talking, reading, sleeping or dreaming was conditioned, judged, praised or condemned by virtue of Suraiya's capricious or irrational unwritten law.

"What are you reading?" she asked Angie.

"It's book on Metaphysics, I got it from the library."

"What nonsense!"

"It's difficult to understand, but I'm trying."

"Have you still got that absurd notion in your head to study Psychology?"

341

It's not absurd, thought Angie; she responded with silence, abrupt concealing her Collins German pocket dictionary before that got confiscated, as well.

"Put that away," said Suraiya, "it has nothing to do with school."

As for Taddeusz, he had definite ideas about Angie's future. "She's going to be a teacher. The city is flooding with immigrants, Italian, Chinese, Vietnamese—from all over—and their kids are inundating the schools. The school boards have started recruiting candidates from colleges and shopping malls, they're so desperate for staff they're practically hauling people in off the street. Angie will have a job for life. Besides, I've already investigated. The training course is dirt cheap, I'm going to enroll her right after Xmas."

"A teacher? Oh, yes, of course, I can just see her, as always sitting on her—*posterior*—at the head of the classroom, reading, marking and scribbling as our headmaster in India used to do while the pupils sat toiling in silence."

Angie seized up; her entire body went on combat alert, prepared yet again to deflect or ignore Suraiya's artillery of belittlement. The roots of her hair stiffened like a cat's crest. Her throat tendons tightened, her breathing became shallow, her throat dried up, her cheeks flamed darkly, her brain became putty or clay; her brain turned to mud.

"Have you noticed how your daughter loves the sound of her own voice? She adores showing off and display, yet at the same time she is lethargic and idle; that's the trouble with her, you know, she was born lazy and born tired."

But Taddeusz ignored the proceedings. He had more urgent concerns than the familiar tension of domestic bickering. News had just reached him that his mother, Mitzi, had fallen somewhere along the Seven Sisters Road in Finsbury Park and been taken by ambulance to hospital. She suffered the classic broken hip that lurks in wait for so many grand ladies of a certain age; it was a messy and difficult operation, after which

Mitzi awoke to find herself held together by a 'plaster of Paris' body-cast and a surgically implanted metal bolt.

Abandoned by most of her loved ones, even she had to acknowledge that she could no longer live alone in her former London abode. A Canadian entry permit was granted on compassionate grounds. Her scrupulously neat, museum-scented flat in North London was emptied, her belongings packed. Once discharged from the Rehab Centre, Mitzi was helped onto a flight leaving from Heathrow. Hours later, she arrived at Dorval Airport, supported upon her two rubber-tipped walking canes, a reluctant captive delivered to her adoptive wilderness home. Who would have believed it? Here she was, for the second time in her long life, uprooted yet again to be blown further westward in her life of flight.

But this was not all. For Taddeusz, the present golden era was fading, its magical '*ambiance*' abruptly souring. The civic authorities now joined their fists in a united front. They had identified a need, an urgent need to safeguard the public weal, to take restraining action against Montreal's dizzy or wily band of practitioners of the mantic arts, who misled or otherwise preyed upon the unwary. Digging back into the law books, the City Fathers chose to resurrect an arcane 17th century statute, prohibiting witchcraft and sorcery. Local astrologers, celebrated soothsayers, psychics, public prophets of every genre were targeted, to be reeled into the larger net, but Taddeusz knew it was his own prominence, his deliberately provocative and goading tongue that had first incited the cross-hair sights of legal scrutiny to be trained upon him.

"Of course, it's the debilitating progress of Saturn in my 12th House," he pronounced, in an unusual attitude of resignation and gloom. This was the domain of hidden dealings, secret enemies and public executions. Fortunately, or perhaps not, he was able to plot the exact constellation of his own nativity, thanks to Mitzi's indelible memory, her compulsive Prussian mania for record-keeping and her lifetime habit of journaling. To this day she treasured her two red canvas-bound ledgers of entries, chronicling her life's events from the banal to the sublime: from the recollection of her first grand ball, at the age of twenty, wearing that gauze-silken party gown in which she danced deliriously the Waltz, the Polonaise, awakening to find herself stricken with the onset of pneumonia the next morning—to that unforgettable, almost Biblical scene of an all-night carriage ride to Timişoara in late November, 1918. Mitzi noted that the night was clear, with a fresh wind, and not particularly cold, she being almost nine months pregnant with Taddeusz, and her husband, Edi, beside her. At five in the morning they crossed a rogue band of de-mobbed military traveling in the opposite direction, their bayonets unsheathed upon their shoulders, searching for unarmed Jews to kill.

There came the sound of Mitzi weeping in her bedroom, her throat rattling and wheezing with the gradual extinction of her breath. It was painful, even embarrassing to watch. To Angie she appeared to be broken, bravely plastered and re-patched but sapped of spirit and strength. In the primrose of her youth she had tramped through the hiking trails of the *Schwarzwald*, deftly eluding the many business-like no-nonsense offers of marriage from village shopkeepers and child-ridden widowers who appraised and coveted her health, intelligence, youth and beauty, a multiplicity of values, enhanced by her quick mind, well-drilled work ethic and eagerness to learn. Instead, independent Mitzi had breezed up and down the country in search of new and interesting paid work. She invaded and conquered the great cities of *Stuttgart, Frankfurt, Munich* and *Bremen.* On one occasion it was a stint in one of the great houses, where she was hired to train the household staff on a new fleet of luxury sewing machines. The elderly *Gräfin* and her husband, the lord and lady of the house, took a particular liking to Mitzi. They ordered her meals to be served in a private suite. They gifted her with personal souvenir photographs (with castle in background), and before her final departure to the train station, they enclosed an ornate tin canister of wrapped fruitcake slices, along with a miniature string purse containing a white silk handkerchief and a new minted gold coin.

"Can you read this—*Kannst Du ein bisschen Deutsch lesen?"*
said Mitzi opening up her precious journals. The yellowed
pages were full of the racing flourishes of her old German
gothic-style script. "Can you understand even a little?" she said
hopefully, producing a miniature pocket loupe.

"I'm trying," said Angie.

Mitzi pulled herself together and wiped her eyes. Together,
they sat complicitly huddled in her borrowed quarters on the
upper floor. The *'Salon-Théâtre'* downstairs was off limits. At
this moment its double doors were slammed shut, barricaded
by the repelling force of Suraiya's contempt.

"Never mind," said Mitzi, "I'm going to tell you my life story
from the very beginning. *Meine Wiege stand in Westfalen—"*

"Wiege?"

*"Just listen, listen, and you will understand. Ich bin am 10.
April 1890 in Essen an der Ruhr geboren—My parents married
very young; Father was just twenty-four, Mother was eighteen.
Her sister, Tante Anna, had married quite well and through her
husband's influence, Father obtained a post as station officer
with the Deutsche Reichsbahn.*

*As I grew older I was often punished for my exuberance,
racing into the street after my ball, or soiling my new white
dress in the mud on the day of the circus. At school, too, I was
chastised for my wild nature, my unwillingness to stop chattering
and sit still, yet I ranked first in class, from the very beginning.
My eyes and memory were sharp; I learned easily, painlessly;
the elegant German script was flowing artistry to my fingers;
notions, dates, facts and figures seeped like golden liquid into my
brain. On the Kaiser's birthday we wore crowns of daisy chains;
only I was selected from the choir and made to sing the special
'Kaiser' song. I treasured every one of my old class reports until
the bombardment of May 23, '43, which rid us of almost all we
owned.*

We moved often in those early days, since Father's 'Stellung' was transferred from Essen to Bochum, then Hagen, and finally to Dortmund. Times were hard, as my parents struggled to raise us as best they could. In the beginning, at least, we were strictly brought up; I, myself, had hardly any childhood. Being the eldest, I was obliged to watch over the younger ones, Else, Franz and Hans, while mother toiled at the black-iron stove, slaved in the kitchen garden, or else washed and ironed 'gentlemen's shirts' by the dozen in our outdoor laundry shed.

Oh, goldene Kinderzeit, nevertheless I do remember, when I was very small, that rare precious time spent at my grandmother's home in Cösfeld, a glimmering pearl-string of holy days, feast days, holidays. I can still see the potted geraniums she nurtured on her windowsill and those baskets of mellow pears and apples that grew like paradisal manna in her fairy-tale orchard-forest behind the house. When I lost the house keys, Grandmother ranted and cursed and chased after me with a knobbed tree branch, but I fled and hid myself in the woods. Then it was her time to feel remorse; she worried and fretted till I returned just before twilight, my sins all forgotten, all forgiven."

There came the sound of little Amarendra, being hauled along the passageway, thrashing and twisting, his cries shrilling the air like tiny pock-marks, defying the notion of being put to bed. Mitzi smiled faintly; she continued.

"At the age of fourteen I was sent away to learn sewing and fine crochet-work at an Atelier in Bremen. I was fleet-fingered and deft although, at heart, I had little interest for the work. Later I was sent to work as an assistant in a hotel but, again, it was tedious and toilsome for me, so I dodged the kitchen and amused myself by playing with my employers' two small children for hours at a time; this pleased them since it saved them the cost of a baby nurse, but when I came home for the holidays, Mother refused to let me go back to Herr and Frau Chemroth's establishment for it was clear that I had learned nothing at all. I thought only of dreaming my way back into my fairy tales and populating my tiny sleeproom with costumed dolls."

There they were still or, at least, their modern-day successors, a harem of stiff, glassy-eyed, woolly-brown or blonde-haired creatures, bedecked with Mitzi's exquisite lacework, multi-coloured silk remnants and fake pearls. Somehow, they had been selected to stowaway on the North Atlantic steamship crossing, packed alongside her irreplaceable journals, photographs, front-buttoned dresses, rolled bandages, elasticized stockings, lavender spray cologne, woollen underwear and silk neck-scarves.

"A decade later, shortly after war broke out, I abandoned these useless occupations and joined a three-month nurse's training course, organized at St. Johannes Hospital by the Red Cross. To test my nerves I was made to observe my first operation, a baby, both of whose legs had to be re-broken. It amazes me even today that I did not feel dizzy or faint at the sight. It was carried out with speed, with detachment, but also with gentleness, even mercy. It surprised me, too, how quickly I learned and how much I loved my work. 'Mein Verlobter'—my fiancé—Herr Yosef Stahlman was sent to join his regiment; at the beginning I received his letters but heard nothing more from him after the summer of 1915. I was serving, at that time, as nursing assistant, traveling on the regular hospital supply trains from Dortmund to Frankfurt. There was also an old transport wagon, slow and quiet, that carried all the returning soldiers—some eerily singing, under the confused, almost hysterical ruckus of shouts and screams—back to the Front. The many wounded were delivered to us and treated directly within the railway carriages. There were five doctors on board and each had his own assistant, carrying supplies of bandages, injections and hot chocolate drinks. It was our duty to remain on board until all the patients had been treated, so often we traveled as far as Frankfurt, before returning to home base. A telephone line had to be installed, a luxury hitherto unheard of at our home, so that I could be reached both night and day. It was exhausting and exhilarating work, but eventually, after two years of 'Bahnhofsdienst,' I became restless for some new adventure. I answered a call from the Austrian Kaiser, Franz Josef, to serve at an Imperial Infirmary in Vienna."

Taddeusz and Suraiya were downstairs talking, or were they arguing with one another? Taddeusz's voice could be heard in stereophonic sound; simultaneously, he was auditing his taped radio program and scribbling notes for the next day. A neighbour's car came crunching over the gravel, over the ice. The engines of a commercial airliner ground slowly overhead; it was gentle enough, yet Mitzi's washed-out milky-blue gaze became alert. Her shoulders stiffened, she listened intently, warily; it was a lifetime's ingrained response.

"Angie, don't forget to bring down Mitzi's supper tray!" called Suraiya from downstairs, before the kitchen door was pushed shut.

"Later, later," whispered Mitzi, "just listen—"

"At the Red Cross Headquarters, near the Stefansdom, I was interviewed by one of the head officers, a multilingual Italian, a Baroness. My experience was considered valuable and it seems that, since I was a genuine Reichsdeutsche, I was given preference over the others. Bus number 38 took me to Grinzing, then I traveled the rest of the way on foot. I discovered that the Infirmary, known as the Lazarett, had been established in a former castle situated near Mount Kahlenberg in the thick of the Vienna Woods.

In each huge room there were up to sixty beds, the officers usually being segregated from the lower orders, the common soldiers. I found that every nationality, even Russian soldiers, were represented here amongst the wounded, a good number of whom were amputees. The apothecary chamber had shelves stocked with drugs, mostly codeine and morphine powder rolled into thin strips of paper, since pills had not yet been invented. I was trained to start my rounds at eight o'clock each morning, serving breakfast and dressing the wounds of soldiers who were bed-ridden; the abler ones helped me to drag around the wheeled trays of food, bandages and drugs. They even helped to make the beds since we were only two nursing sisters at that time. At ten o'clock every morning, the doctors came onto the ward.

Rations were very short that winter and I felt great compassion for the common soldiers who had to survive on so little, coarse bread with no butter at all, for example, whereas the higher ranks fared much better. Once I got to know all the officers, I risked a reprimand by going around at breakfast time, pleading for a donation of one stick of butter from each of them, which I later shared amongst my poor hungry soldiers on the nearby ward. Once I finished sorting and counting the supplies of bandages, disinfectant, plaster and splints in the First-Aid Room, I had a few hours to spare.

The Castle Infirmary had a rear doorway that opened directly onto a private path leading down toward the snow-crunching crystalline woods. From here I could see the public ski slopes and toboggan trails. On weekends, they were filled with Viennese citizens coming out on day trips. They seemed to be relatively untouched by this war, and it felt good from time to time to ease oneself back into the guise of normalcy. I, too, attempted learning to ski, but the trail was so steep, I gave up. The toboggan trail was equally risky, although it was heavenly, wind-rushing down that smooth icy slope, before I ended up almost smashing into a tree. I dared not risk it a second time.

Despite the seemingly never-ending war, the dance halls, cabarets, concert and opera houses of old Vienna were still full; it was in those years that I learned to love the music of Wagner, Schubert and Mozart. On certain evenings we visited Schloß Cobenzl on Höhenstraße, although our Matron Sister would not allow us to taste more than a single glass of new wine; then, like the bitter after-taste of my future, appeared Edi, the Kavallerieoffizier who was to be my first lover, although not my first love. That chance encounter of ours (no, it was surely fated) determined all that was to follow: my wedding in the Registry Office in Vienna, my exile to Hungary, then to Romania, following the Revolution of 1918, the birth of my only son, Taddeusz, the early years of bondage, then abandonment; es war doch eine bittere Zeit."

CHAPTER 38

LA REVANCHE DU BERCEAU

Their clandestine travels covered almost half a century. Mitzi had worn herself out with the effort of retracing her dizzy highland footsteps into forested Old Europe but, for a time at least, she was at peace. Angie left her, snoring gently, within her dark cloistered little space. Her own room, further down along the corridor, vaguely resembled Mitzi's; it was a modestly furnished cell, relatively well ordered, although its shelves were clogged with books, pens, notepaper, collected reproductions of the 'Great Masters,' polished stones, wisps of dried flowers and cherished souvenirs. Like the tormented crannies of her own skull, it was fermenting in darkness, slow-brewing in concealed intellectual ferment, despite—or perhaps because of the veritable Gulag of her existence, the enforced Siberian exile of the Mind. She was Anne Boleyn incarcerated in the Bloody Tower, Princess Elizabeth treading the slip-edge of her own graveside, her prison run, her celebrated 'Parapet Walk.' This nondescript second-storey chamber of hers, devoid of lock or key, was little more than a stink-warren of remembered intrigue, of sharply treasured-to-the-heart censure, Suraiya's absence nevertheless managed to permeate the space with messages of reproach, recrimination and complaint: 'I regret to have to say this, Angie, but you are stupid, weak-minded, unattractive, and dull, although not above being deceitful. I demand loyalty and respect in return for all that you have been given, for everything that we have done for you, something that, for most normal people who have a heart, would come naturally and without asking, but no, you must be a mutant of some kind, ungrateful and hard-hearted, supremely selfish, unfeeling and cold.'

How do I get out of this hell-hole of a prison? thought Angie. *How, how, how?*

'After all these years, I need to be able to depend on you, if you aren't my true ally, then what are you?'

O God, how I detest you, Suraiya!

It seemed to frailer, meeker, more cowardly souls that Suraiya possessed or had forcibly seized the power to resurrect herself in others, to dig into their brains, read their minds and divine the future, sniff out subconscious images and visions, control psychic tidal waves and poison-influence the invisible.

'You may well have no love for me, that I know, I can so easily read your eyes and your soul, nevertheless, I demand loyalty, obedience and respect, above all.'

I'm not the one who's insane, thought Angie, *she is.*

'But I have always known there is something incomplete and vacant about you, an endemic emptiness. You have no convictions, no principles. You drift aimlessly, twisting—as though from an executioner's rope—whichever way the wind flows. The very last voice you hear is the one you heed and remember.'

God, O God, or the Devil (was to become Angie's mantra for years to come), *preserve my enemies, if you must, for the stronger they rise, the more powerful I swear I will become to vanquish them.*

That week's mail brought its usual avalanche of bills, advertisements, governmental tax assessments, queries, fan letters, requests for help, the occasional postcard from overseas. One such card, however, was of local provenance; it featured a back-lit, bearded grinning Beast with a hallucinogenic gaze. *'I thought you might like to know this looks just like you, Dr. Morvaye, on your television show,'* wrote the nameless correspondent, for Taddeusz was now a Doctor of Divinity, a distinction conferred upon him after an intensive summer session at a Theosophical Institute in the United States. Suffering from the flush of a head cold that morning, Taddeusz examined his so-called 'Beast' likeness and laughed till he almost wept.

352

"Make sure you keep that 'Beast' postcard, I'm going to frame it," he said, tossing it to Angie for filing.

But something far more ominous was tucked in with this batch of correspondence; it was a summons from the Municipal Court, a charge of fraudulent abuse of confidence, stemming from a complaint lodged in December of the previous year by a disgruntled former client, Monsieur Réjean Bouthillier: *During the period of June to September, 1964, Mr. Morvaye allegedly obtained a considerable fee from Mr. Bouthillier in exchange for false, misleading or otherwise erroneous information, professional advice or counsel, consequently inducing the said client (on the strength of supposed favourable astrological aspects existing at the time) to invest heavily in a certain commercial venture, resulting in the said client's business failure and bankruptcy.*

"Rubbish!" shouted Taddeusz, flushed both with low-level temperature and an immediate eruption of fury. "Did I create that idiot out of a mudslide? Did I hack out his pulp-brain with my bare hands? Am I responsible for his folly? Did I dictate business decisions to him by mystical transference—or by subliminal instruction? He's suing *me* because he went bankrupt? Angie, get my solicitor on the phone this minute!"

"What do you mean, it's not looking good in the *present* climate? Do you intend to represent me, or do I have to get another solicitor?" ranted Taddeusz on the phone a few minutes later.

Suraiya was trying to comfort four-year-old Amar, who became frightened whenever Taddeusz went into one of his rages. Her expression was grave and judgmental. "Didn't I tell you it would end like this?" she said fatalistically, pouring herself a glass of gold-coloured wine, albeit the breakfast hour. She looked shaky as well, several degrees more disturbed than usual.

"Now don't you start whining again!" shouted Taddeusz.

"You dare talk to me like that?"

"Just shut up, all of you. Amar, stop howling! Where's the phone book, the business pages? Go and find it right now, I'm going to find myself another solicitor today."

Angie scuttled away in search of the phone book; when she returned, a fully fledged battle was in progress. Mount Olympus was flame-erupting again, resounding to the common tirades of domestic Gods.

"What's going to happen to us now?" cried Suraiya, her smooth natural duskiness transformed to a greyish-white pallor. Her throat pulse was visibly racing as a result of her alarm. She looked resentful, even tearful. "What are we going to do?"

"Nothing's going to happen, I've got my contract signed. They won't be able to renege on it, or I'll sue them! This Bouthillier is just some wily opportunist who thinks he can blackmail, or otherwise wring some cash out of me."

"But you do this every time, and *every time* we end up having to move!"

"Do what? I'm the one who deals with the problems, not you! All you have to do is lounge around, dress up, and amuse yourself with—whoever strikes your fancy!"

"Bastard!" The word was issued in a horrified gush of breath, an involuntary response that was too late to retract. Taddeusz had no such compunction.

"Bitch! Bitch and whore!"

"Don't swear in front of the child!"

"Huh?" Taddeusz's intensely gold-flecked eyes glimmered with malevolence—*(that comical postcard Beast-icon came fleetingly to mind)*—his entire body throbbed with anxiety and rage. Angie stood by as witness, ever the silent witness, steeped in resentment, weariness, disgust.

"Angie, get me Amar's snow-jacket and his cap."

"You're leaving? Good!"

354

"I'm taking the boy out for a walk, it's shocking for him to hear your foul language. Believe me, Taddeusz, one day you will pay dearly for what you have just said!"

Angie vanished upstairs and shut the door to her room, drowning them all out, the entire motley caravan, for a time at least. This second storey inner 'keep' served as her secluded shelter and cell, fending off the suffocating oppression of the outer walls and barred doors. Briefly tranquil, it was only a matter of time before her 'Official Keepers' resumed their raucous feuding in the guard-house downstairs. Meanwhile, the walls of her own mind were prison-blocks on which she scratched graffiti-like epistles to God, or to the Devil, whoever happened to be attentive to her dark, rattling stream of myth-spinning, stirrings of hope and dismay, encrypted plots and codes, still-born daydreams and futile visions, swinging batwings of liberation.

Later on, once Taddeusz's elegant silver Rolls had vanished from the driveway, Suraiya summoned Angie downstairs. *"Now, listen to me, something serious is happening behind the scenes. Your father is making plans, secret plans."*

"What do you mean?"

"I have seen things and heard things, scribbled notes, letters, telephone calls; not only will he be fighting a hopelessly costly legal battle, but he also keeps a secret mistress somewhere in the city."

It was just a matter of time, and—true to Suraiya's prophecy—Taddeusz's feisty lawsuits did indeed prove futile against the combined legislative might of his adoptive city. His occult consultancy practice was curtailed, regulated, then outlawed altogether on this historically Catholic island which, for almost half the year, was sunk beneath a canopy of permafrost, transfixed within the glacial-blue expanse of the magisterial *fleuve Saint-Laurent*. Should he hop across the border into Ontario, perhaps head out West as far as Vancouver? No, that would be pointless, what could he hope to achieve in an oversized frozen landmass, dominated by Saturn? He ought to be looking southward to the alluring and mercurial United States.

"I'm giving you fair warning, you'll soon have to fend for yourself," said Taddeusz to his daughter, who was more than mid-way through the deathly tedium of her enforced studies. "You'll do well, thanks to the education we've provided you; meanwhile, the rest of us will soon be moving on!"

"What, Oma as well?"

It didn't seem possible. Surely Mitzi wouldn't survive such another radical transplantation. She was already frail and tentative in her movements, rarely leaving her chamber, except to steer her zimmer-frame to the bathroom and back. She, too, was now an antique Rapunzel, confined to her winter-tower; she wept quietly, confiding only to Angie. Her misery breathed and creaked, infecting the rugs, drapes and walls of her sickroom with the fungus of despair. Taddeusz also seemed perplexed at the notion of relocating Mitzi; his concerns only deepened with this burden of the insoluble. So, the assorted 'family' was moving on without her, and she was about to be abandoned-liberated? Out of respect for Taddeusz, Angie camouflaged her unexpected flight-surge of joy; her heart was rocketing dangerously in anticipation of escape.

"Angie, don't believe him when he talks, he's plotting something, I know it," whispered Suraiya.

For several weeks now she had been looking ill, a giddy planet, pale and unstable. Angie sometimes heard her vomiting in the upstairs bathroom. When she appeared downstairs, she almost resembled Mitzi in her frailness, trembling with the effort of brewing the morning coffee, mixing frozen juice concentrate or soft-boiling an egg with whole-wheat toast fingers for Amar. Even Taddeusz couldn't help but notice her jaundice-tinged skin, her weakness, the uncharacteristic swampy hollows beneath her eyes.

"What's wrong, aren't you well?" he demanded, jolted awake by the essence of caffeine and nicotine, sounding more irritated than tender.

Suraiya's permafrost of contempt, her dogged silence seemed to fray at his nerves. They stared at one another in open antagonism, verging on hatred, across the clutter of the breakfast table; one could almost smell blood. And it was then that it happened; seconds later, Suraiya was crumpled into a heap on the bathroom floor, a flurry of towels soaked red, the telephone ringing and ringing, Amar's pathetic uncomprehending screams and tears, Dr. Martel arriving, then rushing darkly upstairs, his expression a judgmental blend of Coroner and Undertaker, Taddeusz's high-pitched protestations as the ambulance was summoned to the door.

"But I didn't even know she was pregnant—!"

At that same moment, materializing as if from nowhere, perhaps from just the next door dwelling, rushed a gallant looking adventurer, shod in mukluks and wearing a loose coat of aboriginal fur. His gaze was full of compassion and alarm. *"Mon Dieu, Suraiya, what's happened, what's wrong?"* he whispered, his dark thrusting curls afloat in a steam of ice, as he stooped, incautiously lover-like, over the moving blanket-stretcher, his soft tone belying the gravity of his concern. Suraiya ignored him. She was too distraught to notice, or even care.

Like all shocks to the system, this abrupt 'happening' struck, trembled, then dissolved into the shifting fabric of Time. The house, during its Mistress's absence, began to breathe and bestir itself like a resurrected corpse. Angie missed her college lectures in order to stay home and take care of Amar, who fell asleep in front of the television set and was hauled upstairs every evening, partly fed and unwashed, to bed. Taddeusz made a couple of duty visits to the hospital, then spent the rest of the week away from home. Angie and Mitzi stuffed themselves on Belgian chocolates, genuine

Pumpernickel from the nearby Deli, German black bread, Polish salami and *Leberwurst*. Mitzi's prescribed Diabetic's regimen was ditched for a fleeting moment in which they ate like famished vagabonds, while the fugitive house rejoiced in the delicacies of freedom. Mitzi drank her stark sugarless *'Kaffee,'* then became animated, thumping emphatically on the floor with her cane as she bequeathed to Angie the last of her legends.

"Komm doch her, ich muß Dir was sagen!" she cried, urgently raking her memory for the next, and then the next twist in her life-story. She drew in a shallow, asthmatic breath; her frail lips, always ornamented coquettishly with lipstick, trembled. "This is for you to remember, it happened so—*So war es! Mein Mann, Edi Morvaye, hatte schon immer so einen schwierigen Charakter. Eines Tages, als ich meine Familie in Dortmund mit dem Kind Taddeusz besuchte, hatte ich von ihm einen Brief bekommen—*" And so it was, her husband Edi's intractable character, that fatal letter from him, the first salvo of legalese heralding the family schism; Mitzi's defiant recollections of her early love, loss, repudiation and abandonment, the torturous *'Stations of the Cross'* planted along her life's road—all of it soon to be dimmed from existence.

The moment Suraiya came home, unsteady, invalid-like, and in a cast of gloom, she sensed the trace of guilty liberation and unspoken dismay at her return which wafted brazenly, promiscuously through the rooms and corridors of her own house. Her nefarious, disquieting power re-established itself within hours; little was said, but every corner of the dwelling began to reek of her silent recrimination. Weakened and bereft, she fell into mourning for the unborn, the never-to-be-born; Taddeusz showed no sympathy; instead, he overtly shunned her. To the rest of them, too, he was unreachable. Abrupt and business-like, he seemed to be settling something in his own mind; perhaps he needed to disentangle himself from what had become too burdensome. Was he waiting for the opportunity to strike?

Freeze-melded together, they entered January and February, those saturnine months in which the iced-over world hobbles forward, them seemingly backward like a retrograding planet. Angie spoke in whispers and tiptoed everywhere, acknowledging the unseen bars re-secured to every window and door. Their Arctic shelter of a home was now a holding tank, a waiting room for something awesome that had not yet been declared. Suraiya maintained an affronted silence, a silence lasting days and days. Onto that blank enamel-board of her silence Angie inscribed her own sins, her overflowing testament of guilt. It mattered not; in those final winter days Suraiya became disconnected from the remainder of the house.

CHAPTER 39

BELLADONNA

They were visited by Springtime, appearing in the guise of a loved one at the door to the sickroom; with its flush of wind and dewy rain it banished the saint-ridden city of dust and grime, luring out into the open landscape a half-forgotten forest of scent-blossoms, naïve shoots and burgeoning bushes, offering its wayward promises of return. Above Mount Royal the legendary crucifix continued to illuminate the forests of its extinguished vulcan heart. Frère André's ghost dialogued with the Devil, wrestling him nightly to the floor of his former monk-cell and lone stairwell of a haunt below the Oratory dome. The spirit of Jeanne Mance invigilated the apothecary jars of the greystone Hôtel-Dieu. Marguerite Bourgeoys blessed the city's mushrooming schools and colleges. Marguerite d'Youville watched and grieved over its homeless drunks, prostitutes and abandoned orphans. Jeanne LeBer, famed 17th century mystic-anchorite, pursued Eternity warding off the ice tempests and fleets of enemy vessels, massing at the throat of the great river.

But the long-awaited storm of devastation in the Morvaye household was now out in the open. Its foundation of cinder-blocks shuddered; the glass cracked. Suraiya, when faced with the inevitable, was a pillar of holy anger.

"Who is she?"

"You don't have to know."

"I don't have to—?"

"The documents are all complete, you just need to sign, you'll receive support payments once a month for yourself and Amar, that's all been arranged."

"And if I contest it?

"It won't do you much good, after what's happened, and let me remind you that I have witnesses, signed affidavits."

The irony was not lost on her. "You, *you* have witnesses?" She glanced around for support at the two corporeal dread-witnesses present in the room.

"I said this is what's offered, take it or leave it." Taddeusz was adamant. In his mind, it was a done deal. Suraiya was not so easily dismissed.

"Oh, no, this is my home, my family, after all the years I've taken care of everyone—you, your mother, your daughter, your son—you're not going to rob me of what's mine, I won't stand for it," she challenged, standing abreast of her forces, her hostage-allies, Mitzi and Angie, appropriated into her Camp. Mitzi trembled, witnessing her 'Keepers' wage war over her custody in a bizarre twist of 'Habeas Corpus.'

"My mother's going to a Seniors' Residence. I want her ready, her suitcases packed by the end of this week."

"Over my dead body," said Suraiya.

"Angie can stay here a few more weeks if she wants to, until graduation."

"Traitors!" cried Suraiya. "Every one of you, traitors and deserters, you planned this behind my back!"

"Ridiculous!" said Taddeusz.

"You can't leave, Mitzi, how can you do this? After all I've done for you, all my sacrifices! Haven't you got a heart, for God's sake, Angie?" Angie said nothing. She stood there, rigid with dismay. Suraiya understood. "Traitors, and *you're* the very worst of them!" she cried.

Despite Suraiya's defiance, Mitzi was spirited away that Friday morning in a flurry of packed bags and strapped-down suitcases. She clutched onto her knobbed walking canes, her lead-and-silver crucifix and leather handbag, the last precious dregs of what remained. Taddeusz, with the chilling aspect of a pallbearer, dragged the luggage into the open trunk of the car, then assisted his ancient mother on her final journey. She looked grey with the strain. She trembled. She was tearful. She attempted to make amends, smooth over the rift, offering her last helpless farewells, but Suraiya, herself stunned and mortally wounded, did not relent; she froze her out with the fatal silence of her scorn.

Taddeusz, too, was gone, and in the company of his new bride, Inez. How did Suraiya come to know this? Theirs, like so many others, was a 'House of Intrigue,' and Taddeusz was too careless, too cavalier to conceal a trail of indiscretions, crumbs, surely, for sparrows. By now he was approaching fifty, that dreaded knell times five that brings with it the hint, the whisper, the vague sensation and implicit threat that life is over—well, almost over. Yet, issuing from the wings, here he was, the white-haired patriarch at the altar (in truth, the Registry Office of the *Palais de Justice*) beside his serenely smiling new bride. Within a year, Taddeusz had ensnared himself yet again almost before the bonds of the Bond-Mistress, legal or otherwise, had been sundered. With his new family he fled to the United States, heedlessly inviting the curses of disillusioned friends, lost lovers, passing strangers.

Suraiya, left behind clutching her son, Amar, now took on the spectral aspect of a woman abandoned, a woman scorned. A woman who now grafted herself into life's vacuum like a thornbush, a belladonna flowering, flourishing, wilting and withering, then erupting once more in renewed ferocity of strength. Angie dreamed, continually, of poisoning the living head of Suraiya, rooted in the shade-corner of their lounge in an earthenware urn. Why was it that all this time her own Self, her own soul was being forced to grow underground, and in silence?

"No, I won't go to see your grandmother, she betrayed me," repeated Suraiya in bitterness, a bitterness which persisted for weeks, even months.

"All right, I'll go alone."

"But why won't she let me see the little boy?" asked Mitzi, when Angie arrived at the Seniors' Home. "What have I done?"

"I don't know, she just won't."

Mitzi then whispered that she was terrified. A few days ago, upon awakening, she realized she'd lost the sight of one cavernous eye. She showed Angie her arthritic hand, further damaged when a window she was trying to open had dropped accidentally from its casing. Around her already was the scent of death, her aura had darkened, her flagging criss-crossed skin was a pallor of grey; she was almighty terror itself, over-arching pain and distress.

"Promise me that you'll give me a proper Christian burial," she said, wincing as she tried to shift her ancient heap of a body into relative comfort. She gestured for her flattened pillows to be shaken loose and straightened against the metal-spokes of the bed frame. Her eyes, one now sightless, were glittering, angst-ridden, a dilution of blue. Like Angie, she had a horror of the ovens of cremation.

"But you're not going to die, not soon, anyway."

"I said, promise me!"

"Oma—"

"Promise me that you'll take care of everything."

"You're going to be all right, you'll get better, I'm sure of it."

"Promise me, I said, just promise me!"

"All right—I promise."

It was then that Mitzi entrusted Angie with her twice-cast wedding ring, Yosef's glass-framed watercolour of church steeple, reflective lake and mountain, and finally her treasured cloth-bound journals.

"I want you to keep these safely for me, just in case; take them away with you now and never part with them." Trembling with fatigue, with hesitation, she clutched on to the journals a moment longer. "Promise you'll keep them with you always; they are my whole life!"

Angie kissed her hollow cheek, felt the imprint of her sagging body that was little more, now, than the receptacle of a removed soul. "I'll be back soon—"

"One last thing, this is our secret, tell *her* nothing, I don't want her at my accursèd funeral, *verstehst Du?*"

Two weeks later when Mitzi died, Suraiya railed at Angie like a child bereft. "But why didn't you tell me she was so ill?" she cried, in an upsurge of guilt and blame. How was Angie to reveal or betray Mitzi's final commandment? She could not bring herself to do it; she said nothing. There followed a brief and somber communication from Taddeusz, telephoning long distance from the United States. After a tearstorm of protest, Suraiya handed the receiver to Angie.

"You're going to have to handle this now," he said. "I can't come myself, I can't even come to the funeral. Those witch-hunting vigilantes have got my name on high-alert detention order at the Canadian border. Besides, Inez has just had a baby, your baby sister, so she can't travel. Do you understand what you have to do?"

"But how do I—?"

"The funeral expenses are being held in trust. Telephone Madame Rhéaume, she'll help you to arrange everything. I've just spoken to her myself. If you need to consult, you have my phone number here, don't you? What's the matter?"

"Oh, nothing."

"You know I can't ask Suraiya to do this; I'll never hear the end of it. I'm depending on you!"

"Yes."

"How's Amar?"

"He's all right."

"And yourself?"

"I'm okay, too."

"Good, well, I've got to hang up now, but keep me informed and stay in touch."

It was astounding the number of people who flocked to pay their final respects to Mitzi's laid-out corpus, primped-ornamented as though for a ball. She looked thinner and younger, more beautiful than ever, so everyone said, in her deep swoon of ritual and remembrance. How had she managed to reach out and touch so many people during her brief sojourn in this country? Her fellow travelers, white-haired relics of this fin de siècle, living museum artifacts all, shuffled or hobbled into the funeral parlour to sign the visitors' book, grasping Angie's hand and peering into her face, telling her how fortunate she was to resemble her grandmother, Mitzi.

Mitzi was there, too. For three full days as Angie stood in tearfully smiling ambassadorial attendance, she could sense—keenly and unmistakably—a surreal radiance of energy, Mitzi's hovering presence, scrutinizing the décor, approving the ornamental flower arrangements, the virginal lilies and fern-shrouded roses, the Christian prayer books and glimmering prominence of crucifixes, the promised grandeur of her lying-in-state.

Suraiya made an appearance; she could not be kept away. She hovered beside Mitzi's casket, condemnatory and red-eyed from weeping, excessive even for this 'House of Death.' Time, as always, stretched itself around her, a living weave of collected moments—moments belonging to the world—at first light-spirited and frivolous but inevitably transformed to 'Suraiya Time,' imprinted by her presence and densely reeking of recrimination. Angie felt such a dread of returning 'home.' Once this was all over and everyone gone, Taddeusz, Mitzi,

366

barring little Amar, who but herself was left to bear the brunt, the universal punishment for Suraiya's anguish?

Where was that chance, that finger-shaped crevasse in the wall, that escapist route fleetingly promised by Taddeusz? Of course, he had made *his* exit, damn him, but she'd been left behind like a token, a careless sacrifice. Was it possible, *God forbid*, that she might still be here, a Palace prisoner chain-locked to Suraiya, two, three, perhaps even ten years hence?

"I'll be moving out in a few weeks time, Suraiya, just to let you know." This was dress-rehearsal to heresy, to blasphemy; these terrifying words had to be practised in front of a mirror, whispered, then given breath and force and uttered out loud, loud enough to tear down the bleedin' walls—*"I'm moving out, don't try to stop me, I said!"*

Damn it, she knew that in the end she wouldn't be able to do it! Confronted by Suraiya's skewer-like stare and subtle mesmer of intimidation, of course her courage was bound to fail, her resolve would crumble. Whom the Gods would destroy they first render cretinous. Suraiya had been allowed to graft herself into the unresisting, undiscerning grey of Angie's brain. Thus, truthfully, she could blame no one; hers was the real and irredeemable betrayal, the betrayal of 'Self.'

CHAPTER 40

April 1966

LIBERATION THEOLOGY

History teaches us...with what obstinacy they defended their liberty...what vengeance they practised upon those who had deprived them of it, Machiavelli

Angie, imprisoned in Darlene's little rust-chariot, her brain a whirl of leaves and dust, contemplated the streamlined perfection of Interstate Route 93, slicing a path to freedom—the American dream-freedom, plunging through New England's rock forest heart. This was truly a *'Thanksgiving'* weekend, with a touch of class. In the Bostonian university town of Brookline, two thousand literary volumes lined the restaurant's walls as décor; in lieu of rock or musak, Mozart, Beethoven and Chopin raved.

Angie's friend, Darlene, a solidly built, less-than-statuesque libertine, breezed in beside her, flicking smooth her wind-tossed hair which, in classic 'sixties fashion, was aggressively blonded to its shadow-roots. Her nose was blunt and fleshy, her gaze contentious, defiant, like the gleam of oiled malachite.

"Go on, how did you do it, tell me all that again," she giggled, reveling in vicarious revenge. "How did you manage to get sprung from your wickedy stepmother's witch-prison?"

Angie laughed, thinly; she looked guilty, pale, furtive, as though Suraiya's claw-like grasp could stretch out and reach her all the way to greater Boston itself. There was a cultish, swamp-quality to her mind, despite her recent felonious dash for freedom.

"God bless little Amar, I owe it all to him and he'll never know; he provoked it without even realizing."

"So, what happened?"

"Well, I was in a godawful temper, ferociously brushing my hair upstairs in the bathroom, anyway I wasn't being careful and somehow the handle of the hairbrush hooked onto my glasses, and they fell and went skidding over the floor."

"Yeah, and—?"

"The plastic frame cracked, and one lens fell out. It was nine o'clock at night, there wasn't a store open anywhere, and it was thundering rain outside."

Darlene giggled again.

"There I was, half-blind without those damned ugly things—a necessary evil, I suppose—anyway, I went into Amar's bedroom to find some plasticine or glue to fix them. I had to switch on the lamp, and while I was rummaging around in his toy box *she* came pouncing in."

"Get out, get out of this room!" she said—those were her words, I had no chance to explain—"How dare you disturb the child while he's sleeping?"

"Bitch!" whispered Darlene, with feeling.

"She looked demented, like a howling storm-wind; I wanted to kill her!"

"No wonder!"

"I went back to my room, but I didn't sleep that night, my rage was too precious, I couldn't afford to let it go!"

"I told you, didn't I? I told you a long time ago, that dame is sick, man!"

"By four in the morning, half-blind though I was, I had all my stuff packed. I scrounged about half a dozen carrier bags for my rags and my books. There was my one suitcase for my grandmother's things, the things she left me. My passport, my school diplomas, my birth certificate, my citizenship papers, I made sure I had them all. Then I put on the coffee maker to keep me going; it felt like a vigil or a wake, but really, it was a fierce, solitary celebration. I had to be careful, though, not to wake anyone, although if she'd tried to stop me, I think I'd have done her in. I waited till it was almost daybreak to call a cab. Then, on my way out, I tossed a note onto the kitchen table. Meanwhile, the driver was dragging out my stuff; it was still wet outside, there were puddles in the gravel driveway, it was darker than twilight but the air tasted clean and cold. We drove toward the highway and even then I still couldn't believe it—*I was gone, out of there!*"

Darlene's eyes, stabbed by sunlight, were a glitter-stone blue, her laughter so raucous that strangers, even those at the far end of the coffee bar, paused to glance in curiosity, some faintly smiling, some frowning in her direction. "Well, I'm glad you came to stay with me, finally; I've only been badgering you since last year."

Walden Pond in Concord, Massachusetts, when they discovered it, was steeped in the abundance of myth; the air tasted like the elixir of life. Here were the echoes of Henry David Thoreau's universal loon, that trilling ghost-creature whose lone call is so mesmeric, it entrances like the siren-songs of Circe. This was Thoreau country, the quintessence of America. Here lived, perhaps still lives, the spiritual progenitor of '*Civil Disobedience,*' of transcendence, silence, intellectual apartness, and solitary walks of the soul. According to the tour-books, constructed somewhere amidst these *Walden Woods* was a replica of the famed philosopher's cabin, but Angie preferred not to find it. Just the steep-pitched pond, the dense resinous trees were enough—'*Give Me Liberty or Give Me Death.*' The choice was stark and simple. Angie had abjectly, unresistingly chosen Death. Merely a freak happening and, with it, the spark of outrage that had sprung open her coffin lid. The realization made her blush with gratitude and shame.

"Okay, congratulations, it was touch and go for a while, but you finally made it," said Darlene, tramping across the undergrowth, blithely ripping up, impaling and tossing aside

371

helpless wildflowers in her wake. "Now that you're out on parole, what are you going to do next?"

"I'm going to have an affair!"

"Boring!"

"I'll look for another job; I'm no good at this teaching lark, no one told me it was going to be this hard!"

"It pays the rent."

"Humph!"

"Think about your security, your retirement savings and pension plan."

"Oh, shut up."

Darlene erupted in a spasm of laughter. "I may be a rebel, but I make it my business to know the rules. What are unions and collective agreements for?"

"I don't understand any of that, and I can't be bothered. This job is nothing but mind control and intimidation, nothing to do with teaching or learning, it tires me out."

"So what?"

"It's nothing but politics and power."

"So is everything else, believe me, I should know."

"Well, I hate it."

"I'm on permanent staff now, and the kids had better do as they are told, or else. I'm here to stay and the establishment 'brass' can't do anything about it, whether or not they like my hair colour or my shade of lipstick, whether they approve of my twelve-inch skirts, or the slimy trail of men I choose to sleep with, whether I'm invited to join their—what do you call it—*poxy* staffroom tea-making, sanctimonious copy-correcting, knitting, crocheting and gossiping. They're just a clique of wicked menopausal hens, especially Cathy, what d'you think of her, already in the sack with our dear old Principal, haven't you noticed what a cosy little nest they've feathered for themselves?" Angie's startled glance was sufficient. "Don't tell me you didn't know, *Holy Jesus!*"

"No, I didn't, I never noticed."

"Not too perceptive, are you?"

"No."

Upon reflection, Angie was mildly shocked. Did the 'Great Taddeusz' hold no monopoly on betrayals then; did this happen in other people's houses as well as her own? Even these silver-haired professionals, for instance, who dressed neatly and smiled politely, striding through the chalk-scented corridors of Kiddie Academe, past papier-mâché 'Nativity Scenes,' scrap-pasted crayon drawings, cut-out paper snowflakes, jagged Xmas firs and holy candles, stuck between the flaking wood-frames of classroom windowpanes. A revelation indeed—*wake up, will you, for Christ's sake, Angie?*

"And d'you remember 'Creeping Jesus,' Devereux, the Seventh Grade teacher who was 'let go,' the one who had his hand up my skirt at last year's Xmas party? I had to jump out of the car, quick, let me tell you, after he gave me a ride home. Well, get this, he was just pulled in for counterfeiting, I'm not kidding, I read about it in the *Montreal Star* last week!"

Back on the streets in Concord centretown they soaked up the everlasting benevolence of Emerson. Hawthorne breathed and dreamed quietly beside his bride, Sophia Peabody, up at the solitary Old Manse. The Alcott sisters, Louisa and May, were still ghost-trailing along in their well-worn bonnets, criss-crossing paths with their pensive neighbour, Thoreau, as he fled even these furtive glimpses of civilization—*I would as soon think of taking his arm as the branch of an elder tree,* apparently Louisa once whispered of him, with a wicked smile. More than a century later, a preternatural hush still prevailed over Concord's pastoral streets and its spellbound tourists.

Louisa Alcott herself was rediscovered in the second floor sitting-room of the Orchard House in the guise of her official portrait, dour, forbidding and plain, like some mature matriarch of letters. Unlike anything Angie could have imagined. Where then was Louisa's tempestuous fictional embodiment, teen-aged Jo March, 19th-century rebel and archetypal tomboy? Perhaps it was, after all, part wish-fulfillment, part legend, part lie, those idyllic images of home life with *'Marmee'* and Father, the lofty-minded educator, thinker and dreamer, who refrained from performing day labour any more than was necessary to earn his daily bread; so often, in fact, that when there was no bread at all, the family resorted to surviving on plain boiled rice, without molasses or sugar.

Louisa, of necessity, became the breadwinner, training herself to write with the left hand when the right became cramped and useless, while scrubbing other people's houses or posing as governess for the well-to-do merchant class of Beacon Hill. Given her intimate acquaintance with and deadly horror of poverty, America's best-selling authoress-to-be milked her days, distilling her life's passion and rage-sorrow in the deadwood of her books, and this, despite a mind and body eroded by war *'in her Time.'* (She and Mitzi would have a thing or two to share, should they chance to meet in the hereafter). Her sister's transcendental print-impressions still graced the walls, a celestial diffusion of blue, while the spirit of May still presided in the cellar of the old house, whose rough-hewn floors were inlaid with the stones of pilgrimage. And everywhere was the deliberate slow, slowing down of time—Thoreau Time—which meant to 'bathe one's temples in Eternity.'

"If only I could stay here," said Angie, "here, there, anywhere! I just need to get away. I dread going back."

"Why?"

"I half expect to see the 'Sorceress' one day, lurking in wait for me at the school gates."

Darlene laughed. She seemed incapable of understanding how 'Time' snapped and ground its bitter jaws together, the closer they approached what they called their home—how for Angie Time tolled and rattled in its forge, shoed her foot-soles in iron, reined and choked her in its bit. She felt breathless and leaden, leaden in heart and spirit. Was it possible just to run away, to take one's leave like the Almighty Taddeusz, who had broken free without so much as *by your leave*. What blubbering nonsense she was talking and thinking; her entire body was closing down in its rigid cloak of exhaustion. Tomorrow, or the thought of tomorrow, and every other possible tomorrow pervaded and poisoned. Her shoulders, legs and chest ached with the resistance of blocked motion, with the duality of Super-Ego at war with itself.

Was it possible to witness, as in a projection of crystal, oneself rushing to catch the bus the next morning, a futile and lacklustre Monday morning in which one arrived late, despite having risen at the proverbial 'crack.' How much precious time would elapse while Angie twirled uselessly around Darlene's miniature flat, resembling Lily during a *Luftwaffe* bombardment! What had she forgotten this time? The pupils' copybooks, their test scores and their book money, odd bits and pieces that may well have dropped behind Darlene's sofa, her room-mate's universe being a serene anarchic dive, a chaos of clutter to which she was oblivious. Angie saw herself hurrying back to the apartment to re-check the deadbolt, the water taps, the gas ring, somehow she finally succeeded in missing the regular seven forty-five a.m. bus, her mind strangled in a weir of ghoul images—of Giacomo Manotti, King Jack, their school's second lieutenant, oily dark, squat, and as powerful as a wrestler, despite the tragic sporting accident that had claimed the sight of one eye. There he'd be, in his wind-buffeted shirt-sleeves, clipboard in hand, beside the arched school gates.

"But everyone takes the public transport, Miss Morvaye, that is no excuse for being late! I've had to keep your class lined up in the schoolyard for almost twenty minutes, waiting for you," he was sure to say, while even his grim, sightless eye glinted at her in admonition, "I've had to discipline them more than once, and I can assure you that I have better things to do with my time!"

Time, the traveling illusion around which Darlene, for example, skipped nimbly and fleet-footed, in synch, at ease, always in time and on time, her regiment of sixth graders always hatted, booted and champing at the bit to escape at least five minutes before every recess break, dinner and closing time. In contrast, Angie, limp figurehead to a column of anarchy, floundered daily within her cave of mind-demons, amidst the unforgiving surge and crash of Time.

"It's the 'Sorceress' on the line, she wants to talk to you," whispered Darlene, at around nine-thirty that Monday evening.

"I'm not here," whispered Angie, in a flush of dread.

"I've already told her that, the last five times running; sooner or later, you're going to have to face down your demons, so come on, be a brave girl, tell her to go to hell!"

"Hello?" Angie heard her voice falter; her throat, all of a sudden, felt like parchment.

"Angie, didn't I tell you to phone me back? You know that I phoned here every day last week and left a message; how dare you behave this way?"

"I'm sorry."

"You're sorry, very sorry indeed, I'm sure, after what you've done!"

"What have I done?"

"You know very well." Her tone, always genteel, stung the air in its thirst for revenge. "I need to talk to you urgently. Come and see me tomorrow after work."

"I can't, I'm sorry."

"Why can't you?"

"I've got too much work piled up, mounds of corrections, I'm behind in just about everything." Even should she summon the resolve to re-enter Suraiya's cave, mentally, at least, Angie knew she'd never emerge intact.

"That's an excuse, don't forget I know you so well, always dawdling and daydreaming; you won't keep that job for long, I'm certain."

Was this the *'Oracle'* again, the voice of prophecy? Angie judged it best to keep silent.

"I'm calling to tell you that you must get in touch with your father at once. He doesn't return my phone calls either, and I haven't received a penny from him this month. He's not human, Angie, he's made of stone, and so are you! I don't wish you ill, but I do wish that one day you, too, will inherit a stepchild; perhaps only then will you understand what it's been like for me all these years."

"All right, don't worry, I'll phone him. Maybe it's just a delay, it might be a bank error or something." *Welcome, welcome to Lily's world, my lazy half-mad mother, as you once called her,* thought Angie.

"Whatever it is, *ça m'est égal*, just get in touch with him right now, tonight, this minute. Make sure he understands we're on the verge of starvation! How can anyone do this to his child, to his own child?"

CHAPTER 41

WANT

Lily, resembling the multi-limbed Hindu shade-goddess Durga, wrings one of her many pairs of hands, ceaselessly washes another pair, while a third bony hand conceals an ornate blade rammed—deliberately—into her heart. Clinging to her rag-sari are her twinned daughters, one dark, one fair, the interchangeable goddesses of Ignorance and Want.

Within the depths of her East London poverty Lily gazed at her hands, then down at her feet which were bare, exposed and derelict. She looked as though she'd been half-buried beside Lazarus, then abandoned to decompose above ground. Greta had removed her mother's discoloured socks; then, despite her sense of revulsion, she'd unwound the shroud-like cloth from around the toes. There came a reek of rotting corpses, as grime floated to the ground like sand.

"Oh, my God—"

It made her stomach lurch. Untended since Lord knows when, the rims of Lily's toenails had curved into ram-like horns that pierced her flesh, flesh that was raw, purplish with trauma and bathed in slime. Her toenails resembled a row of petrified rosebuds, or whorled nuts. Two patches along the top of one foot had lost the flesh completely; these were replaced by dark-green gelatinous pools at the bottom of which, unbelievably, were the neat white segments of bone.

"What have you bleedin' well gone and done to yourself?"

"I don't want to see no doctor, I'm not going to the hospital. Just get me that plastic bucket under the sink, please, and help me wash my feet."

"Rafael, run up the Chemist and get me a bottle of disinfectant," said Greta, fishing into her old-fashioned leather clip-purse. Then she turned around to look at her two-year-old, who was balancing on tiptoe, cat-like, tugging away at Lily's tablecloth. "Emily, you little bitch, stop that, I said."

Lily grimaced, contorted with guilt-panic and on the verge of tears. She gazed tremblingly from one to the other. "Thank you, darlings, both of you, for helping me," she said.

"I just can't understand how you can get into this state."

"You know I'm half-blind, I can't see to cut my toenails."

"Don't give me that load of bollocks, you're just lazy."

Lily went silent; it was a stubborn, resentful silence. She tried, feebly, to raise one foot high enough to be able to examine the damage.

"I wouldn't be surprised if they have to cut that toe off; that looks like gangrene to me."

Lily screamed. "Oh, no, they won't, I won't let them touch me."

"Emily, sit down over there in a corner and be quiet, or I'm going to hit you."

"No, Greta, don't, she's too little."

"Mind your own business."

Lily fell silent again.

"Where's that kid gone to? He'd better not be buying sweets again."

"It's only been five minutes, ain't it?"

"I told the little bastard to run, you heard me."

"Oh, Greta, please, don't call him that."

"Didn't I just say to mind your own business? Even the Bible says children need to be chastised when they go astray. He's an evil little sod, always has been—*Rafael*," she called out, as he appeared suddenly, ghoul-footed, in Lily's passageway, "you took bleedin' long enough to get back, you'd better not have stuffed your pockets with anything else; where's my change?"

Sidling close to Lily, as if for protection, Rafael delivered up a small paper bag and thrust out a palmful of coins, defensively, like a poverty king's ransom. At the age of eight, he was a robust and silent presence, with a spirit of suspicion and wariness about him. His eyes glimmered like guardhouse lamps. His glistening-with-sweat, rose-dark face reminded Greta too much of Luc, revolting in its beauty, almost preternaturally so, especially for a boy; his thick spiked hair was a halo of dark.

"Flo wouldn't have let you get into this state, if she was alive; it was Albert who sent me the message, all urgent-like, to get over here and see to you."

Just the mention of Flo's name was enough to start Lily weeping again. The universal injustice of it, to have been abandoned, yet again, by one of the few of this world who truly loved and cared for her—"I don't understand how she could have died so early. She was always the strong one; out of the whole lot, she was the one we all depended on."

"*Yeah, yeah,* well, I didn't have no love for her, specially after she tried to get my Rafael away from me. And him, the hypocritical little bastard, running away from home, telling her tales, lies, about all the things I'm supposed to be doing to him. What he don't tell you is how wicked he is, how deceitful and wilful he is, what he does to deserve it—*Careful,* I'm putting the bucket down here now; don't neither of you kids come sloshing into it."

How deadly ironic, this Biblical pageant transpiring in Lily's attic kitchen—the attempt to salvage Lily's mind from its own madness. Meanwhile, each day, Greta was forced to tread the precarious edge of herself, of her *own* damnation. Where was Erskine now, where was her priestly lover? He had not managed to save her, or perhaps he self-destructed in the attempt, like some frail wizard susceptible only to her poison. The truth was, she knew, that there was no saving of her, not on this earth anyway amongst earthlings; any man who got too close to her might eventually kill, or be killed. Like Kenny, perhaps like Erskine (although he had fled before being tried), like Iain, whom she had taken in consensual marriage before Jehovah's Witnesses of the true Church, Iain—her lawful husband, who was at home waiting for her now, willing to smash a wooden ruler across her cheek if ever she dared cross him. There were rules. She acknowledged that there were rules, the rules of their Church. If she remained steadfast and blind, delicately skirting or banishing her real 'Self,' while treading that narrow consecrated path decreed by Jehovah, just like all the world's simpletons, the blest, the prosaic and the holy, she could evade stumbling into the very pit of herself; she would remain safe, the devil couldn't grasp her, as he had tried countless times to do.

It was at those times that you felt disconnected, the way you do in dreams or nightmares where, try as you might, you can't set foot down upon solid ground. It doesn't exist for you, the way it seems to exist for other people; the best you can do is to float, waft, from moment to moment, from crisis to crisis, hardly ever touching down, like a mystical moonwalker, a lune-walker, bound to an umbilical locus, adrift in outer space or inner space. It is here that the 'Path to Righteousness,' the safe path—that lifetime anguish of a path trodden by so many—can be recognized from afar, a topography of ruts and rules, dividing mankind from its own evil, its sought-after occasions of sin. Yes, she had scorned them all once, Erskine and his draughty rattling churchful of saints-in-progress but, at least, by veering toward that safe path, they avoided contamination with her peculiar 'Circle of Hell,' the one located somewhere in middle earth, rank-smelling and inhabited by trolls, ever prone to the compulsions of a destructive planet.

Back at home, once again the family supper hour was fraught with tension and malaise.

"All right, so you don't want to eat what we give you, so starve," said Greta. Rafael's response was a scowling flush. Perched as though on a bar stool, resentfully kicking the table leg, he looked at his barely touched cooked greens, Cornish pastie, which to him tasted like stone and glue, a half glass of diluted lemon barley water, and a dollop of condensed Nestlé milk over a cupful of rice pudding.

"What's wrong with him, then?" said Iain, tall, blond-haired and sinewy, ambling along the passageway into the kitchen. He crossed Rafael in mid-flight as, briefly, the boy smacked into his stepfather, like a bald fist into a cupped palm.

"He won't eat, so I sent him to bed."

"He'd better not wake up Emily or he'll catch it!"

"He keeps trying to get his own way, every chance he gets, but he'll learn in the end that he can't cross me. I'm telling you, he'll give in long before I do!"

Meanwhile Rafael crawled into bed beside little Emily. It was already too dark to read or play. Early winter's eve, and this nursery bedroom was already the colour of midnight, the colour of space. A faint sighing, a rumbling baby snore issued from the amorphous hollow. His half-sibling, Emily, was grappling with her own traveling images of mind.

"Wake up, Em, wake up,"—Rafael shook her tiny shoulder, wrapped in warm, baby-smelling cloth—"I want to show you something."

She was still half drowsing as he lifted her up against the windowpane. He rustled the curtains aside to reveal a mangle of shaded brick tenements, security lamp-flares, a deserted courtyard four flights down. "Look, Emily, we're going to fly down there soon, you and me. You're growing wings, I can see them already; I'm going to lift you up over the balcony one day, *I'm going to show you how to fly!*"

"Right, you little demon!" said Greta, later that night, smashing open the bedroom door, "didn't I tell you not to sleep in Emily's bed? You won't listen, will you, but this time I'm going to make you listen—!" Rafael screamed. Roused from his first sleep, he was dragged bodily onto his own mattress. In moods such as these, Greta blazed with preternatural strength. She flung a bowlful of ice-cold water at his head, drowning his nightshirt, the sheets, the blankets—"And if you're wondering what all this is for, remember the dinner you didn't eat tonight and, worse than that, you little traitor, this is for the time you went sniveling off to Aunt Flo, trying to get away from me. Well, I've never forgotten that and, let me tell you, you're going to pay for it *for the rest of your bleedin' life!*"

Predictably, as so often had happened in the past, at around five thirty next evening, Greta hammered at Lily's front door. No answer. She pushed on it and found it open. Lily was cowering upstairs in the attic kitchen, anticipating the inevitable storm.

"He didn't come home from school today, where is he?" said Greta.

"Oh, God, he ran around here to see me, I couldn't get downstairs with my bad foot and all, so Albert opened the door for him and he scuttled up here. I told him he had to go home, I'm told him you'd be worried, I told him to be good."

"And what did he want this time?"

"I don't know, he was upset, I just—"

"Yes, you do, stop lying, I know what he's up to."

"Oh, Greta, stop that, please, he's only little."

"Don't you tell me what to do with my own kid."

But Rafael did not come home at all that night, a white night for Greta, who raved as in a scene from Armageddon, driving the local constabulary out to search for her son along the wharves, the warehouses, the pencil-thin alleyways, the mossy flagstone steps that led down to the open water.

Dear God

Watch over little Emily
and Rafael—wherever they are
protect them from their mother
who, in Your name,
fastens them to bedposts
locks them in cellars
bashes, then flushes their brains
down the sewers
feeding the subtle spirit of terror
into their gut; unbreakable hold
that will drag them behind her
all of their lives
when she dies
it will rise
like her spectre
straight from the gut.

CHAPTER 42

THE HIDDEN YEARS

Far far from there, across the half-darkened globe, the *'Taddeusz Mystery'* still glimmered darkly under its bushel—*the hidden years*—part unveiled, part dissembled. For Taddeusz, truth gazed upon too obsessively was tantamount to the disintegration of personality; it was the living, flourishing personality that must be transformed, preferably exalted through archetypal myth and lie.

As such, he chose not to harbour certain demeaning images of his early years, such as the memory of Mitzi's flash-fire of a temper as she slammed his miniature buttocks upon the enamel ridge of the chamber pot when he dared resist her fierce cleanliness training. Meanwhile, his paternal grandmother hovered nearby, wringing her long ropy-veined hands, chanting—*Oy vey, Oy vey*—and exuding the essence of vinegar. He no longer remembered his perpetual baby hunger of those sinister *après-guère* years. The iron-grinding train journeys from the age of twelve onward he did recall, though, those headlong flights through the countryside whose man-made borders demarcated the chasm between *'Mutter'* and *'Vater,'* fostering his endemic rootlessness, the gift-curse of the Nomad.

As an adolescent, then later as a young man dispatched for his own safety to Timişoara, Taddeusz chafed under the requirement for fluency, even glibness, in the state-instituted Romanian tongue. His father, Edi Morvaye, an established Timişoarean banker, had naturally learned to minimize his ethnic Hungarian Jewish-ness as a matter of good business practice and pragmatic survival.

'Vorbiti Romaneste,' Speak Romanian, was the edict printed on flyers and public posters everywhere.

Nevertheless, they lived well. As the son of a Romanianised town 'burgher,' he was sent first to complete his *Bachelor of Letters* at Diaconovic College, and then to the Military Academy in Ploesti. Edi probably sensed that war was on the horizon and wanted Taddeusz to obtain his commission before it erupted. In vain did Taddeusz try to dissuade his father from the idea; for one thing, he disliked the notion of being a soldier in peacetime.

"But those officers are such a dim-witted lot, they look like a parade of pimps in corsets and face powder—"

"Enough of that!" replied Edi, in a thunderous tone. He had lost none of his gloomy intractable nature; in fact, he was one of those few persons whom Taddeusz had learned to respect and to fear—which, to him, was one and the same. Edi had aged, of course, but there remained the expressionless dark eyes, the oddly squarish skull, receding hair, straight-ruled and of an indeterminate muddy brown colour, the sallow grooves and shadows of his features cut deeper, severer than ever. "That's the height of disrespect. I said that you *will* finish your military term, and then I promise I'll send you straight on to university."

Ploesti, a town in central Romania that was home to the great oil refineries, boasted a few modern clubs and cinemas built in the Western style; nevertheless, it was a place that stank of pigs and tar. It was to be Taddeusz's home for a full year. The cadet training school of Infantry Reserve Officers was a long, low, whitewashed structure on the outskirts of the town. Two white-gloved cadets stood erect on the left and right side of the building, patrolling stiffly and criss-crossing one another in perfect time. A yellow stripe around their caps and yellow tape on their shoulder straps identified them as the 'Master Rookies.' This nomenclature they interpreted as a mark of great esteem.

Taddeusz, one of the newly inducted 'Rookies,' was posted to the fourth company under the command of their tactical instructor, Major Radulescu, an aging soldier of genuine Romanian ancestry. While Herr Hitler was proclaiming his threats of '*Drang nach Osten,*' their Major, not quite into his dotage, was lecturing on abstract military strategy interspersed with risqué anecdotes about the pursuit and conquest of the fairer sex, those who chose to frequent the streets and boulevards after five o'clock in the evening, at any rate.

It did not take long for Taddeusz to suspect that, although outwardly the Romanian military enjoyed great prestige, as an institution it was practically worthless. The general leadership was unhealthy and over-sexed, its officers resembling orgiastic revelers, hollow-eyed and sallow-pale under their mandatory powder masks. The lower ranks, however, were beaten, sometimes even tortured, deliberately underfed and treated like animals. Taddeusz witnessed, with mild alarm, how cartridges often misfired during shooting practice and 'dummy' bombs exploded when least expected. One solitary plane was able to be commandeered for a routine manoeuvre involving air support, and even that was forced to land because of engine trouble. The machine guns failed; the gunnery officer had forgotten to inspect them before the exercises started. Taddeusz grinned sardonically at the news of this outrage; the man must surely have been detained the night beforehand in one of Ploesti's dark '*speakeasies*' by some Greek beauty recently released from the local VD clinic.

Despite his former schoolmaster's opinion—'*Very erratic irresponsible character, may improve if guided*'—Taddeusz understood that in cadet school it was salutary to at least appear as a model of behaviour. After all, he was now a nobody amongst nobodies, the protégé of no one in particular. He knew better than to challenge these incompetent despots who were his ranking superiors. Besides, there were spies everywhere. Somehow the Company Officer seemed capable of reading their thoughts. Innocent remarks spread like viruses, returning to haunt the most incautious among them. Mishu, the priest-poet (for even priests were drilled in Romania at that time) was suspected of carrying tales to the C.O. Taddeusz learned to trust no one; it was just a question of time, of biding his time until this harsh and dreary year of weapons-training, guard duty, interminable inspections and parades was over. One needed to keep a low profile as well, avoiding the unwelcome notice of any burgeoning fascist-racists among the ranks. *'Foreign elements'* were suspect. Even in cosmopolitan Bucharest, two hours away by train, it was reported in the newspapers, with an air of jest, almost of approval, that some youthful pranksters, students at the Law Faculty had publicly stripped down the pants of two fellow colleagues suspected of not being genuine 'Romans.'

Was it this, then, that accounted for his arrival, penniless, on the British mainland, sometime in 1939? According to his own account in the memoir, *Permission to Land, Denied,* as a fully fledged officer of the regiment at Timişoara (his father's former regiment), having run afoul of commanding officer, Lieutenant-Colonel Procop, he was ordered to lead a raid into the perilous no-man's land abutting the Hungarian border. Later on, once his official protest up the chain of command backfired upon him, faced with court-martial or the insane asylum, he escaped the military hospital in which he was incarcerated and somehow, under a hailstorm of iron and fire, succeeded in making his way out of the country into Spain. He moved unobtrusively through the bipartisan lines of Spanish civil warfare just as Franco's troops were mopping up the last pockets of resistance that remained. Taddeusz chose not to dwell on the humiliating necessity of having to feign loyalty to one group and then the other, as circumstances dictated. His facile grasp of languages helped him to dissemble his position and, by his own dark-humoured account, most of those he encountered took him for a reliable fascist. Deserting the country by a circuitous route which took him first to Morocco, then France, he managed to get on board a vessel that was crossing the English Channel. By 'accident of fate,' he disembarked finally as a destitute alien-exile, somewhere in the vicinity of 'hell-fire corner,' the fortified chalk cliffs of Dover.

As a survival-bent species, having eluded the immediate danger, was it not ironic that Taddeusz should then gravitate, straight as the crow flies, toward the poverty-stricken East End of London, which was on the verge of being blitzed out of existence by his own maternal countrymen? This was where, had he realized it, the unborn generation of Morvayes loomed expectantly like 'Shades'; yet to think, had he attained his first choice, had Lily's sister Ruth accepted him in matrimony, not a single one of them would have been born. The East London borough of Stepney, this was the entrenched city-seat of the Herman tribe. Twelve or thirteen sons and daughters, presided over by their abjectly poor father (later driven insane by his own invisible demons) and raised miraculously to adulthood by their Magna Mater, Renie, who created the semblance of a home out of virtually nothing, somehow managing to stretch pennies into pounds, making loyal allies of the local East End tradesmen, roaming the open markets to scavenge for end-of-the-day bargains. *'We don't know how she did it,* they said, *but Mum always fed us well; it's almost miraculous, really, we're all strong and healthy, and none of us ever caught TB.'*

And so what to make of Taddeusz's hasty war wedding with a native Briton of second choice, somewhat too poor and too dark-complexioned for his taste? Was this little more than a sentimental convenience, offering him the coveted immigrant's status in a 'safe' country? Somehow they had all lived through the terrifying *Blitzkrieg* then, later on, the relentless wave after wave of V1 rockets that pierced the clouds like fleet-finned crucifixes and it seemed the whole of the screaming city was driven underground. They fled into shelters such as the Tilbury Goods Yard, where hundreds, perhaps thousands of civilians cowered together head to toe, all along the bays. At the beginning there were only four earth buckets at the far end, behind screens for toilets, and the whole place, he remembered, with a shiver of disgust, was a stinking cavern from hell.

And then, of course, was his own inevitable 'dance with death.' On the night of the 21st January 1941, the Norwegian merchant ship, the *SS-Kronenberg*, under the stewardship of Captain Akse, sailing at a moderate speed of five knots on route from Reykjavik to Kirkwall, encountered two columns of an Allied convoy outward bound. Unexpectedly, due to signaling failure or misjudgment, the *SS-Kronenberg* was struck on the port side by the British vessel *Castleford* which was sailing directly toward them, without lights and at full speed. The stricken Norwegian vessel, smashed in half, sank rapidly by the head and was lost less than half an hour after impact. In the resulting terror and confusion, 22-year-old ordinary seaman, Taddeusz Morvaye, escaped onto a port-side lifeboat that was lowered into the heaving icy sea and immediately flooded with water. Somehow, it remained afloat with most of its half-frozen occupants inside. Like the legendary Christ figure on the storm-tossed waters of the Galilee, bolstered not so much by faith, but by his own primitive will, Taddeusz escaped destruction; unlike Christ, he did nothing to salvage his fellow kinsman, able seaman and gunner Laszlo, lying exhausted, stunned or perhaps punch-drunk in the ship's hold. Were the 'Shades' of his many yet unborn gathered bleakly around him during the hours spent, tempest-tost, amongst the ice floes of the North Atlantic? If so, surely they knew that their future incarnation depended solely on his brutish determination to stay alive and afloat, at the expense of his drowned comrades if need be.

It was after this soul-forging event, that Taddeusz began to believe, as never before, in the powerful forces that had kept him alive for a distinct purpose, surely, whatever purpose that might be. It was at times like these that he felt invincible, almost luminous, a gleam of metal slicing, butchering a path toward his destiny. Somehow this conviction sustained him even during the months that he languished in an internment camp for Alien citizens on the remote Isle of Man. Finally released, further interrogated and debriefed, he was ushered into the *B.B.C. Foreign Service* as a trainee foreign-language news announcer. Then, at the climax of the war, the British War Office recruited him from amongst the most promising of registered

Aliens in their midst. Taddeusz's particular blend of attributes, a quick intelligence and excellent knowledge of languages, his complex ethnicity and ease of contact with an enemy nation was potentially, at least, a national treasure. As a fluently German-speaking disenfranchised son of a *'Mischehe'*—a racially impure coupling—he was officially briefed, made to take a solemn oath of secrecy, then summoned to a meeting of the 'underground' Astrological Research Bureau which met at Grosvenor House in Park Lane, under the leadership of Hungarian-born novelist and astrologer, Louis de Wohl.

In this group were five or six recruits who spoke perfect German and were willing, in the national interest, to delve into the study of astrology. It was believed that Herr Adolf Hitler consulted regularly with the famed Swiss astrologer, Karl Ernst Krafft, who was not a Nazi himself, just a hapless 'servant to the King.' Absurd though it may seem, British Intelligence Services began investigating the possibility that the entire war effort might be being guided, if not directed, under the influence of Hitler's own natal chart, that of Germany's in general and of Hitler's Chiefs-of-Staff in particular. Cryptically labelled the 'Black Group,' these multilingual recruits, while assisting the operations of the British War Office, were advised that their personal beliefs in the 'Science' of astrology were irrelevant; the urgent task, for which no one but De Wohl was paid a penny, was to fathom the complex system that astrologer, Krafft, was using and strive to anticipate what kinds of predictions and recommendations he was likely to make to Hitler himself.

After a three-months' crash course, Taddeusz was required to practise his new skill. He was secretly incensed at De Wohl's complaints that his efforts were not 'profound' enough; later on, whether to encourage Taddeusz or to boost his ego, De Wohl remarked that his recent work had helped focus attention on the future actions of some particular German commander or otherwise pinpoint some imminent attack. It would appear that during Hitler's first favourable Jupiter aspect, he overran France, Belgium and the Netherlands. However, as of May 1941, the

Führer's astrological chart was more and more dominated by maleficent aspects. During the famous attack on the Island of Crete he lost a great many ships and sacrificed countless lives. Similarly, for Rommel's engagement in North Africa, as well as the grand turning point in the war, the abortive Battle of Stalingrad.

Taddeusz liked to think, no, he firmly believed that his clandestine efforts had influenced the outcome of the war which, by then, engulfed half the territories of the globe. This conviction, as the years progressed, was writ large into the memory lobes of his brain. He was proud, too, that his nightly *B.B.C. Foreign Service* bulletins, his trademark gravelstone voice, broadcast in English, French, German and Romanian, penetrated the consciousness of even the most oppressed by feeding accurate up-to-date news reports on the progress of the war, whether for good or for ill, combatting the gluestream of Axis propaganda, which was routinely false or distorted. Not that the *B.B.C. Foreign Service* did not use Taddeusz for their own brand of propaganda, which was to try to indoctrinate the concepts of Western-style democracy into countries like Romania, Hungary and Bulgaria; however, to him this was a fair exchange of goods. He prided himself on his far-reaching reputation for credibility in those dark years, the hidden years; once, he was able to warn the citizens of Ploesti about an imminent air assault on their town by British and American Forces.

Of course, the right hand had to be employed to spy upon the left one. The British Naval and Military Intelligence Service conducted an independent study into Astrological research and, from time to time, Taddeusz was contacted by anonymous agents for the purpose of verifying the accuracy of their own calculations and charts. Not a single member of this clandestine group was above suspicion and, besides, no single person should be entrusted solely with the mission, there being a very real danger that their leader, De Wohl himself, might become a casualty of war. In the course of his 'duties' Taddeusz was required to compose a series of articles in German, mainly interpreting the astrological charts of Hitler's chief generals. They were certainly intended to be used as propaganda, since only maleficent interpretations were solicited; the more positive ones were destroyed. Within this sinister vortex of systematic disinformation, did he act as 'secret agent' for Britain as well? Years later, Taddeusz hinted as much in a chance remark to his cousin, Anneliese, which was promptly forgotten. During the Allied bombing raids over the Westphalia region, even his mother, Mitzi, had lost contact with him. She had no way of knowing whether he was dead or alive, having fled Dortmund for the countryside at the height of the bombardment, leaving no forwarding address in her wake.

In those years leading up to the armistice, Lily slept very little in the only flat they could afford to rent near the Elephant & Castle Tube Station. Waking or dozing, she lived in dread that the family of rats, nesting under the cracked floorboards, would one day become emboldened enough to attack her own babies in the cradle. She expressed her rage only once—it was a daring move—flinging a handful of soiled nappies at Taddeusz's precious framed diplomas from the *London School of Economics and Political Science*, which was located near the studios of the *B.B.C.* Her abashed penitence was futile. Beget in wealth and privilege, despite their present hellish accommodation, Taddeusz scorned the craven servility that often stigmatizes the very poor. Later, of course, there followed his many lovers, both overt and clandestine—*Gilly, Mona, Florence, Lena*—a revolving door of facile conquests and facile desertions. His rocky climb to notoriety, to the semblance of prosperity, was fuelled by rage. Post-war Communist Romania was a lawless, 'no-go' zone. Occupied Germany, now riven in two, had stripped him bare, thanks to its designation of him as a spurious citizen, a *'Mischling,'* a demi-Jew. *'But is it true,* his children once asked, *why don't you tell us, are we really Jewish?'* From that Holiest of Lands and eastern skies sounded an ancient cock-crow, signifying betrayal: *'Us, Jewish?'* responded Taddeusz, *'Whatever gave you that insane idea?'*

Once abandoned by the *'Motherland'*, Taddeusz never truly settled anywhere; his soul was indelibly branded with the mark of the *F-U-G-I-T-I-V-E*. From the age of five, shunted onto trains between '*Vater*' and *'Mutter,'* belongings forever being packed and unpacked, he was in continuous flight, a wingèd seed. It was this, his inbred fugitive mentality, his self-styled 'gypsy streak.' At the dawn of the 'fifties decade, it would sweep him half way around the world into the tumultuous lap of Mother India.

Yet, what remained of his leading lady, Lena, whom he had borne along with him? He'd witnessed her in light and in shadow, buried now under a heap of stones in one of those leaf-enshrouded ancient Hindu cemeteries, gorged with atmospheric *tristesse*. She was buried under Time itself, for he could not, would not saddle himself, his surviving Self, with any residue of guilt over her destruction. During his first attack of malaria, the stomach-wrenching agony, the fever, the sweating and trembling, the hallucinations, he witnessed how she stood over him in unspoken vindictiveness, how she failed to lift a finger, how she watched gloatingly as—*damn it to hell*—he almost died. Meanwhile, his enemies were her allies, Ranjit Ghosh, for example, she may well have been sleeping with the bastard, for all he knew. That surface-smiling nemesis of his, spreading poison in the Maharaja's hearing, yes, indeed, this must be the man responsible for his undoing. The scandal issuing from Lena's death was the final blow. He was compelled to relinquish everything he had worked for, all he might have hoped to acquire—*but he would have his revenge*—having seduced Ranjit's beloved niece, Suraiya, one day without warning he would abscond with her under his arch-enemy's nose.

That vast chaotic country, with its hallucinogenic visions, scents, sounds, debilitating heat, disease, mosquitoes and monsoons, was overwhelming, often terrifying. Soon after arriving in Calcutta, caught in an abrupt deluge and wading, waist-deep, across the street toward the safety of a nearby building, he'd tripped and almost drowned. It was at times like these that he questioned his sanity in coming, certainly in remaining there. Yet, gradually, the place began to evoke his fascination with its occult currents of energy, its sinister mystique. Enticing and heroic, too, was the notion of striding into the cave of unknowing, of revealing and taming its antique mysteries, with himself as mouthpiece, to the Western public at large. Judging by his sheaf of notes (one of the few authentic scrolls to have survived the time, or Eternity, spent in the mountainous vicinity of the Lamasery), the events he witnessed there shook even his hardened composure.

'Carrying my letter of introduction in Hindi from the Maharaja himself, when I reached the temple I was awfully disappointed. Hundreds of disciples had been living here for centuries; it appeared that each succeeding generation had added a little more to the surrounding filth and squalor. It was overwhelming, this reek of gloom and decay. Although the place seemed deserted when I entered, I could hear the chanting of OM MANI PADMI HUM in the distance. Inside the wall I noticed dozens of whitish bowls, some suspended, some placed along the ground with food in them; I could see that they were the upper sections of human skulls. Trying to quell my revulsion, I looked away. Further along, within a large, almost empty chamber, incense was smouldering on a low altar before a statue of the Buddha.

A lama greeted me. "We know who you are. We know why you have come. We know the Ramgarh Raja sent you."

"How? I thought that no postal or telegraphic communication exists here."

"True"—his voice was melodious and heavily accented—"but we always know everything beforehand."

Although doubts assailed me, I listened in awe. He ushered me into a smaller temple where three other lamas were seated in profound meditation, heads bowed, eyes closed. These spirit-men had mastered the art of telepathy and clairvoyance. Furthermore, as I watched, one of them descended into a deep trance, then slowly began to levitate. He hovered about three feet above the ground for several minutes before descending gently in front of a statue of the Buddha. Far more than the extreme reaches of self-hypnosis, this was a violation of the laws of Newtonian physics. I found that my own body was trembling in almost clinical shock. After this, I was led into the presence of Nyang Bas, one of the visiting lamas from 'higher up' who was said to have unusual powers. He had the air of looking not at, but through me, as though I were a drop in the whirlpool of Eternity.

"You may become world-famous, should you be granted the time to complete your life's work, but you will face grave obstacles, high tragedy and tribulation along the path of your destiny." Nyang Bas may have read my mind, for he shook his head benignly and smiled. "Once one reaches Samadhi, there is no need for primitive aids of divination."

That evening, after a ritual feast of rice and goat's milk, curd and fruit, the assembled monks drank a strange brew, which was probably intoxicating. They conjured up dogs, cats and ghosts, which they called 'tulpas,' and played with them like children. I, too, had the same hallucinations, yet I was not offered a drop of their brew. I felt sober, but not sane; I could not rationalize, nor explain away what I had witnessed. Within a few days, my nerves were so fragile, I felt I was on the verge of slipping into a kind of madness—unless I mastered this diabolical skill.

"Can you teach me your art?" I asked.

"It is no use, it would take you an entire lifetime of meditation," replied Nyang Bas. "You are a man of action; in your own way, you are destined to become a great teacher, but you are not one of us."'

CHAPTER 43

Wᴵʟᴅᴇʀɴᴇss ᴘʀᴏᴘʜᴇᴛ

There was a flurry of recording tapes, twining, squeaking, flying to the end of each reel. The network news boomed in between live broadcasts. Taddeusz's headphones and mouthpiece slipped down around his neck. The 'ON THE AIR' sign lit up. With luck, he might just about manage to grab a coffee, vile tasting though it was, before the news bulletin was over.

On the console in front of him was a row of multi-coloured buttons to launch this morning's tapes; there was a pile of cartridges to slide in and out for the canned commercials. Computer printouts were ticker-taping busily away in one corner of this cramped studio cell, whose plastered walls were the colour of vomit. It was furnished with narrow tables, crowded bulletin boards, coils of wiring underfoot and a few swivel chairs; its single doorway opened into a labyrinthine complex of airless twisting corridors that looked as though they might, in the days of legend, have concealed a Minotaur. As Taddeusz chewed minute bites of his sandwich, he kept an eye on the closed-circuit monitor that guarded the building's entrance; the flick of a switch permitted free access to visitors through the main door downstairs.

"Good morning, ladies and gentlemen, this is Count Taddeusz Morvaye at Radio WIKN, returning after a brief absence. In these intervening weeks, I have had, shall we say—a slight brush with the '*Grim Reaper*'—but, I am thankful to report that I am now well enough to resume my duties as morning host and moderator. Our guest speaker, Dr. Steinhof, is on standby ready to talk to us live from Philadelphia about the latest research into cancer treatment, and also to take a few of your questions, but first, let's listen to this important message from our sponsor."

Taddeusz's somber, gravel-textured voice, sounding more hollow than usual, faded out beneath the barrage of canned jingles. Ensconced in his well-worn, downright ratty looking swivel chair, he presided over the airwaves like a lone prophet in the urban wilderness of—*shall we call it*—generic small-town, USA. Here, at the heart of his final isolation, only the claptrap of modernity seemed out of place, anachronistic, like those frantic tunes grinding out of the sound mixer, followed by hysterical directives to get out there to your local shopping Mecca and *buy, buy, buy*. As all this faded into the aether, Taddeusz checked the digital chronometer, re-adjusting his headphones precisely on cue.

"Welcome, Doctor Steinhof, and thank you very much for joining us this morning. I know that many of our listeners will be keen to hear your views on this seemingly modern phenomena which troubles and disturbs us all—the dreadful prevalence of cancer—that it seems we are beginning to witness so often amongst our colleagues, our friends and our families, even very young children. Now before you begin to tell us exactly what cancer is, and about some of the preventive techniques and orthodox treatments that are presently being developed in this country, could I ask you, as an authority in your field, what is your candid opinion, Dr. Steinhof, on the profusion of 'fabled' miracle remedies that have been prominent in the news lately, particularly the natural substance known as 'laetrile.' At the present time, I believe it has not been approved, but has even been banned as an import by the FDA."

"Well, obviously, Taddeusz, so many people, when faced with the knowledge that they are suffering from a malignancy, especially those who have been diagnosed in the terminal stages of the disease, will need to cling onto some hope, some shred of hope that what they perceive as—*pardon me*—an inevitable death sentence might somehow be able to be reversed. This is a normal and completely understandable reaction but, at the same time, let me stress to all of your listeners, that it can be exceedingly dangerous to put one's faith in the efficacy of scientifically unproven substances that, from time to time, are publicly hailed as miracle all-purpose healers—"

Taddeusz stopped listening and his thoughts began to ramble even before the interview drew to a close. Have you ever witnessed, Steinhof, a yogi tread the surface of the Ganges? I hear your impervious and rote-learned platitudes, but what do you really know about the nature of spirit, the nature of flesh? What if mortal sickness is nothing more, or less, than the profound will or subconscious desire of the organism simply to move on, to progress beyond this corporeal stage of existence, in other words, to die?

Himself, for example, trapped for how much longer in this ailing, and now alien body? Only in recent months was he able to immerse himself in the fabled, womb-like healing waters of the patriarchal mother-country: the quasi-mythical Romanian 'Herkulesbad' spa. Ringed by limestone peaks and pierced by caves, it was a green and tranquil place of healing and atonement. Somewhere amongst the surrounding beachside cottages was the ancestral 'dacha' of his childhood memories, no longer existent or recognizable. True, during these past four decades he had not dared to step inside official Romanian borders, so paranoid was he about being forcibly detained, but now—*now that it was almost too late*—he'd taken the precaution of surrounding himself, on this organized V.I.P. tour, with a bevy of well-heeled, well-connected American matrons who unknowingly served as his chaperones, his advance 'garde du corps.'

In a final flourish before the end of their sojourn, they were honoured at a banquet of the grandees, President Ceauşescu and his stone lady, Elena, presiding. In the midst of such decadent largesse, perversely mirrored by the mute hunger of millions of his invisible countrymen, Taddeusz stopped short of rising to his feet, *although he was tempted,* and demanding restitution for his 'Lost Kingdom,' for what would it profit him now?

At least he had managed to salvage his heraldic title, that of Count Morvaye. Delving into the annals, he'd unearthed traces of that mediaeval branch of nobility from which he probably, no, certainly stemmed. His Draculaesque cape and cloisonné-enamel coat of arms he wore on ceremonial occasions such as these.

"Friends, for the record, I must say that I abhor the notion of so-called family, *truly grave robbers in disguise,* disputing, sharing or otherwise rending my garments after my death. Just let me say, I expressly wish to be buried in this—" He confronted the astonished guests around the banquet table with a careless flourish of his cape and a macabre smile. "Believe me, I am not being morbid, truly, I have lived a marvelous life, *a virtually charmed life,* I feel as though I have lived seven lives in one."

CHAPTER 44

January 1976

Book of Revelation

Forcibly grafted within the New World, Suraiya, robbed of what was hers and virtually deserted, was steadfastly approaching her fiftieth year, her birthright of three score years minus ten. Angie was compelled to confront her again, hours after the death of Taddeusz. Who would ever forget it? That fir-enshrouded glacial hinterland of a night during which she was sleepless for no particular reason. Or was there a reason? She, beside the fringed forest-shade of the table lamp, dreaming and scribbling, scanning some worthless pocketbook or glossy mag; he, the escape-artist supreme, performing his 'final act' of abandonment.

Perhaps he was still present. During those pre-dawn hours, were his thoughts, his voice trying to reach her from some 'brave new world' beyond the known universe? If so, she wasn't struck by the certainty of his presence as she had been at Mitzi's death; instead, she lapsed, collapsed rather into a state of numbness. Emotionlessness. How could this be? Wasn't he legend—vibrant, fearless, indestructible? He, who had torched away his life in extravagant fireworks, the chain-smoker, the coffee drinker, the voracious eater, consumed by his own insatiable greed for LIFE. Consumed by his own death. Undeniably, he was her father; in this frost-dark hour, obscure and solemn, in this hour of parting, she must keep vigil with him; there was no possibility of sleep.

A few hours later, she and Amar joined forces, departing together on a noon-hour flight for the *'Land of the Free.'* For the record, here was yet another fatherless teenager, clearly shaken up and confused. After all, like hers, his was a lifetime's dichotomy of loyalties, of double abandonment. They sat, side by side, in their cramped imprisoning seats, airborne, further benumbed by the drone of the engine, miles away from one another in thought, hardly speaking, each contemplating the anarchic loose ends of their father's erratic career. Amar, representing the spectre of his mother—Angie's stepmother—evoked in her that familiar sensation of dread, for, of course, there would be Suraiya and her raging trauma to deal with later on. Was Angie one of the rare females in Taddeusz's orbit who had not been deliberately, even casually driven mad? Long ago, on a vacationing cross-country tour in his *'Open Road RV,'* her father had half-concealed a black Pekingese (the one who bathed in the bathtub with him) under his arm. 'Sorry, Sir, we don't admit animals on this trailer site,' he was told, while briefly being barred at the gates. 'What are you mean, *animal*?' responded the great Taddeusz with an astonished, mildly malicious smile. 'This is no animal, this is my child!' Amar laughed as Angie related this legend but, later on, he wept.

So, if this was his *final repose,* where was the serenity one seeks in the face of the departed? The immortal relief, or even the blankness? Taddeusz's features were stern, unaccepting, with the kind of look that plainly protested, *'Lord, I am not ready.'* Reduced to his mortal remains, his life—and the very real-ness of his death—collided head-on with the 'Myth.' Here was this rime-bearded old man, diminished and tamed by a stillness he had never known in life. In earthly sleep, he'd tossed, plotted and schemed, belched, dreamed, snored and smiled. Within this permafrost of unnatural stillness lurked the tyrannical schoolmaster, the feudal lord cloaked in theatrical black. Faint shadows beneath closed eyes; sensuous lips gummed shut with embalming fluid; cosmetic flush dissembling the grey. With a tongue lashed rigid and tight, how could he still shock and charm and arouse his listeners? In those last instants, drifting from consciousness to coma, he saw visions—a young boy, a young girl. Who were they? Witnesses record that he smiled incredulously, a kind of transient simpleton's smile, then made one last superhuman effort to rise from the deep. He could no longer speak; his final hand-scribbled words were: *'Get me Antidote to Thorazine—I have to wake up.'*

Given Taddeusz's air of the dissembler, unresigned, and lying grimly in state, Angie preferred to resuscitate his more vibrant days when he held court in his expansive sky-blue carpeted living room: ever the capricious monarch, seeking proof of an eternal soul. He watched guardedly for the truth of his fledgling prophecies. Perhaps doubting his own psychic powers, he wheedled and coaxed as soothsayers and sycophants paraded by his earthly throne. He interrogated faith healers who came calling, armed with Kirlian cameras. He sought out clairvoyants, mediums, channelers, phoneys and quacks. With his well-worn smile or scowl, he heard them all out, despite an ingrained distrust of potential Communists, fascists or anti-Semites amongst them. His own hard-core loyalists were a mix of devoted apostles, credulous misfits, soul-lost loners, all basking in his reflected starlight. There was Jolene, former cult victim, who ran up and down the stairs for him, emptied ashtrays, washed cups and delved into his Tarot cards, his Ouija board and books on the occult. There was faithful Jamie who ran daily errands; there was also his quiet-spoken ally, the very mystic Reverend Loon.

But who was the 'real' Taddeusz Morvaye, self-fashioned prophet of the airwaves, scholar, visionary, schemer, compulsive provocateur? In every file drawer, dozens of grand hopeful schemes were taking shape: the early drafts of an astrological board-game, personal self-improvement courses pre-recorded on cybernetic tapes, blueprints for a hydrogen-powered automobile, an electronic system of coin-operated horoscopes-on-demand. Nothing was too outlandish to contemplate: invisible bodily auras, ectoplasmic manifestations, silver threads linking beyond the grave. Approaching the age of sixty, while flirting with the notion of campaigning for public office, Taddeusz was still restless, forever probing, questioning, doubting, enforcing a path around the bumps and corners of life. Here was the ultimate survivor, although fashioning his own undoing, sowing seeds of enmity everywhere. Limitation, resignation, sacrifice and self-denial, these were alien, even dangerous concepts to him, never absorbed in childhood and purposefully evaded with age.

His insatiable curiosity propelled him half way around the world and back, in a circling trajectory of 'East to West.' His artfully tended public persona, his disastrous investments, his reckless flirtation with beautiful women and also the 'Black Arts'—where was it all now? What did it signify? Little more than virtual ruin at the end of his life. Having rocketed into middle age, he was already burnt out, finished, yet he chose to conceal his 'Truth' from the world, from them all, till the end. Connected only by headphones and 'mic,' enthroned on a ratty swivel chair, to his last breath he radiated his magnetic aura over the airwaves. This disembodied voice, this man, could not live—did not truly exist—without the existence of his admirers, his listeners and followers. So be it. He chose, or was chosen for, the public not the private heaven.

Officially of the Orthodox faith, Taddeusz embraced no established religion, he himself was his own God, his own Church, his own Creator of Myths. Yet, with the chastening recognition of his own mortality, he probed more than ever for proof-positive of the Eternal. A tentacled monster had begun to spin itself inside him, digging into his peripheral organs—*not enough time, O not enough time*—a dark rubbery gaseous creature was belching, rumbling, one could almost hear it growing, sprouting its spores of death. Advised, beyond doubt, that he was waning, Taddeusz filled the house with the icons of his hope and fear, vials of bootlegged laetrile, hawthorn berry powder, megavitamins, Aloe Vera and carrot juice. In time, these bottled and packaged elixirs remained untasted on his sick tray while the toxins floated further and further toward the brain. Bilging up undigested food and phlegm, bile and blood, frail though he was, barely weeks after surgery he dragged himself back to the studios of Radio WIKN. His voice was slower, more hollow, more measured. It bled him white, this last superhuman effort to appear normal.

Ladies and gentlemen, I would like to tell you that I have faced, fought and—for the moment at least—vanquished the Grim Reaper.

Beyond cancer, it was the sapping weakness that finally took him down. For a hundred days he fended off the truth-seekers, savouring at his grim leisure the foretaste of oncoming death. A wounded animal in its winter cavern, vain and proud, even as he shrank smaller and smaller into mortal stillness, his magical cape of myth unfurled grander than ever. He, who ought to have lived at least twenty more vibrant years, had burned himself out. Excessive gain and loss, reward and strife, admiration and enmity, as he often said, his was the lion's share of life. Now, divested of his magic, punished for his excess, he was merely a worn-out old man, used-up, obsolete, a straw-stuffed prestidigitator crumpling in the flames.

His funeral rites were a soliloquy of sound, orchestrated by a flame-robed priest of the Eastern rite. It resembled the lyrical wailing of a *gitane*, a soulful klezmer played out before an almost empty collection of pews: present were his remnants of family (Inez and child long lost somewhere in the sands of Time) Angie and Amar, Taddeusz's attorney, the WIKN radio station manager, an up-and-coming congresswoman named Edith Wright, faithful Jolene and Jamie, the very mystic Reverend Loon having died some months before. Side by side with Amar at the head of this meager procession, Angie moved feebly toward the graveyard, fending off the nausea and the blinding stabs of pain behind the eyes. At the squared-off gravesite she dropped a clod of sticky earth, a violated purplish rose onto the sleek wood coffin as it descended into the pit. Where was the huge motley crush of public mourners, anticipated at Taddeusz's passing? Most of them failed to appear on this drizzly January day of raw, unadulterated misery. But there was more—dark-humoured Fate decreed that half way around the globe, Lily, his first consort, should be vomiting up blood on the corner of Commercial Road, vainly striving to choreograph her 'great exit' with the first and only love of her life. It was a grim duet, a '*pas de deux*,' their swan songs rehearsed, unknowingly, upon separate stages. Flesh-and-spirit bonds are fragile; links do stretch and break. Yet, when crossing these high-tension lines twixt life and death, such bonds become imperative, even mystical.

It was no less so for his great amorphous audience of 'the Unseen.' An open-line memorial program in honour of the late Count Taddeusz Morvaye was broadcast the evening after he died. Due to the deluge of callers, the program was prolonged for almost four hours. Listeners from all over middle-America phoned in, many of them weeping. A woman caller suggested that a plaque, a stele or a statue should be erected to his memory. Suddenly there was a rash of phantom sightings, followed by other callers, convinced that they had seen and heard from Taddeusz in a dream.

In the days that followed, poring through his dank unwholesome cellar storeroom, Angie came upon a heaped chaos of self-published books and pamphlets, recorded radio broadcasts and lectures, archived press-cuttings, tearsheets, expired passports, visas, travel permits, postcards, slides and photos, the residual detritus of an ambitious life snapped short. The dust-coated hoard of correspondence spanning several decades she found most intriguing, and revealing. Clad in her thin-soled shoes, with feet of frost, she stood there leafing page by page through a heap of recrimination, threats, insults, accusations, like so many dubious treasures addressed to her father by unknown men and women who had crossed him upon their life's journey, usually beginning, occasionally ending in this fashion: *Taddeusz, I feel compelled to write to you to express my profound disappointment. At the beginning I was (naïvely, as it turns out) of the conviction that we were friends, at least comrades, who trusted and would not knowingly have deceived or betrayed one another. How wrong I was—!* Angie winced as she skimmed through these collections of familiar lines, tossing them one after the other, groaning as she did so, into the bin. Far better that Amar should not stumble upon this, not now anyway, this posthumous trashing of his father's name. What good could come of preserving the written denunciations of the world? No doubt it might all come out later but, for the moment, it was she who vowed secretly to recollect and honour his truth, even to the dark patches, the indefinable darknesses in his canvas of light.

It was at this moment that she caught a whiff of incense. The scent became stronger. And stronger. It was issuing from the recessed closet where he stored his 'cybernetic' tapes, his discarded toys and tokens of the occult. It streamed into every corner and crevasse of the cellar and remained, palpable and alive, for at least twenty minutes, before literally vanishing into thin air. (Could that be Taddeusz and his diabolical sense of humour?) *Idiot!* she thought to herself, although that night she avoided sleeping anywhere near his bedroom, with its final décor of cloth-covered sicktray and turned sheet.

At around one o'clock, from across the wide frost-silenced street, (which she imagined, in a more rational vein, might be explained away as the reverberation from some neighbour's late-night television horror film) she detected, once and only once, the celebrated 'wail of the Banshee.' So this is it, she thought, in a state of doubting wonder—*so this is the legend, this is the truth*—although why is it that no one heard it but she? By the third day came a galloping sense of malaise. Her breath was becoming short, irregular and shallow; she had a continual flutter, a keen palpitation beneath the rib cage. It was definitely time to go, to pack up the essential remains and get out, abandon Taddeusz's dreary edifice of pre-empted dreams, its sagging roof menaced by rotting cedars, its stagnation of cellar.

As expected, Suraiya lay in wait for them upon their return. With the infamous Goddess Kali presiding, the dark-lit salon that Angie remembered radiated the aura of Inquisition. Tea and Indian sweets were served, followed by well-rehearsed, sanctimonious remarks about a dead man's sins being buried with him; he should now be allowed to quit this world with dignity, despite the inequality of the will, a travesty, anyway, given the virtually bankrupt state of his final affairs.

"I feel sorry for you, very sorry," said Suraiya, perhaps because Angie had inherited little more than the executorship of a bankrupt, forlorn and contested estate. "You now intend to write his story? Well, if you choose to record honourable things, preserve your father's legend, I have no objection, but if you dare to flaunt the Morvaye name as a shame and a laughing-stock, I'm warning you, I will come and put the torch to his private papers myself."

Silence. Angie's eyelids narrowed, conjuring up from somewhere, deep in Time, a vestige of Taddeusz, or perhaps his avatar, furtive, rebellious, gitanesque. So be it, if this was the sole legacy he was able to bequeath her, the merest shred of his arrogance, his Olympian courage, his cruelty—*then grant it now!* She confronted Suraiya with a glance of profound hatred, a masque of stone.

"But it's not right for a father to have favourites amongst his children! Besides, don't you remember how he abandoned you time and time again! He is nothing to you, and he's surely nothing to Amarendra, he's nothing, nothing, nothing—!" Abruptly, Suraiya hurled an engraved cigarette case, gracious relic of nostalgia, across the fringed Persian rug. A votive candle on the Indian mosaic tile flared yellow, smoked thinly in its glass. Teacups rattled. An ornate silver spoon tinkled to the ground. On this most deserted of battlegrounds, stalking a spectral foe, here again was Suraiya and her unrequited rage.

As for fifteen-year-old Amar, he sat beside his mother in a fug of morbid silence, awkward, restless, knowing better than to try to speak for himself. Angie understood. As Paschal offering and Palace prisoner, was he the one now fated to remain behind as Suraiya's treasured hostage ten, twenty, perhaps even thirty years hence?

So be it.

Then why did it all strike her as some netherworldly joke? The storming of antique chains, of dungeon cells, prophetic stars unhinging from their orbits in a crash and clatter of maniacal glee. Was the Great Goddamned Taddeusz to be falsely redeemed, lime-washed and sanitized? Impossible. Must she purposely suppress fact and twist history? To what avail? Despite whatever forces of intimidation, hysteria, threats of bonfire, she could not, she would not do it.

CHAPTER 45

Xmas 1983

VIEILLE SOUCHE

The ancestral home of '*la famille Lavigne*' was a fieldstone dwelling, with a metallic sloping roof, at the juncture of '*rue de l'Espérance*' and '*chemin Sansregret.*' Like most other houses, its grave-like foundations had been dug out from amongst the Laurentian rock, within a vast amorphous territory responding to the general nomenclature of '*le grand Nord.*' Here the air tasted like the sun-struck breath of angels, glimmered like a blessing. Its scattered lakelets soaked up the blue of the sky; gigantic, centuries-old pines, living fortresses, shaded and flavoured it with a pungency of resin. A universe away receded the soiled congested jack-hammering metropolis of Montreal; at least, that's how it seemed to Angie as she warded off the grasp of the 'Arch-Sorceress,' Suraiya, by taking refuge in this bastion of northern Quebec. Had she distanced herself far enough into the wilderness?

'*On va t'appeler Évangéline, tu sais, parce que tes origines sont éloignées,*' said the matriarch of the family, Madame Marie-Marthe Lavigne. '*Tu es transplantée en somme—comme les Acadiens—on ne te le reproche pas, bien sûr, les Anglais ont fait la même chose avec nos ancêtres.*'

Madame Lavigne's son, Raoul Simon, the eldest, was a failed priest, sorrowfully recalled some years ago from the Grand Séminaire de Montréal. Even his name evoked a wolverine howl of emptiness, thought Angie. Wasn't he precisely her own mirror image, his dreadful need, her dreadful emptiness? Legitimized by Raoul's dark and thwarted presence, ensconced among these virtual strangers by virtue of her pregnancy, Angie now carried the Lavigne family name and legal succession.

413

'Tu es quand même la bienvenue chez nous : on aime bien notre jolie petite Anglaise. Et, en plus, tu es catholique,' they said, including the Uncles, mon oncle Jacques, mon oncle Donat, mon oncle Étienne, each of them forged in an air of miscegenation, bearing forward into this century the wind-graven features and characteristic hawk-like profile of the dormant Iroquois. True, they were genuinely accepting, genuinely kind. In a natural, even painless evolution, Angie had already begun to attach herself to her adoptive captors.

Mon plus vieux, Raoul, c'est un solitaire. Il est plus compliqué que les autres, confided his mother with a glint of angst and of pride, as she and Angie sat together at the scratched sunlit pinewood table, scraping carrots or shelling peas for dinner. Raoul's *mésalliance* with someone like Angie—a wayward mongrel of a Brit, of all things—was further sign of his apartness, as was his evident need to transcend the familial world, spurning its laws, traditions, even its natural mother-comfort as though it were a facile, even worthless seduction.

Marie-Marthe's sister-in-law, ma tante Ghyslaine, yoked in unholy Matrimony to grey-bearded bonvivant, Jacques Lavigne, spoke frankly of his penchant for illicit lovers of the looser kind. Her jaundice-tinged features, lined and overwritten in pain, were now transformed by an air of detached, faintly smiling irony. 'Let him do his worst—*j'en ai vu de toutes les couleurs dans ma vie, je m'en fiche royalement!*' she announced, when her spouse over-indulged in firewater (as she called it), becoming flushed and tipsily amorous with all and sundry at their family ritual *'veille de Noël.'* Sitting in state between the baking fireplace and the over-decorated Xmas tree, with a glance of resigned severity, ma tante Ghyslaine monitored her 'Other Half,' stumbling around the room as though he were a dog tethered to its leash, pissing outside in the snow. To the women of the household, in grave-dignified tones, she turned and declared, *'Qu'est-ce que vous voulez ? Il a toujours été comme ça : des fois, il faut savoir pardonner.'*

414

In the ensuing silence, mon oncle Étienne, a widower with the serene brow of a Jesuit and body of a dwarf, squinted circumspectly around the room; he took up his fiddle and scraped its miniature bow once or twice across the strings. Mon oncle Jacques broke into song.

> *O Maman, j'ai si mal*
> *J'erre comme une âme en peine*
> *Qu'est-ce que tu as, ma fille ?*
> *Pourquoi te plaindre ainsi ?*

"*Ferme-la!* Jacques, shut up, you're drunk," shouted mon oncle Donat, setting down his own glass and stroking his tumbleweed of flouncing white hair. Étienne's fiddle bow went wild. Jacques, crystal-eyed, purplish and slightly dribbling, grabbed Raoul's 14-year-old daughter, Marie-Ève, around the waist and attempted a slovenly jig. He winked at his brother, Donat; in provocatively falsetto tones, he bawled louder than ever.

> *O Maman, j'ai le cœur gros*
> *J'erre comme une âme en peine*
> *Qu'est-ce que tu as, ma fille?*
> *Pourquoi te plaindre ainsi ?*

> *Mon mari ne m'aime pas*
> *Il ne m'aime plus*
> *O ma belle, qu'est-ce que tu dis là ?*
> *Qu'est-ce que tu dis là ?*

> *C'est vrai, Maman, je les ai vus*
> *Je les ai vus s'embrasser*
> *J'ai tellement mal, j'ai le cœur gros,*
> *J'ai le cœur brisé*

"*T'es bien niaiseux, Jacques, act your age, pour l'amour du ciel!*" cried Marie-Marthe. "I said leave the girl alone!"

Wheezing slightly, overcome by Bacchanalian hot flashes, mon oncle Jacques, still gripping tightly onto Marie-Ève, paused for a gasp of air before continuing.

> *Mais qui t'a volé ton mari ?*
> *Mais qui est-elle, ma fille ?*
> *Je n'ose pas le dire, Maman,*
> *Je n'ose guère le dire*

"Come and sit down," said Raoul, gazing darkly at Marie-Ève. *"Je t'ai déjà dit que ton oncle Jacques, c'est un vieux fou!"*

"De grâce, un peu de respect, mon cher neveu!" said ma tante Ghyslaine, displaying her affronted sensibility. Her lips tightened, her yellowish cheeks flushed. Raoul responded in morbid silence. Wine-soaked, oblivious to the familial crossfire, mon oncle Jacques steadied himself against the mammoth pinewood dresser, rattling the blue-and-white display China, knocking over the spiky gold immortals in their vase. As he brushed the spittle from his lips, the ivory sheen of his dentures glimmered like live candlewicks.

> *O Maman, j'ai si mal*
> *J'ai le cœur brisé*
> *Va, ma fille, va-t-en donc d'ici*
> *Ton mari t'a trahie*
>
> *O Maman, je suis malade*
> *J'erre comme une âme en peine*
> *Va, ma fille, va-t-en donc d'ici*
> *Tu seras bientôt mourante*
>
> *O Maman, j'ai si mal*
> *J'ai le cœur brisé*
> *Pars, ma fille, pars loin d'ici*
> *Tu ne dois plus y retourner...*
> *Tu ne dois plus y retourner...*

"That's enough, Jacques, I'm warning you, *ÇA SUFFIT,"*
declared Marie-Marthe, raising her magnificent voice. "It's time
to raise a toast to Raoul and Évangéline. Please God, bring them,
bring us all a healthy baby in the coming New Year."

To Angie, smiling faintly, this Saturnalian week-long reveling
was becoming burdensome after only the first day; it was little
more than sleeping and waking, eating and drinking, chattering
and yawning. Her bouts of morning sickness had waned, but
still she felt fragile and liverish, confronted with the lard-
rich Xmas pies, frosted angel cakes and walnut-'*cassonade*'
confections. In those swift-reeling days of the winter solstice,
it was stultifyingly hot sitting near the fieldstone fireplace, and
punishingly cold outside.

Ma tante Henriette was becoming tearful, remembering
her older sister Margo. "I do not wish to speak ill of our Holy
Mother Church, but it was through that despicable zealot,
Père Deschênes, that we lost our sister. She died after her tenth
confinement. 'I need to see an infant in the cradle every single
year,' he used to tell her, even when she had no more strength.
'C'est le commandement du Bon Dieu!'"

"Que le diable l'emporte, ce maudit prêtre!" said Henriette's
husband, Donat, with startling ferocity. "Of course, Étienne
couldn't cope, so we adopted the three youngest, and all the
rest were dispatched to the nun's orphanage. Lord only knows
what happened to them there!"

"But now, suddenly, there are no more rules and no more
sins! No more fasting before Communion, no veils in Church,
no Penance, no fish on Fridays. Frankly, it makes me bitter!"
said Marie-Marthe.

"Fairy tales for the soul," said Raoul. "If you only knew!"

Perhaps he needed to escape this rambling, wood-scented
oven of a room where the co-joined members of his tribe were
already responding to the enforced Saturnalia of togetherness
by becoming maudlin, drunken or bitter. Before sunset there
might still be time to wander down to the little pond, the one

417

Angie had discovered at the far end of their *'rang.'* It was transformed now, of course, to a bluish-green membrane of wind-rippling ice. Frozen in time were the rusty stems of the water plants, trapped in silt shallows, the colour of sepia struck gold now and then by the sun. Paradisal. Surrounding this pond, low, severed trunks protruded here and here like unmarked tombstones of themselves. Beyond the primeval forested peak was an immense and dominant sky, nothing but sky, turbulent, gigantic and wild.

In her mind's eye, Angie sensed Raoul get up and leave the room; she made no attempt to follow. His daughter, Marie-Ève, his own mild shadow, faintly morose and withdrawn, was also nowhere in sight. Angie's new stepdaughter—how bizarre, exactly as Suraiya had once prophesied. Was this some weird happening of synchronicity, or else the *'Oracle'* and her maledictions?

"Pauvre petite Marie-Ève!" said Marie-Marthe. "She lost her mother too, already four years ago at Xmas. Our Gisèle, only thirty years old! *Pour l'amour du ciel,* that day I shall never forget; in the space of just a few hours, her skin turned yellow, like the colour of old gold. We thought that perhaps it was some virus, some weird 'flu, but the doctor said no. So we drove her all the way to the Emergency in St-Jérôme, but she lost consciousness even before we arrived."

"What was it?" said Angie.

"To this day, they don't know. They admit they haven't a clue; it's an act of God."

Mon oncle Donat grunted. "Is that what they call it, *calice!*"

"I thought I would lose Raoul as well. He disappeared for days on end. No one could talk to him. I was so afraid."

Angie stared at Marie-Marthe and noted how grey, how saturnine she suddenly looked.

"I was afraid he'd go hang himself out there in the woods."

"Oh, you women, you frighten yourselves to death with your own terrors," exclaimed mon oncle Donat. "Why so melodramatic? These things happen in life; Raoul needed time to get over the shock, it's normal."

"What do you know about it?"

"Okay, so I'll shut up then, *maudit!*"

"Le cœur est fragile, tu sais. Raoul avait tellement de peine."

"Well, we all have our cross to bear, look at Étienne, his whole family decimated. You still have your grandchild, at least."

"Yes, and, as she's getting older, Marie-Ève is the image of her mother—*des fois, quand je la regarde, j'en ai le souffle coupé*—Évangéline, I feel that you have an understanding of these things, and also that you have a tender heart. Forgive me if I am upsetting you with ancient history.

"Notre famille est de vieille souche; our roots run pure and deep. You understand that when we speak of our country we mean Québec. It was our forebears who were the first to cut down the trees, to build the palisades, to cultivate the fields, and make peace with the First Nations people. We can trace our roots back thirteen generations. Mon oncle Onésime, who studied with the Jesuits, researched the archives for us and found that one of the very first 'King's Girls' who stepped off the boat from France was our direct-line ancestress."

Marie-Marthe bent her head over the chopping board, wrestling with the excess gristle and fat on this day's roast, carved from her annual frozen quarter of beef. To Angie she resembled an Aboriginal saint, a contemporary spirit-guide with a stream of moon-whitened hair. She seemed to be endowed with a light, an intangible gleam that flickered and waxed from within, whether in tragedy or adversity, as well as the unbearable humdrum of the 'day-to-day.' *Le quotidien.* She had her fixed place in the universe, and she acknowledged that place.

What could Angie possibly dredge up in response, what roots could she disinter from her own skeleton's closet of impoverished ancestors, that litany of tradesmen and women to whom she owed her existence and racial memory, the parasol makers, ostlers, milliners, hackney drivers, kitchen maids, seafarers and stablemen that populated the Herman family tree? At this moment she actually felt unworthy, even envious of them. They had no false pretensions to greatness; at least they knew who they were, and where they came from. Besides, how could anyone label or explain away Lily—Lily of the Valley of Death—her nearest flesh-link to the past? Living casualty of war? Human statistic of collateral damage? Unfortunate by-product of military experimentation? What about her other direct-line ancestor, Taddeusz, a cross between Renaissance man and philandering wizard of the 'Black Arts'? He would surely not have been lost for words; he'd have flaunted his new-found mediaeval coat of arms, the heraldic Morvayes, upstaging the Lavigne family by several generations at least. Angie had neither the spirit, nor the will to follow his lead.

"Are you going out?" said Marie-Marthe.

"Yes, for some fresh air," replied Angie.

"Then be careful, it's slippery, you'll need boots with a better grip; borrow those grey ones over there beside the fire, I think they should fit."

When the Aboriginal peoples wished to spare their captives they allowed them to keep their shoes; traveling barefoot with one's abductors signified an almost certain sentence of death.

Raoul was nowhere to be found. For most of this festive week he'd vanished as natural wildlife is expected to disappear soundlessly behind leaf and wood. He merely tolerated these prolonged familial feast days, birthdays and death days, like so many shackles on the calendar. Angie understood, she sympathized; she, too, had begun to chafe, secretly, at their enforced although cherished incarceration. Guided more by sense than by sight, she confronted her chosen beloved beneath the twilit fortress of pines.

"You're unhappy, what's wrong? Tell me."

"I don't know."

"You don't want this baby?"

"No, no, it's not that!" Raoul closed his eyes. Turned away. White-faced and haggard, he was actually shaking.

O my God, thought Angie, *what's wrong!* Her own voice she kept submerged, as one would deliberately drown a kitten, or a child. She waited, waited him out, buffeted by the ice-flush of wind, the frenzied night pallor of darkening green.

"Is it my fault?"

Silence.

"Is it?"

"No."

"Well?"

Raoul pressed his raw-boned body against hers until it hurt. "You know I love you; I do love you, but one day—"

"What, WHAT—?"

"You're going to leave me, I know it."

What is it, what's the matter? she wondered, with a sensation of gagging, of choking, as though some invisible gargoyle was crawling upward from somewhere inside her throat. *It's always the same, I don't understand, what is it that goes on inside his brain!*

AFTER THE FALL

Leaves wrinkling
Seared around the edges
Glitter in lamplit puddles like hearts
While the wind filled with ghostly droplets
Batters me through this parkland
With melancholy force
A leaf disconnects from its anchor
Criss-crossing
and blessing me
A moment before my numb sole
Imprints it into the mud.

Now a windslanting veil of snow is trapped
trapped in the fretwork, etched into the roots of trees.
Deep crevasses ingrained
Like battle scars sustained
In duel with the wind
that howls through the parkland—my heartland
Hoarfrost clings to the trunks
Sunk deep
Into a lake of ice

Into the primeval thickets are
Deep curving circles, like arrows sprung—scimitars
Ruts in the road
Leading nowhere but back to the heartland
Black hollows between the trees
Mists rising
from the corpse of the earth
Too deep and cold to throw back
Even an echo
My footfalls are swallowed whole and alive
Into the ground

Still I force my way onward
Ice crackles on the branches
Shatters to the ground like hearts.
Thornbushes fling themselves at my face
As I climb through the lacerating darkness,
My blood has turned black
And is trickling back
Into the earth.

CHAPTER 46

Goddess Ceres

Under a netting of drab cloth in a twilit room was the body of Taddeusz, stretched upon its bier. His skin, the grey of the newly dead; his crucifixed wound exposed to the air. Angie found herself smearing ointment over the flesh, shrouding the cut with a layer of gauze. It should have been repellent to her, but it wasn't. Steadily, Taddeusz began to revive; he sat up. Hurry now, hurry! She helped him into his dusty grey tux just as the church bells outside, jangling and clanging, proclaimed his wedding day.

A kaleidoscopic shift, and he was gone. The chimes ceased. Puffing, grinding and clanking, a train began pulling out of a station, the train she knew must be hers. Although racing toward it, breathless as a hound of hell, she missed it by inches. A momentous defeat, she did not know why. The pale scowling face of Taddeusz, framed by the train's coffin-like window, whizzed by.

Raoul then crept into bed, pressing against her like a coffin lid. "What is it?" he whispered, hot and close, suffocatingly close; his caress was a breath from the Inferno.

"Nothing, just a strange dream."

"That same nightmare?"

"No, not the same, what's wrong with me, why I can't I sleep?"

Down she went, once more, into that awesomely familiar dream-space. Down a hexagonal spiraling of wide wide steps, each bearing the identical pattern of rich, ochre-and-white mosaic. As she trod further downward to the lowest level came that recurringly eerie sensation, the vision of baby-blue coverlets

423

quilting twin beds. And she was compelled, one more time, to confront a queasy apprehension, a reluctant recognition, as a whirlpool of air breathed dark and electric around the room. Palely emerging from the corners, smooth and plastic, a pair of twin mannequins, seemingly inanimate, engendered their own toxic radiation, the unmistakable 'frisson' of evil. Angie witnessed, electrified with dread, how the white white walls and doors of the bedroom—which surely were locked—vibrated and rattled like a malediction, flew open upon their hinges, provoking the two alien dolls to jerk their arms, twist their heads, roll their eyeballs, wrestle with one another, entangling and disentangling their plastic limbs—"Take those things OUT!" she screamed, awakening to the blast of her own voice, detonating inside her head.

Even the crisp pearl-like sheen of daylight the next morning couldn't neutralize the malaise she carried with her, like a weird encryption of the mind. She'd started to feel anxious even at the prospect of falling asleep.

"Don't worry, I have a good natural nerve tonic for you," said Marie-Marthe, smiling, benevolent but uncomprehending.

Mon oncle Jacques, with sweat-glossed skin and spirit-pickled breath, idled beside the fireplace, topping up his glass of home-brewed dandelion wine, which was a thick orangy-gold colour and mystically potent. Its effect was to loosen whatever reserve he might have had; fatuously grinning, he dropped a couple of remarks that were incomprehensible to Angie, although Marie-Marthe flushed and Raoul turned upon him like a savage. Blustering his excuses, mon oncle Jacques recanted; he went silent, shamed, turned his back on them all, seeking refuge in his favourite ancestral wicker-backed rocking chair.

Now, more than ever, it seemed that the great outdoors would be fresh and welcoming, offering renewed life to human lungs clogged with hearth-smoke, bloodstream sated with grease, spirits and sugar, limb muscles immobilized by eternal sitting, and brain cells benumbed by the universal talk. The bracing winter woods were a refuge, an antidote, if only through their serene non-judgmental silence.

On her way out, Angie noticed Marie-Ève sitting alone, talking to no one. The girl appeared flushed, slightly red-eyed and resentful. A typical adolescent, petite, dark-haired, a beauty in the making. I suppose I know what she must be feeling, yet I'm powerless either to earn her love, or deflect her hate. Through no fault of my own, I'm ensconced at the pit of this devastated family. I, the unwelcome, the unholy, the alien stepmother. How ironic—it makes you want to die laughing—what a curse, what a curse upon us both! Unexpectedly, there arose a twinge of belated sympathy for Suraiya, uncharacteristic and rare; after all, how could Angie honour or even acknowledge a shared trait, make common-bond with a mortal enemy? It was a weakness to be resisted; she re-hardened her heart.

Anyway, perhaps all she needed was to get away from this house, disengage from this family and their grim-ritual of togetherness for a few hours at least. Shod in Marie-Marthe's grey leather boots, braving the ferocious wind, she slithered along the humped ice-path toward the backwoods pond, the one fringed by a tumult of long-stemmed water plants, congealed now in their winter sleep, their sly dissembling. After all, do plants feel and do they dream? Do they seek revenge, plot and scheme for their deliverance? Sealed for half Eternity by a merciless murderous climate, this gigantic saturnine wilderness was the haunt of Goddess Ceres, hair streaked in rime, ice tears, frost-bitten heart; like Angie, prisoner of flesh, prisoner of circumstance, prisoner of memory.

CERES UNDERGROUND

Your love flows ripe and red for me
Its drippings stain the corners
of your lip; your smile is bittersweet
I sense the tremors of your writhing
reaching, clinging hand

O haste,
haste,
the time is now...
this fatal fruit I crush
between my teeth and tongue

Now let me taste my love for you
fresh dripping sweet
don't let your tangled hair sprout winter grey
your plaster-mask peel down; your rasp
descend into a wail
and grub into the earth

Crawl back
upon your mighty pedestal
I want to kneel and pay you homage
Hate Perennial
In flowerbloom.

CHAPTER 47

IGNORANCE

Angie's breath rasped in her throat, her pulse raced. Although she appeared to be sleeping, her entire body was convulsing, mind, body and soul fixed and fixated, even hypnotized by an unfamiliar whiteness, a curtain-shroud floating powerfully on an evil, evil breeze. Behind this blanched floating veil, which ran the length of the blank bedroom wall, some menacing spirit-Entity was irradiating her dreamscape with a potency that left her quaking. She recognized it only in its diabolical namelessness, its omnipotent capacity to evoke and instill fear. Now even the chambers of sleep were labyrinthine partitions, throwing up a succession of transparent walls to forbid her escape. For wasn't she conscious by now, experiencing an eternity of entrapment inside a wide-awake dream? An element of her brain was undeniably alert; within this luminescence she detected the familiar fuzz through her closed eyelids, which were nevertheless sealed, immobile, seemingly drugged. Finally, as she burst out of her catalepsy, flinging the fright-vision away, its hallucinatory vestige lodged behind, pulsating and fibrillating for such a long, long time; even the foetus she was harbouring jerked and lunged in terrifying sympathy. Gradually she absorbed the return of the natural darkness as a blessing, a comfort in its banishment of white.

Within this darkness, she put forth her hand. Beside her was a cold empty hollow in the mattress; Raoul was not there.

Where was he? Should she go looking for him? She didn't relish the thought of stepping out at night along the corridors of this smoke-and-cedar smelling house. Its rough barn-wood walls were hung with vintage hunting rifles, moose antlers, dried flowers and woodcuts, anarchic swirls of driftwood,

427

niched crevasses harbouring dark ancestral portraits, like so many treasured or forgotten relics. This deep voluminous space, bonded in stone under a brooding roof, felt ice-damp now that the hearth-fires had died out. Natural age scents assailed the house like the mouldy draught-passages of history. Then came a footfall on the staircase. The door opened. It was Raoul.

"What's wrong?" said Angie.

"Nothing."

"Who's that crying?"

"Marie-Ève."

"Oh—" Of course she's miserable; and it's my fault, thought Angie. Raoul looked grim, disturbed, almost panicked. He's having second thoughts about us; maybe he regrets the whole thing, specially this baby.

"Is there anything I can do?" It was an abject query, hardly worthy even of the 'village idiot.' Raoul's response of—pity? anxiety? contempt?—was not lost on her. His furtive glance of malaise both troubled and rankled; but then, what else was she, reviled and pregnant stepmother, expected to do?

"Never mind, it's all right now, go back to bed," he replied, stern as a patriarch or dormitory prefect.

This Saturnalian week, heralding the New Year, dragged itself out like a mini martyrdom. How much longer before it was over? The following morning, the entire day, was as wearisome as the next. For company there was none other than Marie-Marthe, who was a darling but, even then, there was not enough of her to go around. Mid-mornings, Angie toiled beside her as domestic ally, grateful to have something to occupy her hands, if not her brain, although resentful of their common feminine enslavement. It was a priori, axiomatic, a given. In concert, they worked with implements of war, the carving knife—*If I were violent, I could commit atrocities with this*—the saber-edged vegetable slicer could amputate, the cheese grater could easily shred flesh. Of course, Angie managed to cut only herself, clumsily. Marie-Marthe said nothing, but sent her to find some disinfectant and an old-fashioned plaster. Yes, I'm an urban wastrel, poorly adapted to life in the wilderness. An ill-fated choice, she must be thinking, as wife for her son. Surely she can sense how bored and weary I am just with the tedium of maintaining our day-to-day existence. And to think that I'm on the verge of inflicting this onto my own baby. Oh, my God, I might actually have a girl!

Odd remnants of the Lavigne brood began rattling in and out, shouting their cheery *«bonjours»*—and even cheerier *«saluts»*—chewing on Marie-Marthe's festive roll-sandwiches, creamy herb-onion dip, sculpted radishes, celery and carrot sticks or chocolate-frosted *bûche de Noël*. They raised toasts with home-brewed plonk, jesting, pontificating, staring into the vacuum, falling silent, becoming uneasily social, then at times avoiding one another entirely. Angie smiled behind a veil of courtesy. Did anyone care whether she followed the gist of their private jokes or familial recollections? Secretly, she counted the minutes and the hours. Most of the time she felt bereft. Raoul, when he reappeared from God knows where, swung moodily, erratically between silent ardour and silent indifference. Despite everything, this was his remote realm and kingdom. No matter what, he was rooted here, *'chez lui'*, whereas she, since time immemorial, was marooned.

The Lavigne tribe mostly trickled away except for mon oncle Jacques, who seemed to have staked permanent claim to the rocking chair, *la vieille berceuse, à côté du feu*. Perhaps he was evading his wife Ghyslaine's watered-down wrath, her acerbic condemnation and righteous rage. Winking roguishly at Angie, he raised a toast with his stein of flat beer—*'À votre santé, ma jolie dame!'* As ever, he had one mode, one rôle, one register of address, that of moth-eaten philanderer, whether at cottage hearthstone or palace. Without apology and without pretense, he was a branded-on-the-forehead adulterer, perennial womanizer and unsalvageable reprobate, in short, nothing exceptionally noteworthy or surprising. Reduced in status to a bittersweet joke, he was a mere offshoot from Taddeusz's own vibrant stock.

"Où est votre cher mari?" remarked mon oncle Jacques in a tone both provocative and hostile.

Angie shrugged her shoulders, offered up a lukewarm smile. *Since when am I my husband's keeper?* she thought.

Mon oncle Jacques rolled his eyes, curled his lip. Clearly there was no love lost between them. *"C'est vrai que c'est lui, le plus instruit de la famille, mais il se prend pour un autre, je te jure!"*

"Pardon?" said Angie.

"Écoute, je ne veux pas te blesser, ma fille, tu nous as rien fait (he lowered his tone, in deference to his sister-in-law, Marie-Marthe, in the nearby kitchen) *mais moi, en tout cas, je le trouve révoltant, ton Raoul. Ce n'est qu'un—"*

Angie averted her gaze, feigned not to understand. Raoul? Who was he? What was he to attract such venom even and especially amongst his own family? The runt of the litter, *le chétif,* Marie-Marthe had called him, despite his being the eldest. 'Of them all, he was the one I most feared to lose. When he left home, so young, to enter the Seminary, I almost fell into a depression—'

More and more mysterious, thought Angie, *look into your own soul.*

Bone-thin, tall yet stunted-looking, pale and morbid, how had Raoul attracted, seemingly without effort, how did he persist in ransoming her love? *C'est le plus brillant de la famille,* the most educated of the lot, mon oncle Jacques acknowledged with frankly smarting envy. Indeed, Raoul was the revered 'family genius,' whose burgeoning infantile brain must have absorbed the lion's share, leaving too little to nourish his sickly body. The truth was, and this was disconcerting to contemplate, Angie loved her husband with what felt like a pathological passion. A feverish void, an abyss. *But was this love?*

He was, after all, the one who'd first recognized and claimed her. Did this mean he was bound to her and she to him in some pact, forged before their conception? If so, what was the nature—more significantly—what was to be the consequence of this pact? Otherwise, like a chance gash in the fabric of Eternity, did it exist merely of, and for itself?

Who could tell? In any event, before it was fully daylight the next morning, there they all were—somehow still bonded together—heading southward between split chasms of mountain rock. Raoul was speeding toward the autoroute, traversing the familiar stretch of grooved roadway with its patchy membrane of blitzing gravel and ice. *My God,* thought Angie, *he's going to kill us all!* She witnessed him peering intently through the fogged-up windshield; once in a while, under his breath, he swore. In the back seat, Marie-Marthe, appearing ashen, seemed to have aged a century in a few hours. She held Marie-Ève's head in her lap. The girl wasn't moving. Angie sensed a wrenching in her gut; a lump in her throat; her lungs felt jammed up somewhere inside her chest.

"It must have been something she took, something she found. Oh, my God, why didn't she say something was wrong, why didn't she come to me?"

This is my fault—

Marie-Marthe seemed to read her mind. "No, no, don't blame yourself, Évangéline."

Raoul slowed down, briefly, during a fit of coughing. He harboured an aspect of death himself; he looked ill, unkempt, utterly fatigued.

"It feels just the same, like the day we drove Giselle to St-Jérôme four years ago, it feels like a curse!" said Marie-Marthe.

Raoul grimaced, as though he would curse his own mother for saying so. Watching in the rearview mirror, Angie witnessed the look in his eyes; it was the aspect of a victim condemned to hurl himself through solid rock. Cradled in the back seat of

431

the car, his only beloved daughter, like her late mother before her, was hovering beyond the pale of her own life.

In the hospital waiting room, whose walls were the colour of ash, Angie sat beside Raoul. As the minutes, then the hours elapsed, fear reeked and oozed from his body, vainly attempting to contain, to suppress itself within the shifting glitter of his eyes. She observed Marie-Marthe, immobile as a totem figure in the shadows, and sensed the jittery palpitation of the man crammed closely beside her like a heap of barely contained explosives. She couldn't breathe either; her lungs felt as though they had caught fire.

"I'd like to speak to the patient's parents," said Dr. Pelchat, finally coming toward them in professionally somber guise. What was being veiled behind his eyes—bleak hostility, condemnation, surprise?

Raoul and Angie looked at one another; then he stood up and followed the doctor along the corridor until they were both out of sight. Angie couldn't bear to look at Marie-Marthe; she kept her head bowed and her eyes closed, like a sinner at the confessional.

"If, when she pulls through this, she'll be kept under observation for a long time," said Marie-Marthe. "And then, there'll be the Official Inquisition."

"Yes."

"I should have done something to prevent it."

"How could you?"

"For some time now, I have felt something, something—and now I'm certain."

"Of what?"

"Évangéline, I think I knew, I guessed without really wanting to believe. It's not you, it's him, Raoul."

"Raoul?"

432

Marie-Marthe's compounded sorrow, her gaze of somber cynicism flared like a lurid eclipse in which, suddenly, all became clear. *"Ma fille, ça m'donne envie de vomir, tout simplement, mais, c'est comme ça, on connaît notre enfant."*

At sunset, as they drove home, leaving Marie-Ève behind under the doctors' care, the landscape was a pall of grey, the clouds were all embers and smoke. Then it darkened with the abruptness of a hammer-stroke. Raoul remained mute. Marie-Marthe said little; she, too, had closed up into herself, into her own private act of mourning. As for Angie, she was completely sheared away from them both.

They returned to their ancestral home, during their absence, transformed to a haunt of silence and recrimination. Drawn to the pine-framed mirror in Marie-Marthe's foyer, and then to the antique swing-mirror in the bedroom, Angie confronted herself and was frightened. Revolving back, again and again, to its aged quicksilver surface, needing to reassure herself that though her mind, her thoughts, were quivering, vanishing down some abyss, she herself still existed—in the flesh—that she was actually still there. Robotic, in slow slow motion, she dabbed a film of scented cream over her skin, re-touched a veneer of colour over her reflected effigy in grey. Strangest of all were her eyes; there was now a quality of stillness, a stroke of deadness to them. Something she had never experienced or witnessed before. As for Raoul, he'd been stricken ill. A relapse. An agonizing war waged against an ancient adversary, chronic inflammation of the lower spine. Angie turned to observe him as he was now, a mangle of bone and shadow. Hostage to pain. Maimed, crippling, slithering from armchair to bed, undetected, the way he had done in the beginning, creeping soundlessly toward her out of the darkness.

"Put out the light, I need to sleep, I'm tired to death," he said.

Late New Year's Eve, when it was Angie's turn to be transported to the Saint-Jérôme Emergency Ward, there was bitter humour in the irony. Dr. Pelchat, who was just going off duty, recognized and examined her briefly, then gave her up to the care of the night duty intern. She was bleeding, seized by cramps, whether from false labour or fully fledged miscarrying. She felt stone cold, mortally cold, and pincered in the grasp of a shrieking, gasping pain. In the Intensive Care Unit, an oxygen mask was lowered lightly into place; someone stretched out her arm and rubbed a forefinger carefully over the skin, searching for a vein. Angie drifted away; the rest of the world vanished as well, leaving her alone and unattended for a long, long time. How long? It was impossible to know. All she could do was inhabit this remote floating space in which pain was free to return and assault her with impunity. Her whole body felt like a contortionist-spasm, the breath knocked from her lungs as though she'd been whacked across the spine with an axe. Then came a voice, a taunting voice, like that of a peevish minor demon vindictively close to her ear, a high-pitched falsetto rasp of '*Schadenfreude,*' deliberately goading, gleefully mocking: *Of course you're in pain, what do you expect, of course you are, of course you are!* it ranted and shrieked.

It mattered not. She closed her eyes, beyond fearing and beyond caring. Anything—to stop the pain. Then came a presence, a presence issuing into the room. Angie glimpsed it, sensed more than saw it close by. Something dim, dark. Some nameless, warm and loving presence. An expanse of lucent energy and, between them both, a mystical recognition. Insistent and mildly chiding, this 'presence' edged the taunting creature out of the way. Angie sensed it working deftly, soundlessly on her mangled body until she became warm and sedated, safe and comfortable. Now all she wanted was to sleep, all the way to death if she could, under this beneficent spirit-hand, whatever it was, so spirit-warm and cherishing, faceless and calm. But its grasp was insistent; it forbade her to sleep—*There are choices, Angie, come, come with me.*

Together, they floated over Walden Street, over the brick wall and over the débris where Aunt Ruth's spurned gift of a Xmas doll, given so many years past, was still alive and crying amongst the rubble. Then they soared to the ocean's edge—was it Ramsgate or Ryde?—a scalloped coastline of ochre sand, littered with iridescent shells and waving kelp, from which the tide was running out. This time the live doll had fallen underwater; it was lying on its back, eyes open, pale hair streaming like seaweed, lips rapturously smiling. Angie stretched out her hand, burdened all of a sudden with the premonition she might somehow do it harm. Then it was gone and she was hunting for it, lamenting like a bereaved mother cat, fearful at having to confess to Raoul that she'd mislaid it. Although she couldn't see him, she sensed his shade commanding her to search for the thing. A heinous crime that she failed to find it. Like a skipped gramophone record, her footsteps tumbled along the identical forlorn and barren pathway. Round and around she traveled in search of nothing. The thing was gone. Vanished. Lost. It was her fault. Raoul still threatened from afar with his morbid gaze, his menace of reprisal. She kept searching, calling out for this thing that seemed to be hers and his, yet was nowhere to be found. It became dark, too dark to see anything and she knew, somehow she knew even before she stumbled upon the thing again amidst the débris, no longer crying, not moving, irrevocably mangled, soiled, crushed. 'No, I don't want it, take it,' she said numbly, tearlessly, without hesitation and without remorse, as the 'presence' hovered in waiting.

Descending further into sleep, she discovered Taddeusz in her forest garden. He appeared tanned, flourishing and happy, interconnecting mind-to-mind with her as in a dream. A giant poplar, gnarled and putrid from root to trunk, he seized with one hand. Then he was crashing his way through this forest, hurling down the rot, wrenching away the shade-trees from her confining wilderness—*Oh, careful, careful!* she protested, but already half her garden was felled, and she herself was stretched upon a tuft of grass, in some drugged-like sleep, as luscious bird droppings began falling on her head.

A scattering of translucent-green mallard ducks, wild spotted deer and sheep were dashing frantically around for cover now that their shelter was demolished; yet, in contrast to the protectively gloomy wood it once was, this naked liberating sunshine felt good, it felt right, it felt serene—*O my lost child, I grieve for you to the end of my being and beyond, yet I'll be damned—yes, I WILL BE DAMNED—if I twist and squirm like Lily on my solitary cross. Watch me wrench out these nails, heave the blasted stone, crawl away on my bleeding hands and feet.*

CHAPTER 48

FAIRY TALE

𝕿he 𝕰nchanted 𝕴sland

There once lived a Princess whose mother died when she was very young. When she reached her sixteenth birthday, her father, the King, arranged for her to be married to a fine young Prince from a faraway kingdom. On her wedding morning, after the ceremony was over, the Princess retired to her private chambers for the last time. She peeped into the polished steel mirror and made a wish. She wished that the Prince would remain forever as handsome as she was happy, this very day.

At that instant, a sunbeam blazed in through the archway, striking the mirror like the touch of a magic wand. Her wish was so fervent it seemed to whirl around the chamber like a powerful spell. It actually made her dizzy, so she closed her eyes. As she opened them again, her young bridegroom's face was reflected beside hers in the mirror. He had come in search of her, he said, for their royal vessel was waiting for them at the dock. The weather was fair enough for them to start their journey and, besides, her stepmother, the Queen, was impatient for the young couple to be gone.

Once launched upon the ocean, their ship was buffeted by a freakish storm. The captain, the sailors, the servants, in fact, almost everyone on board ship was lost. When it finally ran aground, the Prince and Princess discovered they had reached an island so small, it was either unknown or not worth the trouble of recording on any map. To make matters worse, they were not able to salvage anything, since their beached vessel shifted and heaved until it crashed to pieces against the rocks. It seemed that this island would have to be their new home, at least until help should chance to arrive.

After a few hours, the Prince and Princess found the ruins of an abandoned castle-like dwelling where they could at least take shelter for the night. Inside they found an antique storehouse with some supplies that hardly looked safe enough to eat. They began to search the castle grounds for any fruit trees, wild berries, seeds or nuts. Later, they ate whatever fish could be caught in the nearby stream.

They lost count of the days that passed, but certainly more than a year must have elapsed in this fashion, by which time the young couple had almost given up hope of ever being rescued. The Princess then gave birth to a baby daughter, who was the absolute image of her, and whom she named Desirée. For a few days she was deliriously happy until she realized that the nameless island on which they lived must be enchanted. For some reason every month she lived here, she, and only she, became one year older. She examined her reflection in a tiny hand mirror and observed with dismay that she was aging at a tremendous speed. What had caused this dreadful state? Could it be that her former innocent wish had been transformed upon herself into an evil spell? After all—exactly as she had wished—her cherished husband, the Prince, appeared not a day older than on their wedding day.

The Princess cried bitterly. She tried wishing the spell away but to no avail for, as time passed, she kept growing older and older and older. The sorrowful day came when she could hardly recognize her own self, so altered was she. Naturally, the Prince failed to recognize her too, so he searched the length and breadth of the enchanted island for the beloved young wife that he remembered. When he failed to find her, he imagined that somehow she must have accidentally perished, either on land or at sea. In great sadness, he returned to their dwelling-place and when he set eyes on the unfortunate Princess, he may be forgiven if he mistook her for a haggard old crone who might wish to harm their beautiful child, Desirée. He issued a stern warning to the Crone-Princess and drove her away at the point of his sword.

438

But what no one knew was that little Desirée had also now fallen under the spell. Within a few months she grew up to be a beautiful young woman, the very image of her mother. The Prince looked at her and believed that she must be his long-lost Princess miraculously returned to him, and he embraced her with great joy. But my name is Desirée, said the young girl, whereupon the Prince, of course, did not believe her. To escape his anger, she was obliged to run and hide herself along the cavernous seashore beside the turquoise waters of an inland lagoon. Here, Desirée gazed upon her own reflection in the water, then screamed with fright. A human statue was watching her from amongst the rocks, or was it a reflection? It looked grotesquely old but, at the same time, eerily familiar. Its voice sounded as hollow as Time itself.

Darling child of mine, we must depart this accursèd place if you wish to escape the cruel spell, said the voice. Trust me; although I appear to be reduced to stone, as long as my child lives, I shall retain a glimmer of life. Make haste now, climb onto my back and, with all your strength, heave us both out onto the waves.

But, mother, are you my mother? Why should we plunge into the midst of the ocean?

Make haste! Your father, the Prince, is waving to us from the clifftop; as he gazes at you I hear him calling my name! We must leave now, now!

And so it was that the very instant Desirée and her mother crashed forward into the waves, the maleficent spell became reversed. Time seemed to travel back upon itself with dizzying speed. The aging Crone-Princess became younger and younger, stronger and more beautiful. She and her infant daughter watched from afar as the Prince, poised upon the cliffhead like a tragic statue—with slow slow darkness descending—aged more than a hundred years.

CHAPTER 49

London, Spring 1995

Second coming

I, Angie, alias Évangéline, twice-named, twice-cursed, predetermined evangelist, remember and record the vision of my mother, Lily, standing beneath the brick arch of our open doorway on Walden. The aging, eternally abandoned child, deathly pale and shivering, shoulders hunched inside her dog-hairy olive-drab winter mantle, tears glittering through steamed-up lenses, her voice extinguished to a feeble vibration—*"Don't go, Angie, please, don't leave me,"* she said.

The wrench of that calculated desertion became a virus, an infection that took root that very moment, that hour, that day of remembrance and un-atonement. It has flourished across the years in my mind and heart like a tree fungus, a mystic carbuncle. Stake plunged into my heart at the fateful crossroad, I was made to choose whether to tread further into the mire or scuttle to higher ground. Taddeusz tossed me a poisoned barb of a lifeline. I grasped it. More than three decades later, re-impelled to my mythic source, I breathe the green-sighing wind of my homecoming; I contemplate the mystery, the enduring mesmer of London east, of Whitechapel, of Walden.

Islam now sweeps across the displaced Yiddish 'Mittel East' bringing its oriental jewelry, sari, curry and sweet shops, its mosaics, minarets and perfumes of arabesque. At four p.m. exactly *Al-lah*'s ineffable name floats across London east. Brick Lane is now reincarnated Banglatown; a transplanted nation of Muslims pray beneath the nearby dome, crowned with a star and a crescent moon. Claustrophobic it feels, at times, on this tiny isle compared to the territorial expansiveness of the New World, yet the city of London stretches in all directions like a Benelux nation; it offers every landscape from ghastly to sublime. Its streets are paved in soot and gold.

Absent-mindedly, I step off the curb facing Bow Road Tube Station in the pathway of a passing car; it's a black hearse-like monster whose driver honks ferociously as he whips past, a hair's breadth from my body. It is at that moment I am reminded that everything, and nothing matters. An abrupt stroke of Fate and the game could be over. It matters till your last breath, not a moment longer. Still I must play, and play the game as though there were no ending. Sodden leaves stick to the path like rumpled coins; it seems that all of London's vast chaotic greenery is rippling underwater. The wind flows, roars like a gentle storm, the mild sun glitters. Even from here, the sound of the Bow bells is deafening; a native east Londoner saunters past, throws up his arms and yells, *"Quiet!"*

Clambering up the steps of Whitechapel Tube Station, I head in the direction of Commercial Road; as ever, it's battered by the swirling winds, the brash fragrance of centuries' old soot. The vanished Jewish Market in Hessel Street harbours the ghosts of its former needle-shop, newsagent, kosher butcher and synagogue, slumbering behind a gauntlet of rattling grates. On a whim, I meander east and southward to the far end of Watney Street. The looming pillar-wharves of brick that span the hump bridge in Wapping Lane are smaller, humbler than I remembered. Map and compass in hand, I hazard the clustered tenements of Wapping. And then, of course, it is Greta, my blood-sister, who—reluctantly—opens the door to her dockside domain. Hostile. Contentious. Her quaint, outmoded frock is of shiny oriental crimson silk; it puckers where her breasts should be and floats around her little girl's waist, incongruous, for like me, she is now middle-aged.

Accursèd Time, as in the fairy tales, has exchanged our days for years.

With her long loose iron-grey hair, her frail dark eyes, she has the wasted air of a mediaeval anchorite, spiritualizing in her own flame; lank and empty, like a she-wolf from too many litters, to this day she clings on to Emily, the only one left who hasn't been hauled away 'into care.'

442

"Well, what're you back here for, to stage a 'Second Coming?'" she says. "I suppose you think you've come back like the bleedin' Saviour that you ain't, to salvage us all?"

"I didn't come here for a fight, Greta."

There is no other reply, for I am weary; our feuds have the air of being locked in childhood. Greta resumes the age-old battle while rattling teapot, cups and spoons onto the kitchen table, supremely familiar in her contempt, as if I'd just dropped in from around the corner, more than thirty years ago.

"All right, Lady Muck, don't you stare at me like that! Who do you think you are, some High-and-Mighty Countess or something, come down here to inspect the lower orders? All right then, so take a look at this flat, look at these bleedin' filthy walls, look at that mouse-hole in the corner. You see my shitty life, don't you? Well, it's *my* life. I'm treading in stink up to my eyeballs, but at least I never looked away. I never pretended it wasn't there. I never tried to cover it up, or change it into anything else. Not like you, *you coward,* I never ran away."

"So, you fashioned your own personal hell out of seeing; I fashioned mine out of not seeing, or seeing something else. What's the difference, either way, life is hell!"

"Don't tell me your troubles," she says, with a glimmer, a smirk of satisfaction, "you should never have deserted the place where you belonged, you should have married one of your own."

Want and Ignorance; Ignorance and Want, nothing has changed. For centuries past and centuries to come, we are the interchangeable Sisters of Poverty.

Suddenly, for no reason, I am reminded of that day years ago when I came upstairs and found Greta sitting at our old kitchen table in the attic, discomfited, the blackish-brown sheen of her hair transformed to a sickly shade of dark orange tea. *I wanted to dye it blonde, but it didn't work,* she'd said in remorse and, to assuage her disappointment, flung me a sharp slap, followed

443

by a twist-lingering pinch on the cheek. Decades later, the breathless 'ambiance' of her own narrow little Council flat is dismal, yet tense; it flickers and swirls like a migraine, like the haloesque aura of *Aides—of Hades—the Unseen.*

It evokes the dream, the *'cauchemar'* I once conjured, then inscribed as if on tablets and still remember: Greta menacing me with a skewer-like weapon, gripped Samurai-style. Each time I disarmed her, she produced another, and yet another blade, concealed inside her back pocket. The level of terror rose until, desperate, I stuffed her into a cardboard box, so small, she must have shrunk like Alice among the mushrooms, and I carried her, dense, heavy and struggling toward the sea. I felt cruel, and I was cruel; I told her I was going to drop her to the bottom like a stone. When she heard that, she struggled all the more; yet even before the box stretched and strained and broke under her force, I was already collapsing in pangs of guilt. How could I do this to anyone, even my evil twin? As she burst out of her confinement, promising to be good, I already relented the horror I had become.

"Where're you staying?" says Greta, reluctant. Also relenting. "You can sleep here tonight, if you don't have no other place to go."

"Thanks, I'll be gone tomorrow."

O Greta, I've always known it was never to be, but I persist in imagining that once upon a time we might have been soul sisters, part of one another, a Charlotte & Emily duet. The only time I ever saw you cry was when your tortoise was bitten in half by the Alsatian; or, after your own staged 'Kristallnacht' in Lily's attic bedroom, you came back that last time for a handful of trinkets and rags, masking your bruised cheek, your bleeding hands and feet.

CHAPTER 50

THE HAUNTING

I contemplate the tail-end of my elapsing life with the hypnotic wonder of a musically charmed snake. Trying, always trying to grip onto the story that must be told. It lodges in me like a live thing, cascades through my memory, both chastisement and lullaby, drumbeat and pagan psalm. After Taddeusz died, I dreamt I steered a tall cumbersome black hearse, drawn by a single horse. Inside the hearse sat all the mourners, the Hermans, the Morvayes, our mismatched caravan of a family. Climbing the stepladder to the driver's seat, I grabbed the reins, cracked the whip and tried to steer the unwieldy vintage hearse over sloshing mud roads to its destination. More than once the entire carriage tipped sideways, almost crashing into the muddy trenches on either side. Yet, throughout the long arduous dream, I held on, heroically, and drove it safely onward. But where?

Mine is the battle of two souls; Taddeusz and Lily continue to wage war in my body, leaving behind a predestined sickening, an exhaustion of waste.

My emerging Self, the one lovingly engraved by Suraiya, is the pitched confliction of polar souls—I am Taddeusz raging out of Lily's inertia. He (although dead) sometimes appears in a whiff of incense—(am I going mad?)—or as cue-master, a powerful mental prompt, an obsession driving me hither and thither, as he once did in life, a phantasm that haunts my dreams with explicit messages and unjust reproaches.

Goddamned Taddeusz, this body of mine is tired, this heart is cloven, bleeding and unrequited; yet still you loom over me, spectral Obermeister, more potent than ever, seconding my still quickening hand into service as your Necromancer, your synoptic gospel-scribe.

Yes, my story is spawned from yours, for I have been fabricated with a porous soul; reluctant host to the death-masques of the living ancestors. I glimpse my face, imprisoned in this traveling mirror. Sometimes I am the grave, stretched stone-forehead of Taddeusz; at times the baffled terror of Lily lurks at the corner of my eye. And then again, and again, I own the bliss-smile of my grandmother, Mitzi, as I delve amongst the stones and starving soil into which I was planted; I become the live crust of a wound at which I hack and hack.

For the past few months I've begun to suffer a mysterious hardening of the throat tendons, making me feel as though I am choking or drowning. A homeopath, a young Asian woman with a private clinic in East London's Tower Hamlets, listens to me pensively, laying her own empathetic palm across her throat and upper chest—*the area of buried grief*, she says—the throat and upper respiratory tract, a sensitive spot, often conspicuous, often afflicted in would-be artists, writers, evangelists. She rustles through the pages of her Homeopath's Bible, on prominent display beneath the Indian veils and hangings, wind chimes, and burning sticks of incense. From a huge wooden spice chest, secured with ornate gold clips, she selects a vial of tiny white pills, *Ignatia Amara*. 'Careful, you mustn't touch these with your fingers,' she says, and pops one directly under my tongue.

I find myself alternately blazing into Taddeusz, re-sinking into Lily. I show all the signs of someone too-long steeped in solitude. For some time now Lily has been oozing over me, a gentle pool of glycerin; back home here, at last, within this eastern gloom-land of legend, smothered beneath her memories, I know I am becoming forgetful, don't trust myself any more with water taps and gas stoves. I grope around in a protracted dream state, mumbling, reminiscing, crying or laughing, arguing with myself out loud. Anchored in Lily's cramped kitchen, surrounded by the comforting reek of darkness and decay, I wash the cups, pour the milk, fill a decrepit wire strainer with tea-leaves. Lily dozes beside me in an armchair, dreaming and navigating to the sea bottom of memory.

"Oh, thanks, Angie, you've made the tea," she says, waking suddenly, and before I can hand it to her, she remembers something and starts to laugh.

"Would you believe it, two days after the wedding your father went into hysterics, he threatened to annul the marriage. He was going to lay our case before the Pope himself because he suspected that I was Jewish. Oh, the bastard! God forgive me, I mean, God bless him, I don't have a drop of Jewish blood. And what if I did? Is that a crime or something? Just imagine your 'mishuggeneh' father accusing *me* of being Jewish."

Lily laughs again and so do I, although she is almost gruesome to watch, a grinning cadaver with scarcely enough flesh left clinging to her bones to be called human. Frail, dust-grey and decomposing above ground, Lily calls up her last reserves of strength to summon her beloved Taddeusz back to life— "'Woman, why did you lie to me? You *are* Jewish, aren't you, you little whore! Well, now were finished—' Oh, Angie, if only your father had meant it, you'd never have been born, it's true, but what a blessed escape it would have been for me."

Tears well up in Lily's eyes. Then she is giggling again. She can't stop. I think her feeble heart will burst, trapped in a hilarious spasm that shakes her rickety body, but then gradually her laughter dies away to a gentle hiccup. She grins at me, a skeletal grin, conspiratorial. Teardrops twinkle in her eyes. Her teacup rattles on the tray as she takes it from me with trembling fingers. She gazes at it as though it were a divine happening.

"I can't believe it, Angie, how did you make the tea so fast?"

Although she is clearly waning, clinging to whatever shreds of mortgaged time, in certain ways, my mother seems almost better than before. She no longer mentions the hazard of catching my eye on a protruding nail as I climb up the dark staircase. Now her fears are more prosaic, more grounded; she fears I will catch something from an unfamiliar toilet, she listens for news of plane crashes whenever I'm in the air. She

447

frets that I'll get robbed on the train, or strangled in the park. She anguishes with equal passion over the spattered birdlime on her kitchen window. A very real and raucous flock of pigeons have established their nest-quarters in an abandoned flower-box on the outdoor balcony.

"Angie, come and shoo those 'orrible filthy birds away, I can't stand them—"

"I'm coming."

"'Ere, did I ever tell you about my job as kitchen maid at the Colonial Restaurant, Plantation House, on Mincing Lane? It had a Dickensian-style kitchen, with deep wooden troughs for sinks. From my very first day, Arthur, the cook—he couldn't stand me—he used to make my life a bleedin' misery or else go out of his way to take the piss. Once, he stuffed a live eel down the back of my blouse, and another time, he sent me down the street with a bucket to buy two shillings' worth of steam! Oh, he did love tormenting me, although I couldn't help liking him, in an odd way. One day, not long before I left, this bloody great heap of skewer irons came crashing out of the lift, injuring my leg—(look here, look at my shinbone, see this scar, see how the skin's discoloured after all these years?)—and almost killing one of the kitchen workers, as well.

"Later on during the war, before Greta was born, we heard the air-raid sirens going off, and I said to your father, 'Come on, Teddy, get up, we've got to get up!' 'No,' he said, 'I'm too exhausted, leave me alone, I don't give a damn even if we do get hit'—but just then, the whole building shook, and you should've seen your father, there he was leaping down those stairs, miles ahead of me, half-naked, with one trouser leg on, and one off as he scuttled across the street. I followed him and we just had time to take shelter under the lintel of the pawnshop, when it struck—Oh, God, was he cursing! We raced all the way down to the Tilbury Goods Yard Shelter, but there was hardly any room, we had to crawl over a heap of barrels, looking for a place to sleep, and then, my life, you won't believe what happened next!

Your father caught sight of a couple of whores from down Cable Street and he went white, chalk white. The next thing I knew he was gone, God knows where he managed to hide, right behind that pile of barrels, I should imagine and, as they walked by, I heard them both talking, they were looking for someone, someone they swore they were going to kill!"

As a foreign national, Taddeusz was registered with the Police Station on Leman Street and was required to carry an Alien citizen's identity book, inscribed with words to the effect: *The Bearer is permitted to land on condition that he respect the regulations therein, i.e., that he does not circulate beyond a five-mile radius from this address.* Not long after Britain declared war on Romania, Taddeusz was seized by two 'seven-foot tall' military policemen who literally burst their way into the poverty-stricken flat. "Yes, Sir, I understand, I've been following it on the news; I was expecting you," responded Taddeusz, jumping to his feet and stuffing into his pockets a roll of tobacco, some small change, and his leather wallet of personal papers. Speaking with a meticulously cultivated foreign tongue, he offered no resistance as they led him away under arrest, right there and then.

He was to languish for months, holed up in a fortress on the Isle of Man until he managed to regain his freedom through the intercession of Felix Zsolt, his transplanted Magyar uncle, a grain merchant whose commerce boasted a brass nameplate on London's Leadenhall Street. In a letter, Taddeusz had instructed Lily to implore, no, request or otherwise demand help and relief from his established kinsman, Zsolt, while he himself was being interned. And so it was that Lily ventured out in search of Mr. Zsolt among the monuments, the fluted columns and grey stone buildings of the City. She remembered him as a shriveled cornhusk of a man, scant-haired, with a feathery moustache stained white, here and there, amongst the grey. Zsolt stared quizzically at Lily; his thin lips, in perpetual flux, compressed themselves until they almost disappeared.

"Well, Mrs. Morvaye," he said, genuinely astonished by this visitation of bashful poverty, this dark-haired Cockney damsel and her babe-in-arms, "why have you come here?"

"Well, my husband sent me to ask you for help, Sir."

"What can I do to help?"

"Well, I, we were hoping that—" (she managed in a few moments to rattle off her miserable tale).

"Indeed, I'm very sorry, but I'm afraid that I can't really be of any help. What I would suggest is that you buy a loaf of bread, dry it in the oven and toast some rusks for the baby and yourself, you know, and that way you will have enough to eat."

I listen again and again to Lily's stories, then I nod, yawn with exhaustion and fall silent. The frigid grave-gloom of a winter evening is closing in and, everywhere, east London's shade-terraces huddle close together like vessels in a mystic harbour. The dense airlessness, the endemic swamp of Lily's kitchen has the capacity to waterlog the mind. Her voice rattles on and on with the asthmatic breathlessness of outrage, insisting upon the injustice, the cruelty, the extraordinary drama of her life.

"Can you believe it, the heartlessness of that Mr.—*what's his name*—Zsolt! Greta was only about a year old at the time, and I was receiving less than two pounds assistance a week!"

At last, gradually overcome with fatigue, she drifts into a quieter mood.

"Angie, I never asked what happened to you while you was over there, by yourself, in that horrible cold country; do you want to tell me?"

"What happened?"

"I'm sorry, I'm sorry I never listened to you before."

"It's all right, it doesn't matter."

450

"Well, tell me."

I remain silent.

"Don't you want to tell me?"

"No, it's all over, it's past, it's finished, I'm recording it in a volume of stories, grotesque tales—" Lily stares at me wonderingly, and then she laughs. "It's true, believe me, I'm writing it all down in a book of fairy tales—too frightening for children."

That same night I dream of washing Lily in the small metal bathtub, the one with rusty handles, stored long ago beside our blackened gas stove on the third storey landing of Walden. A flutter of plague-pigeons circle and perch along the rim of the tub, as I sweat and stoop like a weary grave-digger. Lily whines, resists and weeps, a fetal coil of lamentation, as I soap and soap her pale skin, finally rinsing her small skull and almost hairless body with a saucepanful of tepid water. *It's all right, don't fret any more—* With a swoop of my arm, I try without success to drive off the brash invasion of pigeon fluff and feathers—*"It's all right, it's all over now, you're finished, you're finished, you're finished!"*

CHAPTER 51

Consider the Lilies

Doped on the extract of poppies, Lily is already floating away on her hospital bed. Her eyelids struggle to open, then lodge at quarter mast. The eyeballs roll slightly skyward, the mouth agape, revealing the mare's teeth with which Nature has furnished her; just one is missing along the lower left jaw. Her throat is no more than a knot of bone; two wing-bones for shoulders are set astride hollowed gullies of flesh. Even her shrunken breasts are those of a mummified queen. She's a feral creature. Thunderstruck. A drunken vessel, listing slowly to port on pulsating rivers of slate-blue blood.

Fairy cakes, cherries, bananas, buttered beigles, slices of cheese lie heaped on the side table, votive offerings untouched by this skeletal goddess. Her breathing is regular, although shallow. Occasionally, she draws in a lone deep breath like a sigh. I feel hungry, restless, resentful, sitting beside her on this grainy red plastic chair. In the next bed the bald-headed woman calls out for a glass of orange juice. She struggles out of bed.

"Where are you going, dear?" says the nurse.

"Out of my mind."

The nurse rolls along her tray of poisons, and then later on comes the leek soup, ice cream, mash and baked beans. "Lily, do you want to eat something?"

"*Uh?*" Lily's breathless, unformed mouthings can be heard, but only barely. Indifferent, the nurse drifts away. I hurry after her to retrieve a cupful of tepid soup, which I manage to spoon between Lily's chapped lips. But it's her flesh itself that continues to sag, dripping steadily away, leaving loose flaps of crêpeskin folded over bone. I finger her shrunken skull, just a

453

ridged circle of crenellations; two sunken hollows mark the spot where the temples once were.

A procession of visitors, centuries' old friends, relations, hover around her bed-frame and at the open door. *Thank you for coming, I love you all,* she says, with a regal wave of her bone arm. Solipsistic by nature, she believes the world revolves around *'Herself'* and *'Hersickness;'* she has been so so sick for so long. But then the crowd begins to unnerve her. "Stop bringing me flowers, they're going to get knocked down and splinters are going to fly into my cup! I said *no more flowers,* (in rising hysteria) I feel like I'm being buried alive."

As each day slips away from her, she can barely mouth the words. Drugs have overpowered her skeletal flyweight of a body. Is it a matter of weeks, days, hours? Twin chestnut-shaped bones now protrude from the base of her throat; a couple of hollowed-out troughs are what's left of her thighs. Lily can't get comfortable. Her bedsores are leaking, paining, staining the sheets. I stroke the squared knee-bone, the long stilled femur. Her bed reminds me of a Saxon burial pit of scattered bone shards. Her knees are drawn up, resting sideways bone on bone; her matted, stone-grey skull foams damp with sweat. Deep mauve aureoles encircle her sunken eyes that glitter—urgently.

"Listen to me, *listen*—this time I'm not going to get better, Angie, I'm really frightened, this time I'm going to die."

Oh, how I wish I could hurry her along that mystical gloom-corridor, I just want her to go, to go.

"Mum, when the time comes, they'll all be there to meet you, I promise."

Yet instead of being comforted, she gets angry, thrusts away from me, frets and fusses for her water beaker, her tissues, her comb. I feel that if she lives much longer she will bury me under a mountain-weight of anger, resentment and fatigue. In these last days—these dread days—I too feel immobilized, crippled, unable to move forward, as though some great 'Denver Boot' has locked down my soul. But then comes an urgent summons and, reluctantly, I am here. In St. Joseph's Hospice, I watch as they prepare to administer morphine, liquid nutrients, directly into a vein. Lily crouches in a heap on the mattress, whimpering. "I've still got a pain, a dull pain, I've got palpitations, why am I so hot?" Surely it can't be long before the lamentations are over. Soon she is attached to the diamorphine-dispensing drip. Its red light flashes, indicating a continual flow, but still she hangs on, snatching oxygen from the air with a deep, regular almost soundless gasp.

Her grandson, Rafael, a raven-haired shockingly handsome 'thirtysomething,' barges into the ward, ostentatiously ignoring me, checking her pain-control apparatus, spraying moisture onto her tongue, everything I have already been doing for the past four hours. He will now keep vigil for the rest of the night, so I retire for a time to the visitors' lounge. There's nothing like an incipient death to raise up high-tension lines between family relations. Rafael now leaps into Lily's dying days and nights with a martyr's rage, a convenient rationale for this family's pre-cooked hatreds. As I sit alone, some scarcely known relation enters the lounge and sidles up beside me, keen to share a stream of familial intrigue, gratuitously black-mouthing one and all like some maleficent 'Book of Revelation.' And all this time, my eyes burn, my temples throb. I can hardly muster even the pretense of politeness. At midnight, I rise abruptly to talk to the night nurse, who has just arrived.

"We're taking your temperature, Lily," she says, placing the thermometer under Lily's inert armpit. She nods to Rafael. To me she whispers over her shoulder, "It's just a courtesy to tell her what we're doing; they say the hearing is the last to go."

Back in the lounge, I note that my gossip-monger of a companion has vanished. Sleep, or the semblance of it, becomes a torturous abyss, a desolate cave, a centuries-long void for saints and sinners to wander without hope or respite. Yet, somehow, even this passes away and suddenly, it is pre-dawn; my mind and body leap instantly awake with the certainty of premonition. Rafael grabs at my sleeve.

"Come quick, come!" he whispers.

Together we rush back to the bedside to witness Lily's final shudder, her gentle death croak, a muted, lingering rattle. She passes from our midst on June sixteenth, at 4.55 am.

And now it is time for me to hover in the desolating dawn, contemplating my mother's remains—a crumpled mound of bone-flesh, inert and stilled, a small grey head docked against the regulation pillow. The morphine-dispensing lifeline, steadily pulsating, faithfully flashing, is her only visible attendant into the 'Other World.' As for Rafael, he can hardly wait to make his last farewells. He clamps his raw white knuckles, ruffles his spiked black hair into disarray. Perilously white, swamp-eyed and glittering, he fails to master the familiar nerve-tremble of his smile.

"Well, it's over—finally—I promised I'd stay with her till the end, I'm going home now. I'm knackered."

"All right, good-bye, Rafael, thank you."

"Can I do anything?" says the nurse, coming in. I stare at her. She checks Lily's vital signs, or absence of; it seems the most natural thing in the world. She nods efficiently, soberly, then says, "Just sit down here for a minute, dear, and I'll bring you a cup of tea."

Silence returns with the emptiness, which is its own relief. I sit, gratefully inert for a time, who knows for how long, then all at once I tense up, straighten my head and shoulders, stare attentively into the hollow. Invisible, above and around Lily's body, streams an unmistakable charged and tender energy, a sort of translucence sing-quivering in the air. I can almost reach out and touch it—this palpable séance of visitation—an encircling all-powerful *Peace Frieden Pacis*. For several minutes I watch and listen acutely, as 'it' floats gradually toward the ceiling with the multitudinous sensation of Spirit-Force. I know, of course, *I know* that it is Ruth, Flo, Tweetie and Renie returning briefly to gather their beloved, benighted Lily back into the fold.

At the funeral home, this sepulchral *'Chapel of Rest'* is too dark, despite the blond-wood panels of its catafalque. Twin candlelights glimmer and burn in their deep wells of glass. A white porcelain vase of cultivated flowers rests on the shelf between them. Directly beneath, Lily's bones are swathed in lace and white satin. Her eyelids are closed in weariness, perhaps in disgust, her clay-like features distilled in agony. Nature's death mask is a paper-thin layer of grey skin with deep folds at each cheek. Her upper lip, slightly unclosed on one side, bares a prominent front tooth, lending her a grimacing, predatory look. In death, as in life, Lily appears tortured; this pose is so familiar to her, so familiar to me. The narrow veneered lid of her casket stands upright in one corner; its bronze plaque is minted with her last farewells: Lily Herman Morvaye, born 9.6.1920, died 16.6.1996. The slatted door swings backward, clicks shut, jams and imprisons me for a few seconds in Lily's sepulchre of gloom. I panic, clumsily push my way outside into the hall.

O mother, mother, you are, you were the blind accidental portal through which we tumbled to earth.

Here deep in the East is Lily's earthwork fortress, her own *Chosen Land*. St. Mary's and St. Michael's Church is jam-packed on the day of her funeral. Such a contrast to Taddeusz's paradoxically lonely deserted burial, presided over by some lone priest of the Roman orthodox rite in the distant *'Land of the Free.'* The dizzying speed at which he burnt up his earthly years contrasts and conflicts with the ultra slow slow pace of Lily's wanderings. She, who produced babies without plan or desire, was used and used up so that I, and three others, could taste of Life, and of Death. Ravenous-for-life Taddeusz is long since underground; who could predict that Lily's stricken mind and derelict body would outlive his?

For the funeral service I select the voice of Jeremiah from the Book of Lamentations: *I, too, am one who has seen affliction by the rod of his wrath. He has led me and brought me into darkness, and not into light; surely against me is he turned.*

My flesh and my skin hath he made old; he hath broken my bones; he hath hedged me about that I cannot get out; he hath made my chain heavy. Also when I cry and shout, he shutteth out my prayer. He hath enclosed my ways with hewn stone, he hath made my path crooked; he hath turned aside my ways and pulled me in pieces: he hath made me desolate. He hath bent his bow and set me as a mark for his arrow; he hath filled me with bitterness, made me drunken with wormwood; he hath covered me with ashes, and broken my teeth with stones.

Into her coffin we place *'Grave Goods,'* her precious glasses, her rosary beads, a souvenir postcard from Benidorm, a framed photograph of her beloved Peter, her lost boy. In those ritual days of visitation my sister, Greta, can be reached neither by letter nor by phone; yet, on the day of the funeral feast, she appears at our door, unexpected, describing the compulsion she felt, some irresistible force which impelled her to arrive at this very hour, this very day.

One step beyond, as Lily herself, grinning obliquely, would say.

That entire week I also sense Lily's posthumous agitation all around me, or am I projecting my own poltergeisted spirit? My telephone message-taker flashes continually from the very day of her death; the elevator-lift in her Council dwelling (a *malheur* she fiercely dreaded) gets stuck between floors; Lily's own telephone line goes dead and needs to be repaired at the BT Exchange; a framed ceramic tile, imprinted with a red rose, bounces off my bathroom wall during the night, makes a rationally impossible trajectory in the air and crash-lands four feet away onto the floor of the adjacent wall.

During these days, these lost days, I am determined not to cry. It is only later, much much later, one solitary evening as I am sorting through her dusty worthless scraps of treasures, I pause, stricken in my armchair, and weep as I remember her. It is a sense of desolation, not for her, but for myself, and not for having lost her, for I know she was never mine to lose.

I weep for my pity, hatred, love, and resentment of her, for Lily, my mad sick jailor, leaching her plague of sickness onto me, smearing the walls of my prison with the attar of sickness. I weep for my stone-heart, my stone-heartedness, for her love strewn along our infant pathways like pebbles instead of bread. I weep for her blighted life, her ruin of a mind, her blameless bloody sick-sick-sickness which is the sole legacy she was able to grant us.

O Lily, with your horse-neighing laughter and puling tears, Lily, with your palms prune-white from soaking and your belly stretched from carrying. Lily, with your guilt and innocence preserved in amber, your bashful caught-red-handed smile, your Olympian fears and spacey shrieks, your terror, which was more than equal to your love of life. Long ago, because of your frailty and your angst, before I had even chance to taste of your joys and sorrows, you tried to snuff me out of the womb, out of the world; but I clung on, clung on for dear life, pushed my way through the portals so I could give birth again—to you.

CHAPTER 52

CHIAROSCURO

Greta in recent years has, inexplicably, mellowed. As she ages, she complains of the reek of corpse on her, of dangerously high blood pressure and shredded kidneys. Although near-blind, she fashions with nail-polish on wood an angular mythological creature, a warped translucent female body with webbed feet.

I can't put her framed gift up anywhere on my walls, it repels and frightens me.

More and more she travels backward into the pastness of Time. She disremembers her husband, Kenny; to this day she repudiates her first-born, Rafael, but her artist's total recall of Luc does not fail. Indelible. Her first adolescent love. The scrolled emblems of the 'de Peyrac' coat of arms, the ancestral *Château,* Luc's arrogant rose-dark face, a memorial in living stone, the vague haunting memories of the novelette *'La Petite Princesse.'*

"It's a bit like our story, Angie," she says, "but ours is of riches to rags."

I feel and I look weary; my smile, I am sure, is one of inexplicable fatigue.

"You don't remember because you wasn't even born, but this is how it was, I caught scarlet fever when I was a baby; they took me away and put me in an incubator, in the isolation ward, for ten days."

"I didn't know that."

"Yeah, and the nurses just picked me up with their surgical gloves on and masks over their faces; they just fed and changed me, then left me alone to see whether I would live or die."

461

"What?"

"That's what I'm telling you, how could you know? I always thought there must be a reason for the way I am. Even after that, I always hated to be touched. I can't stand having too many people around me!"

"I know."

"And that time I saved you, you was drowning, that day daddy took us to Torquay, and he fell asleep in the deckchair—*the bastard*—and it was me that pulled you out of the water!"

"I can't remember; God, how can I not remember that?"

"And remember that fable he told everyone about how he fought in the Spanish Civil War? Well, what really happened was, he had to leave home after a row with his father over a pregnant maidservant—'ere, what's that you're scribbling?"

"Oh, nothing!"

I can't quite bring myself to tell her that even now I'm writing us all into our own chiaroscuro tapestry, this living weave growing secretly under my hand.

Greta, the gifted self-advocate, with her rhetorical skills honed from so many hours of proselytizing the Scriptures, relates with malicious pride how she, years ago, took on Portia's rôle and challenged the Goliathan weight of local government to win back her own child, Emily, from the grasp of the Social Services Agency.

"I defended myself all on my own. I simply destroyed them," she says, with a pale smirk of remembrance. "It was child's play. I just wrote to those prats down at the Council, those interfering High-and-Mighties: *'On what are you basing your decision? Just because one of your spying emissaries happened to notice on the corner of my kitchen table a library book entitled: Mediaeval Legends of Witchcraft and Sorcery; just because I happen to be interested in Demonology and Greek and Roman Mythology, how does that prove that I'm*

462

an unfit mother?' Well, they couldn't do nothin' to me and, as soon as I got Emily back, I requested a transfer to a new Council estate all the way away in Suffolk. They put up a fight but, in the end, they had to give it to me, especially after I left the bleedin' kitchen tap running and accidentally flooded out the whole five storeys underneath."

Greta's reclaimed daughter, Emily, is taller than me. She is as dark and lithe as a witch-hazel plant, and I sense that we are deformed mirror-images of one another. Emily has inherited her mother's gift of rhetoric, of dramatic persuasion. Her power to mesmerize stuns me into inarticulate mumblings, ill-expressed fragments of thought. We celebrate, observe and envy each other's youth or each other's age, each other's perceived power. Somehow, I have rolled up life's invisible staircase and become a matron aunt. From the narrow viewpoint of the world, I appear quietly benign. Time has touched me, blessed me, for my face is engraven, my once-blond hair is whitening. The blossoming Herman tribe of assorted cousins, second-cousins, nieces and nephews, miniature aliens all, have started to gather around me, as once we all gathered around Aunt Ruth. But I haven't the same inner assurance, the same ballast, I feel no more their matron aunt than a bullfrog on a lily pad.

"Auntie Angie, don't you know how often I ask about you? I talk about you constantly," says Emily, "and I write, letters and journals, verses, stories; don't you realize how much influence you've had on me?"

"Have I?"

From the vacuity of legend, Emily has created her personal arcana, her dream-wish of a soulful and picturesque life. I protest that I am nothing but a hollowed-out fountain, an antique statuette, pitted with holes and sorrows and inadequacies, but to no avail; Emily has chosen to erect *my* masque-image into the pantheon of her imagination. Yet (and this dismays and saddens) I recognize the undertow of quicksilver in her eyes and in her mind. She suffers memory blanks and disconnected terrors, distractedly leaves live candlewicks and leaking gas jets unattended, slips underground, then resurfaces—abruptly, erratically. For some years now, like me, she has been sucked back into the stale and comforting familiarity of impoverishment. Upon her lapsed soul-journey, Emily abandoned school, eloped with a lover, drifted homeward, disappeared into some abyss then drifted home again. The strain, the angst and foreboding is taking its toll on her mother, Greta. A dark patch of matter has detached itself inside her right eye and is floating around within the eyeball. A blood clot, the beginnings of a detached retina, perhaps? Greta refuses to submit to treatment, to relinquish her distrust, justly inherited, of medical care.

"I can hardly see any more, I can't do any needlework, or painting, or reading. The Church keeps sending us 'Watchtower' pamphlets, but I know we're troublesome to them. We always were, and we always will be; never mind, put my tape on, Emily, go on, play Vivaldi, '*The Four Seasons.*' I love it, it always makes me cry."

After over 40 years of faithful adherence to the Witness Church, Greta can quote many of the Scriptures fluently from memory: Biblical admonitions of chastisement, intimations of Armageddon and the 'Second Coming,' of Annihilation and Salvation, *of September 11, which is Rafael's birthday.* The significance of this may, indeed, be terrifying for her; she falls silent, refuses to speak. Good that Lily didn't live to witness that day (I think secretly). Her fragile mind and body would not have survived the dread of yet another earth eruption, the world at war again, the potential annihilation of her scattered seed.

That same afternoon, I patrol the cemetery path, seeking out and attempting, uselessly, to scrub the Herman family gravestones of birdlime. At each grave I leave behind small clutches of flowers. Are any of them still here, floating guard over their earthly remains? Surely not, for they respond in devastating silence, Aunt Ruth, Aunt Tweetie, Uncle Georgie, Grandfather Karl, Grandmother Renie, a formidable and ever-united tribe of guardian angels.

464

But this cemetery—*ugh!*—has hardly any greenery. It's a petrified forest of white statues, sinister, crowded close together like a top-heavy gathering of nobles. The wind is mournful, too; the heavy sky is drizzling with rain and blackbirds. Further away, in double burial, one on top of the other, beneath a boxed coverlet of mauve chippings and sculpted white Italian marble, lie Lily and Peter. Aunt Flo's final resting place, erected by her son, Jezz, below the moss-live cemetery wall, is a stark greystone of a monument bestrewn all around with crumpled Coke cans, garish neon-plastic refuse, waterlogged newspapers and foot-high feathery grasses, accidental, mongrel-like, untended and unintended, all having the forlorn aspect of irreclaimable débris. Atop the monument, a stone chalice or an urn is emblazoned boldly, even defiantly: *MOTHER*

Is it possible that already I am beginning to forget the faces of my ancestors, forget even their voices? Their imprint on my psyche is like the faint lettering on these tombstones, a tearstream etched on some faraway mountain crag. Later on, in Kensal Green Cemetery, I search for my sister Larissa's grave which, according to Lily's tragic memory, is located near the main entrance in the shadow of an enormous mausoleum and marked over sixty years ago by a white wooden cross. I can't find it, of course, although I wade through marshes of leather-tough ivy, growing in the shadow of the trees. The cemetery, rebellious in its greenery, looks as though it has been flooded or stormed; the wet, clay earth is loosening, disgorging so many of its monuments, Celtic crosses broken at the spine and lying face down under the ivy, a rash of spreading ivy that veils the worn inscriptions, here and there, stone angels without arms or wings, funerary urns overturned, rampant grass unmown. Evidently, the grave-keeper has given it up for lost. He sits in his pick-up truck, parked along the cemetery path, sipping at a soft-drink can and reading a newspaper. He glances at me curiously as I pass, a sightseer in muddied white running shoes, a North American oddity lurking amongst the graves.

How can I honour my grandmother, Mitzi? She lies in the pink granite shadow of a tombstone, under the glaciers, three thousand miles from here in the fabled tragic town of Saint-Eustache. I can only proclaim in silence, and to the whole world, that she was the one who saved me by gracing the pre-conscious years of my life with her presence. In remembrance, I celebrate her life and her death, I treasure what is left of her, her shiny branch-like walking sticks, her canvas-bound journals, her twice-cast wedding ring of thick yellow-gold.

A few miles from here, the former cloisters of St. Victoire's Convent in Hackney are over-run by latter-day Huns and clod-footed lay teachers. Our vintage-framed photographs have been pillaged from the upper galleries, a desecration of thumbprints smudge the pillar-stones of the Sacred Heart Chapel. I remember the early morning choir-song of the Paschal Mass, the attar of frankincense, the sacred fast before communion wafers; it was here, once, that I fainted amongst the gilded walnut pews, to be revived by Headmother Celestine, sallow-skinned angel of mercy.

I am relentless, for now I crawl back around Whitechapel, snapping photographs as though I were a journalist, an evangelist in futile search of my mythic days, my mythic home. Inside the Royal London Hospital itself, where Lily breathed the penultimate days of her life, the Infirmary wards and corridors are still vintage Victorian. Time has moved on, though, for now a bay of cashpoint machines illuminate the bustling mezzanine and a helicopter is perched, facing the mosque minaret, on top of the hospital roof. I watched it not long ago, dispatched at a moment's notice, grinding arrow-straight above the East End terraces to plummet amidst a torrent of noise and wind, a scene no less than Apocalyptic, to rescue a stabbing victim from the crowded High Street.

Consulting my street map, I circumnavigate the maze from Whitechapel along New Road into the western end of Walden Street, left on Turner Street, right on Ashfield Street into Philpot, then right again into the eastern end of Walden. For some reason the street has been cut off and truncated by a slab of wall rising like a cement spore, an anonymous erection probably of the Royal London. Today, our former street seems privately owned, a gated enclave with individually marked parking places for a car-fleet of surgeons and consultants. Lily's painfully treasured vision of the bombed-out terrace has been buried with her, it no longer haunts and terrorizes. The once walled-off débris, that sunken unholy ground, is now reclaimed in favour of a sedate-looking Nurses' Hostel; its dove-grey multi-storeyed cement flourishes genteelly from the depths of the bomb crater while, implanted all around, is a trail of flower bushes and lawn-grass, an anarchy of forsythia.

I stand on this multi-million treasure of real estate, directly beside the vanished brick wall, observing what remains of our street, newly gentrified and immaculate in its re-conception. Our former front door is refurbished in antique blue, its enduring civic number re-forged in brass, under a heraldic arch of sober sand-faced brick. At its eastern end, the *'eye of God'* still gazes down from its porthole in brick, but swept away are all the pigeon sheds, the spider-ridden outhouses, Lily's blackened gas stove and the funereal mauve shingling of her attic gable. No trace of crimson wax smears the raised doorstep. Repellent is the brazen elegance of the letterbox to my loitering eyes. Aunt Flo's former coal cellar below the rib-iron grate I witness, both with satisfaction and remorse, has been scrub-laundered of cobwebs, banished of sins and grime.

EPILOGUE

PRISON SHIP

I must have been about four or five years old when Taddeusz floated me up onto his lap. I remember how he placed a wine-coloured clothbound book, '*Permit to Land*,' between my palms and opened the fresh-minted pages to *Chapter One*. "This is my story, I wrote it," he said (I can still hear the ringing sternness of his pride). "Now, (placing my fingertip under the first line) can you read this word? Go on, read, read it to me aloud."

'If you give away or sell a single one of my books, I'll come back to haunt you,' said Taddeusz, in the shadow-knowledge of his last days.

Yet, with whitening fury and cold heart, before deserting the New World I donated or otherwise banished Taddeusz's vast library (a twenty-four-foot U-Haul, or was it a Ryder Truck, crammed with 140 boxes), his self-fabricated shrine of laminated images, plaques, books, diplomas, yellowed newspaper clippings in which he confronted in arrogance the camera lens, those black-and-silver poses of Himself, flanked by flamboyant ex-Members of Parliament, celebrated psychics, Councilors, television starlets, the Mayor, even fabled *Péquiste Premier ministre, René*. I tossed thousands of his carefully hoarded publications into a plastic green city bin, located beside a treed and mythic green in the shadow of '*Maison St. Gabriel*' in Point St. Charles.

Taddeusz, I called to the woods, the leaves, the roots, to the air all around, *you are being recycled, released and reborn, you are leaking back into the earth.*

469

The teachings of Gurus and sages may lodge in remote corners of one's brain and heart, lighting up transient little parts of oneself, but I know that the fullness of enlightenment is a personal art-form, to be forged and re-forged in darkness, emptiness and pain.

For me, life's grand imperative is to steer creatively through the Ocean of Free Choice on the Prison Ship of Fate, to fix my gaze on the dream realizing, breathe in the universe to power my journey. My return journey eastward (in counterpoint to your frantic westward flight), for now I am bent on gathering the preserved fruit of my days, all of our days, to honour the obsessional need to inscribe my story, all of our stories. You hacked, uprooted and displaced me for my own good, I know, but there is a vital growing part of me that is still missing. I am settled and at peace neither here nor there, my mind and heart are cloven, each divided from itself; I know that I can never grow myself into an oak tree in any deep soil.

And so I come in search of you, Edi Morvaye, unknown patriarch and elusive ancestor of abandonment. I own only one scratched and dented photo-image of you and your betrothed, Mitzi, seated together in 1918 on the summer verandah of the Schloss-Lazarett near Kahlenberg. Your dour, thin-featured face, none of which was inherited by Taddeusz, haunts and saddens.

'You will find no trace of Edi; he vanished in the smoke of eastern Europe during its second war—but when you reach Germany, you must seek out Yosef's burial place, promise me you will plant over it with forget-me-nots and daffodils.'

But where are you, Edi? Who and what are you, unholy Grail that I am driven to pursue. Stalking you back to your source, I come face to face with the Ultimate Creator and Ultimate Abandoner; I contemplate the conundrum of Original Sin and Redemption, neither of which has ever made any sense to me. What else do these doctrines portray but the Holy Trinity as a dysfunctional family and God, the Archetypal Child Deserter?

Biblical lore records some Almighty Sadist, enforcing motherhood on His unsuspecting unconsenting daughter. The 'act' is consummated through some mystical lechery on the part of the Holy Ghost, producing God's flesh-and-blood Son, Jesus, who, some mortal years later, is abandoned on His cross on the spurious premise—and promise—that His preordained death may somehow buy back, redeem the world. It's a divinely diabolical and, to my view, irrational transaction. A falsified ledger of accounts, a cosmic fraud, or merely a patriarchal paradigm springing from the male-dominant side of the brain.

What about Mary, her 'free will,' her freedom of choice? Did she consent, would she have consented to witnessing her son die, uselessly, I am tempted to think? Or is there some deeper truth that I do not, that I *cannot* understand? I embody the eternal question, the everlasting conundrum and non-answer of divine silence. How has, or how will this deceased Judeo-Christian, alias Jesu Xristus, by virtue of His celebrated death by crucifixion two thousand years ago in Palestine, manage to salvage, preserve and deliver me, Greta, Peter, Larissa, Lily, Taddeusz and the rest of the world from evil—for all time?

Quotations

Cited from the Christmas carol, We Three Kings.
Author and Composer John Henry Hopkins Jr.

Cited from the nursery rhyme, The Old Woman
Who Lived in a Shoe.

Cited from Puccini, La Bohème, Your tiny hand
is frozen, Che gelida manina, (Rodolfo) Act I

Acknowledgments

Many thanks to **Louis Bouchard** and **Marie-Elisabeth Morf** at '**La Librairie Das Buch,**' Montreal, Canada, for their generous assistance with German language revision.

To **Saidye Bronfman Centre for the Arts,** Montreal, Canada, for their asssistance with Yiddish translation.

Published by

Prince Chameleon Press

www.princechameleon.com

Invisible Cities Network

www.InvisibleCitiesNetwork.org